Scientific Proof
of the Existence of God
Will Soon Be Announced
by the White House!

SCIENTIFIC PROOF OF THE EXISTENCE OF GOD WILL SOON BE ANNOUNCED BY THE WHITE HOUSE!

Prophetic Wisdom about the Myths and Idols
of mass culture and popular religious cultism,
the new priesthood
of scientific and political materialism,
and the secrets of Enlightenment
hidden in the body of Man

BY DA FREE JOHN

The Dawn Horse Press
Middletown, California

First edition October 1980
Printed in the United States of America
International Standard Book Number
        paper 0-913922-48-X
Library of Congress Catalog Card Number
        80-81175

Produced by The Crazy Wisdom Fellowship
in cooperation with
The Dawn Horse Press

Contents

Every living being has the instincts and the Destiny of Infinite Life.

Da Free John

AN APPRECIATION

by Robert K. Hall, M.D.

1

*Robert K. Hall is Co-founder of Lomi School
and The Gestalt Institute of San Francisco*

Da Free John talks sanely about real sanity. His subject is always the same: a way of living this human existence without fear and without obsession. He talks about surrender to God as only one who has done so can, with luminous clarity and ecstatic precision. But those are just words. To appreciate the good fortune we all enjoy from his being here on earth, one has to meet him in the heart as well as the mind. He is a man of God and he talks of a way through the heart to direct experience of God. At times his words appear out of the murk of human ignorance like fireworks in a July night sky. It is hard not to hear him!

This is a difficult book. At times the language soars to such esoteric subtlety that only another Adept could understand. In between the peaks of ecstatic language, though, are long stretches of very straight and shocking description of the human condition. Da Free John reminds us that we are declining, out of fear, to live our lives in harmony with the creative life force. He points to our obvious failure to give up the fear of living fully in the moment. Over and over he challenges us to give up the contraction of fear around the heart so we can get on with the creation of community among all people that is based on loving contact with each other and the Divine.

In our world of political chaos and potential nuclear holocaust there must be many men and women who are awake to the madness around us and ready to hear the voice speaking in these discourses. I pray that this book inspires them to expand in love and to become guides for the millions who are still blinded by fear and mistrust. The need for truth is urgent.

On Heroes and Cults

by Ken Wilber

Ken Wilber is editor of Re-Vision *magazine
and author of* The Spectrum of Consciousness
and The Atman Project

K nowledge is not democratic; creativity is not egalitarian. I realize that sounds contrary, but consider: When we want original, concise, and brilliant insights into any field of knowledge, we almost always go to the acknowledged masters of that field. In physics, we look to Newton, then to Einstein, then Heisenberg and Schroedinger and Wigner and Bohm. In biology, we go to Lamarck and Darwin and Wallace, then Morgan and Muller and Watson and Crick. In psychology, to Freud and Adler and Jung and James and Piaget. And why not? Genius is genius, and the more the better.

Although that is what we do in fact—consult the geniuses—I sometimes think we all like to imagine, on the contrary, that enduring knowledge is discoverable by all and sundry, that insight is democratic, that you and I could produce the same truths given the right opportunities. That is probably not the case, however, and the practical fact is that humanity has always relied on, and looked to, Heroes—real Heroes, men and women of great genius, men and women who happen, for one reason or another, to be able to see more, understand more, create more, and know more, than you and I can at our present level of evolution, or adaptation.

People are always the philosophers of their own levels of adaptation, and—how can we deny it?—some are more adapted to, and grounded in, the Reality of Truth itself, whatever the particular field of knowledge through which that Reality might express itself. And those individuals, so grounded, have simply been in fact the Heroes of times past and present. They were and are the Heroes of the True, or the Good, or the Beautiful—and ultimately they are all simply the servants of our own evolution.

This does not mean that these Heroes—the Einsteins and Darwins and Freuds and Nagarjunas—have a higher status than you and I, because all people are equal in the eyes of Divine Mystery. But it would be fair to say that they do serve a higher function: seeing and communicating those truths that you and I cannot or have not yet seen and understood, truths that are to you and me only potentials. And, I will soon argue, Da Free John is a Hero—a quite extraordinary Hero at that.

Yet, in America (as well as the world at large, I think), we have an awkward stance towards Heroes. I mean real Heroes—actual geniuses, men and women of truly brilliant understanding. It is as if we all wished to deny that real Heroes could be among us, since—I suspect—we all hold out the dream that we, that you and I, could and should be our own Heroes. To acknowledge a real Hero seems to deny our own worth, and so we are terribly suspicious and sometimes downright antagonistic towards any who might rise up, in these democratic and egalitarian times, as a real Hero. Let our "heroes" be movie stars, let them be astronauts looking for rocks on dead moons, let them be tacky politicians—but real Heroes? real above-the-crowd geniuses? Why, we seem to say, they exist only in the past, far away from our own hoped-for heroics.

And especially religious Heroes, Spiritual Masters, true Adepts in the Divine Mystery—let them abound, we seem to say . . . but only in the past, only yesterday. I cannot be the only one who marvels at the fact that some forty million Americans accept, as absolute truth, that miracles were performed in the past, that someone way back when walked on water, healed the sick by touch, turned water into wine and fish into feast, raised the dead, and healed the lame. Yet none of those Americans would accept any of that if it happened now, here, today. Oh, we all would like to think that we could recognize one such as Christ if he returned. But the sad historical fact is just the opposite: We—you and I—have from the start rejected our true spiritual Heroes when they walked among us, and, if history is any guide, we would probably do the same thing today. It seems that, while they are alive, real Spiritual Masters are met with benign neglect (or worse). The fact is that Christ (or Buddha or Moses) might already have returned—and been summarily rejected. What evidence could we offer otherwise, given our past performances?

I do not want to sound moralizing or condescending about this—I am in no position to do so. It is just that the issue of real Spiritual Masters is so complicated, so touchy, so sensitive, so complex—and I only want to set the problem in the strongest possible terms so as to point out what is involved. We seem to have mixed emotions about Heroes in any field, but we become almost hysterical in our reactions to spiritual Heroes. The point is this: All true spiritual Heroes are, while alive, by and large rejected, shunned, denied, or worse (consider the horrendous fates of Giordano Bruno, al-Hallaj, Christ, Eckhart). But while all true spiritual Heroes are initially shunned, not all those shunned are true spiritual Heroes. And we—you and I—will simply have to try to decide who is a Divinely empowered Master, and who is a fraud, or, at best, whose realization is incomplete.

This problem has today reached a critical point with the events of Jonestown and the growth of so many apparently strange cults. The world at large now looks with even more terrified suspicion upon any movement that appears "cultic"—that is, any group, large or small, centered around a "heroic" or "charismatic" leader.

"Cult" is the new anathema; cult is the new terror. But here again we face the same dilemma: All truthful and beneficial causes are initially "cultic," but not all cults are either truthful or beneficial. Examine any major historical phenomenon, and you will find it is cultic: headed by a Hero surrounded by devotees. This is not necessarily bad. How could the American Revolution have survived Valley Forge without the hero-figure of George Washington and his cultic followers? Where would modern psychiatry be without Freud and his slavishly cultic disciples? Or on the religious side: Christ and his cult of disciples, Buddha and his cult of monks, Krishna and his cult of devotees. Could we seriously wish that none of those cults ever existed?

Politics is cultic; religion is cultic; philosophy is cultic; even science is cultic—and cults, in the broadest sense, simply represent groups of those who acknowledge and try to follow in the steps of the Heroes of a particular field of endeavor. But, as I said—and it is worth repeating one last time—while all truth is initially cultic, not all cults are truthful. We in the West have a long list of cults and their Heroes

5

that we generally think are harmful: Stalin, Hitler, Mussolini, and, closer to home, many of the new "cultic religions" that enslave rather than enlighten. But please notice: What makes these movements deplorable is <u>not</u> the fact that they are "cults," <u>nor</u> the fact that they have "heroes," but the fact that they are based on ideas or principles that reasonable men and women would eventually agree are erroneous or immoral or even heinous. But whatever you think about moral or immoral heroes, can you start to see how extremely tricky is the problem of followers, of truth, of heroes, of cults?

And so: Da Free John is a Hero and Da Free John is surrounded by devotees. What, then, are we to make of this spiritual Hero? Realize that we cannot reject him simply because he is viewed as a Hero. And realize that we cannot reject him simply because he has dedicated followers. Rather, we must look to his teaching, look to his life, look to his example, look to his message. We would not deny such "due process" even to a common criminal, so let us not deprive our potential Heroes of at least equal courtesy.

What, then, do we find? Let me offer a personal opinion. I have put forward four or five books and some thirty-odd articles devoted to a synthesis of Eastern and Western religion and psychology. Freud and Jung and Adler, Piaget and James and Sartre, Hinduism and Buddhism and Taoism, Christianity and Islam and Zen—I have spent my life studying these systems, profoundly sympathetic with their concerns, sincerely interested in their insights. I myself am no hero, but I honestly think that, by now, I can at least recognize <u>genius</u>, real genius when it comes my way.

And my opinion is that we have, in the person of Da Free John, a Spiritual Master and religious genius of the ultimate degree. I assure you I do not mean that lightly. I am not tossing out high-powered phrases to "hype" the works of Da Free John. I am simply offering to you my own considered opinion: Da Free John's teaching is, I believe, unsurpassed by that of any other spiritual Hero, of any period, of any place, of any time, of any persuasion.

I would hope that I would not make such a bold-faced statement without being able to support it. And so, consider: If you survey carefully the world's great and enduring religions, you tend to understand that, taken as a whole, the great spiritual paths announce four or five major themes. Islam is based on the truth of only-God; Christianity, on the truth of only-Love; Buddhism is based on the truth of no-self and no-seeking; Judaism, on the truth of the Divine as formless and imageless Creative Power and Mystery; Hinduism, on the truth of formless absorption in the unmanifest; Christian mysticism centers on the descent or reception of the "Holy Spirit"; and Taoism grounds itself in "Eternal Flux."

From a slightly different angle, the great world religions can be divided into three major classes. The first is the "path of yogis"— the path of hatha and kundalini yoga, which deals with all the "energies" leading up to the highest centers in the core of the brain. The second is the "path of saints"—the path of subtle halos of light and sound secreted within and beyond the higher brain centers, the path of realizations apparently beyond gross mortality. The third is the "path of sages"—the path of formless absorption and meditation in the causal realms of consciousness itself, the realms of only-God, beyond manifestation and beyond any form of the subject-object dualism.

And here is my point: The teaching of Da Free John includes, even down to the minutest of details, every one of those five major themes and every step of those three major paths. I personally have found that not one significant item of any of the great religions is left out of Da Free John's teachings. Not one. And it is not just that these points are all included in his teaching: They are discussed by Da Free John with such brilliance that one can only conclude that he understands them better than their originators.

One cannot help but reflect on why Da Free John's teaching is so balanced and basically complete. I think one of the reasons is that Da Free John himself has tested, and passed through, all of the major paths as we discussed briefly above. Although born natively predisposed as the Ultimate Transcendental Consciousness, he himself underwent years of discipline in and re-adaptation to perfect Ecstasy in God, an evolutionary discipline that, because of its completeness, seems destined to be revolutionary as well. He spent years in the disciplines of the "path of the yogis," under the acknowledged teacher known as Rudi (Albert Rudolph or Swami Rudrananda). He spent years in the "path of the saints," meeting and then surpassing the well-known Master of the subtle realm named Swami Muktananda. Beyond those stages, he "met," "saw," absolutely acknowledged, and gracefully bowed to such transcendentally awakened saints and sages as Swami Nityananda and Sri Ramana

Maharshi. At the summit of those paths, he seemed then to stand complete, possessed of a teaching and pointing a way that included and transcended all through which he has himself passed.[1]

Perhaps you will disagree with my intepretation of Da Free John's life. But I think you would at least have to agree that his intellectual brilliance and moral fortitude mark him as a true Hero—a beneficent hero, a good hero. Disagree with him if you want; fail to be moved by him if you choose—but please do not toss him off as a "weird cult hero." Besides, Da Free John himself has spoken out so often against "cultic hero worship" that it would be very odd to overlook his own thoughts on the matter.

From the start, in fact, cultic hero worship is precisely what Da Free John has tried to expose and argue against. And he was doing this years before the present-day national hysteria about "cults" and "hero-frauds." And he has spoken out not just against the cults of so-called spiritual masters, but against cultic allegiance in any ultimate form: scientific, political, religious. Six years ago, as but one example, he was already explaining that "the cult of this world is based on the principle of Narcissus, of separated and separative existence, and the search for changes of state, for happiness. All of the cultic ways are strategic searches to satisfy individuals by providing them with various kinds of fulfillment, or inner harmony, or vision, or blissfulness, or salvation, or liberation, or whatever. But the truth is that there is no such one to be fulfilled. Therefore, it is the fundamental responsibility of all to continually undo the practice of the cult. Such a cultic existence has no fundamental value at all. Not only hasn't it any value, it is an absolutely negative influence in the life of persons."

Da Free John acknowledges that certain (truthful) cults have an intermediate function—as we said, all truths tend initially to be cultic/heroic, so why press it? However, as Da Free John puts it, "The negative tendency in cultism is the tendency to forget that mere enthusiastic association with an object, an idea [whether of a new scientific discovery or of an evangelical revival], a person [a hero-

1. For accounts of Da Free John's discipleship under these individuals, please see *The Knee of Listening*, by Da Free John (Los Angeles: The Dawn Horse Press, 1973) and Part I of *The Enlightenment of the Whole Body*, by Da Free John (Middletown, CA: The Dawn Horse Press, 1978). -Ed.

figure] or whatever, is basically a superficial or 'beginner's' state of mind. All mere enthusiasm, or belief, or ritualized consciousness is at the novice level of human existence, and if it persists beyond its appropriate term [emphasis added], it becomes an expression of either childish or adolescent neurosis." Such has been Da Free John's stance from the start, and such remains his stance today. In this book he states unequivocally—and probably for the thousandth time—"I don't believe there is stupidity, delusion, and casual ill-will manifested anywhere more than in the domains of religion and spiritual cultism."

Ah, we may say, Da Free John speaks against other cults—from science to religion—but what about his own? Does he not encourage his own cult of Heroism? Does he not also ask and claim followers? Is he not himself the perfect example of the new cult Hero?

Those are harsh questions, but I think they are ultimately fair, and so deserve a fair answer. First of all, Da Free John, like any genius, is and will forever be surrounded by a group of followers. There is no way to avoid that, and no reason to—any more than we would want to prevent Jung and Adler and Rank and Jones from gravitating towards Freud. Eventually, Freud was wildly praised by Jones and wildly denounced by Rank—so what? When we judge Freud, let us look to Freud, and not hold him responsible for the vicissitudes, often irrational, of his followers.

But more importantly, we have the whole example and teaching of Da Free John himself to those who would be his followers. And nowhere is he more critical of the "cultic" attitude than he is towards those who surround him. This is a short foreword, and so I will not inundate you with supporting quotes. But make no mistake about this affair: I have never heard Da Free John criticize anyone as forcefully as he does those who would approach him chronically from the childish stance of trying to win the favor of the "cultic hero." Look to his writings, and you will find the constantly repeated argument that those who see him as a personal, cultic hero do not see him at all, but are merely involved in narcissistic self-love and "movie star" fantasy-hallucinations about their relationship to him. I have seen no other Spiritual Master take that anti-cultic stance from the start so consistently, so forcefully. Fortunately, I do not need to document that point—Da Free John's writings are in print, dated from the start, and thus what he has been saying for the last seven years can only be taken <u>more</u> seriously—not less seriously—in light of the recent "cult disasters" and belated national panic about "cults" in general and "hero-frauds" in particular.

The last thing I would say is this: Perhaps your approach to Da Free John will not be that of a pure devotee; perhaps it will not even be that of a helpful "friend" of his work. But it is becoming quite obvious that no one in the fields of psychology, religion, philosophy, or sociology can afford not to be at least a student of Da Free John. At least confront the teaching; at least study what he has to say; at least consider his argument. Since he is indeed a true Hero—an authentic and supremely enlightened Spiritual Master—please make use of him while he is alive, while he can serve you in direct, living relationship. Do not repeat the past mistake of denying such a Spiritual Master while he walks among us. Do not meet him with benign neglect. Do not wait until decades or centuries after his death to acknowledge what he is. As a simple start, study his written teaching. And I think that if you will work carefully through even one of Da Free John's books, you will find you have been taken apart and put back together again in a form that will be only Mystery to you, only Release in God, only Radiance in the Divine, and only Joy in the obviousness of it all.

Who Is Truth?

W ho or what is Truth?
Truth is not a person, or a thing, or a knowable object, or a thought.

Truth is a Process.

Who or what is "I"?

"I" is not a person, or a thing, or a knowable entity, or a thought.

"I" is a Process.

The Process that is Truth and the Process that is "I" are one and the same.

What is the Process that is "I" and that is Truth?

It is positive (or self-transcending) bodily submission to the Radiant, All-Pervading Life-Principle.

It is the bodily love of Life, done to the absolute degree, until there is only Life.

This is the Law, and it is all you need to know.

Do this, be this, and you will Realize Happiness, Enjoyment, Health, Longevity, Wisdom, Joy, Freedom, Humor, Ecstasy, and the Radiant Way that leads beyond Man and beyond the Earth.

Eternal and total freedom, wisdom, and happiness are the primary needs and ideas of Man.

Da Free John

CHAPTER ONE

The New Reformation

The time has come for a new and worldwide reformation of human culture. The impact of this cultural conversion of mankind will be comparable to that made by Copernicus in the natural sciences and Luther in the domain of religion. But this new reformation will be universal. It will include all of mankind and every aspect of human culture. It will include all aspects and all traditions of religion, all the sciences, the communications media, economics, and politics. And it will transform the intimate and relational conditions of all people.

This new reformation will continue the cultural gesture begun in the time of Copernicus and Luther. That is, it will extend the cultural and scientific tendency of Man to acknowledge and also surrender to what is beyond and more primary than Man, and beyond and more primary than the Earth. This new cultural gesture will base itself on full recognition of the more radical and modern discoveries in science and cosmology, such as those proposed by Einstein and his theories of "relativity." And it will also base itself on full recognition of the more radical and modern realizations in the area of human religion and spirituality, such as I have considered and communicated in *The Enlightenment of the Whole Body* and other books, and which represent the highest Wisdom of actual Adepts who have lived the Truth of the Spirit (or the Living Reality in which the World and Man are evolving).

Therefore, this new cultural reformation will step beyond the old and childish mentality, wherein Man is surrounded by the Parent Deity and the Parental Universe. And this reformation will also pass beyond the adolescent conceptual rigidity of scientific materialism, so that mankind may not only acknowledge the Paradoxical Condition of Nature, but also participate and surrender within that Paradox. Only in that case may we continue to grow and evolve as Man, and ultimately transcend Man and the Earth.

All of this means that we must now begin to escape beyond the conventional Man-versus-Object mentality in religion and science. We must realize and presume God to be greater than an Object to us—greater than the Sun or the Creative Other. And we must see Earth and Sun and our own local Universe within an Infinite Paradox of space-time, which arises, and floats, and changes, and passes away within the Paradox and Living Radiance that is the true Divine, the Mystery or Condition in which all present conditions are arising.

Conventional and traditional science objectifies Nature as the "It" of observable processes. Just so, conventional and traditional religion objectifies God as the Eternal "Other" that creates the World and Man. Thus, both traditions, in their conventional mode, create objective and independent Idols, which Truth belies. In Truth, God and Man and Nature are Coincident, and thus Identical as the Paradox and Process of the totality of Existence. And only when God and Man and Nature are thus conceived to be perfectly reconciled, as a Unity, can we observe and experience and surrender to the Divine Paradox of the Process in which we exist.

Science must abandon the conventional conception of the "It" of Nature, and religion must abandon the archaic conception of the "Other" that is believed to be God. We must all acknowledge and point to and surrender to the Single Paradoxical Reality and Process. Both science and religion must abandon the strategy of separation from Nature and God. We must all acknowledge our inherent Unity with the Paradoxical Reality and Process, and, therefore, we must all surrender into the Living Reality, which never begins or ends, and which sustains all that exists, and which is ultimately beyond all knowledge (and thus is Transcendental). And we must establish the unanimous and universal validity of the cultural disposition of human self-transcendence, or heartfelt and intuitive surrender into the universal, All-Pervading Current of Radiant Life-Energy, within which all worlds and beings are arising, floating, changing, and then apparently passing out of sight or knowing (but never passing out of the eternal realm of Existence itself). Only on such a basis can we live in personal and social pleasure, creativity, peace, harmony, and immortality. And only from such a point of view can we also rightly establish religion, practice science, and create communities that are human, intelligent, and sustained by continuous submission to the Truth, Process, and Paradox of the Living Reality.

15

The Reality in which we "live and move and have our being" is not actually or merely Other than all beings and things. The "Otherness" of God and Nature is an archaic conception shared by both conventional religion and conventional science. In the case of both conventional religion and conventional science, Man, and thus every individual, is, by virtue of a false conceptual understanding of the process of "knowing," established in the mode of the independent observer, the experiencer, the believer, so that his very being is separated from ecstatic participation in the Reality that is both Nature and God.

The God who is irreducibly separate from Man is an Idol, a false God. Such a God is not the God who grants Life and who is Life.

The realm of Nature that Man may only observe and know is a Mirage, a terrifying Illusion, a Lie. Such a World is not the World that is Alive and that is not other than our own Life.

God is not the Supreme Object, related to the body of Man like the Sun is to the Earth.

Nature, or the World-Process, is not the Supreme Object, related to the modern analytical mind like the ancient God was to the ancient religious mind.

God and Nature are a single Paradox, incapable of existing as an Object or Other to Man. Man is inherently involved in the Paradox of the World-Process. Man is inherently one with the Living Presence of Radiant Existence.

All our conventional knowledge and all our archaic beliefs are motives toward Illusion and Idolatry, unless we constantly transcend both knowledge and belief, by intuitive self-surrender into the Ecstasy of Unity with the Living, Radiant, Transcendental Reality, the

Paradox in which childish religion and adolescent science constantly dissolve and are transformed.

The radical and more mature (and thus more "esoteric" or less popularly understood) scientific knowledge that is now beginning to emerge (since the original work of Einstein, and others) is pointing beyond the archaic mentality of the mechanical sciences that produced the modern movements of scientific materialism and conventional technology. The radical new scientific movements are founded in the higher and paradoxical physics of Nature, and these movements are less associated with the rigid, mechanical conceptualization of the universe (and the development of absurd technological inventions) than they are with the creation of a new cosmological understanding of the paradoxes of "matter" and of "bodies" and of "things" and of "mind." The radical new scientific movements are approaching a Divine Conception, in which the primary Destiny of Man is Ecstasy, rather than one or another kind of self-binding success.

Likewise, a radical new understanding of religion and the spiritual process is also now beginning to emerge, and I am a servant or prophetic "midwife" of that understanding. That understanding points beyond the archaic mentality of the ancient religions and the naive mysticism of traditional spirituality. A radical new movement in religion and spiritual science may now be founded on the higher and total psycho-physiology of Man, rather than on naive cosmologies that are nothing more than symbolic extensions of the neuro-anatomy (or nervous system) of Man himself.

Therefore, the new or emerging culture of Man will be religious or spiritual in the highest evolutionary sense, but it will be associated with a rational cosmological understanding. Likewise, the scientific basis of that new culture of Man will be associated with an essentially Ecstatic or participatory view of Man within the World-Process.

There will be no conflict between religion and science in that new and future culture of Man. Religion will not be irredeemably distorted by the illusions of "subjectivity," and science will not be irredeemably distorted by the illusions of "objectivity." Rather, all human beings will engage in common disciplines of knowledge and of self-transcendence (or Ecstasy). It will be a higher human culture, established in the ultimately unknowable Paradox of the Divine Unity, the ultimate Identity of God and Man and the World. And the higher or religious and scientific dimensions of that culture will not be subservient to the vulgar subhuman drama of present-day economics and politics. Rather, the religious and scientific dimensions of the new culture of Man will be the very foundation of the culture— and all matters of economics and politics will be guided and determined by the higher Wisdom of that foundation itself.

17

There is no Truth higher than love. There is no method greater than ecstasy, or self-transcending love of the Radiant Life-Principle. There is no Destiny to which we may evolve that is more profound than the ultimate and spiritual sacrifice of the self, and mind, and body of Man.

Da Free John

CHAPTER TWO

We Have Outgrown the Cult of Childish Religion

Note to the Reader:

In this relativistic era—when we can only speculate on how things seem to be, and wonder when they will be proved otherwise—the unequivocal voice of a true religious prophet may be disconcerting. Prophets speak with authority, based on direct realization of the truths they declare. They have already submitted to the self-criticism and self-discipline they ask of others.

Therefore, those who honor wisdom are invited to test Da Free John's words against their own experience. He is not a speculative or systematic philosopher. His written teaching is part of his entire response, emotional, intellectual, and spiritual, to his own students and to the problems of modern humanity.

The essays and talks in this book were created over a period of one and a half years and they were not written in the sequence presented here. Each is a self-contained statement, often addressing subjects that are discussed in other essays. Some elements of these considerations may be repeated, elaborating and supplementing previous writings. Thus, each chapter is a many-sided, often paradoxical, argument, full of prophetic emotion and inspired wisdom.

The Intuitive Experience
That Produces <u>True</u> Religion

20

True religion has its origin in the nonverbal intuition and direct experience of the Reality, Life-Power, and Consciousness that pervades and transcends the world and the body-mind of Man. There is truly no verbal-mental argument that can convince anyone that there is this Reality. That is why mere objective science and technology fail to produce a higher human culture, and it is also why archaic and conventional religious belief systems are inadequate and false means of associating with the Divine Reality. There <u>must</u> be direct and personal intuition and even bodily experience of the Transcendental Reality if an individual is to become truly religious and practice the personal, moral, and higher psycho-physical disciplines that are true religion.

The process wherein anyone may come to the point of this Revelation of the Living God is generally a rather random and chaotic affair, until the individual confronts the influence and Teaching of someone who has not only experienced this Revelation but also practiced the life of self-transcending Communion with the Living Reality to the point of ecstatic transformation. But, until the reader avails himself or herself of the opportunity for such a confrontation, there are two forms of consideration that he or she can engage at this moment that will provide at least a modest intuitive and experiential awareness of the Reality of which I speak.

First, set aside for a moment all of your knowledge <u>about</u> the universe and all your religious or scientific presumptions <u>about</u> how it all developed to this point in time. Simply consider this: Even if all processes and all beings evolved or appear to have evolved mechanically and by accidents of association, rather than Mysteriously, as an expression of an eternal Divine Radiation of events, then why does anything or anyone exist at all? How does the <u>existence</u> of anything and everything come about as an accident? Where did that accident occur? Within what is it all occurring? <u>Where</u> is space?

I cannot consider the very existence of anything and everything without developing a thrill in my back and head, so that it feels as if my hair is about to stand on end. We do not know what even a single thing is, or why it is, or where it is, or when it is, or how it came to be. We are confronted by an irreducible Mystery, and that Mystery is profound. If you will truly consider, even for a moment, the matter of the paradox of the existence of anything whatsoever, you will feel intuitively in touch with the Mystery that is Reality Itself. The mind falls away in that moment, and even though you will not have come up with any "knowing" explanations for the world, you will enjoy a tacit sense of Communion with the Living Reality of the world and of your own mind and body.

As a second exercise, examine yourself for a moment and feel any and all forms of bodily contraction, emotional reactivity, and mental concern that possess you. If you will do this deeply and truly, even for a moment, you will become aware of your chronic state. We are, except in the attitude of total psycho-physical Communion with the Living Divine Reality, in a chronic state of reactive contraction or tension, simultaneously in mind, emotion, and body. If you can observe and feel this for a moment, you will sense how it is all a single gesture—a withdrawal or contraction from release into the condition of unqualified relationship. And once this becomes clear, on the basis of a moment of insight, you will be able to relax and feel, beyond thought and reactive emotion and bodily tension, into a sense of self-releasing intimacy with all the conditions of the world. And that release will establish you, at least for a moment, in the wordless experiential sense of Communion with Life, or the Nameless Radiance that pervades the world and the body of Man.

These two considerations or exercises are a moment's cure for too much knowledge about things and too much self-possessed reacting to things. In the moment in which we stand free of the self-defining contractions of mere knowledge and mere reaction to experience, we stand in direct experiential intuition of the Divine Mystery or Living Reality that is the Truth of the world, and that is the very and eternal Urge to religious consciousness and the higher evolution of Man.

God and Doubt

People today talk about God as if one could thoroughly deny that God Exists. The puzzlement about whether or not God Exists is not a true question at all. There is no genuine doubt that God Exists. Obviously you did not create yourself, nor can you sustain yourself independently, nor can you spontaneously uncreate yourself. You can only be confused by illusions of doubt, and these illusions can create the sense of separation from the Living Divine. Such doubts are only illusions whereby we become self-possessed, self-destructive, loveless, and incapable of Ecstasy.

We are lived. We are part of a Great Process that is ultimately mysterious, a Process in which we do not know. God, or the Inherent and Transcendental Reality, clearly Exists. Each of us is inherently obliged to relate to the Divine through love and to fulfill the Law of sacrifice that is Revealed to us in every moment of existence. The Divine Reveals Itself, in our sacrifice, through intuitive illumination, and through a process of psycho-physical transformation and ultimate Translation of self into the Real. Only the Awakened devotee truly understands or Realizes the Nature of God, the Reality of God.

There is no justifiable reason to doubt the Divine Reality. Doubt is simply a reflection of ourselves, our reluctance to fulfill the Law of sacrifice and to become Lawfully oriented to Infinity. Doubts about whether or not God exists are descriptions of Man in his recoil from Infinity. Impenetrable doubt cannot be logically justified in the midst of things. Concepts or beliefs about "God" may be doubted, but that which is Divine and Eternal is always perfectly obvious—and, therefore, inherently beyond the conventional disposition we feel as doubt.

You are always "capable" of doubt, because doubt is a condition of yourself. It is a form of contraction. And when you involve yourself in contraction, you become mad—neither relational nor ecstatic. You have no clarity, no understanding, no capacity to transcend your own reactivity and isolation. Find yourself in that position, and then you start wondering if God is Real or if God Exists. But God is Reality. God is Existence. The mind may know doubt, but it cannot know what God, or Reality, or Existence _is_. The Divine is, therefore, beyond knowledge and doubt, which are only ordinary conventions of mind and experience. The Divine is Realized only through ecstasy, or self-transcendence, beyond knowledge and doubt. The Living God may be neither doubted nor known, but only Realized. God may only be loved.

Therefore, hear the critical argument of this Way of Divine Ignorance. Through Awakening to the intuition of the Divine, the unprovable and undoubtable Divine is simply, tacitly obvious. God is simply Reality. God is the Process of Existence altogether, and God ultimately Transcends the Process and the manifestations of all manifest experience.

23

The Existence of God Can Be Doubted, but Not Proven

Academic philosophers continue to persist in the silliest kind of sophomoric debates about the "existence of God." The arguments still range between the "proof" offered by Reason and the "proof" offered by Revelation—but both kinds of "proof" are nothing more than the poor servants of the adolescent dilemma of "rationalism."

To ask if God exists is already to doubt God's existence absolutely—and it reflects a commitment to the presumption that God does not exist until it is absolutely proven otherwise. Once it is presumed that the existence of God is in doubt or in need of proof, the dreadful dilemma of separation from God has already solidified, and neither inner Reason nor outer Revelation has sufficient Power to liberate the individual from the subtle and fundamental despair that is inherent in Godlessness.

I am in a different Mood, which I also propose to you. The most fundamental Mood of Man is one in which God, or the Living Divine Truth, is presumed to be obvious. God must be Realized as the obvious, not proven to exist. We must abide in the Mood of God-Realization, or inherence in the obvious, rather than that subhuman mood or irreducible dilemma wherein the obvious Truth must be proven to exist. We must proceed on the basis of prior inherence in God, or ecstatic surrender of the psycho-physical self in God, rather than on the basis of mental and physical separation from God. We must Realize God through our inherent, fundamental, and absolute Ignorance, rather than seek to prove or return to God through accumulations of knowledge and experience.

24

Reason and Revelation are the gods of separated and self-possessed Man. Only Ignorance itself makes possible the direct Realization of God. And only those who first Realize and then constantly surrender to the Only, Living, and Obvious Divine are also capable of right understanding of the experiential processes of the body-mind.

The search for proof of the existence of God is really a search for reasons to be happy. But the existence of God cannot be "proven" to the point of ecstasy, or the awakening of the opposite of irreducible doubt. The question "Does God exist or not?" is itself a proposition— it is doubt, it is the idea of separation from ecstatic Fullness, it is the self-image of Narcissus, it is the emotional contraction of the body-mind from God, Life, and all relations. Reasons and Revelations are only a hedge around the pond of Narcissus—a false sanctuary for the wounded self, who presumes himself to be trapped in the dead ends of the Machine of Nature.[1]

Only the Realization of God is the unique and actual healing of the self-bound and heart-wounded Man. And to Realize God we must first enjoy profound insight into the irreducible dilemma behind all our questions, which means we must confess the awful despair that lingers in us even in the face of all our answers. On the basis of that insight we are able to perceive that there is no inherent doubt or

---

1. Narcissus is one of the key concepts in Da Free John's criticism of the usual life. In *The Knee of Listening* (page 26), Da Free John describes Narcissus as follows:

He is the ancient one visible in the Greek "myth," who was the universally adored child of the gods, who rejected the loved-one and every form of love and relationship, who was finally condemned to the contemplation of his own image, until he suffered the fact of eternal separation and died in infinite solitude.

I began to see that same logic operative in all men and every living thing, even the very life of the cells and the energies that surround every living entity or process. It was the logic or process of separation itself, of enclosure and immunity. It manifested as fear and identity, memory and experience. It informed every function of being, every event. It created every mystery. It was the structure of every imbecile link in the history of our suffering.

separate self, and we will thus Realize the Radiant Transcendental Being that is obvious prior to the functional contraction of the body-mind.

Certainty, Doubt, and Ecstasy

Conventional certainty is a selfish pretense, always based on limited experience.

Conventional uncertainty, or chronic doubt, is a selfish presumption, always based on limited understanding.

Ecstasy is the only and selfless absolute, based on the transcendence of limited experience and conventional or limited understanding while yet being itself the basis for unlimited experience and unlimited understanding.

Salvation and Destiny

Conventionally religious people often think that "salvation" (or release from the negative implications of change and death) is a matter of belief, or a mere change of mind, and they are reluctant to follow any such change of mind with profound and persistent changes of emotion, bodily habit, and relational disposition. Likewise, they think that to be "saved" (or to believe they will be released from misfortune and death) is directly associated with an immediate passage to Heaven, or a World in which God is overwhelmingly in Power, after death.

Truly, the categories of belief (often mistaken for "faith") are the common and gravely superficial substance of popular religion all over the world. Ordinary people, full of themselves, crave release from their inevitable difficulties, and there is no absence of authoritarian and imaginative religion to console them. But God or Truth is not the substance of those consolations.

Our encounter with the most fundamental questions or considerations of our experience must go beyond belief and mental changes to become profound psychic, emotional, physical, and moral (or relational) transformation. And only such transformation is truly religious, because it makes us happy, free, benign, compassionate, and loving in the world and in all relationships.

Just so, the conversion of the total body-mind releases us beyond belief and consolation to ecstatic Communion with the Living Divine Being. And only such Communion, rather than the believer's hopes of eventual reunion with God, is salvation.

Salvation, or present Communion with God, is the primary religious principle. But that principle is not a promise of a mechanically inevitable Heavenly future. Communion with God—not travel to a place where God will be found—is salvation.

Communion with God is the sufficient and only substance of happiness. And God-Communion is itself the ultimate Process whereby or wherein we are positively changed or Transformed in our appearance and destiny. Therefore, those who Awaken to God-Communion are surrendered in ecstasy to the point of real Transformation. They are Transfigured and Transformed, grown and matured and evolved, by the Radiant Divine that is released to Work in them and in all their relationships. Thus, salvation, which is God-Communion, does not signify a mechanically guaranteed future, in this world or beyond. Rather, God-Communion is a great Principle and Process, sufficient in itself for happiness, which, over time, and depending on the profundity of our surrender or ecstasy, Works changes for the good. And all devotees are set out on a Divine adventure, to see the changes and the Destiny that God will make of them or to which God will move them, now, and now, and now.

God Is the One in Whom We Are Sacrificed

The Divine Reality, or God, is not ultimately the Savior of our lives. The Divine is That to which our lives must be a sacrifice. Indeed, it is the intuition of the Divine that permits us to live as a sacrifice rather than a Narcissistic, reactive, and self-possessed struggle for ultimate survival.

27

The Truth is not that we survive forever as we now are or conceive ourselves to be. Nor is God, or the Divine Reality, the Instrument of such permanent survival, immortality, or salvation. We are necessarily changing and mortal in our present structural form. But we tend to react to this sense of our destiny by seeking to protect, glorify, permanently fulfill, and immortalize ourselves as we are. The discovery of the Divine through true hearing of the Teaching of Truth, and through intuition, self-observation, functionally appropriate discipline, and responsible higher growth, permits us to be at peace with the mortal or finite destiny of our present independent form and circumstance. We become capable of self-release or sacrifice in the case of the Intuition of the Real.

Therefore, we must awaken to the Reality that obliges us to be born and to change and to pass out of sight—or else life is a tormented absurdity and a mean, unrescued center of illusions. Those who awaken to the Divine Reality and become a continuous sacrifice into It find each moment to be either a passing lesson, or a test, or a temporary blessing in the Mystery of Amazement in which we appear and into the State of which we are always dissolving.

The arising of lives and of all changes is inevitable. Our responsibility is to be the fulfillment of the Law, which is sacrifice or love. Thus, we will persist as selves and changes as long as these persist, but we will in every moment be the release of these into the Reality or Intensity that is their Source and Bliss.

Cultism Is the Beginner's Level of Human Existence

28

The word "cult" means, simply, a system of externals (such as beliefs, rites, and ceremonies) related to the worship of a deity, or any deified object, person, place, event, etc. Therefore, all formally organized exoteric religious institutions or communities are cults. Cults are at the roots of all human cultures.

By extension, any organized gathering of people associated with a common source of enthusiasm and commitment may be called a cult. Therefore, "cultism" is associated not only with religion, but politics, intellectual studies, science, the "professions," entertainment, sports, the news media, animal and flower breeding societies!—nearly every area of human endeavor tends to produce the centralizing phenomenon or centripetal motion of cultism.

The negative tendency in cultism is the tendency to forget that mere enthusiastic association with an object, an idea, a person, or whatever, is basically a superficial or "beginner's" state of mind. All mere enthusiasm, or belief, or ritualized consciousness is at the novice level of human existence, and if it persists beyond its appropriate term, it becomes an expression of either childish or adolescent neurosis. (Such is true of individuals and also of human groups or cultures.)

When participation in the "outer circle" of life is prolonged, and the higher or esoteric culture (the "inner circle" of life) does not begin, we see all the classical signs of human failure. Human beings need their childhood and even a kind of adolescence, but they must eventually "put away childish things" and enter into the mature and higher domain of human possibility.

This transition to human maturity requires profound and self-critical understanding on the part of the individual. And if such a crisis of understanding does not characterize the greatest number of human beings alive at any one time, the social order of mankind tends to be more or less childish and adolescent, expressing all kinds of irrational dependencies and equally irrational needs for ambivalent independence.

But this is precisely the situation in the world at the present time. Everyone is clinging to the "outer circle" of human existence. The popular religious, scientific, political, and other cultural and social characteristics of our time are all generally immature, aberrated, exclusivistic, and bereft of the higher Wisdom of true evolutionary and spiritual acculturation.

In the domain of religion, the cults are almost invariably founded on irrational and archaic beliefs, and many cults claim exclusive possession of the absolute Revelation or degree of Truth But exoteric religion is not in possession of the highest Truth in any case. Exoteric religion is only the "outer circle" of Truth.

The childish neurosis that overcomes exoteric cultism is just this clinging to superficial levels of understanding (or even mere belief, without much understanding), coupled with a righteous sense of exclusive possession of Truth. And this frame of mind is in evidence in every area of human occupation at the present time. It characterizes the cults of science and politics just as much as it does the cults of conventional religion.

It is time for everyone to awaken from the spell of childish, subhuman, self-possessed, subjective, intellectual, and lower physical obsession. It is time to grow up! The Truth can become obvious to our understanding, and the cultural situation of mankind can become harmonious and benign. It is a matter of serious consideration of the higher Wisdom of Life as it is communicated and demonstrated by true human Adepts. It is a matter of entering into the yet hidden or esoteric domain of awakened intelligence, self-restraint, acceptance of Life-positive habits of physical, emotional, and mental activity, and conversion from the separative and self-possessed disposition to the truly ecstatic moral and spiritual disposition of self-transcending Love-Communion with the Life-Principle and Transcendental Reality of the World-Process. That Way, and only that universally true Way, permits the child to grow into maturity. That Way is the evolutionary Way that is hidden or natively built into the psycho-physical structures of Man.

The "problem" of cultism is prolonged exotericism, which produces fanaticism, delusion, and exclusivism. Freedom from false cultism depends on human growth, from the exoteric (or superficial levels of understanding) to the esoteric (or higher, evolutionary, and transcendental levels of understanding). Exoteric religion must become nothing more than a means of preparation for higher spiritual and evolutionary acculturation.

Therefore, every religion must be submitted to the <u>universal</u> Truth and the <u>universal</u> Wisdom of Adepts who have fulfilled the higher Way through actual practice of it. Conventional religions must abandon all things superficial and exclusively true, and they must submit to all that belongs to the universal, profound, and transcendental Truth.

Likewise, all other popular cults—such as the cult of scientific materialism—must abandon the irrational exclusivism of their preferences and see that Wisdom is higher than knowledge.

Everyone, in every field of human endeavor or commitment, must be awakened to a higher intuition, and to a critical understanding of all the superficialities of conventional and popular human awareness.

True and False Religion

People who irrationally accept various religious beliefs and so adhere exclusively (and often fanatically) to a particular historical cult of belief are engaged in false religion. This is not true merely of the so-called "cults," or non-establishment religious groups, that characterize one aspect of the contemporary scene. Rather, it is true of all conventional religious institutions, and it is especially true of the broadly based "establishment" of religious institutions that proliferate in the entire world.

True religion is not a matter of uninspected belief, or fanatical adherence to an historical system of objective beliefs that excludes all other systems of belief from the right to Truth. True religion is a higher human process. It is a process enacted in the body-mind of the individual and in the communities of all individuals who are consciously involved in that same process. It is a process that can only begin if it is founded on profound self-critical consideration and insight, followed by conversion, or release, of the entire body-mind into the Life-Power, the All-Pervading and ultimately Divine Energy, that may be directly and bodily experienced and also clearly revealed to the intuitive mind.

True religion is the mechanism in Nature whereby Man evolves and transcends himself, both individually and collectively (as a species and as a cultural and social order). Therefore, true religion transcends the chaos of conventional and exoteric cultic beliefs. It transcends even all of the sects and offshoots of the so-called "great religions," such as Christianity, Judaism, Islam, Buddhism, and Hinduism.

31

What Are True and False Religion, Spirituality, and Meditation?

W hat is popularized, hyped, and commonly believed to be religion, spirituality, or meditation is invariably a form of self-meditation, self-glorification, and self-survival. Such subhuman games are sold to masses of people via an appeal to naive and neurotic needs for certainty, hope, fascination, superiority, a positive self-image, and egoic immunity from fear and death. Thus, religion, spirituality, and meditation become diluted, reduced to the worldly or self-preserving levels of less than human interest. The typical follower is childish, ultimately irresponsible, self-involved, amoral, experientially undeveloped, weak and out of balance in the dimensions of action, feeling, and thought, and irrationally attached to the enclosures of cult and belief.

Just so, in the popular view, religion, spirituality, and meditation are considered to be inherently different or separable things. Thus, meditation tends to be embraced as a merely psychological or physiological technique, even "scientifically" respectable, without religious significance, and often without spiritual content. Religion is commonly embraced without esoteric spiritual understanding or the higher responsibility of meditation. And spiritual or esoteric notions are popularly accepted in a vacuum, as an alternative to true religious and moral responsibilities, and with a simplistic view of meditation that is really a commitment to subjective illusions, self-glorification, and self-survival rather than to sacrifice of self in the Divine in every area of experience.

The popular promotability of religious, spiritual, and meditational ideas, cults, personalities, and practices depends on the subhuman and childish state of the general population. The responsive audience of such propaganda is the same subhuman mass of "consumers" that is the target of TV and the common media all over the world, and little more is required of anyone than to dutifully purchase the "product." To actually use the "product" is not demanded in any profound sense. Just buy it, praise it, own it, believe it, and glamorize yourself by association with it.

The whole matter of the popular communication and acceptance of religion, spirituality, and meditation is as obnoxious and absurd as any area of vulgarity in the world. It is all an appeal to the sense of self-divided fear and the general absence of intelligence that keeps people irresponsible and dependent, locked into problems, forever searching for solutions without becoming responsible for the problem and the need itself.

Truly, neither religion, nor spirituality, nor meditation expresses the human relationship to Truth unless each is directly and rightly integrated with the others. Religion, which is founded on personal and moral self-sacrifice, or truly human ecstasy, must maintain direct and conscious association with higher esoteric processes, the secrets of the spiritual adaptation of Man. And the religio-spiritual understanding of human sacrifice in the ultimate Reality must be associated with practical disciplines and transcendental means of higher or more perfect human adaptation through the full technical range of meditative and self-sacrificial processes. And all of this must be integrated with a right understanding and valuation of the Spiritual Master and the radical or perfect Destiny of devotees, or true practitioners.

The religious, spiritual, and meditative Way of Truth or Eternal Life is a process of personal, moral, and higher psycho-physical sacrifice. It is not a superficial and private remedial technique, but a form of culture, a profound and total way of life. The leaders of popular cults tell their fanatic followers: "Meditate on yourself, in yourself, for yourself, and by yourself. Come and get it.

What you get—and it will be easy—will make you happy, fearless, superior, right, invulnerable, lovable, and immortal." But, truly, what is thus acquired only reinforces the loveless moods of those who are already constantly acquiring and buying for the sake of ultimate results and satisfactions.

The Way of Truth cannot be understood by children or fools. It is of no interest to the vulgar daily personality refined and developed by TV and the mob of peers. It requires the most profound intelligence, commitment, responsibility, and moral force of persistence in practice. It requires the most creative and easeful force of love. It requires great freedom from the destructive force of irrational reactivity, fear, and self-protectiveness.

33

Therefore, the communication of such a Way truly takes place only in the forums and with the speed of the highest kind of human consideration. To the degree such communication is introduced into the media streams of popular "culture," it must creatively struggle, through constant criticism and depth of information, with the profusion of subhuman propaganda. And the useful or effective communication of the Way of Truth requires a continual mindfulness of the ordinary tendencies, demands, and illusions of the subhuman mood of the usual state of human beings.

The message is this: You, as you know or may experience yourself, are not immortal, nor yet even fully human. What you tend to be, and think, and live is exactly what must be overcome—through insight, change of action, and the fullest working out of the disposition of sacrifice. Your reluctance to resort to the Divine and to the higher Agency of the Spiritual Master, neither of which is within you or even merely outside you, is a sign of the very dilemma from which you must be liberated. Your moral and relational weakness or reactivity is the dominant fault that binds you to the illusion and torment that is yourself. Your tendency toward confinement in inward and mental and physically self-possessed states is not at all reinforced by the truly spiritual Way. The entire Way of Truth is immensely difficult and creative. The entire Way is a Sacrifice. The Way of Truth is the only matter of ultimate significance in the life of Man. Let us yield our very bodies and minds into the Reality and Destiny that is both Spirit and Truth.

The False Viewpoint
of Religious and Spiritual Cultism

I don't believe there is stupidity, delusion, and casual ill-will manifested anywhere more than in the domains of religion and spiritual cultism. Those who would truly live as a sacrifice in God must struggle every day to maintain a level of wit and good humor in the face of ceaseless disheartening confrontations with believers and aspirants in the various traditions. There is a righteous kind of sheer and pious madness that seems almost always to infect those who should be the enlightened minds and friends of mankind.

The reason for this is that religious and spiritual persuasions do not commonly require intelligence, freedom from illusions, or a fundamentally moral relationship to the world. Most often, just the opposite is true. Religious and spiritual cults and institutions typically thrive on human neurosis, fear, gullibility, childishness, amoral self-possession, and the need for fascinating experiential consolations of either a bodily or mental kind. The conventional religious and spiritual point of view is oriented toward the primitive egoic search for indefinite independent or personal survival. It is the preservation and glamorization of self that is commonly served by the conventions of institutional and mystical grace. Wisdom barely enters into the whole affair, and the moral disposition of honor, manly trust, positive compassion, humor, love, and service extended to all is casually bypassed by most of those who pervade the world with ultimate beliefs and salvation techniques.

Those who cling to one or another religious or spiritual way must realize that the foundation of all such ways is the disposition of sacrifice. Every way is, above all, a system of self-sacrifice—not of self-preservation and of immunity to life through internal or subjective fascinations. Religious and spiritual activity is, above all, moral activity. It must be expressed in a new, free, sober, and truly compassionate disposition. Such a disposition freely anoints the world with help and intelligent consideration. It finds great pleasure in the intelligent and truly human companionship of others, and welcomes wise and thoughtful confrontation. And in the face of the persistent dullness of the cults such a disposition often becomes fierce and aloud:

The whole Earth, the cosmos, and every separate being is a great Sacrifice! Therefore, let us consent to fulfill the Law! Let us give ourselves up, so that each temple—each bodily and mental person—may become a temporary and perishable altar of self-giving into the Mystery that pervades us!

The Evil in Man and Religion

The Living God is Present under all conditions. However, the fact is that all conditions may be perceived, experienced, conceived, and altogether known in themselves and for their own sake.

Phenomenal conditions themselves are a force, a machine, a cycle of beginning, change, and end, a destiny, and a presumption that always contain an equal balance of positive and negative factors. The entire realm of phenomena, or "Nature," is, in itself, a binding form, an inevitability that is without freedom or ultimate happiness. The phenomenal realm is, in itself, what has traditionally been called "evil."

Phenomenal conditions, including one's own body-mind, are recognized in Truth only when they are seen arising within or as modifications of the Transcendental Power and Person or Being that is the Living Divine Reality or God. Such recognition, and only such recognition, is the necessary basis of freedom and ultimate happiness. Such recognition, freedom, and happiness, under whatever conditions are presently arising, are what have traditionally been called "goodness."

Many human individuals presume themselves to be religious when they are merely persuaded, in their minds and to a partial degree, by certain consoling ideas, or "beliefs," relative to their own future, the conventional "rightness" of their behaviors, and so forth. Typically "religious" people suffer from profound separative tendencies, fears, and doubts, which are always present in the unliberated psyche of Man in Nature, and which cannot be dissolved by concepts or forces in the superficial mind and body. And, unfortunately, such people project themselves via righteous opinions that tend to exclude and negate other individuals, whose social (and particularly sexual) behaviors and "religious beliefs" are different from their own.

The righteous presumptions and behaviors of superficially and conventionally religious people are a Life-negative and socially pernicious influence, based on a failure to recognize the phenomena of human experience within the Being of the Living God, Who is the ultimate Self and Destiny of all beings, things, and processes. Such individuals give lip service (or mental acknowledgment) to the Divine, because such service consoles them in their fear. But they do not Realize the Living and Present God, and they do not truly serve all beings in love, as an expression of the liberality and wisdom of their prior and eternal happiness.

The conventionally religious mind is not free, not liberated from the force of phenomena, or the dreadful and marvelous Machine of Nature. Therefore, even though so-called religious people may be full of God-Talk, curious beliefs, and mystical profusions, they do not typically acknowledge or Realize the present inherence of all beings and things in the Transcendental Reality. And this absence of direct Realization obliges them to function, and experience, and presume within the domain of phenomena, or Nature in itself. In this manner, conventional religion is often bound up with tendencies, motives, expressions, and philosophies that are "evil" and not "good." Therefore, anyone who is moved by arguments of a religious kind should consider all of it to the point of ecstatic surrender, awakened wisdom, and a profoundly activated love of all beings (expressed through non-threatening service, tolerance, compassion, and help).

Be more sensitive to the "evil" that is always persuasive in your fear, regardless of the glamor of your "experiences" or your beliefs. And oblige yourself first of all to surrender the self and all its internal and external possessions to the Infinite Being and All-Pervading Life-Radiance that are God.

Moving beyond Childish and Adolescent Approaches to Life and Truth

I n the current exchanges about the true Way of life, people are alternately invited either to submit themselves in childish, emotional, and cultic fashion, usually by grace of "hype," to one or another glamorous tradition, personality, or possible effect, or else to assert their adolescent independence from any Divine Influence, Master, or Way by engaging in any one of the seemingly numberless, cool, mental, and strategic methods of self-indulgence, self-possession, self-help, deprogramming, or certified sudden transcendentalism now available in these media-motivated times. In the midst of the pervasive language of these offerings is all the implicit crawling fear of children and adolescents, surrounded by Parent, waiting for Wednesday, wasting weekends on authorities who preach against authority, or who promote peculiar enthusiasms for secret, unique, scriptural, and wholly fulfilling techniques for bodily, emotional, and mental absorptions in the One True Reality, which everyone advertises, but very few find sufficient. Religious, spiritual, and philosophical revivals are so plastic and popular, as mindless as soap, and yet they seem always to distract the world.

I am not the usual man. All that I Teach has been awakened and tested in my own case. There is Grace. There is Truth. There is God, which is both Real and Reality. There are true and false or fruitless ways to live. There are partial revelations. What is only distraction and foolishness has always been part of the theatre of mankind. This need not concern us, if our need for true illumination is strong enough. What we are obliged to do is realize, in our own case, a heart that is the center of our life, that is neither self-indulgent nor foolish, and that is responsible only to Truth.

"Experiences," high and low, are required by those who are still lingering in the conditions of their childhood and adolescence. Everything a child does is a manifestation of one underlying assumption: dependence. When you are a child, the assumption of dependence is eminently realistic and useful. But it should be a

38

temporary stage of psycho-physical life, in which one's functions are nurtured and developed in conventional ways. However, there is commonly a lag in the transition to manhood, man or woman, because of the shocks experienced in the immature attempts to function in the world. Thus, to some degree, every man or woman lingers in the childhood asumption of dependence. And, insofar as men and women are children, they seek to enlarge that personal assumption of dependence into a universal conception in the form of the God-Cosmos-Parent game, the game of dependence upon and obedience to That upon which all depends. That childish aspect in each of us seeks always to verify the condition of dependence in forms of safety and relative unconsciousness. That childish demand in every man and woman is the principal origin of religion, which means "re-union," or, literally, "to bind again." It is the search to be reunited, to experience the vital and emotional reestablishment of some imagined or felt Condition or State of life that is previous to responsibility. It is the urge toward the parented, enclosed condition. This urge always seeks experiences, beliefs, and immunities as a consolation for the primitive cognition of fear and vulnerability. And the "Way" enacted by such a motivation is principally a game of obedience to parentlike enormities.

It is in the childhood of Man that the idea of God-apart or Reality-beyond is conceived. The sense of dependence initiates the growing sense of separate and separated self through the experiential theatre of growth. The intuition of the Whole, the One, is the ground of birth, but "growing up" is a conventional pattern of initiation in which the sense of difference is intensified. At the conventional level of the life-functions themselves, there is a need for such functional or practical differentiation, but the implications in the plane of Consciousness are the cause of an unnatural adventure of suffering and seeking in dilemma.

The passage of childhood thus becomes the ground for the eventual conception of the mutually exclusive trinity of God-apart, separate self, and world-in-itself (any world, high or low). The drama implied in the added assumptions of independent self and objective world is generated at a later phase of life than is realized by the child. The child barely realizes the full force of implication in the ego-concept or the world of things. His or her principal concern is relative to the God-Parent-Reality, That on which all depends, and his or her growing but as yet not fully realized sense of separated self-existence. Separate self and objective world are yet hidden in unconsciousness for the child. They are themselves a mysterious and later realization of that which is at first only felt, not conceptualized, as fear and sorrow. Therefore, the child is always grasping for permanent security in an undifferentiated, unborn bliss, wherein the threats implied in life are forgotten and unknown. Reunion through obedience is the way the living child learns in secret, while the life that grows the child through experience continually demonstrates the failure of all childish seeking.

There must be a transition from childhood to maturity. That transition is also commonly acknowledged as a stage in the psycho-physical development of a human being. It is called adolescence. This stage also tends to be prolonged indefinitely, and, indeed, perhaps the majority of "civilized" men and women are occupied with the concerns of this transition most of their lives. The transitional stage of adolescence is marked by a sense of dilemma, just as the primal stage of childhood is marked by a sense of dependence. It is in this transitional stage that the quality of living existence <u>as</u> a dilemma is conceived. It is the dilemma imposed by the conventional assumption of separate, egoic, independent consciousness, and thus separative habits and action. That whole assumption is the conventional inheritance from childhood, and its clear, personal comprehension, felt over against the childish urge to dependence, is what initiates the ambiguous conflicts of the phase of adolescence.

The dilemma of adolescence is a continual goad to dramatization. It is the drama of the double-bind of dependence versus independence. Adolescence is the origin of cleverness and, in general, of mind. What we conventionally call the conscious mind is a strategic version of consciousness that is always manufacturing motivations. And, in the adolescent, these motivations or desires are mutually exclusive or contradictory. This is because he or she is always playing with impulsive allegiance to two exclusive principles: dependence and independence. The early or childhood condition yields the tendency to assume dependence, but the conventional learning of childhood, as well as the general growth of the individual psycho-physical state, yields to the growing person the equally powerful tendency to assume independence. The result is conventional consciousness or conscious mind, as opposed to the unconsciousness of childhood, but it is strategic in nature, and its foundation is the actual conception of dilemma. Therefore, adolescence is the origin of the great search in all men and women. It is an eternally failed condition, an irrevocable double-bind. It is the very form of Narcissus, or eternal self-reflection (immunity) achieved by impulsive, psycho-physical flight from the impositions of relational conditions.

40

The solutions developed in the adolescent theatre of mankind phase between the exotic and exclusive extremes of either yielding to the states of egoic dependence (thus tending to disintegrate character) or asserting the status of egoic independence (thus tending to rigidify character). Both extremes remain tenuous, threatened by the possibility of the opposite destiny, and involve an ongoing sense of dilemma. We make culture and adventure out of such mid-learning. In the case of the yielding toward the childish condition of dependence, we see more of the mystical-invocatory-absorbed tendency. In the case of the revolutionary assertion of independence, we see more of the analytical-materialistic-discriminatory tendency. In the adolescent range between these two extremes are all of the traditional and usual solutions of Man, including the common understanding of religious and spiritual life.

Traditional religious spirituality, in the forms in which it is most commonly proposed or presumed, is a characteristically adolescent creation that represents a balance between the extremes. It is not a life of <u>mere</u> (or simple) absorption in the mysterious enclosure of existence. It is a life of <u>strategic</u> absorption. It raises the relatively nonstrategic and unconscious life of childhood dependence to the level of a fully strategic, conscious life of realized dependence or absorption. Its goal is not merely psychological reunion, but total psychic liberation into some imagined or felt previous Nature, Position, or State of Being.

When the child of Man fully realizes the way of obedience to That on which all depends, he or she has also entered the phase of adolescence. At that point he or she also has realized the assumptions of the ego-self and the world as apparently independent or objective dimensions, exclusive of or other than the Reality that is the goal of all dependence. Therefore, the way of obedience, fully developed, is already a way of dilemma, of conflict, of struggle with self, as every religious person realizes by experience. Truly, then, the experiential realization of the way of childhood, or dependence, is fully demonstrated only in the advent of human adolescence.

In every form of its adventure, the way of experience and attainment conceived in the adolescence of Man is a struggle for solutions to a principal dilemma. And that dilemma is itself the characteristic demonstration of all such adventures, as well as of the mere suffering of the usual man or woman. In the adolescence of Man, the separate, separated, and separative self is the motivating assumption in our common suffering and our common heroism, both in life and in spirit. The sense of permanently independent existence is the source of that dilemma that undermines the undifferentiated dependence of mere birth. In the adolescent, there is the unrelenting search for the success, salvation, realization, transcendental security, survival, immunity, or healing of the assumed ego. The ego, self, or soul as Self is the primary assumption of the adolescent man, even as the assumption of God, or That on which all depends, is the primary assumption of the child of Man. Therefore, in the usual man or woman, who is embedded in the adolescent conception, the idea of God becomes in doubt, or is chronically resisted. Thus, "sin" ("to miss the mark") enters into the consciousness of adolescence. And the world becomes merely a scene of the adolescent drama wherein even the very "stuff" of the world is viewed as a problem, a principal warfare of opposites, in which manipulation of manifest things, rather than radical intuition of the eternally Present Nature, Condition, Form, and Process, becomes the hope of peace.

There is a mature, real, and true phase of Man. Our maturity is radically free of all childish things and all that is attained, acquired, and made in the adolescent adventures of our conventional life. In that mature phase, the principle of separation is undermined in Real Consciousness, and exclusive God, self, and world are returned to the Condition of Truth. In the maturity of Man, the world is not abandoned, nor is it lived as the scene of adolescent theatre, the adventure in dilemma. Exclusive God occupies the child, and exclusive self occupies the adolescent, and both see the world only in terms of their own limiting principle or suffering. But in the real or mature person the world, or the totality of all arising (subjective, objective, high and low), not in its exclusive sense but in Truth, is primary. In the mature individual, the world is felt as World, as a single, absolute, nonseparate Reality, implying no separate "self" or outside "God," but including the Reality they each imply. For such a one, the Absolute Reality and the world are the same. The World is the inclusive Reality, the Divine Nature, Condition, Form, and Process. It includes all that is manifest, and all that is unmanifest, all universes, conditions, beings, states, and things, all that is within, all that is without, all that is visible, and all that is invisible, all that is here, all that is there, all dimensions of space-time and all that precedes space-time.

42

Clearly, the search for realization via experiences of all kinds is the principal characteristic of both the childish and the adolescent or conventional and traditional stages of human development. The experiential or life dimension of the Divine Transforming Power contains every possibility for the holy or unholy fascination of children and adolescents. But I must always work to disentangle men and women from their lingering and strategic life-motives, so they may realize the Way of the final or mature phase of life. It is only in that mature phase of functional human existence that life in Truth may be realized and the experiential drama of unconsciousness, egoity, conventional mind, and strategic motivation be understood.

The mature phase of life is not characterized by either unconscious dependence or the strategically conscious dilemma of dependence-independence. It is the phase of intuitive attention (rather than dependence) and real responsibility (rather than exclusive independence). As in childhood, there is no problematic strategy at the root of the mature phase of life. But childhood is a realm of unconsciousness, whereas the mature person is freely conscious, because, unlike the adolescent, the mature man or woman conceives no irreducible dilemma in life and consciousness.

This mature phase of life requires conscious, intuitive, and radical Understanding, the Divine disposition or presumption of Ignorance, for its ongoing foundation. The separate and separative principle of independent self, the strategies of mind and desires, the usual self-possessed life of the avoidance of relationship, the urges toward unconscious dependence and mechanical or wild independence, and all the mediocre and mediumistic solutions that balance or fulfill the extremes of experience, all of these must be obviated in the radical presumption that, no matter what arises as apparent experience or knowledge, "I" do not know what a single thing is. Therefore, understanding initiates the mature phase of life.

The mature or responsible and truly conscious phase of life is thus the origin of the real practice of life, or true action. And to this mature phase of life, perfectly realized, belong not the usual religious and spiritual solutions, but perfect or radical Ignorance as the Principle of life. Such maturity or true humanity is characterized by no-seeking, no-dilemma, no orientation toward the goal of any conceived or remembered state or condition, but radical Enjoyment, the perfectly prior, and thus always present, Nature and Condition that is Reality. Only a man or woman thus free enjoys manifest existence in the very Nature and Condition and Heart of the Divine, which is also the Process and Form and Light and Fullness of the worlds.

43

Beware of Those Who Criticize but Do Not Practice Religion

A talk by Da Free John

D A FREE JOHN: Members of departments of comparative religion in universities, along with other intellectual commentators on religion, have become the popularly acknowledged "authorities" in the field of religion. They seem to take a systematic and intellectual view of their "subject," and, because they have university degrees and may even be professors, they possess the glamor of the scientist, who is the model of the ultimate authority in our society. However, if we examine the point of view of these people (and there are many, as it is a common kind of scholarly profession) we can see that their view of Man's existence is different from that expressed by their own subject of study.

We would presume, because they study religion and new religious movements, and because they appear to be people who possess a thorough understanding of religion, that these individuals are congenial to the possibility of participation in a truly religious Way of Life—but, most typically, they are <u>not</u>! Like the scientific and university establishment in general, they tend to work <u>against</u> authentic religion and spiritual practice. Like most scientists and university intellectuals, they represent a left-brained, exclusively verbal mentality that is addicted to analysis and comparison and to the <u>fixed disposition</u> of one who analyzes and compares. Therefore, they do not represent the consciousness or the state of adaptation that may become truly religious, or committed to the practice of a spiritual Way of Life.

These so-called authorities on religious life represent the adolescent mentality that pervades the scientific and intellectual establishment in general. In the mood of adolescence, people cannot commit themselves to the higher evolutionary activity of the whole body and to surrender to the Transcendental Reality. Indeed, such people are primarily interested in maintaining their position of strategic superiority to the childish (or dependent) mentality with which they are always struggling. The professional intellectual is, in most cases, not fundamentally devoted to higher Truth and evolutionary responsibility, but he is basically devoted to a struggle with his own primitive, preverbal mob-consciousness, the childish consciousness that always seeks a lie on which to depend, as on a parent.

In our society there are basically two characteristic mentalities: (1) the childish mob-consciousness of the uneducated (or merely "officially informed") mass of popular culture; (2) the adolescent mentality of those who comment on the childishness of popular culture, and who try to analyze that culture and awaken it to the independent mood of adolescence. The adolescent, by virtue of his acts of self-definition (or defensive separation from all outside forces), remains perpetually independent of childishness and psychological dependency, yet he never matures into higher or truly human development and, ultimately, to evolutionary spiritual responsibility.

The intellectual study of religion, which is the analysis and comparison of the religious movements and cults of the present day as well as of the past, has potential value. And it might even help humanity to outgrow its childish and adolescent consciousness about religion, were it not that, in general, those who make the analysis themselves represent the dogmatic and rigidly analytical state of mind of the adolescent (rather than the liberated understanding of the true practitioner and the true Adept). Thus, at best, scholars of "comparative religion" are critical of childish motivations in religious movements. Yet, even these analyses are relatively superficial, because the critics do not represent the disposition of the subject they study. They are not, in general, practitioners of a religious or higher spiritual Way of Life, although some may attempt to be practitioners on the basis of merely intellectual presumptions about the various traditions. Because of their personal background or their "student" view of the world, they may harbor casually friendly feelings toward the most superficial aspects of a particular religious tradition, such as Christianity. But, for the most part, these professional critics are engaged in the eternal study of "comparative religion"—in which basically no commitment to religious and spiritual practice is ever made, but, rather, religious and spiritual movements are forever contemplated and analyzed and compared.

45

The nonparticipatory, analytical disposition of scientific intellectualism has become so much the standard point of view that whenever a "reporter" within the mainstream of the popular communications media wants to learn what is happening in the world of religious movements, he consults the professional critics. Whenever young people consider seriously, perhaps for the first time, their doubts about religion, they enroll in the department of religion at a university, to study comparative religion and to meet the same critics. Whenever the ordinary man is engaged in considering the matters of religion, he buys the books of these same critics, whose works are published under the seal of major publishing houses. Thus, the charisma of authority in religion has been vested by our society in the intellectual establishment, and those who actually practice and Realize the Truth are regarded suspiciously, as if practice and Realization disqualified them from a true or "objective" understanding of their own most direct experience and intuition.

In the mature levels of human culture, adolescent analyzers are understood just as clearly as children, and they do not become acknowledged as "authorities." In such a mature culture, it is not the anti-religious or conventionally religious analyzer of religion who becomes the authority about religion, but it is the true mystic, the saint, the experienced yogi, the true prophet, the full Adept, and the Spiritual Master who become the resort of those who are seriously interested in the matters of religion. The work of bringing the insight of higher Wisdom to the childish and adolescent motivations and tendencies of the subhuman world belongs to those who have realized their true humanity and who have also transcended their mere humanity through self-sacrifice in the Living Truth.

However, in our modern scientific society it is the out-of-balance man, the adolescent, the one-sided man, the man who is yet to find wholeness, and who is yet to surrender to Truth, who represents the highest level of development that is popularly conceived. More highly evolved individuals, who have realized the maturity of the higher stages of human and super-human development, are generally relegated to the world of "kooks" and social outcasts, and they are identified with all the childish, antisocial qualities of dropouts from society.

The sophistry of the "pharisaical" commentators who are the conventionally acknowledged "authorities" on religion can be summarized as follows: "Religious movements are an answer to a need. People who become associated with such movements are motivated by a genuine need that is not satisfied by the buttoned-down, media-mad culture of our daily existence. They seek to fulfill this need through the experiential revelation of religious and spiritual phenomena. Since established religions are not generally oriented toward experiential realization, people may tend toward religious movements that involve experience." In this manner, the commentators on religion seem to support the religious search for Truth, and they seem to consider religion to be an "appropriate" human activity.

Ultimately, however, the intellectual critic of religion is likely to caution his audience against actually finding an ultimate "answer," a solution, or a commitment that ends their seeking. Thus, the master of comparative religion is as effective as a doctor who tells his patients they are sick, and even provides them with a detailed analysis of their disease, but at last recommends that cure be avoided at all costs! On the one hand, such caution is, to a degree, warranted. Many, and perhaps even most, religious sects thrive by stimulating the childish and irresponsible motivations of ordinary people. On the other hand, the point of view of the intellectual authority on religion ultimately would prevent serious inquirers from going beyond childish and adolescent conceptions of life and religion and becoming truly committed to higher religious and evolutionary spiritual practice. Yet, such higher or unconventional practice is indeed possible and available today.

The intellectual masters of comparative religion generally fail to differentiate between the negative manifestations of popular religious cultism and the positive manifestations of higher spiritual culture. The adolescent fear of being parented is a kind of disease that prevents mature commitment to the higher Way of Life communicated by Adepts, as well as commitment to the initiatory and guiding Company of Adepts themselves. Professional commentators seem to be possessed by a most profound and critical fear of Spiritual Masters, of full and complete spiritual Teachings, and of spiritually oriented communities. They are fundamentally and personally unable to yield to these three kinds of good company. They are rigidly fixed in the separative, adolescent, and analytical position, from which they strike out at superficial failings and secondary faults and engage in nondiscriminating attacks on unconventional Adepts, true Teachings and practices, and communities of practice. In this sense, the commentators on religion belong to the same popular culture and mob-mind that they criticize, and that is perpetually struggling against the Living Reality by which Man may evolve and transcend himself.

But the critics almost never fail to offer themselves or their point of view as the ultimate resort of those who consider religion! They have become the new charismatic authorities! They are the small-minded gurus of the mob-culture of our TV world. The ultimate practice to which they lead those who would become like themselves is the relatively sophomoric educational program of an eternal course in comparative religion. The "curriculum" is the new Cult of religious intellectualism. And the curriculum requires the student only to make analytical comparisons between religious movements, while yet remaining eternally uncommitted to anything except the procedure of analysis and comparison. One who persists in this "yoga" ultimately becomes the enemy of his own subject, because he cannot commit himself to the process he is studying so obsessively. He is only committed to the obsessive study itself, which is motivated by the fear of commitment, the fear of becoming parented and losing the self-indulgent liberty of adolescence.

This discussion has been a very critical and even negative summation of the intellectual and scientific establishment—and it is not made casually! In fact, it is made urgently. We have arrived at a time in the history of our technological society when the adolescent state of Man has become the model for human existence. The higher culture of Man, which is attainable only when both childhood and adolescence have been transcended, is more and more profoundly suppressed by the adolescent intellectualism and materialistic scientism that are now in league with the State everywhere in the world. If the criticism that Adepts bring to human acculturation is not heard more generally in the world, then the higher culture of Man will be more and more suppressed by the official Cults of worldly understanding, until the true Way of Life becomes "secret" again, and disappears from the common world.

48

True Religion Is the Natural Evolutionary Process of Human Existence

True religion is the product of the inherent human biological (or total psycho-physical) urge to the evolutionary fulfillment and ultimate self-transcendence of Man in the Radiant Reality, or Life-Principle, in which he and the world are arising. Religion is not a matter of belief in the evidence or results of religious activity on the part of a certain few historical individuals. Religion is not exclusively a matter of "revelation" in the sense of the specific historical communications made by rare and prophetic individuals. Rather, religion is the process itself—the evolutionary and self-transcending process of the psycho-biological transformation of Man.

The process of true religion is inherent in the psycho-biological structures of every human being, except that it is only more or less developed in each individual. The structures of the religious process are already in the biological anatomy of the human individual. But the development of those structures depends upon cultural adaptation.

The problem is that religion is not commonly understood as a native psycho-biological function in Man. Religion is associated with symbolic cosmologies, archaic belief systems, and illusions of mystical flight from the world. In that case, true religious acculturation is suppressed and obliged to remain at an infantile level. And the more adolescent movement of scientific materialism is gradually, and also rightly, destroying the credibility of such childish religious culture.

The phenomenon generally and popularly known as religion is a childish, even infantile, expression of our possible higher acculturation and evolution. It is always associated with childish cultism, symbolic rituals, and irrational belief systems that can never be penetrated to the point of establishing the true and universal religious process.

Religious cults are nearly always antagonistic to one another—each claiming some kind of righteous superiority for its special historical revelation. And the level of participation in the limited cultures of such cults is largely a matter of uninspected beliefs, external rituals, and superficial codes of social conduct. There is nothing morally, humanly, or spiritually superior about such "religious" consciousness.

Indeed, the whole affair of conventional religious cultism is childish and subhuman, and only rarely do we find any individual attaining higher human and evolutionary transformations of his own character or body-mind as a result of participation in the popular cults of religion.

Even so, such religious cultism does represent the first evolutionary level of the ultimate religious process. Conventional religion is primarily an ancient achievement of Man. The primary developments of such religious cultism began to occur in the general time frame of approximately 1500 to 1000 B.C., and it became gradually and essentially fixed and changeless by approximately A.D. 700 to 1500. After that period, the institutions of ancient religion began to decline, and the modern era of the institutions of scientific materialism began to ascend in importance.

However, the higher dimension of religion has also always been practiced by a relatively few uncommon individuals. Indeed, it was largely the response to the more conventional or superficial aspects of such extraordinary personalities that produced the great cultic movements of exoteric religion among the masses. But such cultic movements are created by and designed for the instruction and social improvement of ordinary people, not men and women of the more highly evolved or awakened type. Therefore, alongside the development of exoteric religions there have always been secret societies and esoteric groups founded on practice of higher personal, moral, and biologically evolutionary disciplines.

The esoteric societies of higher religion have recently begun to become publicly communicative, particularly since the late nineteenth century. This is also a sign of the evolutionary trend of true religion. On the one hand, the bearers of esoteric wisdom will be responsible for turning the tide of the anti-religious and scientifically materialist trend of modern societies. And, on the other hand, the higher religious or evolutionary and spiritual process that is communicated by such individuals will replace the old cults of the conventional and subhuman religions (which have now become false religions, since we have fundamentally outgrown them).

Let me briefly state the nature of the new religious culture, from my own direct experience. It is a process of psycho-physical transformation engaged directly by the individual. It is not founded on archaic beliefs or philosophies, nor is it designed to achieve symbolic ends, such as heaven after death, or cultic membership in the future kingdom of some Teacher who is exclusively identical to Truth and God. Rather, it is a process founded on self-critical insight into patterns of mind, feeling, behavior, and experience, both subjective, or internal to the body-mind, and objective, or in the plane of relations that are apparently external to the body-mind.

The mechanism of this higher and true religious process is in the biological structures of the human body-mind itself—not in the imaginary world of archaic religious cosmologies. And that evolutionary mechanism is not merely present in extraordinary individuals, but in every human being. It is only more consciously activated or served in extraordinary or more perfectly awakened individuals. But it is present in everyone, and it may be awakened in anyone through self-critical insight and higher disciplines of the body-mind. And the process may be quickened in every case through right spiritual association with more highly developed and living Adepts and through natural acculturation in mature spiritual communities.

The higher evolutionary mechanism in Man has not generally been considered or studied by the scientific establishment. The mechanisms that are commonly studied are generally of a lower order, belonging to the subhuman structures in Man, whereby he is seen in his likeness to the less evolved life forms and the less-than-human motivations of living creatures. Thus, to the degree that religion is studied, it is considered only in these lesser terms, and its limitations become more and more obvious as the era of science progresses.

However, the higher evolutionary mechanisms in the nervous system and brain have yet to be studied and understood from a modern scientific point of view, and thus the future evolutionary and higher religious culture of Man has yet to receive its scientific justification or "go ahead" signal in the popular mind. Humanity in general is now in a period of transition from the childish cultism of archaic religion and the adolescent exclusivism of scientific materialism to the future age of higher and evolutionary religious and spiritual culture.

51

I have, in such books as *The Enlightenment of the Whole Body,* considered in detail the evolutionary mechanism associated with higher and previously esoteric religion. Let it suffice for me to say here that the evolutionary mechanism is essentially associated with the central nervous system.[2] And the human individual is natively or structurally disposed, through the stimulating effect of the universal Life-Current in the central nervous system, to grow beyond his present limits via a process of higher personal and moral acculturation, and via superior religious or esoteric spiritual disciplines. Those disciplines involve participatory submission of the individual body-mind into the universal Life-Current, via the total awakening and activation of the central nervous system.

This wisdom is not a new invention of my own. It has been the basic presumption behind esoteric societies all over the world for countless centuries. All of the extraordinary phenomena and prophetic revelations exhibited by religious leaders of the past were either the consciously achieved or spontaneously demonstrated results and expressions of this evolutionary process in their own psycho-physical being. There is no other basis for religion and religious report (or even science and scientific report) than the yet only partially demonstrated biological mechanism that is Man himself in

2. For a full discussion of the esoteric anatomy of human evolution and self-transcendence, see Chapter 4, "The Culture of Eternal Life."

his cooperative submission to the Radiant and Living Reality (or Life-Principle) in which he and the total world are appearing, changing, and, ultimately, dissolving.

Leave God Alone

L eave God alone. Let God be. Allow God, the Reality and Power and Being in which the world and all beings arise and change and pass away, to be whatever God is. It is impossible to know what God is or to gain power over what is All-Power. Simply surrender to God. Yield the body-mind into the Radiant Transcendental Being. Then there is only God-Realization, whereas, while you seek God (rather than surrender to God), there is only the experiencing, partial knowing, and mortal reluctance of a being trapped in the dilemma of its own limitations. Simply to surrender is to enter into Freedom and Fullness.

Therefore, leave God alone. Allow God to be what God is. Transcend the dilemma of the independent and limited psycho-physical self. What you experience is simply more limits of body-mind. Therefore, do not appeal to God to become known or to appear in any manner whatsoever. Simply surrender the body-mind self into That in which it is arising. Do this always and you will constantly be liberated and saved by Grace.

True Religion

R eligion is sacred activity. It is a formal, specific, and even bodily sacrifice. It is a total, whole, and present sacrifice or offering of that which is oneself (not that which is other than oneself). That sacrifice must be made regularly and, at last, even continuously. It is a process of love, or unobstructed and free feeling-attention, in which all the functions of the bodily being are yielded into That which is intuited at Infinity (and with which one is identical at Infinity). The sacrifice is a specific functional process of the whole bodily being, and it must be learned through testing, purification, discipline, insight, meditation, readaptation, and transformation of all the presumptions or tendencies of body and mind.

Such religion or sacred practice is inspired and communicated via human Agents who already abide in the ecstasy of this sacrifice. One who is such an Agent becomes attractive to others, so they become polarized to him through love. Such devotees are tested and instructed, initiated, raised up, absorbed, transformed, and sacrificed in the face of the one whom they love as Master of the sacrifice. He is their advantage, whereby the Way of sacrifice is not only learned but quickened.

This is the ancient secret that few have heard. It is the hidden part of all the cults and institutions of religion. It is absolutely so. And those who do not learn and become this sacrifice, performing it moment to moment like priests before a sacred fire, do not yet have their eye on Truth or the Way to be restored to very God, the Radiant One Who is the Mystery in all experience.

The idea of scientific materialism provides the archetypal self-image of Man in this time. The chronic mood of "Everyman" is a popularized version of the scientific mind. It is the disposition of separation, self-possession, and doubt. Its chronic forms of relationship to the world are the self-conscious gestures of question, analysis, emotional dissociation, and recoil from the limitless Infinity that lies behind all the patterns of mere experience. The scientific attitude of mind is a useful device for knowing about things in an ordinary or conventional fashion, but when it becomes a world view, a fixed and obligatory idea, then it becomes the enemy of free emotion, higher aspiration, and unqualified happiness.

There is an alternative and more fundamental form of association with things, within which the "scientific method" may be used as a practical tool without becoming our essential point of view toward all existence and the limit of our Wisdom. It is the gesture of ecstasy, of prior unity with all things, of heartfelt Communion with the Radiant Life or Transcendental Light-Energy in which all things and beings are arising. It is the self-transcending disposition of love, surrender, cooperation, and trust in relation to the ultimate Reality and Condition of the world and Man. This disposition is senior and superior to all forms of conventional knowledge, including those of scientific materialism and all popular or exoteric forms of religious cultism and belief. It serves the Truth, and it evokes the real Way or practice of Life. It is the key to the awakening of the psycho-physical transformations that comprise the esoteric or "hidden" aspects of religion. It is the Secret of Enlightenment, and the only Path to the ultimate Destiny of Man.

Da Free John

CHAPTER THREE

Scientific Proof of the Existence of God Will <u>Not</u> Be Announced by the White House

Religious Stupidity and Scientific Genius

The Age in which we live is culturally distinct from times past, in which tribal and nationalistic movements, founded in ancient popular ideas and ideals, produced society, and politics, and religion. The Age in which we live was brought into being with the worldwide emergence of the industrial technologies of scientific materialism. Therefore, mankind has lately been obliged to root itself in the disposition of larger purposes, and our concept of the future must be projected against the infinite scale of the total universe, rather than the provincial scale represented by gross self-interest, ancient tribal and national divisions, or even the scale represented by the Earth or by Man himself.

The broad political, social, and technological movements associated with our Age would inevitably draw mankind as a whole

56

into the most sophisticated universal order, founded upon the more or less exclusive and even esoteric influence of the sciences. I say "esoteric" influence because the knowledge represented by scientific disciplines is not truly popular knowledge. It is the kind of knowledge that, because of its special intellectual, educational, and industrial requirements, may be fully acquired and possessed and used only by the very few. And, therefore, since knowledge is the measure of power in any Age, scientists, along with their academic, technological, and political extensions in the common domain, are tending to acquire the positions of power in this new Age.

In contrast to such men of power, I speak for the primary element inherent in all human experience, knowing, and culture. That element was allowed a level of acknowledgment and even primacy in Ages past, but in this new Age of scientism it has been propagandized out of the mainstream of human understanding and acculturation. I speak for the truly religious or spiritual dimension of our conscious existence. What is commonly recognized and sometimes defended as religion in our Age is only the most superficial and factional and often dim-minded and perverse expression of ancient national and tribal cultism. Therefore, I speak for the Truth of religion and spirituality in the highest, most universal, discriminative, benign, and rightly esoteric (or profound) sense. And, like Teachers in Ages past, I am not merely a scholar or a worldly revolutionary, but I come full of spiritual experience and hard-won understanding and the powers of blessing that Radiate through Man in the Presence of the Living God.

The popular apologists of our academic and scientific culture argue for a human future that is founded entirely upon the rule of scientific materialism. If they consider or honor religion at all, it is almost invariably the superficial and factional exotericism of the "great religions" (which are nothing more than the historically dominant cults). Therefore, true or ultimate religion, or the universal spirituality of the Adepts (which was the foundation of all great religious movements of the past), has not yet emerged in our Age as a dominant cultural influence, and the prospect of a future human culture founded upon a new religious and spiritual understanding of Man in the universe is not yet seriously contemplated in the popular realm. Indeed, the Adept, or spiritual genius, is, in our Age, as subject to abuse by the dominant worldly and cultic powers as in any previous Age.

Consider this. In the Age of worldwide political and social interdependence, of super-technology space migration, and the atomic bomb, and of esoteric sciences of the kind initiated by intellectual geniuses such as Einstein, the people must not fail to be equipped with a true, practical, supremely intelligent, universal, and full esoteric understanding and practice of spiritual religion. If they remain in the embrace of the archaic, myth-laden, exoteric, divisive religions of the past, they will only be subject to exploitation and negative dominance by the superior esotericism and popular persuasiveness of scientific materialism. To persist in the old cults is, in effect, to be bereft of religion in the Age that is upon us.

57

The True Culture
of Prior Spiritual Unity
vs. the False Culture
of Analytical Separation

Modern "science" began as a method or way of knowing or finding out about the structures and workings of natural processes. It was presumed to be a superior method, based on rigorous observation, conceptualization, and analysis of events. However, it is not the only or even necessarily the best method of finding out about the world of events. And, in any case, this method has, over time, become more than an intellectual method of specific knowledge. It has become the popular world-view of the modern world. It has become not merely a means of gathering information, but the very form of our relationship to the natural world and to each other and to ourselves. Indeed, it has become the only officially and popularly acceptable form of relationship to anything whatsoever.

Even though the scientific method of inquiry may serve as a means of analytical knowledge, it utterly fails as a right and true form of moment to moment relationship to things and beings and the totality of existence. It is properly only a special form of relationship to specific events in specific moments and for a specific purpose. If it is allowed to become the standard form of relationship itself, the natural process of our participation in the play of existence is retarded, suppressed, and even destroyed.

58

The scientific method is fundamentally an exercise of the verbal mind in relation to events in or via the autonomic nervous system. As such it is only a partial development of the total body-mind. Also, it is a method that requires stark and strategic conceptual separation between the observer and the observed. And when this exercise becomes the primary mode of one's relationship to things and to experience and to existence itself, it becomes separative, and a kind of warfare or opposition develops between the self and all relations of the self.

Science has become the popular and chronic form of the everyday or casual approach of all people to the events of experience. As a result, the process of relationship itself has become disturbed. Science would pretend to be able to create a true and superior human culture, founded on technology and analytical knowledge, but in fact the scientific method has no capacity to create a true or human culture, since the scientific method is founded on analytical observation and conceptualization, rather than on nonverbal or tacit participation in our inherent unity with the total world of existence.

We are inherently one with the World-Process. We are only secondarily knowers about the World-Process. Therefore, if we adopt a form of relationship to the World-Process that is founded on separation, observation, and analytical knowing, rather than on intuitive, self-surrendering, and self-transcending Communion or participation in our unity with the World-Process, then we will tend more and more to interfere with and even lose sympathy with our unity with the World-Process and with the ultimate Condition in which we are presently arising.

This in fact is what has happened, and we are now in the midst of a dehumanizing, anti-religious, and even anti-cultural technological revolution of the entire order of mankind. The method that is our science is no longer seen in a right perspective. And, as a result, the unitive, intuitive, mystical, self-transcending, ecstatic, evolutionary, and participatory culture of Man is being displaced or prevented by the authoritarian propaganda associated with the Cult of scientific materialism.

I am not arguing for an end to analytical science, but I am arguing for a cultural return to the primary mode of human existence, wherein we must transcend ourselves and all our knowledge through surrender into unity with the World-Process and heartfelt intuitive Communion with the Transcendental Condition of all things and beings. Once any individual does that, he is on the way to human well-being and spiritual as well as evolutionary growth. Only such an individual can also apply himself to the method and the data of analytical science without becoming deluded and Godless. And only when the leaders and the general population of mankind begin to awaken to this realization will human culture begin again, free of the tragic pride of knowledge, even while we are also given to know and understand all things. (And much of that knowledge will be attained personally and directly by each individual, as an intuitive phenomenon, prior to the assumption of the analytical point of view of the verbal mind and the presumptive strategy of manipulatory exploitation of the body-mind and its relations.)

The False Religion
of Scientific Knowledge

S cientists tend to imagine themselves to be "humanists," or individuals who possess a superior regard for the well-being of mankind. Indeed, organized groups of scientists commonly promote themselves as a kind of independently superior and humanistic conscience, whereas in fact their general effect on the world is often quite the opposite. (At the very least, their effect is no more superior or ultimately beneficial than that of any other organized and socially powerful point of view, past or present.)

The scientific establishment has been organized in league with the highest levels of concentrated political, economic, and propagandistic power in the world today. Science is simply the primary method of knowing in modern societies, and its rule is

60

established in no less an irrational and authoritarian manner than was the case with any religious or philosophical principle that ruled societies in the past.

The method of science has now become a style of existence, a mood or strategy of relating to the world and to other human beings. That method now describes the conventional posture taken by "Everyman" in every form of his relationship to the conditions of existence. Science has become a world-view, a presumption about the World-Process itself. It has become a religion, although a false one. And modern societies are Cults of this new religion. Can this new religion establish us as individuals and communities in right relationship to each other and to the World-Process? Absolutely not! Science is only a method of inquiry, or knowing about. It is not itself the right, true, or inherent form of our relationship to the conditions of existence. No matter what we may know about the conditions of existence, we cannot acount for existence itself. And we are, regardless of our personal and present state of knowledge about the natural mechanics of the world, always responsible for our right relationship to the various conditions of experience, to the beings with whom we exist in this world, and to the World-Process as a whole. Relationship is inherently and perpetually a matter of individual responsibility, founded in intuition, prior to the analytical mind.

The method that is science is inherently incapable of establishing us in a right relationship to the conditions of existence. Love and self-transcendence are realized outside or prior to the play of conventional knowledge. The scientific method is not a moral or a spiritual and intuitive disposition. It is a strategy for acquiring objective knowledge. If it were a moral disposition, then scientists would all be great moral beings. But in fact, the daily application of the scientific method is not itself a moral practice, or a kind of meditation that transforms the practitioner. Rather, the application of the strategy of scientific inquiry is only a special intellectual discipline, and it forever stands outside the higher intuitive and radical psycho-physical processes whereby the individual may be transformed in either evolutionary or moral or spiritual terms.

Those who embrace the attitude of verbal thinking, observing, analyzing, comparing, categorizing, and so forth must understand that to do so is not the same thing as to exist and live in the most fundamental and responsible terms. Rather, it is merely a way of observing and verbally considering the patterns of phenomena, in order to know about them. And if one abandons the fundamental process of self-transcending Communion and unity with the World-Process, and opts instead and exclusively for the position of the separated analytical observer, then one begins to operate in defiant opposition to the primary conditions of human existence.

Science must again become simply a method of inquiry, and it must be renounced as the universal style of our very relationship to the conditions of existence. It must cease to characterize the totality of Man himself. Rather, it must again become an "employee" of Man—a specialized instrument for certain kinds of work. Otherwise, Man will cease to be capable of either the moral or the spiritual and evolutionary exercise of personal responsibility.

The verbal mind, or the left hemisphere of the human brain, is not suited to be the Ruler of Man. It is only an attribute or potentiality of Man. Therefore the "urge" to science, which is the ultimate method of the analytical or verbal mind, must be disciplined and held in right perspective by a higher or more complete understanding. Every exercise of a part of Man must be understood relative to Man as a whole, and submitted to the process and ultimate Condition that includes and involves Man prior to all his knowledge.

The right hemisphere of the human brain was once the Ruler of Man, in early societies founded in the methods of magic, psychism, and a truly active and inward religious consciousness. But the method of psychic inquiry proved to have severe limitations, because of the variables involved in personal subjective processes and the competitive conflicts between societies organized around different historical accumulations of conventional religious belief. Therefore, the functions of the left hemisphere of the human brain began to evolve and to achieve cultural prominence. And now they are the dominant characteristic of modern verbal and analytical Man. But the results of the dominance of the left brain are equally as limited, troublesome, and psychologically devastating as the results of dominance by the right brain.

The right-brained or "oriental" Man enjoys psychic attunement with the World-Process, but he cannot differentiate himself sufficiently to acquire responsibility for his destiny in the natural world of psycho-physical phenomena. And the left-brained or

62

"occidental" Man, even though he is committed to responsible analysis of natural phenomena and control over the laws that govern the World-Process, is incapable of the higher morality or disposition of self-surrender, self-transcendence, psychic illumination, and participatory Communion with the Radiant Transcendental Reality that may be intuited to be the Truth of the World-Process and the Source of the Happiness of Man.

Therefore, we must awaken from our solid pose of intellectual superiority and our irrational belief that knowledge <u>about</u> the processes of natural phenomena makes a superior humanity. A superior humanity will not be derived from authoritarian scientific decrees, imposed through powerful technologies. Man cannot live happily, nor survive long, without the intuitive certainty of Transcendental Love, or Spiritual Communion with Divine Power, Bliss, and Purpose. Without higher religious consciousness (free of the dogmatic nonsense of conventional religious beliefs), the future made by scientific acculturation is an abominable fiction, a mechanical contrivance in which Man is, paradoxically, both satisfied in his desires and desperate in his being.

And I do not argue this point of view out of despair. I have Realized the Truth, and I see the present and the ancient errors in Man. I am also a knower about the natural world, except that I have been committed to the higher discipline of Man as a totality, and Man as an inherent Sacrifice in God. Therefore, I have seen all the mechanisms of our evolution, and I have understood all the necessary structures of a true culture of Man. But it is extremely difficult to be heard in the midst of a society that is bound and determined to follow its present strategy to the end of its course. The Wisdom of transforming our disposition <u>before</u> we fail is considered disdainfully by the popular and intellectual mentalizing of this day. Everyone is endlessly chatting, comparing concepts, looking for consoling pleasures, fascinations of mind and body. Everyone is possessed by a lust for knowledge about the natural world and about the experiential mechanism of Man. But it seems that very few are interested in <u>being</u> Man at this present time. Very few seem willing to accept the discipline that is the totality of Man and to fulfill the destiny of personal transformation in bodily, emotional, psychic, mental, and Transcendental unity with the Radiant Mystery of the World-Process, which is eternally prior to all our knowing.

Awakening from the Word

The conventional culture of contemporary Man is primarily a culture of the verbal mind and the discrete or discursive languages of the left side of the average or common brain model. Thus, it is a culture that tends to be dominated by verbal and other discursively symbolic language systems (such as the potent visualism of television and movie theatre, which make inverted use of visual or spatial and right-brained phenomena in order to serve the purposes of the verbal or discursive mind). The contemporary individual is propagandized constantly by exclusively left-brained appeals, powerful verbal influences, promises of ultimate egoic glamorization and fulfillment, and the parentlike authority of analytical "knowledge." Our experience and our understanding are dominated and determined by these means—so much so that the media of discursive mental culture, such as television, and all other officially-reported knowledge, are more fundamental to us than what we experience in our living relationships and our intuition of the ultimate Reality. The "word" has finally become our Parent, and we are being eaten alive.

The exoteric or common order of verbal and left-brained culture is the daily "TV world" of verbal conventions and commonly communicated "knowledge" or "News." But there is an "esotericism" or "esoteric" cultural core that is tending more and more to dominate the lives of individuals. The political and common social world of our too-spoken lives is the "exoteric" level of the dominating influence in our common culture. But the "esoteric" order that is the inevitable extension of our verbal or left-brained world is tending more and more to dominate us, whether openly or more or less indirectly, like a secret and high priesthood. And, like all high priesthoods, the Super-Church of our time is in league with the State, and ultimately seeks to control the State.

The scientific, rationalist intellectual, and technological core-culture of our social order is the secret "esoteric" "Mother Church" of the left-brained congregation of ordinary people. It is through the growing and pervasive influence of this exclusively left-brained "esoteric" or most highly developed core of our verbal culture that the

63

holistic, intuitive, psychic, or right-brained communion with the conditions and the Reality of our world is being gradually eliminated as a possibility. In ancient times, the exoteric and esoteric influences that dominated the daily culture were predominantly right-brained and hallucinatory, and this exclusivity produced its own symptoms of imbalance. But in a fully evolved human culture, the right and the left, or the psychic-holistic and the mental-analytical, aspects of the human potential must be mutually integrated and balanced, and then the whole and entire body-mind must be submitted to the All-Pervading Life and Divinity that animates us. If human societies cannot evolve into whole brain and whole body levels of adaptation, then the human being and the human world will inevitably be reduced to a mechanical and self-possessed destiny that is mortal, loveless, and absurd.

It is not that the rigorous and intelligent use of the verbal or discursive mind is not necessary. It is indeed culturally necessary. And both scientific and technological advances can do much to improve even the political and economic as well as intellectual estate of mankind. But the exclusivity of that influence and its pervasive philosophical disposition toward the contracted, analytical, and independent or analyzed-self orientation are a negative extension of the egoic or exclusive and self-possessed disposition of the individual in his fear. From that exclusive viewpoint, the pattern of totality may be analyzed, but the viewpoint itself cannot be sacrificed into the pattern, nor can the ultimate and All-Pervading Reality or Condition of the whole and of every part become the dominant factor in the daily life of the individual or the society. Scientism and the left-brained predisposition can produce an age of analytical knowledge but not an age of faith (in the highest sense). Therefore, we must be culturally and personally awakened to the Mind and Intuition that is obvious only to the whole brain and the whole body-mind, or else the Parental Word will slay the Radiant Children of our Mystery.

The Priesthood of Science

A talk by Da Free John

DA FREE JOHN: I have recently read some books that attempt to summarize the current state of physics, astronomy, and cosmology based on scientific observations. These texts summarize the history of the material universe, from the moment of the so-called "Big Bang" to the present, and they also describe its evolution in the future. Each of them is written in a different mood and comes to a different conclusion. In each case, the conclusion has philosophical or spiritual and religious significance, but it has nothing whatever to do with the summary evidence. The conclusions are purely emotional persuasions. One of them has something like a religious feeling about the whole matter. Another has a completely atheistic feeling about it. One sees the universe expanding and contracting in eternal cycles. Another sees its genesis once and its coming to an end only once. But none of these events has actually been observed. The writers of these books are surrounding the collection of physical observations with a structure of childish or adolescent philosophizing that is at the same level of thinking that existed centuries before these physical observations.

Thus, the old dogmas persist. We have different priesthoods, that is all. And the current priesthood is the priesthood of the scientists. Modern scientists certainly perform great services for humanity in many ways, but we tend to misinterpret their influence and their level of understanding. We tend to feel great awe in their company, but they do not have any more sound basis for making ultimate assumptions than people did hundreds of years ago, before our present scientific capacities. In other words, our scientists represent the same mind, the same disposition, the same state of evolution, as men of old, and the same variability of viewpoint, from school to school, from person to person.

It makes no difference whether we are scientists looking at sophisticated measurements and data or ordinary people walking down the street and casually commenting on the weather—we cannot say anything more intelligent than our state of adaptation allows. We cannot enjoy greater insight into what we are examining (regardless of what it is we are examining) than we have the adaptation from which to communicate. We are always the philosophers of our present state of adaptation. Modern scientists are scrutinizing sophisticated data, but they are not making truly sophisticated or higher cultural sense out of it. The data itself may contain all kinds of hidden clues to the same Wisdom that was enjoyed by great seers in the past. But the conventional scientists cannot communicate that Wisdom. They can only communicate the dogma of their own adaptation. Since they have not stepped into a different evolutionary process, they do not know anything about the physics of real meditation and the process that is evolving in the higher structures of the human being. They know nothing about it. Despite their best intentions, then, they are basically just chattering about their own immature or subhuman condition and communicating the vision, the emotional understanding, of which they are presently capable.

People tend to misinterpret modern scientism just as they misinterpreted the priestly influence in the Middle Ages. There is always a kind of glamor surrounding the official priesthood of any time. People presume all kinds of omniscience in these people, but it is the data, the information itself, that glamorizes the people associated with it. The data glamorizes scientists today, just as religious phenomena and beliefs glamorized priests in times past. What they are talking about in itself glamorizes them, but they do not have any capacity to make the greater sense out of it, or to perform a greater service for other human beings than those others can for themselves. Therefore, modern scientists do not introduce into human time another process that would permit human beings to advance on the scale of evolution. On the contrary: They are providing us with highly technical information about the state of adaptation we have already achieved. They are providing us with highly sophisticated information that gives us powers over the elemental life with which it is possible for us to destroy ourselves, because we have not yet developed the evolutionary capacity to make use of this information in a more civilized and benign way.

The more sophisticated the information or the technical powers we acquire, the more we have to mature in the culture of love and freedom, or true psycho-physical morality. Scientists are not offering such a Wisdom-Culture, based on a higher evolutionary level of functioning. But without such a culture, human beings cannot advance, no matter how comprehensive their information.

Thus, it is a matter of great urgency for modern men and women to come into a true understanding of what the true Adept or Spiritual Master represents to Man, and what the devotional relationship to such a one actually entails. The Teaching of the true Spiritual Master serves the moral transformation and ultimate evolution of Man. He incarnates and communicates the necessary Wisdom-Culture of Man. In his Realization and his argument, the Spiritual Master, or highest Adept, represents a radical criticism of the usual man's standard of functional existence and all the forms of his resistance to the real spiritual process, the life of intelligent sacrifice, or love.

At the present time almost all human beings are more or less mechanically insisting upon the repetition of an essentially subconscious, controlled life, not a free and creative and spiritual life. Modern scientism and all the other influences of our day, both secular and apparently religious, represent doctrines and presumptions within that limited, not yet conscious form of life. The conventional institutions that advertise growth, freedom, creativity, and spiritual transformation all in fact tend to become spokesmen for that egoic or conventional, Narcissistic logic. But the Way of Life that I Teach is the most serious and profound and radical, or nonconventional, affair. People must therefore begin to distinguish this radical Way from the so-called "spiritual movement" of our time as well as from the conventional traditions of exoteric religion and esoteric spirituality, both Eastern and Western.

67

Cooperation and Doubt

The world is suffering from a wrong understanding of human freedom and human politics.

Those who value the notion of human freedom tend to think of it in terms of Narcissistic immunity from restraints. That is, they think of freedom basically as separation from parentlike demands, so that the "free man" is conceived of as someone who can do whatever he likes, whenever he likes.

But such freedom cannot be realized or practiced in the world of human relationships. Indeed, it is founded on a fundamental revulsion to the limiting power of relationships and to the moral demands of love and self-sacrifice. It is a false, childish, and ultimately antisocial point of view. It is the viewpoint of private self-indulgence and ceaseless self-meditation. It is the very principle that destroys relationships, love, and the higher processes of personal, social, and spiritual growth.

Yet, this childish point of view is the popular notion that underlies the exercise of freedom in present-day democracies. It characterizes the present popular version of the "American spirit" and the present state of the "spirit" of democratic and capitalistic free enterprise everywhere in the world. It is the root of private and public irresponsibility and vulgar exploitation of subhuman possibilities everywhere in the modern technological world of TV cultures.

Human freedom is not in principle about the ability to randomly fulfill random desires. The true principle of human freedom is a higher cultural concept of the status of <u>superior</u> human individuals, not childish masses of vulgar subhumanity. Human freedom is a mature realization of the status of individual existence in relationship with all other human beings and all aspects of the shared world. Human freedom is a political or relational estate, rather than a separately personal one. It is the disposition in which the higher or evolutionary conditions of one's superior adaptation are chosen, and in which full moral responsibility is accepted for one's social and intimate relationships.

If a State is organized as a democracy, it cannot function as a true democracy unless the people are typically and personally mature in this disposition of human freedom. A true democracy is founded on such freedom, or moral responsibility, on the part of the population as a whole.

But if the people do not mature, if the people do not learn the higher Way of Man and become fitted to personal patterns of self-restraint and moral patterns of responsibility and service in relation to all others, then democracy will inevitably fail. Indeed, it is already fundamentally in a state of failure—or a stalemate in its development—in America and in democratic societies all over the world.

Therefore, the democracies are in a critical moment. The next moment will determine whether the democracies will survive, or whether they will necessarily be replaced by authoritarian and utterly centralized forms of political rule.

We can already see that democratic institutions are eroding, and that the populations of the democracies are becoming more and more lawless, chaotic, and childish. And to the degree the people have become irresponsible, the State inevitably moves to create order by law, authority, and force.

I am suggesting that the democracies are in serious danger at the present time. And there are very few forces at work to turn the tide away from the centralized ordering of mass culture that typifies the present-day non-democratic States. Indeed, the principal influences in American society and other democratic societies are themselves actively, if somewhat unconsciously, working against the development of higher cultural and individual maturity in the populations of mankind.

The principal influences that are currently at work in the world belong to the modern movement of scientific and political materialism. Every great modern State is intimately in league with this movement, as ancient States were with official Cults of religion. And the products of that marriage are all of the technological and manipulative influences that more and more pervade and control the daily lives of people.

The popular media of TV, the press, and the publishing industry, as well as the scientifically indoctrinated intellectualism of the universities, are all working for a common cause, which is the ultimate and exclusive triumph of scientific and political materialism. Such is the character of all of the dominant influences in contemporary technological societies. All contrary or superior voices tend to be excluded, negatively manipulated, or otherwise overwhelmed and minimized in their effects by all of this machinery of popular culture. Certain traditional voices continue to be heard, particularly in the less sophisticated areas of the mass culture, but the traditional voices have already had their day, and the archaic mind that supported the old ways and the old days is gradually dissolving into a condition that is not distinguishable from the dominant voice of scientific and political materialism.

Apart from the popular media of communication, the social order in general daily manifests more and more critical signs of deterioration. Mankind is not permitted to learn the higher purpose of Man, but is continually indoctrinated into a superficial state of mind that is merely observing and reacting to objective events and struggling with mortal psychological states. Human beings are currently learning little more than how to desire elemental bodily fulfillment and how to achieve the goals of material self-glorification. All the rest of what Man can be is kept in a state of perpetual doubt by the propaganda of scientific and political materialism.

We have come to a moment in time when democracy as we know it is beginning to look like a passing romantic adventure. Indeed, it was originally the creation of superior and somewhat romantic idealists who belonged to the old traditional order, but who also maintained an enthusiastic interest in the newly awakening possibilities of a scientifically fabricated culture. Democracy, as we have conceived of it in modern times, was essentially created in response to the new scientific and political possibilities that were beginning to emerge in the eighteenth century. Such democracy not only recognized the new possibilities for the personal and political relief of the burdens of "Everyman," but it also maintained an idealistic hold on the intellectual and religious culture of the old world, in which Man was viewed as an ultimately superior and perfectable being.

The problem is that the religious basis for the traditional idealism that was the original foundation of democracy has gradually and steadily been propagandized out of existence by the emerging cultural, technological, and political forces of scientific materialism. As a result, the people no longer generally or seriously presume the idealism that is the necessary support of democracy as we conceive it. The superior Man and the true cultural, spiritual, and political leadership of superior men has ceased to be popular, and the mood of people is no longer idealistic in the higher cultural sense, but it is materialistic in the sense of subhuman and self-possessed desiring.

Science is properly and originally a method, but it has become the source of the popular world-view. And just as science is a method of self-isolation for the sake of objective observation of events, the mood or strategy of "Everyman" has become the one of separative self-consciousness and the inability to surrender the self and make it responsible to the totality or total pattern of existence.

The popular mood that the scientific method tends to produce is the intellectual or verbal-mental mood of doubt. The way of science is to question or inquire without ceasing, just as the ancient cultural way was to pray without ceasing. Therefore, science is not about the end to questioning. It is not about finding a final answer. It is about always questioning, and, by this means, increasing the knowledge we have about things. And thus true scientific inquiry is based on the constant and tacit recognition that the present state of knowledge about things is neither permanent nor absolute. (Actually, if scientific and intellectual leaders would fully understand this principle of the tentativeness of all knowledge acquired by the scientific method, the destructive propagandizing against religious, spiritual, intuitive, and higher cultural movements, or persuasions gotten by other means than the scientific method, would be significantly decreased—to the general benefit of mankind.)

Since the scientific method does not admit of a final or perfect answer to any question, the mood or strategy of scientific inquiry remains that of the question itself. Only the questions are forever. Thus, the conventional mood established by the popularization of an exclusively scientific culture is the mood of doubt. And, therefore, the psyche of "Everyman" has become more and more characterized by doubt, or questions without answers. As a result, the only certainties that can be propagandized are questions, doubts, anxieties, objective phenomena, and elemental states of body and mind.

For this reason, the cultural scientism of our day is perpetually, and wrongly (since it is has no direct knowledge or understanding of what it is criticizing), propagandizing against whatever it has not yet proved by its own method. Whatever is not yet proved by the scientific method is still in doubt (or still existing in the form of a question, from the scientific point of view), but the popularizers of the viewpoint of scientific and political materialism (which is the cultural extension of the scientific method and the current summation of proved knowledge) tend always to speak dogmatically. They either imply or directly propose that what is not yet proved by the scientific method is also simply false. And since the scientific mind knows or presumes no other way to enter into relations with things than by objective scientific inquiry, no way is seriously suggested to the general and somewhat closed population of scientifically based cultures for entering into the mind and process of the higher and spiritual way of Man.

Even those intellectuals who comment on religious and spiritual matters have no way to view or <u>recommend</u> religious practice. They ultimately recommend nothing more than questions and doubts, and the intention to "keep on studying the problem." Intellectualism based on scientism ultimately remains in the exclusive mood of scientism. Therefore, it cannot find answers, but only questions, doubts, and so forth. This is because the method of science is not identical to the primary structural process in Man that produces higher human participation in the world, including the moral force of love, the religious force of Divine Communion, and the evolutionary force of surrender into the Life-Power that is the Matrix of the human body-mind and the world. And unless commentators of higher cultural phenomena will attain a wisdom superior to science, they will never understand the disposition that produces love, spirituality, and the superior Man.

The summation of the effects of the predominant intellectual and popular influences of modern societies is dogmatically anti-religious and fixed in the mood of doubting and inquiring, so that anything that looks like an "answer" is regarded as some kind of demonic absurdity. But the intellectual and popular leaders of the dominant mentality have simply failed to understand the true nature of Man and the primary form of the human relationship to other beings, to the events of moment to moment experience, and to the ultimate Reality or Condition of the totality of existence. For this reason, they have failed to allow for a process in Man that is senior to doubt and inquiry.

The childish religious mind proposes that "faith" (or nonrational belief) in "revealed" or preverbal "answers" to great questions is the alternative to the chronic doubt of the scientific, analytical, verbal mentality of modern society. But the viewpoint of "belief in answers" was created in the childhood days of Man, long before the era of scientific inquiry and the culture of scientific and political materialism. Since the era of scientism began, the traditional "answers" have gradually been found to be largely untenable. And there is no right reason for believing something, if it is clearly untrue, simply because belief feels better than doubt.

Thus, the childish and dependent religiosity of traditional Man has been confounded by the adolescent and separative intellectualism of modern scientific Man. But the culture offered by the rule of scientism is bereft of anything but doubt and materialistic enthusiasm. Therefore, we must be awakened to the maturity of Man, beyond childish religiosity and adolescent intellectualism.

The mature Man is a spiritually awakened being who has transcended both the method of conventional religion and the mood of conventional scientific intellectualism. He is established in the primary disposition of Man, which is the intuition of unity with the World-Process and the active disposition of heartfelt Communion with the Reality, Life-Power, or Transcendental Unity in which the entire realm of Nature is arising, changing, and passing away. This mature Man is possessed neither by questions nor answers. He transcends all knowledge and all experience in his fundamental Condition of existence. Therefore, he is able to participate in the higher and evolutionary acculturation of his own body-mind without· resorting to archaic belief systems and childish salvation schemes, and also without succumbing to the self-divided and subhuman fixation of nonparticipatory doubt and intellectual impotence.

Only such a Man can provide the workable foundation for the creation and survival of future human cultures. He must become the new Man to which every individual commonly aspires, or else the adolescent era of scientific and political materialism will destroy not only the child in Man but also the mature manhood of Man.

I have, in this essay, continually linked scientific materialism with political materialism. This is because science, as a dominant world-view, inevitably creates or recreates the social and political order in the image or mood of science itself. And I began this essay by referring to the idea of human freedom. Now I would consider that the failure of true human freedom, or higher human acculturation, will inevitably produce a false politics—and, indeed, is already so doing.

As I have said, the concept of democracy was an idealistic and even romantic notion, founded in the ancient traditional mentality, and produced in the earliest stages of the transition to the era of

74

scientific materialism. But as the era of scientific materialism progressed, a new political design was conceived that was founded in a new idealism, entirely conceived within the "realistic" (rather than "romantic") framework of scientific materialism itself. That idealism is called "communism" and, somewhat more loosely, "socialism."

Simply stated, the communistic and socialistic ideal is associated with a collectivist (rather than an individualistic) social structure. However, the basic foundation of a communistic or socialistic State is not collectivism but the <u>authoritarian</u> role of the Parental State, which enforces collectivism. There are many positive things that may be said for forms of collective (or cooperative) social order and activity themselves. Indeed, it is the failure of the cooperative mentality and the practical politics of cooperation that is the principal sign of disintegration in a democracy. When human beings become obsessed with the motives of exclusive privacy and uninhibited personal exploitation of conventional desires, they become more and more self-indulgent, uncooperative, and antisocial. Then the intimate world of community disintegrates, followed by the disintegration of family structures.

The mass of human individuals must awaken to the Truth of Man and to the higher evolutionary culture of the truly Divine Transformation of the individual and the society as a whole. This means that the mood of both nonrational belief (which produces only the consolation rather than the transformation of Man) and rational doubt (which produces objective knowledge but allows for no fundamental transformation of the knower in the process) must both be transcended in the mood of intelligent self-knowing and self-transcending participation in the spiritual Reality that confronts us directly in our intuitive experience of the conditions of existence.

If the massive populations of human beings will begin to respond to this consideration, and if benign leaders will begin to create a culture that has outgrown childish religion and that transcends science while also making right use of scientific methods and discoveries, then it should be possible for true human freedom to persist as the fundamental characteristic of future societies. However, if such a response and such responsibility do not begin to characterize the quality of "Everyman," then future societies will more and more consist of authoritarian and materialistic States engaged in great centralized efforts to manipulate and control irresponsible populations of disturbed people.

We can already see how the democracies (as is naturally the case with large collectivist societies) are moving more and more toward the political structures of a centralized State that must support and control a large, fragmented population of disturbed and demanding people. The effects of the popular social influences in America, for example, not only tend to destroy or prevent the higher cultural development of the populace, but they actually create and exploit the subhuman and hopeless motivations that ultimately produce social fragmentation and chaos.

The false concept of human freedom produces a mass population that is fragmented into a chaotic and reactive collection of mere individuals. In that case, communities and families dissolve or become weak, and only the State remains as the source of order, help, and security. The next step is the deliberate and total centralization of power in the mechanisms of the State, and the reduction of the population to an orderly machine of production.

But what if the fragmented masses awakened to the truly responsible mood of human freedom and destiny? Then the spell would be broken, and a new possibility for the future would emerge.

And what are the political characteristics of such free and superior beings? The primary urge of the free human being, who is responsible for himself or herself and his or her relationships, is to enter into cooperative relationships with others. Therefore, if the masses of mankind will awaken to the process of higher and truly human acculturation, they will transcend childish and adolescent attitudes, they will make right use of scientific and technological means of knowing and improving the common conditions of human existence, and they will naturally enter into cooperative or relational forms of social order.

It is natural for free or responsible men and women to live in forms of cooperative commitment to one another. Therefore, truly free men and women are not separative and self-indulgent in their actions, but they are fundamentally cooperative and self-transcending in their actions. This means that responsible people create families and intimate communities, and they maintain right and responsible agreements with their intimates as well as with members of other families and communities.

But the current trends in so-called democratic societies are toward self-indulgent fulfillment of individual and lower desires (even through technological means) and away from cooperative commitments, including marriages, families, and intimate communities. The popular mood expressed in the current media of our mass culture demonstrates a general fear and disdain relative to intimate religious or secular communities, and the average citizen lives in a private castle of self-illusions, comforted by TV visions and the degenerative habits of his or her choice.

Even so, human societies must be founded on families and autonomous intimate communities, or else the State becomes the only autonomous political structure, and all culture is replaced by the salt-of-the-earth round of political subservience to State controls over every aspect of human existence. The only defense individuals have against the centralizing tendencies of the State is to break the spell of dependence on the parentlike powers of State and enter into intimate cooperative relationships with one another. Only in that case—when the social order is composed of autonomous, intimate, and higher culturally oriented communites of free and responsible men and women—can the overwhelming trend toward State control of populations by political means and also cultural means (via the official Cult of knowledge at any given time, be it the Catholic Church in the old days or the new "Church" of scientific materialism in the present day) be brought to a halt.

The practical ideal of communism, or socialism, is founded on "realistic" exploitation of the lowest needs of mankind, and it does not "romantically" depend on the higher qualities and superior aspirations of Man. Perhaps for this reason, many people presume that it is the political ideal most likely to achieve dominance in the future world of Man as he now seems, since the general population of mankind is not presently aligned to the processes of higher human acculturation. And even the once "romantic" democracies are vulnerable to the tendencies of the Parental State as a response to the chaotic problems of contemporary societies.

The truly negative aspect of the trend toward communism or socialism and away from democracy is the single one of the development of a Parental State with totalitarian police power over all people. As I have already indicated, forms of cooperative community are basic and essential to truly human and free societies. The democracies are now deficient in this respect, and, as we say in moments of angry despair, "everyone is out for himself." But the communist and socialist societies seem to be prospering through the establishment of cooperative forms of social order. Then is not the communist solution superior? Of course not! The communist solution is only superficially based on cooperative communities. Actually, the communist solution is founded on the principle of the Parental State, which controls the population, maintains the population as a mere machine of production, and, by maintaining the cultural dominance of the propaganda of scientific materialism, prevents the appearance of true communities oriented toward higher human or evolutionary and spiritual acculturation.

True communities must be the foundation of human societies, but true communities must be based on the higher and evolutionary cultural principles of spiritual Wisdom and self-transcending habits of action on the part of every individual. If such communities can begin to develop and achieve a primary voice in the media of daily understanding, then the present trend toward the politics of the Parental State can be overcome. But true communities must arise among the people as autonomous, free, and higher cultural entities. If they do not thus arise, but, rather, if the superficial communal aspect of human communities is enforced as a method of the State, then community simply becomes an instrument of the depressive powers of the Parental State machine.

The State cannot create true communities. The State cannot elicit higher cooperative motives in the people, nor should it be relied upon to do so. Nor can science or scientific materialism create a true culture of Man, since the primary acculturation of Man takes place as a process of self-transcending Communion with the Life-Principle and ecstatic Unity with the World-Process, and it involves the immediate and moment to moment evolutionary transformation of the individual—whereas the mood of scientific materialism is doubt, and the method of scientific inquiry excludes the process whereby the knower himself is transformed. Therefore, the Cult of scientific materialism is fundamentally a tool of the Parental State, and it only serves the establishment of a disturbed and dependent humanity that must resort to the authoritarian propaganda and technological resources of the State and the scientific Cult of the State.

Science is only benign when it becomes the tool of free men, and the State is only benign when it must necessarily respond to the demands of the people. But the people do not represent a power superior to the State unless they become responsible and autonomous through the establishment of free cooperative communities, wherein individuals are obliged in their actions only by the higher culture of Wisdom served to them in intimate company, while they yet remain entirely free of the dictatorial limitations that a Parental State will always apply to their actions—even their most personal, private, and intimate actions. Likewise, the masses of humanity will not enter into true forms of cooperative and higher evolutionary community unless they begin to respond to the Wisdom-Teaching of living Adepts and overcome both their childish and dependent religiosity and their separative adolescent predisposition toward a self-indulgent, analytical, and dissociative view of the world and Man.

The Illusion of the Separation of Church and State

Modern societies generally acknowledge the principle of the separation of Church and State. The origin of this common principle was in the early conflicts that arose between traditional religious institutions and the emerging powers of secular scientism and technology. In the historical transition of mankind from the cultic religious basis of ancient societies to the scientific and technological basis of modern secular societies, the old religions balked at some of the implications of the "new knowledge." Therefore, if scientific technology were to provide the basis for the new era of Man, the dominance of the social order by the authority of official cultic religion had to be brought to an end.

The principle of the separation of Church and State is simply the "civilized" device created to permit the transition from a religious to a secular order of society.

Ever since this principle became the working norm, cultic religion itself has been gradually diminished in power and secularized in its content. And the "new knowledge" of science, which provides the dogmatic basis for what is in effect a new "Church" (or official way of knowing and living), has become more and more a critic of cultic religion. Indeed, the scientific establishment and its spawn of university intellectualism and large-scale technical and industrial enterprise have displaced the ancient culture of religion. In fact, the principle of the separation of Church and State is itself only a strategy for excluding conventional or cultic religion from the creative position of authority over the proceedings of society in general. Truly, that principle does not apply to the official "Church" of secular society.

The State is always in league with the official "Church" of scientific materialism in all modern industrial societies. And the authority and authenticity of every religion other than science is fundamentally excluded by the dominant "Church." The Rule of science moves over the world with the heavy hand of State power, creating scandal and doubt and fear in every area of independent cultural creativity. And all religions are forced to suffer the plundering by this new "Church"—or else convert and be transformed into a species of the "new faith."

As a result, we find that certain religious cults have submitted to a high degree of containment by the secular forces, and so they have been granted a kind of official status as "allowable cults." Such is true of mainstream Christianity and Judaism in much of the Western world. However, even these, along with the other cults of the "great religions," are the subjects of oppression in those secular societies in which the "Church" of scientific materialism is most clearly in power, based on its intimate association with the State, or the practical idealism of political materialism. (Such oppression is true in the absolutist secular States of European and Asian communism.)

The trend of the new "religion" of scientific materialism is to exclude the mystical, evolutionary, and independent cultural motivations of all peoples, and to establish a political ideal of materialistic work-effort in every area of society. Therefore, wherever this trend succeeds, human beings are devoted to individualistic motives and collectivist hopes for material progress that will ultimately permit every future individual to enjoy a prolonged life span of pleasurable self-fulfillment.

Wherever conventional cultic or "old-style" religions are permitted to survive in secular societies, they are able to survive only by adapting to the new social and political idealism and the new knowledge. Thus, cultic religion has become more and more a merely poetic restatement of "humanistic" psychological interpretations of

Man. And the "mysteries" of religion have become merely prescientific allegories for natural events that have now become banal truisms, or "closed cases" in the continuing "detective story" of science. Certain "fundamentalist" religious beliefs remain at the less sophisticated levels of popular society, but such religious beliefs are generally regarded as a kind of harmless and ridiculous intoxication that has no real significance in the daily world of sober social effort.

I am not protesting that archaic religious institutions have ceased to be able to freely dominate mankind via intimate association with powers of State. I am protesting that a new, aggressively anti-religious, secular, and materialistic philosophical trend is everywhere in league with the State. And the true religious or evolutionary spiritual Wisdom-Teaching of the great Adepts of the world is being prevented from achieving its rightful role as the dominant cultural motive of mankind. Indeed, the new "Church" of scientific materialism is not, in this regard, any different from the old exoteric religions that were previously in league with State powers.

The religious institutions that anciently achieved legitimacy and dominance through political association were exoteric "Church" institutions that supported ideals compatible with the secular motives of the State. Those religious institutions are still present today as the "allowable" cults of Christianity, Judaism, Islam, and so forth. But the more basically secular "religion" of scientific materialism has superseded the authority of exoteric religion and, therefore, in most societies, the State is now designed in separation from the old cults, and, in many cases, the State and its new "religion" are in direct opposition to the old cults.

Truly, the exoteric religions of the old world are archaic, and they are fast becoming obsolete. The obsolescence of the ancient exoteric religious conceptions is inevitable and not inherently wrong or regrettable. However, what is wrong and regrettable is the continued disposition in the institutions of popular secular society to exclude the esoteric Wisdom of the evolutionary spiritual Teaching of true Adepts, ancient and modern.

The exclusion of true or esoteric religion has been the business of the State since ancient times. At first this was done via the establishment of the popular idealism of <u>exoteric</u> religious institutions in league with the State. But in modern times the same process is done by the strategic exclusion of conventional religious cultism, mystical idealism, and higher evolutionary Wisdom from the mechanisms of popular culture.

Consider all of this carefully. Observe the dominant powers that influence, propagandize, and rule in our daily lives. Examine the strategies of your own opinions. Criticize the motives of your own desiring. Then you will see how urgent is the need that mankind awaken to a new cultural destiny.

In the realm of popular culture, scientific and political materialism is in power. And the essence of official popular propaganda is fundamentally anti-religious and devoted to an exclusively materialistic interpretation of Man and Nature. The "allowable" or semi-official cults of the yet remaining religious establishment continue to serve as exoteric religious extensions of the secular State. But all non-establishment cults of free religious, mystical, and spiritual experimentation and practice are constantly the subjects of negative propaganda in the popular communications media. And "intellectual leaders" are constantly agitating against esoteric and non-establishment religious cultism—and especially against the possibility that any religious or spiritual leader achieve a position of widespread influence and power in the midst of the secular order. (Therefore, university intellectualism and popular criticism generally oppose, or at least work to maintain the disposition of doubt relative to, religion, religious institutions, mysticism, and the naturally dominant role of the Living God and true Spiritual Masters in the esoteric culture of true religion.)

I am deeply dismayed by the trends of popular culture in our day, and I have grave concerns about the immediate future of the human world. The modern machines of political power and "official" propaganda are immense, and the common mind of even the most considerable intellects of our day is monstrously deficient in higher understanding and purpose. The people are full of righteous needs, but they are otherwise possessed by aggressively self-indulgent motives and all of the self-deluding conventions of the mob-mind.

I am awakened and committed to another understanding than the one that now and traditionally has motivated and controlled the human world. But I can do no more than Teach, by word and intimate demonstration. I have no worldly power to change mankind. My only power is the Truth that I Teach, and the love or sympathy that any man or woman may be moved to grant me as they consider, and practice, and change in community with me. Therefore, I can only plead and beg for your attention and for your understanding of the esoteric spiritual Way that I Teach. And if I am heard by many, then perhaps we can together demand real changes in the cultural basis of the social order, so that Wisdom will at long last become the Master of Church and State.

82

Frustration:
The Universal Disease

Fundamentally, the conditions of experience are not organized around our passive, random, and casual participation, but they oblige us to conscious, responsible, and active participation. To the degree we do not live consciously, responsibly, and actively, we are confronted and overwhelmed by the random force of events. If our will or responsible intention is weak, neither casual inclinations nor essential functional needs will tend to be satisfied by our passively attained circumstances. And even if we become consciously and responsibly active, full of intention in the world, the forces of the material and psychic circumstance of the world will always bear upon us, yielding only occasional and partial fulfillment of our personal desires.

Therefore, frustration of the individual is a basic fact in the Realm of Nature. At best we may enter into the stream of changes, through right intention and appropriate action, but we will in any case more or less constantly suffer the frustration borne upon us by the stresses of the world-changes, which have no ultimate tendency to satisfy or eternalize individuals. The Force of Life we intuit to be within us is moved by our willful or desiring acts to create circumstances of fulfillment. But that Life is truly Universal and All-Pervading, not inward and personal. Therefore, if that Life is manipulated by inward motives to satisfy personal desires of all kinds, not only will that satisfaction be only occasional and mostly partial— but the Force of Life will itself be frustrated, since it cannot fulfill its

Universal or All-Pervading Function or Realize its Transcendental Freedom.

Also, when human beings gather in large collectives, or orders of State, a design is brought to the possibilities of experience, and the collective order moves on in its daily fashion, even if the individual lapses into a passive mood. Thus, it is possible for individuals in any social order to succumb to a chronically frustrated mood, and yet their mechanical or passive participation will be sufficient for at least a minimal satisfaction of ordinary personal desires. Indeed, where the State becomes a great worldly power, and the individual is controlled and limited beyond any hope of truly creative and free movement, either psychically or physically, then every individual is essentially obliged to the mode of passive or mechanical participation. And such is the tendency and common option of most individuals in the world today.

The Wisdom-Culture of Man at Infinity has been arrested all over the world. Everywhere, individuals are dominated by subhuman powers. The politics of human life has been brought under the control of salt-of-the-earth ideologies and gross scientific or technological machines of State. The truly spiritual understanding of Man is suppressed in every area of common education, and official voices are present everywhere to anathematize the deep visions and urges of the higher material, psychic, and spiritual or Transcendental dimensions of the human gesture in the world. Truly, it is always more or less so in the human world, but it is also clearly so at the present time.

The result of this suppression of Man by Nature and by the State is the appearance of a universal and chronic disease. It is frustration, or depression of Life. Everyone suffers this chronic depression, and everyone must struggle to overcome it. But the effects of the propagandistic subhuman powers of the world tend to minimize the conscious, responsible, and active mode of individual participation in the stream of experiential events. We tend to be passively or helplessly aligned to "what is," because our Force of Life is frustrated, in doubt, crippled by a profound despair, which is always present, even if concealed under an exterior gloss of enthusiasm and competence.

Both Nature and the State demonstrate an acknowledgment of the limits of the individual capacity for the frustration of Life.

83

Thus, a minimum but vulgar satisfaction is commonly held out as the constant promise of daily living—if only one will be calm and accept the passive role of mechanical participation in the game of limits proposed by Nature and the State.

But only the most unconscious and childish people can be satisfied by such a meagre destiny. And, for this reason, both Nature and the State are engaged in a perpetual machine of effort to "clone" as many controllable and minimal human individuals as possible. Even so, the usual man cannot easily tolerate the perpetual round of Life-frustration. Therefore, Nature and the State allow some few consoling indulgences that function as periodic and temporary relief, enabling frustration to be discharged in occasional degenerative outbursts.

Nature provides the possibilities of degenerative self-indulgence abundantly, but the State must control these means, or else the mass of frustrated humanity would resort to constant intoxication and become uncontrollable or unproductive. Thus, highly stimulating substances, to be taken internally, as well as highly stimulating entertainments, or outward distractions, are allowed, but more or less controlled by the State. The minimally stimulating substances (such as killed meat food, manufactured or artificial delights, tobacco, and so forth) are minimally controlled. But more intensely stimulating substances are always the subject of controls and even absolute suppression. Thus, alcohol, hallucinogenic drugs, and so forth are always the subjects of preoccupation by the State. Likewise, minimally stimulating and useful propagandistic entertainments, such as television, movies, popular literature, and even the press, are in "spirit" controlled but generally, at least in the West, only minimally suppressed by the State. They are, in general, even exploited by the State. But intensely stimulating "entertainments," such as orgiastic sexual indulgence, criminal violence, and anarchism, are always strictly controlled and suppressed by the State. And the exploitation of these subjects by the otherwise popular media is also strictly controlled, or else, where direct control is difficult, there is constant propagandistic preoccupation, on the part of the State, or the official social media, against such exploitation of sex, crime, and anarchy.

Since the State depends on its power to control the indulgence of individuals in intensely stimulating or intoxicating experiences,

84

which tend to orient people toward unproductive self-centeredness rather than coordinated social productivity, the State also tolerates and often promotes a degree of "religion." Every individual can, through social propaganda and various psychological media, be made at least occasionally critically aware that chronic indulgence in self-centered stimulants, internal and external, is degenerative and antisocial. And Nature provides the core of mortal fear necessary for the rest of the power of the conventional religious argument.

Likewise, the highly technological or scientifically propagandized social order can provide "religious" consolations of its own. Ordinary religion is an argument against the personal and social effects of intoxicated or chaotic self-indulgence (most prominently in alcohol, hallucinogenic drugs, sex, and criminal or anarchistic violence). And such religion is also an argument for the possibility of release from the conditions we tend most to fear—particularly pain, death, and absolute frustration of the pleasurable sense of existence. In less technological or scientifically propagandized societies, religion appears in its conventional form, which is a system of mythological beliefs or glamorous psychological persuasions toward positive social inclinations, or conventional "morality," which is conceived as a means to acquire both satisfaction while alive and immortal pleasures after death. In technological and scientifically propagandized societies, religion appears more in the form of another myth—the myth of "real" or "demythologized" knowledge—along with elaborate technological and political strategies for healing, pleasuring, and even immortalizing people.

But religion is tolerable to the State only to a degree and in a certain mode. The mythological and technological consolations are tolerable only to the degree they reinforce positive and productive social behavior—and they are intolerable to the degree they produce autointoxication, or obsession with mystical and poetic revery. Thus, the State in general propagandizes against the deep psychological, higher psychic, and mystical phenomena associated with the more profound reaches of religion and the radical contemplation of the world by the individual. (All knowledge must be "official," and thus propagandized by the common media of the social and verbal mind, not the private and nonrational media of the psyche.)

If all of this is understood to be true, then what alternative may be offered? If the frustration of Man is even the business of both

86

Nature and the State, then what is the alternative to frustration, despair, chaotic and degenerative self-indulgence, and autointoxication? The answer is that there is no alternative to all of that, unless the individual Awakens to the Transcendental Truth in which the phenomena of Nature (or the world of the body-mind) are arising. And if individuals so Awaken in sufficient numbers, then the functions of the State may become the responsibility of the Wise, or the Friends of Man.

Only if Transcendental Wisdom moves the State can the State cease to be the subhuman Oppressor of subhumanity. The State need not be destroyed, any more than the Realm of Nature must or even can be destroyed. But just as the Play of Nature, or the experiential body-mind, must be transcended, the conventional or subhuman order must be transcended. The world must become the Domain of the Wise (those who are adapted to a degree of functional realization that is more than human), and those who are Elders in the Way of Wisdom must also become the acknowledged Masters of Man. Devotees of the Living God must accept responsibility for the social and cultural order of human experience, and the Wisdom of Transcendental Divine Realization must, with all of its Lawful and practical understanding, become the root of all common education.

The usual man, who is mechanically and passively, if fitfully or neurotically, associated with the conventions of daily experience, is the subject of profound frustration of the Force and Condition of Life. The Life that appears to move him is inherently moved to Realize its Transcendental Condition of Radiant Bliss, the Freedom of Absolute Consciousness. And that Radiant Life would even Radiate as the world and as the body-mind of Man, except that the Force of that Absolute Radiance is confused with the independent self-position of the mortal individual, and thus it is constantly frustrated by all the petty limitations of functionally and socially organized desire and energy.

Therefore, the Condition of our Life must be Realized. We must not merely be filled with Life. The self that seeks to be filled must become a sacrifice. The individual must become Ecstatic, or self-released. We must function in the mode of self-transcendence rather than self-indulgence.

If we Awaken to the Truth of the Living God, then we will cease to be inherently frustrated, since Life is thus released from binding identification with the conventional self or body-mind. And if we persist in such Awakening, or whole bodily Enlightenment, then we will also cease to be <u>chronically</u> frustrated, since we will be conscious, responsible, and active in the midst of the stream of experience.

Until that Awakening, we may crave the ordinary instruments whereby individuals commonly relieve their sense of inherent and chronic frustration. Thus, we may crave self-indulgent and degenerative exploitation of stimulating substances, such as killed meat food, tobacco, alcohol, and hallucinogenic drugs, or stimulating activities, such as degenerative erotic sexuality, and even criminal or anarchistic violence. But if we Awaken to the Bliss of the Living God, then we are inherently released from such cravings, and we may quickly grow out of all our chronic dependence on such degenerative associations.

Likewise, if we Awaken to the Way of the Radiant Transcendental Consciousness, the Way of the Bliss of the Living God, we will be inherently free of the need or the persuasion of conventional religion, all the suggestive consolations of mere objective scientism, and the absurd propagandistic or humanly depressive uses of gross technology. And we will be free to enter into a truly moral relationship with the world and with the society of human individuals. We will cease to be motivated by self-centered desire, and our movements will become conscious, responsible expressions of Ecstasy, or true God-Communion. We will be full of inherent pleasure, and free of chronic obsession with all the degenerative means of acquiring the sense of pleasure that the inherent frustrations of Life chronically exclude.

Likewise, free of false religion (which only motivates and controls and further deludes frustrated or childish and adolescent people), we will become inherently oriented toward the true religious or spiritual process of Life. We will naturally enter into the ecstatic mystical expansion that is structurally inevitable in Man. And we will ultimately transcend the psychic or mystical phenomena of the body-mind, even as we first transcend the physical or vital and elemental as well as ordinary or lower mental phenomena of our experience.

Thus liberated, we will transcend the illusions that all conventional religions and technologies conceal. We will not look for Freedom via magic, just as we will not look to degenerative self-indulgence for Bliss. We will not regard the inner or psychic dimension of the body-mind to be separate from and merely magically related to the body or the world of natural relations. We will observe the Life-Power that is subtler than the gross physical, but we will also Realize that the Power of Life is truly operative only in the simultaneity of the body-mind, or the cooperation of body and mind, rather than the domination of one by the other.

88 Even the Spiritual Master does not heal by magical means. Rather, he works to Awaken responsibility at the heart, the center of both body and mind. At times, the Spiritual Master, or the Divine Power, may appear to Awaken individuals suddenly, or to heal them so quickly that no natural process seems to have been involved. But this does not truly imply any magical activity—only suddenness of the simultaneous Awakening of body and mind, or the Principle of the heart.

There is no spiritual Awakening, nor any true healing or change of Man, unless the heart, or the body-mind as a whole, is coincidentally or simultaneously Awakened. Thus, most of the changes developed in individuals through surrender to the Living God and the Agency of the Spiritual Master are gradual, rather than sudden. In general, time is required for the various parts of the body-mind to be purified, enlivened, changed, and integrated with all other parts, coincident with the Life-Power at the heart. There is no true Awakening without a change of heart, a literal purification, a redress of wrongs, and a change of habits.

In summary, Man is subhuman until he Awakens from mere desire, or self-indulgence, to Love, or self-transcendence, in constant Communion with the Living God and in Lawful or responsible management of all functional and relational conditions of experience. The Awakened or true Man is inherently Free of all the frustrating limitations of Nature and the State. He is Radiant in the world, so that the Transcendental Reality is alive as him. Therefore, a world of human beings so Awakened may create a truly benign and moral Culture, or true State, founded in the Wisdom-Influence of the Radiant Transcendental Consciousness. And only human beings so Awakened and so ordered are free of the inherent and chronic frustrations that produce subhuman societies, subhuman cravings, and subhuman destinies, before and after death.

Radical Politics
for Ordinary Men and Women

A talk by Da Free John

DA FREE JOHN: We have renounced our real and true politics. We have renounced responsibility for our own lives, and we no longer determine them. We do not assume freedom of movement, association, and commitment, but we assume instead that we have to listen to every little bureaucrat, intellectual, commentator, or revolutionary who wants to control or prevent our intimate politics and society. And this assumption reflects and results from our frightened renunciation of the Life-Principle and the exuberant vitality of bodily existence.

Because individuals are afraid of their own vitality, afraid to be polarized to it whole bodily and to enjoy it intelligently and responsibly, we have the present-day world, which is a product of at least 3,000 years of patriarchal, anti-sexual, anti-Life indoctrination. The result is a society of morons and slaves. Many people in this present-day world are no less slaves than the poor beasts who built the pyramids. For the most part, we are an unconscious mass, controlled by shrewder people.

In the most ancient days, men and women were oriented toward delight, toward vital life. They were positively, but not obsessively, polarized to the Life-Principle. But ever since the advent of the modern other-worldly religions, men have assumed that vital life is supposed to be manipulated, suppressed, and even eliminated. People are deeply troubled about their vitality. The whole of modern society is built around the manipulative suppression of Life. Even the State is in the business. Everything has become very humorless. You are supposed to <u>work</u>. That is the asceticism of the common man and woman. You are supposed to be a mere salt-of-the-earth worker, and you are not to be fundamentally and ecstatically involved in delight. You are not expected or permitted to be conscious. Consciousness is not valued. You are supposed to work and buy junk food and television sets, and you are not to be aware of anything fundamentally curious that might cause you to become erratic and profound.

90

Some anthropologists say that Man's uniqueness is that he makes tools. But that is only a secondary and debatable uniqueness. His fundamental uniqueness is that he interiorizes the problem of survival. The sense of existence itself as a problem, as a dilemma, is inherent in the human condition. And, through the tool of desire, Man constantly creates new solutions. He seeks a condition of release that exceeds the limits of both mind and body. Thus, he invents an interior or mystical process, through which he can step out of both mind and body into another world. But he also does other things. By virtue of having a mind, he is able to enter into creative relationship to the functional processes in himself and in the world. So he creates sciences and technologies as practical tools for dealing with the material conditions of existence. But both of these possibilities, both mystical and technological, are extensions of the ordinary game of problem-solving.

Until the common individual begins to grasp some basic understanding of his ultimate Condition, he is exploitable by individuals who arbitrarily assume a creative power and authority beyond his own. So the usual man or woman, who works in a factory or an office and listens to the News faithfully, is constantly exploited by all kinds of shrewd people who are really in charge of his or her political, social, and intimate life.

For the usual person, politics is merely a matter of listening to the News every night. Our politics is either a childish or an adolescent reaction to the fact of being controlled by the State. One individual plays the "system," and the other is a revolutionary. The child buys the "system" and wants it to work, and the adolescent is a perpetual revolutionary. Both types are merely dealing with the Parent Figure in ordinary ways.

If you stop listening to and believing in the News, and if you simply observe what is really going on, you can get depressed and feel that your life is not under your control. But that is really a very minimal insight. Obviously, everybody is controlled. The typical response is to react by joining a revolution, getting drunk, kicking a couple of bad politicians out of office, having a war, getting "high" on drugs or religious and mystical illusions, becoming an anti-communist, or becoming a communist. But reaction is obviously not the way to transform politics. What is needed is to establish a completely different principle of human culture and politics, one that is not based on reaction to all the bad News—because there is only bad News in the ordinary, unenlightened, chaotic world. Instead of waiting for action from sources out in the beyond somewhere—government sources, media sources, Divine sources, or whatever it is that you wait for all the time—become involved yourself in intimate community with other human beings. In a responsible, mutually dependent, and intimate relationship with those people, create and protect the basics of a truly human culture and daily society.

91

The only reason the State can exploit you is that you are in vital shock, or self-dividing recoil from the Life-Principle, and you believe that you need a number of things you cannot get without playing for or against the "system." But if you are already alive, already full of humor, already full of the Living God, you need not be concerned about any of that. You can and must create your own politics—in intimate cooperative association with your fellow human beings.

The existence of the big "system" does not make any ultimate positive difference in the daily life of the individual. You can and must live a humorous, responsible life, regardless of the "system." Of course, it can be done a little easier if the "system" is relatively loose and benign, as it still is in America. You would have to be more inventive to do it in an absolutist society, or during a war in a bombed-out town, but it could still be done.

The true change we must create is not principally in the system itself (in the "Parent") but in the ordinary associations between human beings. Common people must simply live in an entirely different way. They must understand themselves, externally and internally, and they must adapt to a totally new way of life, in which they are each personally responsible for the character of daily existence, and in which they simply live together, without a Parent anymore.

A truly rational politics cannot be enacted merely by investing everything in a worldwide system of Parentlike bureaucracies. The abstract system creates childish dependencies and illusory solutions, and it discourages the general possibility of genuine personal responsibility or involvement. The true politics of the individual is in relation to what is intimate to him. Truly human politics is in the sphere of relationships experienced on a daily basis, where the individual's voice and experience can be heard and dramatically felt.

That, fundamentally, is politics. All the rest is only the vulgar News of the world-machine.

A politics based on truly human or intimate relationships is not likely to take place on a large scale in a present-day city, although that is a possibility. But present-day cities are merely a random collection of subhuman emergencies. People crowd together in modern cities for all kinds of conflicting and subhuman reasons. These are not genuine cities in any fully human sense. A true city would be a large-scale community, an essentially autonomous, cooperative, and intimate order of mutually dependent people who are devoted to the higher evolutionary culture of Man. But we do not have that kind of consciousness in the cities of today. Today a city is just a collection of disturbed and fascinated people, not a conscious, working association of truly human beings. Without a community of responsible relationships and higher cultural agreements, there can be no valid form of politics. True politics is the higher function of the personal relationships between individuals living in free cooperation with one another.

The true community is not just another utopian commune, in which everybody tries to be perfect or perfectly fulfilled—as if such were possible. Higher human and spiritual understanding is the principle of life in true community. Communities are rightly established when human beings understand the functional design of Man as a totality and as a single or simultaneous whole, and when the problem-solving, creative capacities of human beings are rightly measured in terms of their ultimate importance. Human beings must understand and be responsible for their liabilities and their tendencies to live life as an inherent or irreducible dilemma and as a perpetual search for self-glorifying fulfillment of loveless inclinations.

In such a community, every one knows what every one else has the tendency to become (when irresponsible) and the possibility to become (when responsible). And all serve one another at the level of that understanding. They all also know the functional character and capacity of each other, and they amuse and enjoy and serve and employ one another at every appropriate level. But responsibility for functional life must always be assumed and demanded in a truly human community. When it is not, that failure of responsibility will weaken the community and thus enable (or even oblige) other, shrewder men and women to exploit and oppress the members of the community and make them slaves again.

So if men and women will enter into true community, into intimate cooperative and higher cultural relationship with one another, they will no longer be exploitable by any Life-negating Parent source in the social and political realm. The negatively dominant bureaucracy of the Parent State becomes obsolete only through non-use. And, once its negative and Parentlike powers become obsolete through non-use, the State will again be obliged to become the simple instrument of the responsible agreements of the people. If the people do not assume childish dependence on the State, then the State in which they live makes little ultimate difference. And if the people truly become collectively responsible for the mechanisms of the State, then individual freedom will never really be threatened.

Conventional politics has always been associated with an ideal of one or another sort. In the last hundred years, the ideal has switched from a humanistic to an economic one, but all merely idealistic systems tend to depend on temporary, emergency solutions to basic problems. This is because conventional idealism is an abstraction, a basis for a politics of manipulation of people by the State, but not for an intimate politics of practical responsibility on the part of the people for both themselves and the State. The tactics of abstract State politics always relate to a more or less irresponsible and controlled populace, and, therefore, the State tends to be fixed in a view of human life as a dilemma that continuously requires new emergency reactions to solve the constant crisis of new emergency problems. As a result, we get an insane conglomeration of temporary solutions and a bureaucratic State that is oppressive, rigid, immense, and intolerable.

The fundamentals of life must be pre-solved at the local level, at the regional level where the community exists. Within the community, every member should be guaranteed access to the basic necessities of life (provided each individual functions responsibly and cooperatively within the community). Basic solutions to human needs do not generally require resort to any of the resources of the State, but they should be managed locally in one's own community, and in natural cooperation with other communities. (In other words, first establish community and the planned solutions to fundamental needs, and, on that basis, see what kind of agreements are useful in cooperation with other communities and with large-scale cooperative agencies.)

Politics is a human adventure, and our inherent obligation involves the realization of our humanity as a discipline. We do not really have the option to renounce our humanity or the Life that sustains us. Rather, we must assume the burden and the delight of human relationships. We must assume all the structures of Man (both lower and higher) as real conditions of existence. And we must become functionally responsible to the Life-Principle in every area of our experience. To the degree that all of this is done, it obliges us to be committed to existence in the dimensions of time and space, but only then are we also perfectly free to carry on the creative evolutionary and ecstatically self-transcending process of our own lives.

If we do not assume responsibility for our own lives, we deserve all the dreadful results that come down the road every day. The News is our ordinary destiny, our minimal inheritance. Everybody tends to sit like cattle at the feet of the daily News, expecting it will all eventually evolve into some superior politics or fate. But truly human politics or destiny cannot go on unconsciously. Truly human life occurs where consciousness enters the domain of existence. There is no human politics, then, without conscious responsibility. You cannot sit like mice in front of the TV, dutifully listening to the official News every night, and rightly expect or require that somebody in Washington is going to create some super-program or announce some Super-Truth that will liberate you from your lowly estate. You must take responsibility for yourself. It is not by reforming the State in any way, but by consciously stepping apart from your childish dependence on it, that you carry on radical and truly human politics. You must provide your own requirements, in personal and local cooperation with others. You must enter into intimate community with others. You must cooperatively share your functions, your resources, and your vitality with other human beings. That is the only true and liberating politics for human beings.

The usual man's life is built on the idea that the law of life is survival, and that survival is the significance, meaning, and goal of existence, whereas in Truth, the fundamental process of Man, and even the very Realm of Nature, is one of sacrifice. Sacrifice is the Law. The usual life is not built upon the self-transcending principle of sacrifice, but on the self-fulfilling principle of survival, or the aggressive self-glorification of the individualized, separate, and separative entity. This is the common illusion, and this game of surviving as a separate, self-contained, and separative "someone" is what makes human existence the overwhelming chaos of troubles that it has now become for everyone. But the fact is that all specific "somethings" must ultimately be sacrificed, and human existence itself must become a sacrificial affair, in which nothing is maintained for its own sake. As soon as the individual realizes that the Law of Life is loving sacrifice to the Life-Principle, and not survival independent of the Life-Principle, he becomes free. He becomes free of guilt, fear, his entire ritual of obsessive activity, all the assumed dilemmas of subhuman culture and politics, and all the Parent-child games of the usual life in this world.

The Religious Necessity of Community

There is no such thing as true religion without community. The sacred community is the necessary theatre wherein true religious responsibilities and activities can take place.

Over time, religious understanding and responsibilities tend to become abstracted and dogmatized, so that religion is made to seem to be a merely personal or private endeavor. Thus, popular religion tends to be deficient as a true culture.

The State, or the broad plane of politics and economics, is a secular domain. When the people become tied exclusively to the secular environment of the State, they become fragmented into a mass of mere individuals, controlled by great political and economic forces. Therefore, religion must function not only as the Teaching of ultimate spiritual Realization. It must become the working foundation of right human relationships. The Teaching of religion must become the foundation of human acculturation. That is, religion must become the instrument whereby individuals create a cooperative order, a union of human communities.

Popular religion tends to create an institutional order, but it generally fails to create a free cooperative order or true culture. The institutions of popular religion tend to organize the attention and resources of people in much the same manner as the State. That is, merely "institutional" religion fragments the native community of Man into a superficial order of weakly associated individuals. It does not oblige people to create literal religious community, involving mutual cooperation, responsibility, and dependence.

Therefore, practitioners of true religion should orient themselves to the free creation of sacred community, and they should work with one another to create truly cooperative human environments. Truly, this obligation can only be fulfilled by those who are sufficiently mature to be religiously responsible in the moral and practical theatre of human relationships. Thus, all such practitioners should live in circumstances wherein there are constant opportunities to be tested and to be creative in relationships with others, but it is perhaps only among the most mature practitioners or esoteric initiates that the fullest agreements are possible, agreements which oblige each and all to accept the many daily and household conditions of a completely cooperative community of devotees of the Living God.

Family and Community

The great social problem of the present time is not the fragmentation of the family—although this too is symptomatic—but the great social problem is the fragmentation of community and the destruction of the intimate social and spiritual culture of community, in favor of the domination of humanity by the abstracted and dehumanizing Power of the State and all the media of popular indoctrination. Freedom from the Parental powers of the materialistic politics of State is possible only if people enter into responsible cooperation with one another in free communities. In that case, the State can do no more than represent the will and strength of an autonomous, free, and responsible populace.

And freedom from the Parental powers of the Cult of scientific and political materialism is possible only if people respond to the higher, esoteric, evolutionary, and Transcendental Teaching of Wisdom, so that they may live together in a true culture of Man, in Communion with the Living Divine Reality. Then the adolescent and technologically manipulative Cults of official knowledge that tend to thrive on an ignorant or childish populace can do no more than inform and increase the capability of humanity to survive and to fulfill its evolutionary role in the universe.

Cooperative Democracy

Freedom is a matter of consciousness (or real intelligence) and responsibility. It is the duty and fundamental political motive or urge of free men and women to create an intimate cooperative union with other men. Therefore, the basic idea of democracy, or of free society in general, is not mere personal independence (nor impersonally organized collectivism), but it is community, or the culture of responsible intimacy.

The principal obligations or practical responsibilities of any truly free or democratic community are:

1. the practical establishment of truly humanizing and evolutionary cultural and spiritual Wisdom as the basis of the daily education, moral and personal testing, and literal practice of all members of the community

2. the lawful establishment of rights of privacy and personal mobility within the community, and the full consideration and clear enunciation of just laws (or behavioral agreements) as well as right and just means of enforcing and adjudicating the laws or agreements within and without the community (If law ceases to be a matter of abstract and arbitrary rules, but it is simply a matter of behavioral

98

agreements made on the basis of wisdom and compassion, then "law enforcement" and "justice" will also tend to become natural and intimate functions of the human community itself, rather than the duty of abstracted powers that manipulate "criminals." Only if the matter of law remains within the province of the intimate community will citizens adapt to the truly moral point of view, and it is also only within the intimate community that the "letter" of the law can remain secondary to the compassionate and humanizing judgment of wise representatives of the "community mind." Only one for whom the loss of community would be the greatest loss of all will accept the rules and tests and judgments of the community. And such a one generally need not be "punished" if he commits any wrong, but he can be healed by the obligation to serve the people he has wronged, as a condition for his reacceptance into full participation in the community. But "outsiders," or individuals who have never lived within the community bond of a living culture, in fact have no peers and no moral foundation for their existence. Therefore, great authoritarian or Parental States breed outlaws, because they destroy the political principle of autonomous and intimate community as the basic unit of citizen participation.)

3. the comprehensive planning and orderly development or "pre-solving" of the total natural and human environment of the community (both in itself and in its cooperative relations with all other communities)

4. the management of the universal availability of fundamental and necessary goods and services within the responsible community, and thus the guarantee of access to those goods and services on the part of all members of the community who participate cooperatively and responsibly in the community and who can thus offer one or another kind of fair exchange for goods and services (And the community should, in its cooperative relations with all other communities, help to establish the universal availability of necessary goods and services within all other communities.)

The Revolution I Propose

Politics is founded on concern for the <u>availability</u> of the goods and opportunities of human life. Truly human culture is founded on concern for the <u>right use</u> of the goods and opportunities of human life, as well as concern for the higher growth and ultimate self-transcendence of human individuals.

The realm of politics is the realm of conventional striving, and it tends to dominate human life with dehumanizing force, unless Wisdom is valued by the people and by those in power. Until the culture of Wisdom produces individual responsibility and general agreement on the ultimate Situation of human existence, all talk of "freedom" and "justice" is nothing more than political gossip.

Every man and woman must be politically free to enjoy access to the goods and opportunities of human life, but every man and woman must likewise be spiritually responsible for the right use of those goods and the right exercise of those opportunities. Any other situation is subhuman, bereft of culture, incompatible with true freedom and justice, and leading nowhere but toward exploitation and despair.

The true social revolution is a cultural revolution, not a political or economic one. The political and economic necessities become relatively easy to organize once the Wisdom of the truly human cultural orientation is generally accepted. Until we all Awaken to the Situation and purpose of human existence, we will create no lasting peace or order, and each day will bring the world closer to the finite chaos of War and Bewilderment. But if the Wisdom of true Spiritual Adepts is "heard" in the human world, then the true revolution can begin, and all the dreadful destiny that now lies before us can be dissolved in the Heart of God.

The Healing Power
of Community

Only true, spiritual, and moral community provides the human functional basis for the continuous testing and schooling of human qualities. When people exist outside the cultural bond of community, all the forms of anti-social and self-possessed aberration appear, and, once having appeared, they cannot truly be changed unless the individual is restored to the condition of community. (Until community is restored, the responsibility for "curing" antisocial or subhuman aberrations seems to belong to abstract professions and institutions. But neither the State, nor any cult of laws and police, nor the great priesthood of psychiatrists can do what can only be done by the humanizing influence of true cultural demands within the bond of community.)

Therefore, devote your freedom to community. Put your energy into human things.

Refuge, or the Radical
Function of Community
within the Politics of State

The intimate community is inherently free or liberating in function, whereas the State, as a Parentlike Power, is a binding or fixed condition. Free men and women must create a refuge, or human sanctuary, for their growth, and this is not done in personal isolation, but only in intimate cultural cooperation.

The function of community is to be a humorous refuge, a servant of higher adaptation—a refuge from the humorless and grounding demands of the binding politics of the Parental State. The true and right function of the representative State is to ensure the possibility and also the necessity of human community, by acting as a focus for the representation of common needs (legal, protective, broadly economic and social, international, and so forth) and by preserving restraints upon its own actions, so that the fundamental, necessary, and humanizing obligations of communities constantly fall back on communities themselves. (The failure of human community is demonstrated when the State becomes the target of childish demands and the agent of grand solutions that should be the responsibility of human beings in their cultural and social intimacy.)

The community and the State should be a dynamic play, in which the community is the core value and Principle of all basic solutions. The State should, by law and common agreement, yield all exercise and sovereignty over the intimate affairs of communities, and all communities should be autonomous or self-regulating, except to the degree that the actions of any community actually serve to undermine or prevent the very existence of community in the general case. The State, as the limited representative of all communities (or all individuals, insofar as individuals submit or adapt themselves to existence in human community), may guarantee or serve the rights and general obligations of individuals and communities, but the community, which is a cooperative, free, and responsible association of individuals within the State, must guarantee or serve the intimate, essential, and higher evolutionary process of Man.

The State, independent of a society of cooperative communities, is a tyrant. The community, without a benign, true, and free State to protect its rights, is in fear and cannot fully release attention toward the higher realization of human life.

The Discipline of Community

This is the human Law: Whatever responsibility you do not assume must be fulfilled and will be assumed by another. Whatever responsibility men and women in general do not assume will be assumed by an interest apart from their general interest.

If people do not resort to the true form of life, or the culture of intimate cooperation, which transcends the dominating power of the

"News" (or the trend of the world when mankind is irresponsible), then those agencies that have the controlling responsibilities will become mere manipulators and exploiters. Whatever people or institutions are in power will always seek to survive <u>as</u> themselves, unless they are made accountable to the people, or the true culture of Man. (Therefore, when the people are irresponsible, the politics of mankind is reduced to international money politics, wars, and more "News.")

102

We must assume personal, intimate, and cooperative or local responsibility for our individual and collective lives. We must realize the unreality, essential unimportance, and even deliberate lie or daemonic force that is the "News"—or the trend of events when mankind abandons higher Wisdom and cooperative human intimacy (or all the forms of <u>cultural</u> responsibility). We must begin a politics of mutual responsibility and creativity at the level of intimate cultural community, and we must demand that the State become and always remain responsible to us. If we abandon our passive or self-possessed individualism and become active in cooperation with one another, we will become essentially self-sufficient, free, humorous, and unexploitable. This is the only true political movement in the world.

The Hypocrisy of Popular Disgust

The "News and Information" media of popular culture do not often invite the public to the exercise of discriminating intelligence. On the contrary, the popular media <u>thrive</u> on hype, propagandized states of emotion and mind, and nondiscriminating responses to every kind of advertised goods, persuasions, and results.

Until the media that inform the masses of humanity begin to invite the individual to exercise discriminating intelligence in all matters, and until human beings in general become founded in the higher Wisdom-Culture and the intimate politics of authentic human existence, there can be no true wondering about the madness we inherit in the daily News.

Indeed, the hypocritical media reaction of surprise (and sometimes disgust) in the face of all the kinds of fascinating and bizarre news in the world is even the product of a kind of competitive rivalry. The Cult of the News would be senior and superior to any phenomenon about which it reports. (From the popular point of view, the "Messiah," or the "Messenger," is always senior to the Message.) Everyone in the world is in the cult game, including the media themselves. Everyone wishes to be glamorous and right and the center of attention.

The News is one of the principal forms of modern popular entertainment. The Messenger is glamorized by the superior entertainment value of every kind of Message. Therefore, the News exploits the vulgarity of subhuman events and bastardizes the achievements of superior men and women. Then why should there be any wondering if immature people follow false cults, false leaders, false ideologies, and destructive causes? To be enthusiastic and also false is the hypocritical core of the "American Way." Indeed, Western culture as a whole was founded on religious lies, political exploitation, and manipulative propaganda of every kind. And these means are yet to be overcome.

The popular media that "inform" and ultimately control the world's populations are not simply "guardians of human rights and all the truth," even though they may wish to be known as such. Rather, they are also propaganda instruments for the more or less "official" Cult of Everyman, or the Cult of Things As They Can Seem to Be. As nondiscriminating propaganda instruments, popular media are themselves among the primary instruments that actively work against the freedom of Man to transcend mob rule and to create an intimate culture in which the unofficial, evolutionary, and transcendental Wisdom that has yet found dominion only at the fringes of society is allowed to be the center of human existence and the dominant influence on human action.

We must all awaken from the sleep of Wisdom. We must be self-critical, and we must discriminate among all the superficial doctrines that surround us and that arise within us. We must see the childish tendency in "Everyman" to be Parented by dominant, powerful, and official influences. Likewise, we must understand the merely destructive adolescent reaction of despair and clinging to the hopefulness of less popular illusions that flatter the mind and give us reasons to avoid the call to compassion and love.

The mass of humanity is the child of the Parent-State and all of the fake mind of popular culture. We all lie in wait for "official" permission to believe and know and feel and act. We await the theatrical cues that govern universal responses. We seek permission to laugh, the authority to be happy, the right to Divinity and the Fullness of Life. Instead, we must hear the Truth and awaken to the timely demand of our Manhood.

104

Be Informed
by Direct Experience

When all is said and done about the great affair of religious cultism and spiritual community, it still remains true that human beings need to grow beyond the subhuman round of mob societies. Human beings need to adapt to their own higher functions and to the Living Transcendental Reality. And the Way in which this is done is in intimate spiritual community. The process of higher human, moral, mystical, and evolutionary spiritual adaptation is a <u>cultural</u> process. That process is necessarily self-transcending, not merely self-fulfilling. And it requires both technical instruction and practical guidance by one who is an Adept in the <u>total</u> process. Therefore, it is not a merely self-manipulative process of private experience, but a self-sacrificial process—in community with other practitioners, and in a mutually sacrificial relationship with a true Spiritual Master (to whom one may not be related merely as a submissive child or a rebellious adolescent is to a parent, but only as a responsible aspirant, awakened to Wisdom and Truth, is related to an Enlightened Teacher and Initiator and Guide).

The creation and development of an authentic community or culture of evolutionary spiritual practice is an immensely difficult affair—because people are, in general, so profoundly afraid, self-possessed, adapted to archaic and self-defeating patterns of thought and behavior, and constantly disturbed by childish and adolescent motives toward chaotic self-fulfillment. Therefore, even the communities of experimental spiritual culture bear all the evidence of the growing pains, the tackiness, the immaturity, and all the other bewildering deficiencies that otherwise mark the secular and subhuman order of the world.

Some imagine that this is scandalous, and so they criticize even authentic cultural experiments with a kind of negative "gotcha" mentality that implies nothing but a viciously destructive intent. This is a tendency that can easily be observed in the popular media of TV, newspapers, and magazines.

Therefore, resist all attempts to be "officially" and dogmatically informed—whether for or against—about religion and the significance of religious institutions and teachers of religion. Consider and experience that entire affair yourself. And be humored by the realization that the popular communications media are fundamentally motivated by the necessity to propagandize and entertain, through fascinating and alarming messages. That is how they make their money and achieve their power. And we ourselves have taught them to do so, by childishly submitting to be entertained, and even demanding to be entertained and told what is black-and-white true. (Unfortunately, the price we all are paying for entertainment and glib analysis, as a substitute for Truth and direct experience, is our universal reduction to a controllable and exploitable mob that has no reason for existence other than to be pleasurably distracted and consoled.)

Conversion

The right motive of true spiritual practice is not mere belief or any sophisticated strategy of self-manipulation. The right motive of all practice is the Revelation of the Living God. That is, each individual who is truly moved to take up the Way of Truth must have passed through a critical consideration of the total human situation as well as his or her own habits of action, feeling, reaction, and thinking.

Anyone who seriously considers the human situation will naturally observe that we have not brought ourselves into existence, nor can we continue to exist without accepting the relationship of dependence on various primal processes in the Realm of Nature. We are not self-contained beings. We are transcended by and dependent upon a Great Process, Reality, or God.

106   The usual individual, full of desire and fear, does not tend to consider this matter seriously in his moment to moment existence. He generally opens himself to random influences and seeks satisfaction in the conventional or popular stimulations of his body-mind. Thus, he does not truly discriminate between the influences that surround him, and he, therefore, does not tend to be responsible for his personal and relational existence—except for the casual maintenance of conventional patterns of behavior, reactivity, and popular belief.

But once an individual is awakened to the serious consideration of human existence, he or she begins to transcend the stream of casual survival and self-indulgence. The source of this awakening to serious consideration and insight is always a form of crisis. That crisis may appear in the form of personal suffering, the observation of social chaos, and so forth. But it must always be followed by receptivity to the communication or argument of spiritual understanding, given through Divine Teachings, personal encounters with serious practitioners of a spiritual Way of life, and so forth.

Thus, the origins of the Way of true religion are in the psycho-physical conversion of the individual to the Divine and Living Truth. That conversion is made through "hearing," or awakened insight. And it is a conversion from casual and random submission to the conventional stimulations of experience and to responsible surrender to the Reality or Transcendental Condition and Process in which we have found ourselves.

The conventional disposition of human individuals in this time and place is founded in self-indulgence and self-possessed struggles for experience and survival. The social machine as a whole is geared toward the accumulation of objective knowledge, or the attainment of the ultimate power to control and manipulate the Great Machine of nature, including Man. It is this ideal and strategy, coupled with the personal habits of self-indulgence and separative self-interest, that is producing the drama of daily events or "News" that control and at times shock us all.

The individual, and the social order of mankind as a whole, must awaken from the chaos of efforts toward mere domination and exploitation of the World-Machine. And, likewise, there must be an awakening from the disposition of self-possession, fear, self-indulgence, and separative or immoral reactivity (such as violent anger, sorrowful despair, lustful preoccupation, and so forth).

The truly human individual is one who has been converted from self-possession to self-transcendence, from self-indulgence to self-control and self-giving. The truly human society permits truly human acculturation, the development of intimate politics or human communities, and the tempering of all knowledge and technological as well as political power by the higher cultural ideals of the Realization of Wisdom and of the Divine Transformation of the world, of mankind, and of the human individual.

Thus, when the individual awakens to the Wisdom of true, right, and serious consideration of the human situation, he or she becomes converted to a new relationship to the Great Process in which we are all appearing. Instead of commitment to mere knowledge, power, and the ideal of exploitation or manipulation of the Realm of Nature, the awakened individual is committed to an intuitive and cooperative relationship to the Great Process and to the personal and relational or moral conditions of human existence. The awakened individual is intuitively established in a disposition that transcends knowledge about the phenomena of the Realm of Nature. He or she is established in the intuition of his or her actual and eternal situation, which is not that of ultimate knowledge and the power to survive by total and vulgar manipulation of self, others, and the world. The awakened individual intuits that his or her essential situation is one of Transcendental or Divine Ignorance: No matter how much experience or power he may acquire, no matter how much he may know about the conditions of Nature, he never at any time knows what any thing, or himself, or the world is. The world, and all phenomena, and even our own personal qualities always transcend our ability to be independently responsible for them. That is, we do not create the world, or ourselves. We are transcended. We depend on the Great Process. We do not now or ultimately know what any of it is. Existence itself always transcends our knowledge.

Therefore, the awakened individual is converted from experiential and social chaos, mere knowledge, and the destiny of self-possession. He does this by intuiting the right disposition of Man—

108

the disposition of Divine Ignorance, or intuitive surrender of self into the Great Process or Reality in which the self is perceived or conceived.

The origins of the Way of real Life are in this "hearing," this conversion from conventional or self-possessed knowledge and belief and to the intuited disposition of surrender or self-transcendence in Communion (rather than in struggle) with the Great and Divine Process in which Man and the total world are appearing, changing, and passing.

Thus, the foundation of every stage of the Way of real Life is this conversion to surrender, or self-transcendence, in Communion with the All-Pervading, Living, and Transcendental Reality. The foundation of the Way of Truth is psycho-physical conversion from self and self-possession to God and God-Communion. And the initial gesture of practice, founded on this conversion, is adaptation to new forms of action—that is, to right and self-transcending practices in the sphere of personal and relational (or moral) existence.

True religious practitioners are devotees of the Living God. That is, they live—based on intuitive understanding of the human situation—in an active disposition of self-control, self-giving, service, and spiritual or devotional surrender to the obvious Reality or Great Process in which we all exist.

Such devotees value their truly human intimacy with one another—and they also value the establishment of a general social order, or the culture of mankind, founded on higher Wisdom, restraint, and humanizing ideals. Such devotees also enjoy and value the esoteric or true spiritual relationship with a Spiritual Master, or an Enlightened Adept, who has become Full through the intuition and practice of Divine Wisdom.

The Culture of Ecstasy

It is true that mankind must become capable of intelligently distinguishing between true and false religion, or true and false cultism. But it is also true that mankind must abandon the anti-ecstatic or anti-Life disposition of scientific and political materialism. The secret of human existence is Life—the All-Pervading Life-Current and Transcendental Consciousness in which the World-Process and Man are arising, floating, changing, and passing beyond themselves.

We cannot grow beyond the childishness and exclusiveness of archaic and conventional exoteric religion by embracing the adolescent intellectualism of scientific and political materialism. The scientific method does not provide the basis for a sufficient world-view (or a culture of fully human participation in the Paradoxical Reality of the world). The method of science, or the ritualistic subject-object strategy of the conventional mind (both religious and scientific), does not provide for or even permit ecstatic, self-transcending Communion with the Unity and Radiant Energy of the Process of the world.

The presumption of the bodily and psychic separation between Man and the world (and the ultimate Reality of the world) has produced archaic exoteric religion and scientific and political materialism. The exoteric and conventional ritual of the method of scientific abstraction, observation, comparison, and analysis is not different from the exoteric ritual of liturgical worship and belief in the "God of our fathers." Both processes are ritualistic, exoteric, even archaic, and dependent on the establishment of disunity or inherent separation between the ego or self or observer and the phenomena of the world (or the totality that is God). Such a process may produce various kinds of experiential knowledge or belief about the world and God, but the process itself prohibits Ecstasy, self-transcending participation, or surrender and abandonment of the difference or separation between the self and the world (or God).

Only the ecstatic presumption of Unity or nonseparation between the self and the world and the Reality (or Living God) of the world permits the Realization of Wisdom, or direct knowledge, which is prior to but not exclusive of experience.

Therefore, the method of Ecstasy, or self-transcending participation in the Life and Unity of the World-Process, must be the necessary foundation of higher and truly human culture. And that method transcends the archaic disposition of both conventional religion and conventional science. Therefore, it provides an intelligent basis for discriminating between true and false religion, and it also provides a basis for understanding and making right use of scientific experimentation and invention. (However, the archaic religious or scientific mind does not, in its turn, provide a basis for understanding and participating in the evolutionary process of Ecstasy, or self-transcending Unity with Life and the World-Process.)

Fanatic and false exoteric religious cultism and anti-ecstatic or anti-Life intellectualism were the essence of the obnoxious Pharisaism that Jesus criticized so angrily. And it was that same Pharisaism that ultimately brought about the hypocritical execution of Jesus, sanctioned and presided over by the good offices of the State.

That same combination of intellectual and hypocritically religious resistance to participation in the ecstatic Life-Principle is still at work in our own time. And it is still producing the same effect—which is the suppressive undermining of the culture of Ecstasy, or prevention of the emergence of the esoteric and evolutionary culture of a fundamentally free humanity.

Let us not be naive and indifferent. Let us be tough-minded, but let us be self-critical. Let us hear the Truth and submit ourselves, both individually and collectively, to the Living Reality. Let us adapt to the mature practice of human and esoteric Wisdom, as it has been proclaimed and demonstrated by countless Adepts. Let us surrender, from the heart and with every breath, to the Radiant Law that is Life. Now let mankind understand and prove the Wisdom of its highest or most evolved members. Now let the Adept and the practitioner of Ecstasy become senior to the subhuman heroes of the popular mind and all the mechanical priests of false religion and false knowledge.

I Would Find a New Order of Men and Women

I am interested in finding men and women who are free of every kind of seeking, who are attendant only to understanding, and who will devote themselves to the intentional creation of human life in the form and logic of Reality, rather than the form and logic of Narcissus. Such men are the unexploitable Presence of Reality. They will not devote themselves to turning the world to dilemma, exhaustion, and revolutionary experience, nor to the degenerative exploitation of desire and possibility, nor to the ascent to and inclusion of various illusory goals, higher entities, evolutionary aims, or deluded ideas of experiential transformation. They will create in the aesthetics of Reality, turning all things into radical relationship and enjoyment. They will remove the effects of separative existence and restore the Form of things. They will engineer every kind of stability and beauty. They will create a Presence of Peace. Their eye will be on present form and not on exaggerated notions of artifice. Their idea of form is stable and whole, not a gesture toward some other event. They will not make the world seem but a symbol for higher and other things.

111

They will constantly create the form of Truth while conscious of Present Reality. Thus, they will serve the order of sacrifice and liberated knowledge. They will evolve the necessary and good, and make economic and wise use of all technology. They will not be motivated by invention but by Reality, which is the Presence to be communicated in all forms. They will not pursue any kind of false victory, any fearful deathlessness, or any overwhelming survival for Man. They will only create the conditions for present enjoyment, the communication of Reality, the Form in which transcendental understanding can arise, live, and become the public foundation of existence.

Thus, I would find a new order of men and women, who will create a new age of sanity and joy. It will not be the age of the occult, the religious, the scientific, or the technological domination of humanity. It will be the fundamental age of Real Existence, wherein Life will be radically realized, entirely apart from the whole history of our adventure and great search. The age envisioned by common seekers is a spectacular display that only extends the traditional madness, exploitability, and foolishness of mankind. But I desire a new order of men and women, who will not begin from all of that, but who will apply themselves, apart from all dilemma and all seeking, to the harmonious Event of Real Existence.

What is the Ideal of the East? It is Silence, or Stillness, separate from the body and the world of the body. It is no-creation, dissolution of the body in the mind, immortality of the soul (or inner person), or transcendence of the motions of the being.

What is the Ideal of the West? It is Incarnation, or Perfect Fulfillment of the world, the body, and the mind. It is unobstructed creativity, incarnation of the mind in the body, immortality of the body-mind (or incarnate person), or justification of the motions of the being.

What is the Way of Truth that transcends the limitations of the East and the West? It is the Love-Sacrifice of the total world, body, mind, soul, and independent self in the Living Radiance and Transcendental Consciousness (or Radiant Being) that is the Matrix of all manifest existence. It is the Way of self-transcending Love, Divine Communion, or Ecstasy, expressed in every moment through creative, functional, total psycho-physical, and Life-positive identification with the infinite, all-pervading, mindless, soundless, formless Radiance and Divine Person that always stands Perfectly Revealed at the heart of Man.

Da Free John

CHAPTER FOUR

The Culture of Eternal Life

Wisdom and Knowledge

Science and mysticism are natural enough occupations or experiences of Man, particularly in the earlier stages of personal and cultural growth or evolution. But they must be understood from a right perspective, and they must ultimately be transcended by the whole bodily disposition of Wisdom, prior to mind.

Method and Ritual

Both religion and science are forms of popular or conventional knowledge, except where each leads beyond its own presumptions into the esoteric and transcendental realms of Truth.

Religion makes profound use of the method of ritual, or the repetition of what has been previously found to be auspicious and revealing.

But science makes equally profound use of the ritual of method, which is also the repetition of what has previously been found to be auspicious and revealing.

The method of religion is to repeat prescribed external or internal rituals of action and attention, until there is a deep psychic encounter with the unknown.

The ritual of science is to repeat prescribed external or internal methods of action and attention, until there is a conscious mental encounter with the unknown.

Therefore, both religion and science pursue the experiential knowledge of the unknown.

Religious ritual is the science of the right hemisphere of the human brain (or the holistic faculty of intuition).

Scientific method is the religion of the left hemisphere of the human brain (or the analytical faculty of comprehension).

Both religion and science are motivated by the absence of perfect knowledge.

Both religion and science are founded upon the urge to transcend the present limitations of the human body-mind.

Religion cannot do what science is intended to do, because religion is not fundamentally oriented toward the mental analysis of the world of manifest phenomena.

Science cannot do what religion is intended to do, because science is not fundamentally oriented toward psychic unity with the world of manifest phenomena.

Therefore, a complete or truly human culture would be both religious and scientific in the highest and most universal sense of each discipline.

And the self-transcendence of Man is also beyond the conventional methods and rituals of both religion and science, even as both hemispheres of the brain must be transcended if the mind is to be transparent to the Radiant Reality in which the world of manifest phenomena is floating.

Science, Mysticism, and Love

Modern science is simply the way of knowledge that is natural to the left hemisphere of the human brain-mind. It is the primarily verbal, temporal, and analytical method of relating to the objects of experience.

Ancient religious mysticism was (and is) the way of knowledge that is natural to the right hemisphere of the human brain-mind. It is the primarily nonverbal, spatial, and holistic method of relating to the objects of experience.

Scientific knowledge is communicated primarily through verbal abstractions, and also visual signs, that are intended to represent "objective" or "concrete" events, relations, and things.

Mystical knowledge is communicated primarily through visual symbols and other nonverbal and archetypal signs (as well as verbal metaphors) that are intended to represent "subjective," "subtle," or "psychic" events, relations, and things.

The left hemisphere of the brain generally controls the right side of the body, and its qualities are most directly analogous to those of the sympathetic division of the autonomic nervous system and to the downgoing and outgoing motor currents of the body.[1]

---

1. In the field of physiology, the human nervous system is divided into two anatomical systems: (1) the central nervous system, consisting of the brain and the spinal cord; and (2) the peripheral nervous system, which is subdivided into (a) the somatic system (voluntary), consisting of both motor and sensory fibers, and (b) the autonomic nervous system (so-called involuntary), which also has two parts, the sympathetic and the parasympathetic divisions.

Medical anatomists point out that the division of the nervous system into a somatic or conscious system and a visceral or non-conscious system, though offering a convenient physiological description, does not imply the presence of two anatomically distinct systems. The two divisions are different aspects of a single, integrated neural mechanism, and they are closely interrelated both centrally and peripherally. In this book and other literature, Da Free John uses the conventional anatomical distinctions to create a descriptive experiential analysis of certain qualities of human consciousness and action.

The central nervous system, comprised of the brain and spinal column, is the primary mechanism of conscious, or voluntary, functioning of the body-mind. Thus, it is senior to the autonomic nervous system, which is the mechanism of the generally involuntary functioning of the viscera or vital organs. In the usual person, attention is fixed in the functions of the lower body, that is, the functions below the brows, and in the autonomic nervous system that governs these functions.

The sympathetic and parasympathetic divisions of the autonomic nervous system contain both motor or outward-directed and sensory or inward-directed nerve currents. Nevertheless, in

The right hemisphere of the brain generally controls the left side of the body, and its qualities are most directly analogous to those of the parasympathetic division of the autonomic nervous system and to the ingoing and upgoing sensory currents of the body.

Therefore, science and mysticism each represents only one primary half of the human structural possibility, but each, in its own time of dominance, wrongly claims to be the primary, right, sufficient, and even ultimate form of human understanding.

Both the left and the right hemispheres or zones of functioning of the human brain contain specific or built-in functional limits as well as limiting presumptions. And, therefore, both science and mysticism represent only partial or half-human forms of understanding. Only the whole body or total body-mind of Man can provide the structural point of view for right and ultimate human understanding. Only the whole body (or total psycho-physical being) of Man can provide the foundation for a truly human and harmoniously integrated culture.

Science and mysticism both represent archaic or partial cultural principles. Each is the point of view of one half of Man

---

general, the sympathetic division is experientially associated principally with outward-directed or motor impulses, and the parasympathetic division is experientially associated principally with inward-directed or sensory impulses. In general terms, the sympathetic division governs the "hot" reflexes of excitation and activity, whereas the parasympathetic division governs the "cool" reflexes of inhibition and stasis.

The usual man or woman is bound, in his or her unconscious and subhuman state, to the perpetual play (and sometimes antagonism) between the sympathetic and parasympathetic divisions of the autonomic nervous systems. When the play between these two is harmonized and raised to a level of Life-positive intensity, through awakening to a participation in Life that is senior to the struggle for mere physical survival, then attention is free to pass into the central nervous system, which is the mechanism for our higher evolution. And, ultimately, even that evolutionary mechanism must be transcended in the process of perfect enlightenment or transfiguration, as described in this book and in *The Enlightenment of the Whole Body*, by Da Free John.

The descriptions in this text of the esoteric spiritual process in relation to human anatomy are based on experience, as well as knowledge, rather than scientific analysis. The author's purpose in these essays is to relate experiential and esoteric descriptions to current anatomical theories. These descriptions are generalized; they are not attempts to create a rigorous description of analytical anatomy that corresponds in detail to current medical theory. Those who find these suggestive descriptions helpful may apply them in practice to the processes of esoteric meditation. Others who wish to consider the matter further in analytical and medical terms should use these descriptions as a broad and general reflection on the analytical anatomy of medical science. They would perhaps find it interesting to develop these general descriptions along the more rigorous lines of medical study.

Science is not truly "objective," but it is simply a style of knowledge and culture that is founded on the independent functions of the left hemisphere of the brain and the expansive motor impulses of gross bodily action. Science is simply the highest intellectual achievement of a cultural point of view that is founded on the separate and separative consciousness of self (or ego), the psychic disposition of doubt, and the motives of physical attachment and even aggressive behavior.

Mysticism is not simply "subjective" in the high and heavenly sense that is promoted by conventional religious cultism. It is simply a style of knowledge and culture that is founded on the independent functions of the right hemisphere of the brain and the passive or inverted impulses of the sensory internalization of consciousness. Mysticism is simply the highest mental or psychic achievement of a cultural point of view that is founded on the undifferentiated state of the deep psyche, and also on the motives of attachment to internal psychic phenomena and to behavior that tends toward passivity and nonrelational self-absorption.

The culture of science is the ultimate achievement of the "occidental" mind, or the primary mood of Western Man. And the culture of mysticism is the ultimate achievement of the "oriental" mind, or the primary mood of Eastern Man.

But what of the culture of Man in his totality—including his total brain and totally integrated bodily being? That culture has no great representation in the human world as it now exists. Man is yet only evolved or adapted to the lower structures of his possibility, and his cultural achievements still reflect only his internal conflict. Therefore, East and West are in conflict, and the parts of human consciousness are culturally at war.

I am at work to awaken a new understanding of Man in his totality, and to help establish a whole bodily cultural movement in the world, that will replace the half-bodily cultures of science and mysticism. That understanding includes the total mind and nervous system of Man, and it produces a culture that is not founded on self-possession, self-division, doubt, exploitation of Man and Nature, or the flight from relationships, or even the flight from bodily existence. Rather, the whole bodily understanding of Man produces a culture of self-transcendence, relational love, bodily service, and spiritually illumined consciousness. Therefore, by this new or radical understanding, East and West will create a World-Synthesis of human culture, on the basis of aspiration and adaptation to the Total World, or the World of Light.

The unevolved or partially adapted and lower-adapted human being is suffering from a darkened or unenlightened understanding of his situation and his experience. Therefore, he <u>reacts</u> to the conditions of his mortal bodily circumstance. This reaction is personally and culturally communicated in one of two ways, because of the bifurcated structure of the human nervous system. Thus, the style of the common human reaction to the mortal threats of experience is either extroversion or introversion.

Extroverted reactivity typifies the "occidental," "left-brained," aggressive style of the sympathetic division of the autonomic nervous system and of Western Man.

Introverted reactivity typifies the "oriental," "right-brained," passive or interiorized style of the parasympathetic division of the autonomic nervous system and of Eastern Man.

Science and aggressive worldliness are the characteristic cultural solutions of Western Man to the primitive reaction to mortal experience.

Mysticism and passive other-worldliness are the characteristic cultural solutions of Eastern Man to the <u>same</u> primitive reaction to mortal experience.

Thus, the basic cultural achievements of mankind to date are <u>reactive</u> and <u>partial</u> solutions to what is felt to be the <u>problem</u> or <u>dilemma</u> of human existence. It is the reactive and partial nature of these solutions that makes them temporary, incomplete, and even suppressive or destructive to humanity. And it is the sense of dilemma—or existence without the Freedom of Ecstasy—that makes individual existence and cultural or social experience into an intolerably problematic bind that needs a unique solution (that is, a solution or situation that is not native to the fundamental situation of existence itself).

The "oriental" and "occidental" methods and solutions of Man are equally founded in a reactive dilemma, and both are partial, specialized, emergency solutions that create an artificial or unreal environment for human adaptation.

The world envisioned by science is equally as desperate, artificial, and unreal as that created, presumed, or invented in the

118

psyche by other-worldly mysticism. Both science and mysticism need to be relieved of the primal dilemma of reactive fear—or recoil from bodily relationship—which is recoil from the plane of natural events as well as from the Living or Radiant Reality in which the natural world is arising, changing, and passing out of sight.

The trouble with both the "oriental" and the "occidental" solutions of Man is that both ways are based on styles or methods of experiential <u>knowing about</u> the world of experience. Both ways are founded in a reactive dilemma, and both ways, therefore, seek release from that dilemma via conventional knowledge—or the power to manipulate and control the conditions of experience. Both ways avoid the simple, original, radical, obvious, and direct path—which is the way of self-transcendence, or tacit, nonproblematic acceptance of bodily existence and the obligation to live as the body in love.

The "oriental" way of inwardness (or mind) and the "occidental" way of worldly and bodily self-indulgence (or the way of the "flesh," separate from the Transcendental Bliss of the Light, or All-Pervading "Sun," of the natural world) both avoid the whole bodily way of self-transcending love. This is because neither one is founded in the primary or native disposition of Man—or freedom from the primal negativity of reaction to bodily existence and the evolutionary trial of difficult experience and mortality.

Both science and mysticism are founded on self-possession, or the self-defining fear of death. Both science and mysticism <u>seek</u> knowledge or power that will release Man from death (and thus from fear). But neither science nor mysticism is founded on an original, primal intuition of the Reality and Truth that relieves even bodily existence of the <u>need</u> for inherent or chronic fear.

The native Way of Man in his totality is the Life-positive Way that is priorly free of fear and that persists as love, bodily, through all experience, and even death. That Way is the Way of true religion, or the higher, truly human and evolutionary spiritual culture of Man.

The basis of false religion is the Life-negative reaction of fear. And false "religion" includes all cultural solutions that dominate Man in his fear. Thus, the cultures of science and of mysticism are equally "religious" in this sense.

The "right-brained" culture of psychic inversion (or psychic "other-worldliness") is founded on loveless bodily fear and flight from the mortal or ever changing limitations of relationship.

Likewise, the "left-brained" culture of self-indulgent extroversion and intellectual worldliness is founded on the same loveless bodily fear and flight from the impingement of relational limitations.

Cultic religion in an "oriental" culture tends to be founded on inverted mystical beliefs. But cultic religion in an "occidental" culture tends to be founded on both irrational beliefs and Lifeless "rational" beliefs held by the verbal mind.

120

Therefore, mortal fear is the bodily foundation of conventional religion and conventional culture, whether "oriental" or "occidental." But true religion is the native and Life-positive response of relational love, expressed bodily and as Communion with the Unity, Eternal Existence, and Radiant Life-Reality in which Man and the World-Process are always absolutely established.

The Living Reality is always already the Condition of Man and the World-Process. Man is bodily, originally, prior to all knowledge and all strategic attainments, in the situation of Unity with the Eternal Reality. Science, or the verbal mind, including thoughts of all kinds, as well as mysticism, or the mind of archetypal images and "uncaused" ideas, are simply forms of knowledge about the World-Process. But true religion, or the true culture of Man, is not about knowledge of any kind. The true Way is senior to all knowledge and to all the implications of experience. The true Way is the Way of love, or self-transcendence via native, whole bodily, or total psycho-physical surrender into positive Life-Feeling.

The world of science and mysticism is the known world. But the world of Man—the world of true religion and higher human culture—is the Living World, the native world of the body itself, prior to all knowledge.

The Way of Man in his totality is senior to the cultures of science and mysticism. It is the Transcendental Way of Love-Communion with Radiant God, Who is Life. It is the Way in which we abide continually as the body in relational love, not qualified by any kind of knowledge or inwardness, and not qualified by any binding reaction to (or recoil from) the changing conditions of experience.

The Principal Doctrine
of the "East" and of the "West"

"Oriental" Mysticism: "Sit up straight, take leave of your senses, and go out of your mind."
"Occidental" Realism: "Observe, think, choose, act, attain, possess, and know."

The Two Ideas of Fear

The occidental mind fears death, or the loss of self. The oriental mind fears attachment to the self, or the lifetime of the self. These two habits of mind have traditionally dictated the two unique and opposite paths of mankind.

The Disposition of the Body-Mind
Determines the Findings of Philosophy

One of the original absurdities to which the "occidental" structure of mind (and of Western Man) was predisposed was the invention of a God who is an explanation for the existence of the world and whose own existence needs to be proven. The "occidental" mind sees the world first and then calculates the existence of God. Therefore, to the Western or "occidental" mind, God (or the Living Reality) is not obvious. God must be thought about and invented or calculated into existence. Since God is inherently in doubt from such a point of view, God can only be tentatively believed or eternally sought. But the world (and the body-mind of the human individual) is accredited with an overwhelming realness, such that it tends to be felt to exist in, of, as, and for itself.

In contrast to the conventional pattern of the "occidental" mind, the structures of the "oriental" mind (and of Eastern Man) are predisposed to the intuitive presumption of a God who not only needs no proof of existence (since that existence is tacitly obvious), but who is attributed with such overwhelming realness that the world and human existence are in doubt. (Therefore, "oriental" cultures tend to be weak in their orientation to the personal and moral reality of Man and to the evolutionary fulfillment of the conditions of the World-Process.)

The origins of the divisions of traditional philosophy and culture are to be found in the chronic neurophysiological self-division of ancient and modern Man. The functional divisions and oppositions between the left and right hemispheres of the brain, between the central nervous system and the autonomic nervous system, and between the two principal divisions of the autonomic nervous system have created the conventional dynamics and also the terrible cultural divisions in the world of Man up to the present time.

It is necessary, therefore, for us to come to a new understanding of Man, founded in his totality. And we must reform the adventure of human existence toward a worldwide unification of the processes of human culture.

We must awaken to the singleness and wholeness of the body-mind. We must transcend our psycho-physical recoil from Life—for it is in that recoil that we become self-divided and self-possessed. In our whole bodily disposition, every part of Man is integrated in a harmony of Good Feeling. And to such a Man, God is obvious, both to intuition and direct experience, as the Transcendental Life and Consciousness of the world. Likewise, in that same disposition, the natural world is seen to be Full of Life—an irreducible Play in which God is to be Realized more and more perfectly, by Man and by all beings (both greater and less than Man), until the Light Outshines the world.

The Idea of Infinity

I n the traditional oriental or Eastern mind, Infinity is pondered as the ultimate Zero, or "no thing."

In the traditional occidental or Western mind, Infinity is pondered as the Maximum Number, the totality of possibilities, or "every thing."

123

These two entirely different conceptions of Infinity, or the Absolute, describe or illustrate the essential cultural difference between the East and the West.

The traditional East is devoted to regression from the repetitive cycles of birth and death, or the reduction of experience to Home Base, before anything exists.

The traditional West is devoted to the progressive increase or the linear and even evolutionary elaboration of experience, until End Time, when everything is perfected.

Each of the two great motives excludes and cancels the other. And the origin of these Two is in self-divided Man—or Man prior to whole bodily Enlightenment.

When the whole body-mind of Man awakens beyond the illusions and ultimately destructive motives of self-division and recoil from the single Life-Principle, then the Paradox of Infinity is Revealed. The Infinite, Absolute, All-Pervading Reality is One. It is simultaneously (and thus paradoxically) Every Thing and No Thing. It is Love, Bliss, Radiance, Truth, Life, Fullness, and Mystery beyond the force of all contradictions.

I am a witness to this One. This is the Holy One, Who is not set apart from the World.

The Present or Living God

T he conventional occidental idea of God, or the Ultimate Reality, is of a Separate Being that is other than the "I" of creatures and that is the creator or independent opposite of all objects or things.

The conventional oriental idea of God, or the Ultimate Reality, is of Being Itself, Which is conceived to be identical to the "I" of creatures, but which is also conceived to be the tacit opponent of all objects or things.

124

The Ultimate Reality, the always Present and Living God, prior to all ideas, may, however, be Realized directly, and thus Revealed to be That in Which the "I" and all objects or things are presently arising as spontaneous, nonbinding, and free modifications of Itself.

The Single Field

The "occidental" objectivists think that the Mystery of Reality is fundamentally contained in everything that is external to consciousness.

The "oriental" subjectivists think that the Mystery of Reality is fundamentally internal to consciousness (or separate from the objects and relations of consciousness).

But the Truth to be Realized is that consciousness (or the apparently independent "nirvanic" self) and its objects (or "samsaric," conditional, changing, and impermanent relations) are a Single Field—Infinite, Uncontained, and Unconfined. And to Abide in this Transcendental Realization is Perfect Ecstasy, or Radical Intuition of the Fundamental and Ultimate Identity, Which literally Enlightens the total body-mind, Transfiguring the consciousness and all its relational objects with the Blissful Living Love-Radiance of Infinite Divine Being.

The Two and the One

There are two prevailing philosophical, cultural, and political points of view at play in the world of Man. They are the point of view of the West and the point of view of the East.

These two unique, comprehensive, and apparently autonomous points of view are not only ancient in the world of Man, but they are <u>native</u> to the body of Man.

The play of systems that are Occidental and Oriental has come to be considered not so much as a dynamic process of continual synthesis, but as a kind of warfare between two opponents who are trying to dominate and destroy one another. But the world cannot be reduced to "one," since what is absolutely single and without possibility of an other is also motionless and bereft of the possibility of play, or growth and change. Therefore, the world is always a dynamic play of opposites, a process that should produce living harmonies, and absolute singularity or "Oneness" is simply the Transcendental Principle we intuit to be the ultimate Ground or Milieu of the play of these processes.

If we conceive of the play of opposites as a form of negative antagonism, then we are reduced to a negative understanding and experience of the world and ourselves. Then the world becomes like a married couple that can no longer confess and express mutual love, so that divorce becomes the only motive and the only vision.

Indeed, the human structural or bodily origin of the play of opposites in the world may be considered to be the play of the sexual differentiation—or the mutual play between the male character and the female character. Thus, the "feminine character" has traditionally been associated with the East (or the oriental disposition of sensuous and intuitive inwardness), and the "masculine character" has traditionally been associated with the West (or the occidental disposition toward physical action and manipulation of physical conditions via rational intelligence).

However, the ultimate human structural origin of the perception of the dynamic play of opposites is native to every human individual, regardless of sex. Our perception and conception of the dynamic play of every aspect of the World-Process is rooted in the relationship between the central nervous system and the autonomic nervous system in our own bodies.

The central nervous system is directly and intimately associated with the All-Pervading Life-Current in which all things and beings are arising, or existing and changing. The central nervous system may be thought of as single or ultimately monolithic—a kind of monad in the body. It encompasses the brain and the spinal cord, and it is via the brain and the spinal cord that the universal Life-Current is distributed or Radiated to the total body of the human individual.

The autonomic nervous system is, in contrast to the central nervous system, bipolar, dual, or dynamic in its functions. It is made of two great parts: the sympathetic and parasympathetic divisions. These two divisions are in a kind of perpetual embrace, like a pair of lovers—unless the body-mind becomes unbalanced, so that the two halves of the autonomic nervous system become more like aggressive or sulky opponents. The sympathetic division is associated with efferent or outgoing motor impulses of an expansive or "masculine" kind. And the parasympathetic division is associated with afferent or ingoing sensory impulses of a more passive or inward-directed or "feminine" kind.

The autonomic nervous system is dependent on the central nervous system for its ability to be animated or brought to Life, whereas the central nervous system is always in direct Communion with the Life-Current (until the moment of death). But the autonomic nervous system is also the basic domain of conventional human awareness. That is, we feel "naturally" associated with processes of physical sensation, bodily emotional reactions or responses, and patterns of thinking that depend on physical or bodily associations. Therefore, human beings who are consciously adapted only to the functions of the autonomic nervous system tend to be unconscious of the higher psycho-physical Condition of the body-mind at the level of the central nervous system.

This in fact is the common state of "Everyman." He is adapted only to the peripheral, dynamic, and lower functional dimension of his own body-mind, and, therefore, he is not founded in awakened awareness of his higher bodily and psychic functions and the Transcendental Condition that he may intuit by ascending to the Consciousness of Unity and Life that is native to the central nervous system.

It is the work of esoteric religion and the Adepts of the spiritual process in the higher and intuitive dimensions of the body-mind of Man to create the <u>cultural</u> circumstances in which human beings may adapt and grow beyond the lower conditions of the autonomic nervous system (the "flesh," the "senses," or the realm of childhood and adolescence) and ascend to the higher conditions of the central nervous system (the realm of true maturity and the "Spirit"). The central nervous system contains subtle structural organs and mechanisms that belong to the higher evolutionary range of human development. But these mechanisms are not stimulated into activity in the "Everyman," who is schooled only in the play of the lower being, and who is divorced from the cultural mechanisms of truly human and esoteric community.

If the higher mechanisms in Man can become the common or universal subject of literal personal adaptation and social expression, then the yet subhuman trend of human societies can be reversed—but not until then. Therefore, it is essential that we make a thorough examination of our individual habituation, and it is necessary that higher cultural obligations begin to be communicated and rightly enforced through the work of humanizing communities that are founded in the Wisdom and Help of true Adepts.

The Occidental versus Oriental warfare in the conventional realm of politics, popular culture, and ordinary philosophy is an expression of the absence of right and thorough self-knowledge on the part of human individuals and human societies. The "warfare to death" mentality that characterizes the political realm today is a sign and an expression of a fundamentally unbalanced and also undeveloped or unevolved state of existence on the part of most people and on the part of <u>all</u> of the great States now in power.

And just how is the lower-adapted individual constructed in his view of the world? He is consciously adapted only to the dynamic or dual functions of the autonomic nervous system—or the lower range of the body-mind. He is automatically, perpetually, and reactively involved in food, sex, manipulation of things and others, the Life-negative play of emotions (such as anger, sorrow, and fear), and the mental stream of verbal and lower psychological patterns and images.

Such is the common and "natural" personal condition of most people. And there is also a broad cultural component in the personal character of individuals. That component imposes a characteristic style of behavior and attitude on the individual. At one level, that "style" is expressed through the conventional behaviors and attitudes of the "male" and the "female" social roles. However, at the larger cultural level, that style characterizes entire nations and regions of the world. Thus, we have the characteristic points of view of the East and the West, or the oriental mind and the occidental mind.

128

The qualities of the "oriental" cultural mentality, as a mood of action, are most like those that are dominant in the parasympathetic division of the autonomic nervous system. The "oriental" cultural mentality is more inverted, passive, traditionally "feminine," and oriented toward the monistic or singular disposition characteristic of the central nervous system. This tendency toward singularity or monism provides a basis for tendencies toward the creation of centralized or monolithic forms of State. The general tendency away from differentiation and expansive activity (or away from the characteristics of the sympathetic division of the autonomic nervous system) creates the "oriental" tendency toward self-effacement (or "egolessness"). And this also provides the basis for a general orientation toward collectivism. (Thus, the politics of the monolithic State in control of a collectivist society is congenial to the "oriental" tendency in human acculturation.)

The qualities of the "occidental" cultural mentality, as a mood of action, are most like those that are dominant in the sympathetic division of the autonomic nervous system. The "occidental" cultural mentality is more extroverted, expansive, traditionally "masculine," and oriented toward the dualistic or dynamic disposition characteristic of the autonomic nervous system itself (and as a whole). This tendency toward dynamism provides a basis for tendencies toward decentralized and libertarian or democratic political institutions. And the general tendency in the direction of an expansively differentiated personal character (or toward the characteristics of the sympathetic division and the autonomic nervous system as a whole, distinct from the central nervous system) creates the "occidental" tendency toward individualism (or the "strong-willed ego"). And this also provides the basis for a general revulsion toward collectivism, and even a reluctance toward positive cooperation with others. (Thus, the politics of the monolithic State and the collectivist society is threatening to the conventionally "occidental" tendency in human acculturation.)

The classical "oriental" orientation is toward the undifferentiated monad in consciousness and in the social order. Thus, from the East we inherit not only the politics of collectivism and the Parental State, but the philosophy of the absorption of the ego in the Absolute, beyond differentiation. Thus, it is from the East that mankind has received the basic cultural methods of esoteric religion and mysticism. And because of the native oriental disposition toward the mechanisms of the parasympathetic division of the autonomic nervous system and toward the status of the central nervous system itself, the East has produced many great individuals who investigated and demonstrated the higher and intuitional dimensions of the human body-mind. The practical philosophers of the East generally were and are esoteric practitioners, who explore the far reaches of experiential possibility that are hidden in the human brain (above the brain center of the verbal mind and the sensory domain of the autonomic nervous system).

The West, on the other hand, has produced the greatest cultural movements toward human political freedom and individualism, and human intellectual genius, including the genius for science as a tool for knowing and technologically manipulating the world of elemental processes known to the human senses.

But both East and West have demonstrated and continue to demonstrate a reluctance and even an incapacity for cultural and political and philosophical synthesis. East and West continue to strive against one another in a kind of irrational competition. Indeed, the East and the West have begun to act like two great Cults, each bound exclusively to its own partial point of view, and each determined to displace or destroy the other. This is a sign of a psychotic split in the cultural mentality of Man, and mankind must awaken to Man as a whole if this split is not to destroy the human world.

Therefore, let us consider Man as a whole. He is not two, but one body. And yet, he is expressed as a play of parts. He is a dynamic system in his active and sensory being. He is male and female, active and passive—that is, in his positive and responsible mode, he is self-regulating, always moving toward an integrated harmony of opposites. But he is also more than he appears to be. In the core of the body-mind of Man is the central being, the central nervous system, which knows only Life, and which, by submission to Life, constantly awakens to higher structural awareness and function.

Therefore, Man is a dynamic animal, and he contains a secret bodily path or part that can make him change and grow and transcend all that he is at any moment. The central nervous system is not only or merely the seat of mystical and intuitive illumination, but it is the mechanism whereby Man himself can grow and develop new functional characteristics, so that these new characteristics may gradually transform even his physical appearance and state, as well as the total culture of his human existence.

If mankind can begin to learn about and adapt to Man as a whole, and thus also begin to break down cultural, philosophical, and political barriers to the synthesis of human activities, then the present and chronic state of conflict between nations and between individuals can come to an end. Then there can truly be peace or harmony in the world—but not before. There will be no peace until there is the harmonious and total acculturation of all individuals within a dynamic world-culture that accommodates all aspects of the human capacity. And there will be no peace until the evolutionary and benign play of humanity begins again, free of negative oppositions. Therefore, first of all, the body-mind of "Everyman," or every individual, must become a harmony, oriented always toward higher evolutionary adaptation and self-transcendence. Then male and female will also play in harmony again, and West and East will embrace like lovers, full of hope.

The Purity of Our House

The separate Ways of the East and the West are founded on the two independent impulses (or circuits) of the autonomic nervous system. These two impulses or circuits are experienced daily by every human being. Indeed, both impulses are active in every moment of bodily existence, and the bodily test of Man is a matter of whether or not the two divisions of the autonomic nervous system can achieve and maintain a functional harmony.

However, we function with a tacit presumption that there are in fact always two <u>alternative</u> modes of attention, or thinking, or bodily behavior, in every moment of our functional existence. These two modes are the modes of extroversion (or outward-directed attention and motion) and introversion (or inward-directed attention and motion). And these two alternative modes of acting or "being" correspond exactly to the two functionally independent impulses in the autonomic nervous system.

Thus, human beings may be characterized, according to our observation of them in any moment, or in their general pattern over time, as relatively extroverted or relatively introverted. If a person exhibits the "hot" or extroverted tendency, the sympathetic division of the autonomic nervous system is dominant. And if a person exhibits the "cool" or introverted tendency, the parasympathetic division of the autonomic nervous system is dominant.

These same mechanisms account for the basic personal and cultural divisions in the human world. The male is more or less associated (at least traditionally) with the extroverted character, and the female with the introverted character. Likewise, the occidental or Western cultural style is traditionally extroverted, and the oriental or Eastern cultural style is traditionally introverted. Just so, the primary method of knowledge and of cultural enterprise in the West is extroverted, scientific (or technological), and analytical, whereas that of the East is introverted, mystical, and intuitive.

Man as a species and mankind as a process are both properly understood only when viewed (and exercised) as a totality, or an integrated whole. Man and the natural world are truly a dynamic or living play, not a self-divided machine of death. Therefore, the great cultural divisions in the human world must constantly yield to the motive of unity and energetic harmony, just as the male and the female must yield to one another in self-transcending love.

Those who speak of an irreducible "Western mind" and an equally irreducible and opposite "Eastern mind" are simply bereft of true understanding of themselves and of Man, and they are not turned to the ecstatic and single motive that is native to the universal Life-Energy and to the central nervous system of Man.

There must be a personal and a universal cultural synthesis of human functional energies. The dynamics of personal and cultural existence must constantly and creatively work toward a living unity —otherwise the play of Life becomes a kind of warfare in which self and other are constantly brought to the brink of destruction. The natural divisions of the autonomic nervous system and of the two hemispheres of the human brain-mind must not be permitted to create a self-divided Man and an irreducibly divided world.

Therefore, the creative and truly human task of Man, in the form of any individual, any group or community, or in the form of the total world of humanity, is to overcome self-division, conflict, and destructive motivations. The separate motives of the two structural halves of Man may seem to demand self-divided conflict in any moment, but the unity of the whole body (and the central nervous system) must constantly be accepted as the prior and dominant Principle of action. Indeed, the acceptance of the personal and cultural Principle of inherent and ultimate unity (rather than inherent and ultimate self-division) is the distinguishing characteristic of the true Man and the true culture of Man.

We must accept the discipline of self-knowledge and of critical understanding of all of our personal and collective motivations. Such is the very least of human wisdom that we should expect of one another—and of all our leaders. It is time for this. It has long been time for this. Now is the time for all of us to purify our houses and embrace one another in the square.

The War between
the East and the West

The separate cultures of East and West express the self-divided quality of the human individual. When the individual is self-divided, then he tends to function obsessively, in a single and exclusive direction, and on the basis of fixed ideas, so that he destroys the true or dynamic play of his own existence. Only the native Unity of Man is the proper basis for a human world-culture.

Therefore, it is not appropriate for us to fix upon or idolize the cultural products of Man in his self-divided enterprises. Rather, we must criticize and understand the unique and exclusive motivations in Man that have created and continue to create destructive and deluded personal and cultural divisions.

Neither the East nor the West is precious or sufficient in itself. We must each become awake to our inherent personal unity in Communion with the universal Light of Life, and, on that basis, we must recreate the culture of mankind as a new, living, and benign unity of superior human beings. Therefore, we must examine and criticize the basic cultural motives that divide the traditional East and the traditional West.

The mystical enterprises of the cultures of the East are presently in a temporarily depressed state, because the technological and scientific culture of the West has been on the rise for several hundred years. However, the mystical cultural movements of the East are, along with the collectivist political motives of the East, beginning to reappear, even within the Western nations themselves. Thus, in recent decades, we have seen the beginnings of the profound influence of oriental mystical philosophy all over the Western world. And the rise, in the West, of the political motivation toward forms of socialism and even communism is also an expression of a more "oriental" tendency than has typified the West in the past.

Just so, the West has invaded the East with all of the social and cultural influence of materialistic science and technology—and traditional men and women of the East feel just as disturbed by that invasion of their domain as do traditional Western religious and cultural leaders who are faced by the invasion of their domain by oriental mystical trends and other tendencies offensive to traditional Western individualism.

The truth of the matter is that we are already witnessing the inevitable breakdown of the ancient traditional divisions between the East and the West. And this process is a good sign! It is a sign that Man, incarnated as the men and women of the generations now living and about to be born, is moving out of the ancient traditional mode of self-division and of cultural exclusivism.

This unifying cultural process has, until now, been largely involuntary. For this reason, the world seems to be trapped within a design of inevitable conflict—as if East and West must someday confront one another in a last great battle. But neither East nor West can or should win. Neither East nor West is the "good" side. The origins of the separate cultures of East and West are in the self-divided and self-possessed mode of human development. To say that one or the other is "good" and must triumph is like saying that one or the other hemisphere of the brain must triumph—or one or the other division of the autonomic nervous system—or one or the other of the two sexes. No, neither must triumph. Rather, Man must consciously transcend self-division and the self-possessed (or anti-ecstatic) strategies of personal and cultural enterprise.

134

We must each observe the inevitable trend toward self-transcending unity in our own person, and, on that basis, we must each begin consciously to serve the self-transcending unity of mankind.

Body, Sex, and God-Realization

Both the anti-sexual mind (or the self-conscious body-negating and sex-negating "oriental" mind) and the self-possessed sexual mind (or the anti-ecstatic body-exploiting and sex-exploiting "occidental" mind) are naturally and inherently transcended in the Mood of God-Communion (or heartfelt ecstatic and self-transcending surrender of the body-mind in the Radiant Transcendental Being). Therefore, in the Way that I Teach, there is no presumed "problem" about bodily existence and sex. If the problem is transcended, the "two minds" of our self-divided state are also transcended.

From the point of view of Transcendental Ecstasy, there is no inherent difference between bodily or sexual experience and the absence of the same. The existence or experience of psycho-physical states is neither inherently problematic nor demanding of either self-conscious suppression or self-possessed exploitation. In the Way that I Teach, the point of view of practice is neither toward nor away from phenomena. Rather, it is, in every moment, a matter of Abiding in Transcendental Ecstasy, or heartfelt inherence of the body-mind in the Radiant Being (prior to the force of experience). In that case, a natural psycho-physical economy develops, founded on the equanimity of Divine Bliss. That economy perhaps develops and changes over time, but it expresses the non-problematic or priorly free Disposition of Transcendental Realization. Nothing is added or subtracted from that Realization by any experience, and there is no profound tendency toward either the "coolness" of suppression or the "heat" of obsessive exploitation of conventional psycho-physical states.

135

For this reason, I have continually stressed the non-ultimate or conventional significance of mystical (or yogic, "upper coil," and higher psychic or psycho-physical) phenomena. Such phenomena are founded upon the suppression, inversion, or sublimation of the vital, "lower coil" functions of the sense-mind. They are merely conditional or conventional experiential states (as are the "lower coil" states which are their opposite or lower counterparts). In any case, whether our present experiences are low or high or positive or negative in the spectrum of our possibilities, they are nothing but apparent modifications of the Radiant Transcendental Being, in Which we inhere, and Which is always already the Condition of "I" and all phenomenal events.

It is only the Realization of Transcendental Ecstasy that establishes us in the Divine Being as the Condition of all our experience. And only that Ecstasy grants us the equanimity, the power of discrimination, and the essential freedom necessary for us to be Happy and rightly oriented while alive.

Beyond the Sexual Limits of East and West

Traditional Eastern (or oriental) and Western (or occidental) sexual orientations lead to two basic psycho-physical scripts.

1. The Eastern: the "left-sided" or "yin" script. The couple avoid exploitation of the outer-directed or motor apparatus and the sympathetic (or "right-sided") nerve currents by embracing without motion, relaxing the brain and breath, and emptying the verbal mind,

while also exploiting the sensory apparatus and the parasympathetic nerve currents through intense tactile awareness, contemplation of internal sensory phenomena of body and brain, and sending of the sensory thrill and attention upwards toward and via the brain (thus releasing genital tension and the need for genital orgasm).

2. The Western: the "right-sided" or "yang" script. The couple exploit the motor apparatus and the sympathetic nerve currents through hyper-excitation of the body, breath, and brain-mind. This has the effect of dulling the sensory apparatus (or suspending the parasympathetic or "left-sided" nerve currents), thus limiting the depth of tactile and internal awareness, and it also sends the energy of the motor thrill downwards, away from the brain, toward the genitals and genital orgasm.

The Eastern sexual script is characterized by calmness of body, emotion, breath, and mind, whereas the Western sexual script is characterized by the excitation of these. The Eastern sexual script tends to develop general psycho-physical equanimity as well as a heightening of energy in the brain, particularly the right hemisphere, which is directly related to the sensory circuit. (And the extreme version of the Eastern sexual script is sex-transcending asceticism, or a habit of contemplation that avoids sexual activity and generally minimizes outer-directed activity of body and mind.) Thus, the Eastern sexual script is related to the general Eastern ideal of heightened intuitive or nonverbal psychic and mental activity and physical calm.

The Western sexual script tends to create a sense of release (and even emptiness, when done to excess) in mind and body. Likewise, it reinforces the general tendency toward outer-directed physical (or motor) activity and verbal (or left hemisphere) brain activity—although both motor and brain activity are temporarily suspended or released in the event of orgasm (thus providing a brief illusion of ecstasy).

The Western sexual script is the universally common practice in modern industrial societies, whereas the Eastern sexual script is generally engaged only by the practitioners of esoteric yoga and ancient oriental medical philosophy. However, the Western sexual tendency has historically always been confronted by systems of cultural and social taboos, which are often anti-sexual in character. The purpose of such social and cultural mechanisms has been to control the built-in liabilities of the Western sexual script, and thus to control or economize the outer-directed sexual force, which tends to produce degenerative excesses and promiscuity. Clearly, such positive control was the original intent of Hebrew and Islamic social and cultural rules or taboos. But the Christian social and cultural taboos, which have long dominated the largest part of human civilization, particularly in Europe and the European "colonies" or sub-states, including the Americas, have invariably been associated with an anti-sexual or sex-negative intent.

There is a clear difference between a sex-positive control of sexual tendencies and a sex-negative manipulation or suppression of sexual enjoyment. And Christian civilization contains an inherent problem or conflict in this regard. This can be understood if we can also understand the roots of the Christian religious message. The centuries have obscured the essentially oriental origins of the teaching of Jesus. Western civilization adapted the exoteric religion about Jesus, but in doing so it unwittingly inherited certain uniquely oriental attitudes. One of those is the conservative Eastern sexual script. The Eastern sexual ideal is the opposite of the Western sexual ideal, as I have already described. And Christianity, while providing the original basis for Western culture, contains an essentially Eastern disposition toward sexuality.

The Eastern sexual ideal, when applied to the Western sexual tendency, feels like a suppressive or anti-sexual message (since it is not disposed toward excitation, orgasm, or the verbal personality). And that aspect of the Eastern sexual ideal that Jesus apparently represented was the ascetic or sex-transcending ideal (which is commonly regarded as the ultimate fulfillment or extension of the Eastern sexual practice). Therefore, the inherent orientalism of the Christian sexual disposition has always worked in opposition to the basically Western (or outer-directed occidental) ideal to which Christian civilization has historically been devoted. And, for this reason, the recent trend in Western and generally occidental (or industrial) societies has been toward a revolutionary overcoming of anti-sexual taboos. In the process, patterns of degenerative and promiscuous sexuality tend to appear, but the ultimate outcome should be a sex-positive social and cultural disposition that tends toward a rational economy of sexual activity. (Such was indeed the achievement of various epochs of non-Christian but Semitic culture. The great epochs of Judaism and Islam were clearly associated with a sex-positive disposition in which sexual pleasure was properly glorified and sexual control was rationally understood. Thus, such societies made no taboos against wisdom, happiness, sex, childbirth, wealth, health, or longevity, and those "laws" that pertained to sex were designed to create reasonably predictable social structures rather than prevent truly human sexual expansiveness. Evidence of this is that polygamy, as well as sex-positive monogamy, was commonly accepted as a positive social possibility by both Jews and Muslims, whereas Christians have always tended to prefer either celibacy or a kind of compulsory monogamy that is ultimately a form of anti-sexual religious austerity.)

Clearly, the industrial societies of the future must overcome the confusion of social and sexual ideals that we have inherited from the ancient Eastern/Western division of the world (or the like division between the functions of brain and body). The outer-directed social enterprises must be permitted to be intelligent, Life-positive, and, therefore, sex-positive. The self-division of Christian and general Western culture must be overcome, and, therefore, the arbitrary dominance of Man by the ancient exoteric religious cults must be overcome. Sex-positive social structures must replace the old disturbances. But it is also true that Man must become whole and single—no longer exclusively characterized by either oriental or occidental ideals. Therefore, while a sex-positive social economy must develop, every individual must awaken to the esoteric spiritual culture of the whole body. The outer-directed verbal tendencies must achieve a balance with the sensual or sensory and nonverbal or intuitional possibilities. This requires each and all of us to go to school for a lifetime, in order to grow through all of the evolutionary patterns in Man. And, in sexual terms, this means that we must Realize a process of sexual communion, or mutual love-surrender in the Divine Life-Principle, so that our sexual play transcends the inherent and traditional limits of both the Eastern (or oriental) and the Western (or occidental) scripts.

The Commitment to Culture

"Oriental" asceticism, or self-enclosure, is a reversion to nomadic eccentricity, a breaking away from the cultural collective of human order. But collective civilization and personal evolution both depend on our persistence in the cultural way of the human social bond. Therefore, we must embrace our bodily and our social adventure, but we must also move on to a higher evolutionary plane of understanding and action.

The Method of Lust

The phenomenon of lust characterizes the self-possessed illusions of both oriental and occidental men. It is simply that the lust is turned in a different direction in each of the two cases.

The occidental man (both male and female) is characteristically moved by lust for what is below the heart—for food, and sex, and vital possessions.

The oriental man (both male and female) is characteristically moved by lust for what is above the heart—for visions and flights to realms of mind.

In the present epoch, East and West are in confrontation, and, although a true marriage has not yet taken place, each is involved in a process of sharing and duplicating the qualities of the other.

Therefore, the East is adapting to a new "worldliness," through various kinds of political, social, and technological change. And the West is adapting to a new "other-worldliness," through fascination with the possibilities of mind, and the deep psyche, and the higher nervous system.

Experimenters in the East and the West are thus sharing in each other's ancient lusts, and great technological efforts are everywhere being made to exploit both the inner and the outer Man.

But lust yet characterizes the seeking of mankind. Objects of every kind are sought for their distracting power, to save us from the torment of mortal fear, boredom, and unlove—all the symptoms of depressed Life.

The machines of State are overwhelming in their drive toward power and material complexity. Just so, the laboratories of scientific or technological research into the psyche strive to "take Heaven by storm."

140

We are lusting for what will change us. We are lusting for every alternative to the frozen moment of the threatened present.

But we must understand and transcend our lust, our self-division, our deluded fascination with the things of body and of mind. We must awaken to Life, and we must be free of the reactive recoil from Life that moves us to exploit mind and body by every means.

Man can take natural pleasure in his truly creative and self-transcending adaptation to the evolutionary possibilities that are structured into every individual. But the heart, or the radical intuition and ecstatic love of the Transcendental Life-Principle, must precede and inform and even heal all the motives of Man.

Lust is destructive of self and other. Lust is self-possessed and incapable of true Ecstasy and true Wisdom. When lust is transformed by the love of Life, then we are awakened to Wisdom in relation to mind, and body, and all relations. The Truth is not any political system, nor any technological strategy, nor any chemical that can change the mind. Truth is the self-transcending love that is identical to the Radiance of Life itself. We evolve only through adaptation in love. And experience, without the spiritual discipline of total psycho-physical Love-Communion with the Life-Principle, is, at best, only satisfaction—but it is merely a temporary release from the awful distress of unillumined mortality.

The Secret Bodily Path
beyond the East and the West

I t is not only the parasympathetic division of the autonomic nervous system that leads to the central nervous system and to the Infinite Domain of the Life-Current. The sympathetic division of the autonomic nervous system can be followed just as directly to that same Infinity of Life.

The "oriental" way is the way of inwardness, via the parasympathetic and sensory currents in the spine, to the brain-mind, where the Life-Source may be experienced. But this way leads to the experiential illusions of subjectivity or inwardness in the mind and brain, and the Life itself may easily be overlooked.

The "occidental" way is the way of functional extroversion, via the sympathetic and motor currents in the spinal circuit, to the outer functional terminals of physical experience, where the Life-Source may also be experienced. But this way leads to the illusions of merely physical or "objective" experience, and the Life itself may easily be overlooked.

Therefore, there is also a radical bodily path that leads directly to the Life, prior to mind and prior to bodily experience. It is not the way that merely leads up the spine to the brain-mind, nor is it the way that merely leads down the spine and out through the lower physical outlets or functions. Rather, it is the radical Way of the total body itself. It is the Way in which "I" accepts and confesses that it is only the body—the total body, prior to any experience or exercise of its parts.

The radical Way is to be the body-only, awake, without inwardness or thought, and full of Life, prior to all the implications of bodily experience. It is simply to be the body as a whole, prior to all subjectivity, and to abide in direct and self-transcending feeling-intuition of the Life that pervades the total body, including the central nervous system and the autonomic nervous system. It is to be Ecstatic as the body, prior to mind and bodily experience. It is to abide as the Life, by not turning from identification with the prior or radical Condition of the total body.

This radical Way is a paradox. It is the only or ultimate Way of Life. It is a matter of transcending all strategies of inwardness and all strategies of bodily exploitation. Thus, it is a matter of abiding moment to moment simply as the body in direct feeling-communion with the Infinite Life. In this process, the body is Transfigured by the Life-Radiance, which is Love, and at last, after a drama of many apparent changes, the body may even be Dissolved in the Life-Current, which is God.

142

The Mind, the Body, and the Radiant Transcendental Being

Introversion is the anti-relational or "oriental" subjectivist tendency toward consoling absorption in the internal, independent, or "bodiless" conditions of mind.

Extroversion is the seemingly relational but self-possessed "occidental" tendency toward consoling absorption in the experiential and external conventions of the "embodied" or physically expressed mind-self.

Neither introversion nor extroversion characterizes the Way of Life in Truth, and the Mood or Posture of Enlightenment is characterized neither by the strategic embrace nor the strategic avoidance of the patterns of introversion or extroversion. Rather, Enlightenment is a matter of Transcendental Ecstasy, or self-transcending Awakening to the Condition in which all events or experiences or conditions (whether "subjective" or "objective") arise.

Therefore, when there is such Awakening, the Drama of psycho-physical experience is utterly transcended in Ecstasy, or tacit Absorption in the Blissful Realization of the Radiant Divine Self-Fullness. That Radiant Fullness of Being Transfigures or Outshines all experience of mind and body, dissolving all the seriousness or humorlessness of the egoic psyche and its subtle and gross forms of worldly embodiment.

When such Awakening is most profound, there is native or prior Self-Absorption—there is Liberating Dissolution of the contracting, limiting, and self-defining power of psycho-physical states. Such states may seem to continue—from the viewpoint of others—but they are "involving" to the "subject" only in a playful and transparent sense, without binding power. And the individual or "subject" self will seem to be rather "uninvolved," no matter how intense the quality of his apparent action or experience.

It is not that some internal pattern becomes absorbing, but, rather, the Transcendental Condition of Radiant Being has been Realized as the Condition and Truth of all events, internal and external. Therefore, such an individual cannot be understood or identified by his actions (which may be either "conventional" or "unconventional" relative to common behaviors), nor may the profundity of his Realization be determined by analysis of his "inner" or psychic experiences, healing powers, miraculous abilities, or any other evidence in the body-mind.

The Power of Divine or Transcendental Ecstasy simply Liberates the body-mind from the recoiling or self-defining tendency; thus permitting egoless existence (or non-separation from the Radiant Divine Being). That Ecstasy Transfigures the total body-mind with Radiant Life, dissolving all conditional emotions in Love-Bliss, so that world and body and mind are, in effect, forgotten or overcome in the Whimsy of Liberation. More and more, this Blissful Disposition conquers the problem-based, strategic, and self-bound will to experience and accumulated knowledge in the countless domains or worlds of body and mind.

The Whole Bodily Synthesis of Evolutionary Love

The traditional "oriental" (or universal mystical) method of spiritual esotericism is to withdraw attention from the functions of the autonomic nervous system and fix attention in the central nervous system, via methods of prayer, internal concentration, or direct stimulation of the Life-Current in the nervous system (via manipulation of breath, feeling, and so forth). This particularly involves relaxation of the "outer ego," or the expansive mental and physical activity that is generated via the sympathetic division of the autonomic nervous system. Therefore, the principal method is to place attention into the mechanisms of the parasympathetic division of the autonomic nervous system, and thereby force attention to ascend, via the sensory currents, to the brain.

144

This universal and "oriental" spiritual method produces monistic states of consciousness (free of the verbal mind and all subject-object entanglements with the "body," or the dynamic physical and mental being), and, as the process progresses towards the monistic consciousness, it also produces conventional mystical knowledge about the interior or subjective dimensions of the body-mind of Man.

The fault in this traditional mystical process is that it tends to objectify the internal phenomena of mind and to attribute independent reality to subjective states. Thus, the "oriental" men of knowledge imagine they can escape the body of Man through inwardness, and they forget that Man is a psycho-physical being, and, therefore, that mental states are themselves only dependent reflections of physical states. Just so, the "oriental" world-view is essentially amoral, or nonmoral, since it is not founded in fundamental acceptance of the human relational and bodily condition, and the "oriental" Way thus tends to be ascetic, other-worldly, and static.

The traditional "occidental" method of ordinary living is based on natural acceptance of the body and the natural world as an irreducible situation of existence. The "occidental" tendency is anchored in the functional body-mind, or the "navel" (not floating out through the brain). It is individualistic (or naturally egoic) in its point of view, and thus it is verbal, or discursive and analytical, in its mentality and physically expansive or vitally active in its cultural and environmental adaptation.

This "occidental" method of ordinary living produces bodily and concrete mental activity of all kinds, ultimately directed toward positive practical changes in the physical dimension of the body-mind and the world of Man. And it also produces practical knowledge about the exterior or relational dimension of the body-mind of Man.

The fault in this conventional exercise is that it tends to absolutize the exclusive reality of non-subjective or "material" conditions. Thus, the "occidental" men of knowledge imagine they can conquer or master the realm of physical experience, and they forget that physical or "material" conditions are only dependent reflections or simultaneous companions of subtle forces of mind and energy. Just so, the "occidental" world view is always <u>tending</u> toward immorality, since it accepts the human relational and bodily condition, but it generally fails to submit that condition, via literal psycho-physical processes, to the higher or Living Transcendental Reality. Thus, the "occidental" Way tends to be self-indulgent, worldly, and hyperactive.

145

Neither the Occident nor the Orient is sufficient in and of itself. The central nervous system and the autonomic nervous system (and the sympathetic and parasympathetic divisions of the autonomic nervous system in itself) depend on one another as do body and breath—and they are necessarily at play with one another, like man and woman.

Therefore, if we understand Man as a whole, we may understand the cultural disposition and necessary characteristics of the ultimate or right future of mankind. Occident and Orient, West and East, are not mutually exclusive opposites, like Evil and Good. Rather, they are a Couple, a Pair of Lovers, a Cycle, a Cooperative Process. The function of the two limbs of human motion (introverted and extroverted) is to produce a Play, a Dynamic Unity, a Total Culture of Man.

The central nervous system and the autonomic nervous system are two dimensions of <u>one body</u>. The mind and the gross physical body are one psycho-physical body, or <u>body-mind</u>. The experiences we may attain by exploitation of either half or any part of our psycho-physical being are not in themselves sufficient, true, or absolute. And Reality Itself is not rightly Realized by either point of view—East or West. Neither body nor mind is the best symbol for the Truth. Only the total body-mind is intimate with the Living Truth.

The East and the West, in their separate modes, are deluded by the kinds of knowledge—intuitive, rational, and sensual. The Eastern view is like a soul without a body, and the Western view is like a body without a soul. The Eastern view imagines the mind is disembodied and that inward experience is sufficient and real in itself. And the Western view imagines that "salvation" or ultimate evolution can come without inner and higher evolutionary practice.

The Truth is that which gives Life to body <u>and</u> mind. The Truth is Life Itself, which is not separable from the Play of the World-Process. The Truth is the Living God, with Whom the total body-mind must Commune, and toward which the body-mind must grow, through transcendence of every kind of knowledge (subjective and objective), and through surrender of the total self as love.

The higher evolutionary and transcendental Way of Man is not in itself a matter of objective knowledge about natural processes, nor is it in itself identical to internal, mystical, and self-saving knowledge about the internal being. Rather, it is a matter of total psycho-physical sacrifice of self, which is self-transcendence, or Ecstasy, in literal functional Communion with the Living Reality.

This consideration has implications for the esoteric spiritual process itself, which I have described in *The Enlightenment of the Whole Body*. Thus, the radical spiritual and higher cultural Way of Man is that of neither East nor West, but it is a matter of the Whole. It is a matter of submission of the total body-mind into the evolutionary Cycle that is native to the nervous system as a whole. There must be the gesture of absorption in the disposition of the central nervous system (in the "oriental" manner) but this must alternate or coincide with the Radiation of Life in the autonomic nervous system, and the truly moral discipline or practice of personal, relational, truly emotional, sensuous (or bodily), and cultural adaptation.

And Man is ultimately suited only to the intimate culture of concrete and cooperative community, not isolation or the illusion of relationless independence. If human beings are bereft of community, they grow wild, and they do not tend to grow high and true, but in a self-divided manner. Therefore, our independence must be a matter of natural privacy and responsibility <u>within</u> a true and higher human community. And only the cultural solidarity of true community makes it possible for mankind also to create a representative State that serves mankind and does not Parent or enslave mankind.

We contain and create our own negative forces. The world is overrun with us. Therefore, the prophetic demand of this time is for a new reformation, a new understanding, and a new discipline. But the method whereby all of this will be achieved is self-understanding and love.

The brain and the navel contain the two principles at play in the body-mind and in the world of Man. But these two principles must be directed into a dynamic Cycle, a Circle around the heart, for it is from the feeling heart of Man that the Transcendental Divine Radiance Shines into the higher and lower parts of Man and even the world of Man.

When you begin to feel as afraid as you really are, then you will find the energy to reach up and begin to have visions. And you will not stop seeking visions and having visions until you overcome fear completely.

Da Free John

CHAPTER FIVE

The Seamless Garment of Love

Exoteric and Esoteric Religion

Conventional or exoteric religion is communicated in the form of ideas, attitudes, and behaviors. True or esoteric religion is communicated in the form of high transformative experiences and Transcendental Realization.

Transcendence of the Human Nervous System

Conventional and exoteric religion is based on naive submission to the physical and sometimes psychic conditions determined by the structures of the human nervous system.

Conventional religious esotericism is typically based on strategic submission to the psychic and sometimes physical conditions determined by the fully analyzed structures of the human nervous system.

True religion and true religious esotericism are based on conscious and intuitive transcendence of the human nervous system and all psychic, physical, or psycho-physical conditions determined by it.

150 # Divine Descent
and Human Ascent

Exoteric religious traditions are frequently, if not commonly, associated with the primary idea that God has descended or will descend and manifest to mankind, even by incarnating as a human being (or, ultimately, as all beings, human or otherwise).

Esoteric religious traditions are frequently, if not commonly, associated with the primary idea that Man, as each and every human being, must and will ultimately ascend (via the inversion of our manifest faculties) and manifest to God, even by merging into the independent Domain or Form of God.

All such traditions, both exoteric and esoteric, are founded upon intuitive and experiential associations with the structure and structural symbology of the human nervous system and brain-mind. The exoteric notion of Divine "descent" and "incarnation" expresses our feeling of positive association with the extended body-mind, the "material" Earth-world, and the outward or evolutionary play of the sense-mind via the autonomic nervous system. And the esoteric notion of the "inversion" and "ascent" of Man expresses our feeling of positive association with the root-condition of the body-mind, the underlying Essence and Source of the Earth-world, and the unconditional state of energy and consciousness, prior to the experiences of body, senses, and mind, communicated deep within the central nervous system.

However, when the absolute ideas of Divine descent and human ascent appear in the languages of religion, they seem mutually contradictory. If Man succeeds at ascending and God also succeeds at descending, then Earth will eventually become Heaven (since God will be here, but Man will have already vanished), and Heaven will become merely another urban sprawl (since Man will be there, but God will have long ago gone to Earth)! Clearly, the two ideas, when thus considered as equal and absolute propositions, become absurd. But in what sense, then, are they rightly understood?

Truly, the exoteric idea of Divine descent is a popular conception, communicated among the masses of ordinary and suffering humanity, promising help and salvation to those whose lives and minds are bound up in the conventions of outward and mortal experiencing. Such individuals are greatly consoled by the messages of Divine Providence. And, indeed, the Eternal Divine is Revealed to ordinary humanity via extraordinary Acts of Grace and via the relatively rare appearances of those Adepts who surrender themselves in service to the people.

But once any individual has become healed and steadied by the Work of God in the world, that individual begins to become inclined toward the Divine Itself, and for the sake of Loving and Realizing the Divine (rather than the acquisition of any consolations or advantages in this world). In that case, the individual begins to respond to the inverted and higher psychic movements of the being, and he will eventually enter into profound sympathy with ideas and practices of esoteric or mystical ascent.

Therefore, we may understand the independent messages of Divine descent and human ascent to be expressions of two primary stages in human psychological and cultural or religious growth. However, this is not to say that those two stages of growth represent the total possible human pattern, and, clearly, the doctrine or primary proposition of each of the two stages is in itself partial or incomplete.

The partial doctrines of human experiential understanding must all be yielded at last to the direct Revelation of the Living Divine Person or Truth. And that Revelation, to which the completed Adept is Awakened, serves to correct the partial or yet to be completed understanding of Man.

This book is itself a prophetic meditation on many of the partial views that pervade the popular and also the "secret" or esoteric domains of human culture. The Wisdom-Revelation of the Living God is the Principle whereby these meditations or prophecies have been made. Therefore, let us also consider these ideas of Divine descent and human ascent in the same Light.

As I have already said, these two ideas express two characteristic orientations toward our experience and even toward the psycho-physical mechanism (or body-mind) of our experience. But what is the Truth of our experience? Should we receive and incarnate the Divine, or should we invert our psycho-physical consciousness and ascend to God within and away from this world? The conventional "incarnation" idea is fundamentally "occidental" and the "inverted ascent" idea is fundamentally "oriental." Is Truth of the East, or the West?

Truly, Divine Wisdom is whole and One, even as the body-mind is a single and dynamic harmony. Neither East nor West is, in itself, the Sign of Truth. Both are transcended in the Single Vision and the Whole Bodily Enlightenment.

The Living God is Transcendental Being. God is not merely above and separate in absoluteness, nor is what appears below (or in experience) of value in itself or independently. The body-mind must be transcended through Awakening to the Transcendental Condition of self and world. In that case the illusions of our stages of relative maturity are vanished in singular Bliss.

It is not that we are going to leave this world and only then "return" to God, nor is it true that God is going to come here as an independent person, suddenly evolve both Earth and Man to perfection, and stay here to Govern us forever. Rather, our Condition is always already one of Divine Inherence, and our Destiny is always to go on being transformed, in a Process with all other apparent moments of beings and things and worlds, eternally—in the Eternal Play of God.

The idea of the "ascent of Man" is a characteristically "oriental" concept, founded in the esotericism of inversion, abandonment of the body and its relations, and exclusive absorption in the central energy of the spine and brain. And the idea of the "descent of God" is a characteristically "occidental" concept, founded in the exoteric mythology and bodily hopefulness of the vitally extended human nervous system. But the Truth and the Way of Life that transcend ideas and the structural imperatives of the human nervous system are founded on Ecstatic Equanimity, or the Intuition that body, mind, and the world of beings and things and changes all inhere in the Infinitely Radiant Divine Being.

The heart or feeling being of Man is the "place" of the Unity of Vision, or the Harmony of the independent motions of ascent and descent. The heart is zero, the "place" or Way of the surrender of the total psycho-physical self into the Radiant Transcendental Being. From the "point of view" of the heart-surrendered being, God is not exclusively above, nor is Man exclusively below, nor is either mind or body considered to be the dominant realm of human existence. From the heart we may enter, even in body and mind, into the Vision or Love-Intuition of Only God, in Whom self and mind and body and all objects or phenomena are presently arising.

153

The body-mind need not be suppressed. Neither are we even now separated from the Transcendental Divine. If the Living and Perfect God is Realized, the parts of Man, above and below, within and without, become equalized, and God becomes Man indeed.

The Commitment to the Creative Struggle of Life

To survive, we must change, and grow, and evolve.

To change, and grow, and evolve, we must transcend ourselves.

To transcend ourselves, we must become a love-sacrifice into the Radiant Life-Principle.

If we surrender to mortal fear, then we fall back on ourselves. In that case, we contract and separate ourselves from the Radiant Life-Principle, and, therefore, from the acts of love, and evolution, and growth, and change. We will seem to survive even then, but only by regressing into the static subjective illusions of mind, finite self, destructive bodily self-indulgence, and ultimate emptiness. Such survival (while we live, and even after death) is merely withdrawal from the creative struggle of Life, by passing back through the stages of growth, adaptation, and evolution we have already completed, until the motive of Life again inspires us.

Therefore, we are obliged to survive, and change, and grow, and evolve, and love. But that Process is ecstatic, or self-transcending, and always already free. It is a matter of the surrender of the total self, including both mind and body, into the All-Pervading Current of Radiant Life and Transcendental Consciousness.

154

The Trial That Tests Us While We Grow

The true test and proof of Man is not a matter of whether he can attain mystical experiences, or "out-of-body" experiences, or even sophisticated scientific knowledge and power over the world. The true test is a matter of whether Man, as any individual human being, will exist as love and persist as love, transcending himself in the midst of all experience and all knowledge, even when all experience and all knowledge press upon him to be less than love.

The Moment of Man

Man, or human existence, is a moment or stage in the evolutionary struggle of the total Realm of Nature toward a Condition of absolute identification between matter and energy.

Man himself is like the spectrum of light visible to the human eye. He is made up of only a few colors. And what "colors," or kinds of existence, precede and follow Man are a Mystery to Man, just as what kind of experience precedes the birth and follows the death of any individual is a Mystery to that individual.

The Seven Stages of Human Life

Human life develops or evolves in seven stages.

The first three stages of human life are the stages of lower functional (physical, emotional, and mental) adaptation to the universal Life-Energy.

The fourth stage of human life is the stage of whole bodily surrender and adaptation to the universal Life via Love-Communion (the disposition of the heart or deep psyche of pure energy).

The fifth stage of human life is the stage of mysticism, or evolutionary adaptation to the higher brain and mind.

The sixth stage of human life is the stage of ego-death, or transcendence of mind, independent self, and primal fear.[1]

The seventh stage of human life is the stage of bodily Translation, or Transfiguration of the total body-mind and the atomic soul in the Infinite Radiance of the Living God.

155

1. Da Free John has described the evolution of man, from birth to perfect God-Realization, in terms of seven stages. He describes the sixth stage as that of transcendental intuitive adaptation, culminating in the State traditionally known as "Self-Realization." Attention, or mind, dissolves in Divine Ignorance or unqualified Consciousness, at the heart, excluding awareness of body, mind, and world. In the seventh stage, the "eyes of the heart open" and Consciousness is released into perfect Identification-Communion with the Divine Person, or Inherence in the Current of Radiance that Pervades all bodies, minds, and worlds. Thus, in this stage, Transcendental Ignorance and Infinite Radiance become the single Intensity of God-Realized Bliss, until the devotee is Translated, even bodily, beyond all the dimensions of the Realm of Nature, high and low, into the Divine Domain that is that Very Bliss.

This is, of course, a technical description of the most subtle esoteric realization of Existence. In more practical or ordinary terms, the person who has realized the sixth stage of life tends to be extremely inward, ascetic, aloof from life and all relationships. He regards the world and all experience as unreal. The one Awake in the seventh stage, however, is profoundly alive, full of joy and humor in relation to all conditions of experience, and profoundly committed in love in all relationships. He is Alive as God, and to him the world is absolutely real—and yet, paradoxically, utterly unnecessary at the same time.

For a complete discussion of these stages see *The Enlightenment of the Whole Body* and *The Eating Gorilla Comes in Peace*, both by Da Free John.

Birth and Ego-Death

There is neither a negative cause nor a negative purpose of our birth. But we may mistakenly presume a negative cause or purpose, and that negative presumption has power to disturb our equanimity and orient us, via desire, toward negative ends.

On the basis of various configurations of thought and experience, we design a presumed state of mind and body, which we then apply to the moments of our existence. Such is the basis of habit and even philosophy. Where is wisdom to be found in all the acts and talk and thoughts of men? When will we be still and understand our own illusions?

There are no wisdom and no happiness except in the case of utter Realization of the Real Condition of all experience. And that Realization itself is only obvious when the manifest self, or the self-defining and self-limiting body-mind, is utterly transcended.

Previous to such self-transcendence, individuals pursue forms of self-satisfaction, seeking thereby to experience a release from the limits of the self. I have pursued and tested and considered all such possibilities, high and low—for my habit of living has been a spontaneous and freely experimental effort toward Truth, rather than a traditionally programed exercise in sainthood. Therefore, I have seen the body-mind in all its parts and relations. And I finally understood that none of it was the method or means whereby Truth is Realized.

We in our felt dilemma of existence are motivated toward all kinds of bodily action—to enjoy, to know, to influence. And we are also motivated to think, to perceive inwardly, to possess mysterious and shining secret things. Our pursuits in body and mind are all profoundly emotional. They are efforts to solve a basic emotional, or, ultimately, spiritual problem. And that problem does not tend to disappear, even in all the successes of body and mind.

Our fundamental problem or dis-ease will not be overcome unless we Realize the Truth, or the Real Condition of the psycho-physical self, its knowledge, its experience, and its world. And that Realization is itself a form of radical intuition that transcends the dilemma and the self-defining and self-limiting power of the body-mind.

In their pursuit of an "answer," people think and act. They believe and emote. They yield themselves to both internal and external influences that can create temporarily fascinating effects in body and mind. But their experience does not Enlighten them—it does not make them wise, good, truly happy, free, or even more intelligent. And people tend to yield to whatever is most compatible with their obsessions and most likely to produce an immediate experiential illusion of release. People want to read and think and propagandize themselves happy, but they will not engage the discipline of silence. They want to enjoy curious perceptions through arcane meditation, kundalini, and drugs, but they will not understand themselves. They want the consolations of money, food, and sex—or even the paradoxical consolations temporarily created by the absence of these—but they will not accept intelligent moral and personal disciplines in their daily lives.

There is something immensely comic in the subhuman folly of all mankind, but it is outweighed by the sorrowful destiny to which each one of us is being led by a lifetime of benighted self-seeking. The Truth, which is the only happiness, is not Realized in any of the states of mind or body. The Truth is Realized only in Ecstasy, or self-transcending Intuition and Love of the Real Condition of self, experience, and the world of things and beings. And only when this Realization is profound, complete, and stable are we established in a true, right, positive, and happy course.

This Realization of the Truth or Real God depends on what has traditionally been called "ego-death." But ego-death is just another phrase meaning Ecstasy, or the Realization of Love. It is a wholly or ultimately positive Event, and it is not an Event that negates our born existence, nor does it imply that born existence is itself a misfortune.

Until we are awakened in our intuitive and emotional understanding, ego-death, indeed, the whole affair of spiritual Realization, will tend to signify a negative process or Event, wherein the force of the being (felt as "I") is suppressed. And those who pursue ultimate Realization prior to the awakening of true understanding generally engage every aspect of the necessary discipline as if it were a game of self-suppression—whereas in fact true practice is always a form of profound and free Love-Communion between the very being and the very Divine Reality.

We are not born to be destroyed. Even death, we will Realize, is only a form of transformation. The basic force of the being is not intended for destruction. Rather, it is drawn into more and more profound Awakening and Fullness via the evolution or hierarchical development of experience, which tests the being toward self-transcendence. If the basic force of the being is negated in the process (that is, if the experience of the body-mind produces a negative reaction or critical suppression of the basic force of the self), then liberating Help must eventually be given to us so that we may continue to grow.

Paradoxically, the basic self-force or ego-force must be strong if we are to Realize the Event of ego-death. This is because ego-death is not the ultimate suppression or negation of the basic force of the being, but it is the release of that force from limiting identification with the body-mind.

Whenever we become weakened by our experience, we suffer in body and mind. And all of that is a reflection of the frustration and suppression of the basic force of the being. But the basic force of the being is identical to the Transcendental Being. It is simply that it presumes itself to be identical to the limitations of the body-mind. Ego-death is the Awakening of the being to its Real Condition of inherence in the Radiant Transcendental Being in which all things and beings are arising.

The primary symptom of the suppressed self (or ego) is a depression of feeling-attention (or love)—in relation to the Radiant All-Pervading Divine Being and also in relation to all manifest conditions (the world, other beings, and so forth). Ego-depression is shown in a collapse of the energy available for feeling-surrender to God and for serving other beings. The secondary symptoms of such ego-collapse are all the reactive emotions, petty habits of self-indulgence, selfish and mean attitudes, physical weaknesses, and unillumined opinions, beliefs, and philosophies that characterize people at their worst. (From this description it should be clear that, at the present time, mankind in general is suffering from the disease or wound of ego-collapse, rather than too great a sense of self. And this Teaching is an offering of Divine Help in response to that universal disease. It is intended to strengthen humanity through recollection of the Great Life-Light that is the Substance of this world. Such Divine Teaching has Power to Awaken humanity to the Love and Fullness that is naturally ever expanding from that dimension of the being that Realizes its own inherence in the eternally Radiant Life-Light.)

If the being is Awake to its Condition, it is Ecstatic—that is, it already transcends the limiting conditions with which it is conventionally associated. Therefore, such Awakening has been likened to death—but it is simply the death (or spontaneous and natural transcendence) of the presumed limitations of the born self. And once this Ecstatic Awakening is actual in the case of any individual, the process of a lifetime is authenticated and made fundamentally Life-positive. This is due to the release of the Transfiguring Radiance (or Love-Bliss of the Divine Self-Identity) into the plane of the body-mind. And if the Enlightened individual abides in that Radiant Self-Identity, the body-mind and even the world are gradually Transformed by that Radiance—even eventually to the point of Translation, or the Outshining of the body-mind and this world. In that case, the positive purpose of our birth has been fulfilled and our Destiny is beyond all knowing.

Ego-Death and the Chaos of Experience

A talk by Da Free John

D A FREE JOHN: The concept of ego-death is something that most of you, I am sure, have read about or heard about or considered, and as a result of what you have read or heard or considered, you probably believe that the death of the ego has something to do with the mystical process of "serious" religion. But if you examine the popularized dogmas of mystical religion, you will find that they tend to bypass the description of this process of the death of the ego. Popular mysticism is a kind of emotional and bodily enthusiasm through which the individual (and thus the ego) acquires various kinds of experiences that are in the direction of the mind or the non-bodily and "other-worldly" conditions of experience.

Many people today travel around the world popularizing mystical techniques and meditation. Mysticism is "hyped" much like the loony salvation games of popular downtown religion. Fundamentally, popular mysticism invokes the same kind of psychology as popular religion—a kind of enthusiastic believing and attachment to a sect, and to "secret" practices, and, very often, to an individual, and certainly to certain kinds of experiences that are consoling, pleasurable, and distracting, and that are equated with God.

The phenomena of conventional mysticism belong to the ego itself. They belong to the subtler internal realm of the mind and the nervous system. They arise when our attention is inverted, when we are concentrated inwardly, when we relax and give ourselves up to what we feel within, to the energies within, to the states of mind within. Traditionally, these states of mind are valued as signposts or stages in a process that leads toward more and more profound inner vision and inner experience. From the point of view of conventional mysticism, certain inner experiences are regarded to be of the highest type, and, therefore, they are regarded to be the signs of the highest illumination. Certain internal sounds, certain internal lights, certain internal visions, as well as beliefs that are a kind of internal religion— all are valued as the answers to mankind's search for the Divine Reality. Thus, the conventional religious and mystical experience is attained through egoic or self-meditative seeking. Profoundly distracting internal experience is considered to be an answer to the search provoked by our reaction to mortality, our fear. The process of mysticism, of religious belief and concrete experience in the form of mystical inwardness, is therefore a consolation for our mortal fear.

To the man or woman in doubt of the existence of God, mystical sects offer an alternative to mere concepts and all of the objective mythology of exoteric religious beliefs. Mystical techniques offer inward experiences that satisfy an ordinary need in certain kinds of individuals—a need that can be satisfied in others by belief in "Jesus," or in the "afterlife." Conventional religious and mystical phenomena console and mystify the doubting being and the suffering mind. And in the midst of all of this religious and spiritual or mystical enthusiasm, in the midst of all of this consoling "fulfillment" of people who are suffering, there is also the ancient Transcendental

Teaching that the realization of Truth or God or true Happiness is a matter of the transcendence of the limited mind and self, or the death of the ego.

People play with the conception of ego-death as if it were an extension of egoic or mystical practices. The common idea is that ego-death is a matter of mortifying one's flesh, doing without things one desires, even obliterating one's existence. But these are notions of ego-death that the ego itself projects and considers in the midst of its own efforts to survive and to defend itself. The ego is not other than the mind. The ego is the mind—the ego is not contained within the mind. The inner being, the subjective personality, the self-reference, "me," "I," is the ego. It is not by consoling one's inner being with experiences (or states of mind) that one realizes Truth. Rather, it is by the transcendence of the mind, by the death of the mind, or by the overcoming of the false evaluation of the status of the mind, that the Truth is realized.

Popular religion and mysticism serve the self, or the mind, by providing consoling objects of belief, experience, absorption, attractive states that may seem to fulfill us in the midst of our fear. Ultimately, all psycho-physical experience serves the separate being, the separate psycho-physical person that is "I." Thus, what is popularly conceived to be God-Realization, or mystical absorption, or true religious belief is only a state of mind (or of the limited body-mind), a condition or experience. of the manifest personality—Narcissus. Experience, or inwardness, is the hedge around Narcissus, the enclosure of the self. The archetype of Narcissus, who avoids the world by gazing into a pond at his own image, is a metaphor for the ego, the independent self-mind. Like the pond, the mind is a reflective mechanism. Therefore, the ego or the self or Narcissus is a reflection, an illusion of independence. To enter into the realm of the mind, to persist in our flight toward subjectivity, our obsessive experience of separate self, is to be possessed of the self, not of God, no matter how profound the inward phenomena may seem to be at any time.

The various states of mystical inwardness have nothing whatsoever to do with God-Realization, absolutely nothing. They are simply experiential states of the separate personality. Mystical experience is promoted as a solution to suffering, as an answer to doubt and fear, just as saviors and popular religious concepts are offered for the same purpose. But the Realization of God or Truth appears, and spontaneously, only in the instant of self-transcendence, or ecstatic annihilation of mind, of inwardness, of self-consciousness, or the reflection of oneself in experience. Ego-death, self-transcendence, or the transcendence of the mind, then, is the "narrow gate," the necessary doorway to the realization of Truth. Thus, the old saw that Truth is within is not true. The Truth is absolutely not within. Within is "me." Within is the inside of "me." Conventional mysticism and conventional religion are addressed to our inwardness, because the psyche, the inner being and mind, can feel itself to be separate from the body and the physical environment and all the conditions of mortal existence of which we are afraid, all the conditions that can die.

Ordinary mystics throughout human history have separated themselves from bodily consciousness by withdrawing attention from the body and from relations, becoming more or less ascetic and concentrated in the brain through various mystical and religious devices of concentration and contemplation and prayer. By detaching themselves from the awareness of the physical, and by entering into the mind itself, such mystics can feel and believe that they are free of the body and of mortality. They see all kinds of abstractions flashing in the nervous system, and the mind explodes into reveries and dreamlike states that seem to take them to other worlds, while glorious and ego-glorifying archetypes come flooding into the conscious mind, detached from physical sensation. These states traditionally were—and are—regarded to be holy. They were regarded to be the conditions under which God was realized, mortality escaped, and Truth attained. And one who was able to persist in such conditions of internal absorption would participate only minimally and even reluctantly in the daily life of the world until death, at which point he looked forward to going elsewhere, or permanently within. But I must confess that the conventional religious interpretation of mysticism is nonsense. It rests on uninspected believing and the fearful motives of self-protection. There is an evolutionary mechanism involved in mystical experience, and mystical inversion is a necessary phase in higher human development. But the reflecting mind, and the limited self, and the total functional design of the body-mind of Man must ultimately be transcended, whether or not Man is also perfected.

If we are truly serious about the matter of religion and spiritual practice, we must also be consistently self-critical. Religion and spirituality without self-criticism are merely forms of self-protecting enthusiasm, founded on uninspected fear. I have lived the mystical path myself. And I came to the end of it, where ego-death is the price for going further. Therefore, I propose that we consider religion and mysticism from a self-critical point of view.

We are all participants in a vast Realm of Nonsense, and we are struggling to make "sense" of it by attaching ourselves to selected or experientially preferred phenomena. We are confronted by an Infinite Chaos of Experience, and we each try to enforce an order and a limit on Infinity via the self-limiting mechanisms of our own body-mind and independent consciousness. We each try to make a "Universe" out of "Chaos" by continually imagining an inner being, or mind, or soul that is "I" and that is a fixed and independent center of experience. The inner "I" is the "Principle" to which experience is referred, and it is this self-reference that provides a center and singleness to the otherwise open-ended and centerless chaos· of experiences and possibilities. The "I," and not phenomena themselves, is the "Principle" whereby the World-Process is made to appear as a defined and logical "Universe." Then, on the basis of the "I"-sense, we exploit our internal and external experiential possibilities in the "Universe." But the truth of the matter is that we are terrified by our vulnerable mortality, and the Infinite Chaos of the World-Process is not a Condition into which we tend to be joyfully and ecstatically surrendered.

We are afraid, because we exist, and we observe that our existence can apparently come to an end. We also observe that our existence can achieve pleasurable distraction. Thus, we are attached to all the ways by which we can make ourselves feel good, and we are afraid of all the ways by which we can suffer and be annihilated. That fear is our fundamental response to existence. It is what produces common religion, mysticism, conventional spirituality, science, popular culture, everyday life, all the ways by which mortals struggle to be satisfied.

The transcendental Teaching of Wisdom or Truth belongs to a different stream of communication than all the "orderly chaos" of conventional secular, religious, mystical, or spiritual consciousness. The Truth is that "I," whoever speaks it, is the <u>body</u> (or total psycho-

163

physical being), and when "I" am afraid, when "I" contract and withdraw from the conditions in which this body is arising, "I" become self-possessed. "I," like Narcissus, create the "Universe" by reflection, or reaction to phenomena, and "I" look to be satisfied in my separateness by indulging my preferred possibilities, within and without. Any individual "I" can thus create its own known world, its own plan of "salvation," its own self-serving philosophy, its own closed society, its own program of experiential limits (or allowable distractions and fascinations), and its own "official" Truth. But there is no liberating Truth, no liberation from the fear that is native to self-consciousness, until the inner being or "I" that is created by fear is transcended. Therefore, God-Realization, or liberation in Truth, is most fundamentally a matter of ego-death, or the death of the illusion of the inner consciousness, the separate "I," the mind of self-centered presumptions and experiential limits.

The popular dogmas of religious mysticism presume that salvation (or liberation) lies in the exploitation of the inwardness of mind. The popular philosophy is that mind (or knowledge) is the way of salvation, and Truth is within. And the conventional mystic believes that the inner self can and, indeed, must be released from the body. Therefore, he instructs you to invert your attention, to abandon your intimate relationships, to stop all but the most pleasureless eating, to stop having sex, to stop going to work, to stop your enthusiastic play of bodily experience. All of those activities are extremely difficult to sustain, and they are ultimately mortal. Therefore, the conventional mystic advises you to forget about all of that. He advises you to turn within and away, and to begin the inner tour by which you may acquire the self-glamorizing experiences of independent inwardness. But the truly liberated Man, who has passed through and beyond mysticism, must confess to you that the tour within will only lead you to the illusions of inwardness, or the inheritance of Narcissus. And even though every man and woman must evolve and become a mystic for a time, he or she must at last transcend the mind itself, and the independent inner "I" of all experience.

The "sage," or the intuitive anti-mystic, carries the process of inversion even further than the mystic, the yogi, or the saint. Just as the mystic suffers revulsion to the body, the "sage" suffers revulsion to the mind as well. Thus, the conventional "sage" not only gives up the body and the pleasure of relations and of eating and sex, but he also gives up the mind, and, by another inward strategy, enters into the silence of the witnessing consciousness (or the "I" prior to all objects of experience). Even so, he does not bring an end to the Chaos of the World-Process. He has merely performed a trick with his attention, so that his experience is limited to Awareness (prior to objects), and he is thus, temporarily, made immune to the universal Life-Process of Changes.

Only the highest type of mystic or sage proceeds beyond mystical and intuitive inversion, to the point of true Ecstasy. And there is no true Ecstasy except in Love. The binding power of self and of all the experiential limits and illusions of the body-mind is transcended only by Ecstasy, or self-transcending Love-Communion with the All-Pervading Life-Principle and Transcendental Consciousness in which the "I" is conceived and in which the body-mind and the World-Process are always presently arising. Therefore, one must be committed to the fulfillment of all of the lawful or basic functional obligations of one's humanity. You must responsibly live all of the aspects of your humanity to the point of self-transcendence, or Ecstasy in the Living God. You can set aside responsibility only temporarily, because your inherent structural obligations will inevitably be reborn, recycled, and relearned—in this or in future lifetimes, on Earth or elsewhere. You cannot simply abandon attention to the body and its relations. You cannot merely abandon the mind. Mere abandonment of functions and relations is not liberating, for then the body-mind will simply haunt the inner being, the way a ghost haunts a room. All the functions of body and mind arise in the same Divine Reality, the same Universal Energy, the same Transcendental Self. Therefore, body and mind are transcended only by responsible use in the midst of a life of self-transcending God-Communion. Whatever you have not given up, whatever is not absorbed in that Transcendental Love-Communion, remains to distract attention and to cause future experiential bewilderment.

It is true that we must perceive and adapt to the functional activities of this body-mind that are subtler than thinking and talking and eating and sleeping and sexing. All aspects of this body-mind must be inspected, and they must become matters of self-transcending responsibility. But the subtler phenomena within the body-mind are not the Truth, nor are they the Way to Realize the

Truth—any more than the grosser or outer phenomena of the body-mind are the Truth or the Way to the Truth. The conditions of this body-mind, gross and subtle, without and within, must be explored, but in that process of inspection they must also be transcended. They must be understood and rightly interpreted to be not the Truth but only the self-bound artifacts of Narcissus. Ultimately, if this process of inspection of all functional and experiential phenomena, without as well as within, is pursued with great intensity, there is the Realization of ego-death, or self-transcendence, or the transcendence of mind and fear. There may be momentary intuitions of the egoless or mindless Reality—there may be approximations of the Transcendental Truth at any point in the evolutionary spiritual process—but, ultimately, that Realization must be a simple, tacit, direct, permanent, and absolute transition, beyond the "I" of the body-mind. There is no returning from that Adventure. The illusion of the separate and fixed inner being is utterly destroyed. The transcendence of the inner being, the death of the ego in the universal Life-Principle, is the Way of Truth.

You may have read descriptions of this Event, communicated by people who have passed through it. Ramana Maharshi,[2] for instance, clearly described the primary event of his own trans-formation as a permanent moment of ego-death. In his description of that event, he said that he was suddenly overcome by great fear of death. For no apparent reason, he suddenly became terrified. He suggests that during the half hour or so in which this event occurred, he did something like inquire "Who am I?" (or "What is 'I'?" or "Where and how does 'I' arise?") in the manner that he recommended years later to people who came to him for spiritual instruction. However, verbal or mental consciousness does not characterize the actual event of ego-death, and no such mental operation could have had any fundamental significance in the actual "ego-death" of Ramana Maharshi. He was simply and suddenly overcome by fear—by absolute, irrevocable, and unavoidable terror.

2. Sri Ramana Maharshi (A.D. 1879-1950) was a great Sage who lived, taught, and radiated the Presence of God among devotees for more than fifty years at Tiruvannamalai, South India. After his own Awakening in September, 1970, Da Free John found esoteric corroboration of his Realization in Maharshi's Teaching, and in 1973 he enjoyed a living Demonstration of Maharshi's Realized Presence when he visited the late Sage's tomb and former place of residence.

He became so terrified that he was unable to make any of the ordinary inward or outward gestures by which we usually make ourselves feel better. He lost his mind! He was too terrified even to create mind, or the self-defense that is conventional inwardness. He lost himself! He was too terrified to become self-possessed. There was simply fear, which is the primary reaction of all individual beings to manifest experience. None of the conventional methods by which we avoid that fear and by which we are consoled and distracted from that fear was possible for him in that great moment of ego-death.

167

Instead of going within, instead of seeing a vision of Krishna,[3] instead of believing in Jesus, instead of concentrating on psycho-physical states produced by the kundalini, Maharshi became tacitly absorbed in the intuition of the naked Reality that precedes the self-contraction (or the conventional result of mortal fear). That intuition, that direct awareness of the Condition in which we ultimately exist, is the very foundation of God-Realization, or the Realization of Truth.

In *The Knee of Listening*, I have described incidents of "madness" and self-transcending fear in my own case, incidents that finally led to a series of events that culminated in irreversible and permanent ego-death, or transcendence of the illusions of mind and the primary illusion of an independent inner self.[4] What was significant about those incidents, as in the case of Ramana Maharshi, was that nothing could be done to allay or diminish fear and the dissolution of mind. And, therefore, the Event of true ego-death was able to occur and to remain as a permanent Condition of all ordinary and future psycho-physical experience.

The dilemma of our ordinary state is that we imagine, mistakenly, that there are experiential ways to become free of our chronic and primary fear, and we seek, anxiously and futilely, for such methods or consolations. Most people are not very profound in their seeking. They look for ways to achieve a sense of satisfaction or pleasure through ordinary physical and mental self-indulgence. The consolations of these moments of self-indulgence pass, however, and

3. Krishna is an archetype of the incarnation of God in the tradition of Hinduism.

4. Please refer to Da Free John's autobiography in *The Knee of Listening*, and also to Part I of *The Enlightenment of the Whole Body*, for accounts of the incidents of awakening in Da Free John's life and for a description and interpretation of the culmination of his spiritual adventure in the Vedanta Temple in Los Angeles, California.

thus they must be repeated again and again. Ultimately, through practicing the method or fear-remedy of physical and mental self-indulgence, a person degenerates, physically and emotionally and psychologically.

Others pursue the more "creative" distractions of religious belief and discipline. This form of the search for consolation from fear is, to one or another degree, more profound than the method of gross physical and ordinary mental self-indulgence. Generally, religious people moderate their physical life to varying degrees. At the one extreme is the typical downtown American or European religious person, who does not, in physical or even moral terms, live very differently from the ordinary, self-indulgent, nonbeliever. At the other extreme is the more serious religious person in both Western and Eastern cultures, who does little more than believe in some traditional and inward "answer" that will distract him from fear, but who is, at the level of ordinary, vital life, engaged in uncommon degrees of self-discipline, ranging from unvarying moderation to asceticism. (And there is also a rare class of individuals, whom we award with the title of "saint," because of their awesome and uncommonly heroic feats of religious commitment, who actually become devoted to the extremes of religious and mystical inversion of attention. Such individuals become profoundly detached from conventional relationships, and the physical world, and all the forms of physical self-indulgence, or even the "natural" gestures toward physical survival, that others consider to be ordinary, normal, and necessary.)

Those who are beginning their religious search in life generally become associated with either common or extraordinary individuals who are practicing one or another traditional "answer" to fear. Thus, through the culture of intimacy with other religious people and even saints, we acquire the traditional habits of religious practice. One can acquire habits from ascetics as well as from drunkards. When you become associated with people, observing them and hearing them communicate, you generally (and even unconsciously) begin to imitate what they appear to be doing, and you tend to believe what they are believing. In this natural cultural manner, you duplicate the experience of others, and eventually you may discover for yourself to what extent such experiences can or cannot distract you from your primary fear.

Whenever you find an experience that significantly distracts you from the anxiety of daily or ordinary fear, that experience tends, at least temporarily, to become your style, your "answer." But the ordinary mass of acquired habits and beliefs has no power to protect or distract us in extreme moments of naked, primary, and true fear and near-death, when everything that we have done, everything that we have experienced, everything that we have realized, becomes superficial, unavailing, and untrue. Therefore, most people try to keep themselves superficially and perpetually occupied, so that such moments do not occur very often! In fact, most people try to keep any profundity at all from occurring. Thus, we tend automatically to ritualize every aspect of our daily lives, so that we will never in any moment be found incapable of distraction or self-possession. In every moment, we exploit the option of self, of mind, of experience in some form, so that we need not suffer the fundamental fear of annihilation that is native to a separate consciousness. However, this naked and unconsoled fear must and will be experienced, if only somewhere in the midst of death. But if that fear is not met and transcended while we are still alive, there can be no realization of Truth while we are alive.

169

The profound, ultimate, and necessary process of ego-death or self-transcendence is not rightly understood by the popular mind, even though everyone is deeply afraid, and even though the rare testimony to true and permanent ego-death is openly available in the literatures of esoteric spirituality. The process and significance of ego-death is generally misrepresented, and it has even become a popular religious idea. At one time or another, you have probably entertained the idea of ego-death in your casual thinking. You may have presumed that you were involved in the search for ego-death in your practice of conventional religion and spirituality. And you may even believe you actually attained ego-death in some extraordinary moment or experience of your life. But your idea of ego-death is probably nothing more than a superficial concept (or even a self-image!) associated with self-denial or temporary self-transcendence. As a popular idea, ego-death is associated with nothing more than the conventional idea of death itself, or the idea of self-annihilation and the ending of experience. The obvious end phenomenon of a long process of self-denial is death, or self-frustration to the point of emptiness. Thus, ordinary death, ordinary suffering, and self-deprivation characterize both the popular and the professional mystical understanding of ego-death.

The ego, the self, the "I" who is pursuing Truth, consolation, and liberating experience, can manipulate its experience in all kinds of ways, but it cannot bring itself to an end thereby. The ego has no intention of bringing itself to an end. Ego-death is not the result of something that the ego can do to itself. The death of the ego is the cessation of self-possession, the end of the gesture of loveless contraction, and the gesture of fear, the gesture of self-meditation, the gesture of the entire way of life that creates "me" and inwardness and "my experience" and "my Truth" and "my God," "my religion," "my mysticism."

The death of the ego coincides with the spontaneous confession "I am the body." "Egolessness" is in the ecstatic bodily confession of Love-Communion with the Life-Principle. It is the beginning of real existence, the self-transcending Event of true incarnation, the sheer, naked, mindless, bodily birth into Infinity. "Egolessness" (or identification with the Transcendental Self of the Life-Principle) is always already the case—even at the origin of our experience, over time and in this moment, but we have betrayed and abandoned that naked and simple principle out of fear. We lose our "innocence" in the midst of suffering, and thus we come to notice that the bodily "I" can die. As a result, we create a surrogate self, the inner self, the mind, the subjective being with its eternal history, the immune and immortal soul. We embark upon the looking-glass adventure of the inner self, Narcissus in flight from death and all relationships, until at last we realize ego-death, the death of the mind, and return to our original existence as the body in love with Life.

The fulfillment of that process of return to Reality (or Love) can occupy one moment or many years. It can be accomplished in one lifetime or in many lifetimes. In the physics of things, this separate personality, this inner "I," this mind or soul, is made of subtler aspects of the Energy that is manifesting as the total psycho-physical body, and so it continues to exist even after the physical body dies. Thus, mere physical death is not liberating, and it is not the end of the illusory tour of the inner or independent and exclusive self. The illusions with which we are possessed up to the moment of physical death persist as experience even after death, and we resume our looking-glass tour in the physical realm as soon as we can become associated with another physical body, in another birth, in this or some other world.

The compulsive cycle of deluded lifetimes is nonsense. Our seemingly "fulfilling" experiences arise out of the Chaos of Infinity. We make an orderly universe out of our experience by means of the centralizing principle of self-possession, and thus the unenlightened life seems somehow to make sense. If you hold up a finger in a windstorm, all the elements seem to be revolving around it. But if you withdraw the finger, the universe returns to chaos, because there is no center for the whirling.

The transition or Way from ordinary self-consciousness to awakened bodily consciousness (or Enlightenment by the Living Transcendental Identity) is fear. We cannot avoid it. Ultimately, everyone must make that transition back through fear to the original Situation of born existence. The Way through fear is not a matter of watching one's fear, or performing some self-manipulative technique while being afraid. Nor is it merely a matter of being psychotically terrified, of merely being "me" and afraid. Rather, ego-death is a matter of actually passing through and beyond the gesture of fear, even beyond all of the gestures that one is equipped to make in order to be free of fear and distracted from fear. In short, one must pass through all the distractions of mind and become only the body, with pure attention in the Presence of Life. One must be perfectly converted from fear to Love.

There is no Enlightenment, no evolutionary entrance into the truly Spiritual Condition of human existence, without ego-death, or transcendence of the mind. There must be the literal death of the separate and separative consciousness. In this moment, you are holding on to your sense of separate consciousness as if it were something tangible and material. You possess yourself through a great contraction of body and psyche. By virtue of this gesture, you have become rigid, mediocre, deluded, relatively loveless, self-possessed, and isolated. To be without an inner consciousness is, for you, unthinkable. To be incapable of feeling yourself as a separate consciousness is, for you, a terrifying prospect. Nevertheless, that is precisely the realization with which you must become completely comfortable.

There is no "drama" associated with the ultimate realization of Divine Reality. The consciousness is simply different, from that

171

moment onward. One's true consciousness is identical to the Divine Self, or the Identity of Life. The Divine is the actual Identity of the "inner self," and the Divine or Transcendental Life-Consciousness is what the total bodily being realizes itself to be in the instant of ego-death, just as in the previous moment of conventional awareness one presumed quite naturally the limitations of egoic consciousness. This passage through fear, this process of ego-death, is the necessary transition between the conventional higher consciousness of the mystical brain-mind and the paradoxical Enlightenment of the seventh stage of life (or the ultimate process of the Transfiguration and Translation of the bodily being).

The Transcendental Self is not within the body. The body arises in the Transcendental Self, or the Life-Principle. The Transcendental Self is not the inward self that is felt to move and perceive and think, but the All-Pervading Consciousness, the Heart of Radiant Life and Love, even prior to the body-mind of Man. Thus, while we are yet seeking within ourselves for Happiness, Truth, Life, and God, we have not yet realized God, or the Transcendental Self. It is only when we overcome the recoil toward inwardness that we realize the Identity and the Living God in Whom the body and the world are arising. Therefore, in the ultimate or seventh stage of the process of God-Realization, the Transcendental Self, the Heart, stands bodily as Man. The body is not then felt to define existence as a soul or separate consciousness. The body is felt to be in simple, absolute, most direct Communion with the Infinite Radiance or Light of the Transcendental Self. The body exists in perfect, direct, selfless, mindless Communion with the Living Divine Reality. All the inhibitions to Love or Radiance are naturally dissolved, and even the body becomes more and more profoundly transformed, or Transfigured, by that Light.

Ultimately, then, the body disintegrates, dissolves, falls, or yields in the Light of Life, and the transcendence of the body in the Light, Life, Love, and Consciousness of Real God is the culmination of the seven stages of Man. However, if the body dies before the mind, the lesser evolutionary stages of Man continue to arise in the form of the school of experience. It is only after ego-death, or the transcendence of the mind, that the highest stage of human existence begins, and that is the stage in which the body dissolves or yields to Love and Light while alive. The body is, therefore, not truly transcended until the seventh stage of life, when the inner self or ego is realized to be the body-only, and when there is already no illusion of separate existence, separate mind, independent inwardness, or defined soul.

The fulfillment of the process of the seventh stage of life is not necessarily demonstrated by an extraordinary and miraculous disappearance of the physical body. Such a phenomenon may very well occur in some cases, and it may become more and more common among Adepts as the centuries pass, but one can enjoy and demonstrate the Transfigured Enlightenment of the whole body in the seventh stage of life and yet remain naturally or bodily alive. Such an individual can likewise die an apparently natural or ordinary death. The body need not disintegrate into Light at death. It disintegrates in any case at the point of death, except that in the case of natural or ordinary death that disintegration takes place gradually, via the natural organic cycle. In the seventh stage, the body-mind as a whole is given up in the Infinite Radiance of God, the "Transcendental Room" in which the entire world is now sitting. There is no mind, no subjective being that is the Principle of Existence. Even the body is not the Principle of Life. The Radiant Transcendental Life-Consciousness, the Living God, is the Principle and the ultimate Domain of the world. But the body is the Way to Life. The whole body (or body-mind) is the necessary vehicle of the process of Enlightenment. Therefore, we must be surrendered, body and mind, into the Divine Radiance, prior to fear, prior to separate consciousness, prior to all knowledge, prior to all of our reluctance to be foolish and to love. We must surrender to the point of Ecstasy in this Chaos of Joy.

Mysticism and Ego-Death

The conventional mind is a reflection or reaction to psycho-physical experience. The conditions or states of mind may seem to be within and subtler and higher than the body, and even independent of the body. Therefore, the mind tends to imply the

174 existence of a separate, separative, and independent inner self, ego, or soul. Therefore, until the mind is transcended, we are bound and deluded by experience, knowledge, states of mind, and the sense of an independent or threatened inner self. But the mind and the ego (or independent self) are only a complex process of reaction or contraction in the brain, or the body-mind as a whole, and of the reactive or contractive modification of the All-Pervading Life-Principle. Therefore, the illusions of mind and ego must be transcended through prior intuition of the Life-Principle and Transcendental Consciousness that are the true Identity of the individual body-mind. (Only in the case of the radical intuition of the Transcendental Condition and Identity of the body-mind may psycho-physical experience be engaged in total freedom.)

Mysticism is a conventional form of knowledge, or mind. It is a matter of the entrance of attention into the higher plane of the brain-mind. It is a matter of self-fulfillment, or ego-fulfillment, via the inward glorification of independent consciousness. But the Truth is Realized only after ego-death, or transcendence of the brain and the mind. Therefore, mysticism is not the ultimate stage of human evolution. In fact it is only the fifth of the seven evolutionary spiritual stages of human life.

In the sixth stage of human life, the root of mind and conventional self-consciousness is found, and the mental self submits or dissolves in the Radiant Energy or Consciousness in which the bodily self is arising (as a contraction, or superficial modification). This is ego-death—from which the "eyes" of the true Self or Transcendental Consciousness open, beyond all qualification by mind, internal psychic phenomena, or any gestures of self-attention. Then the Radiant Life of the world stands clearly Revealed in all conditions of existence. And the body becomes the single instrument of Divine Communion or Sacrifice in the Living and Radiant Reality.

Therefore, in the seventh stage of life, when the independent inner being is no longer the basis of existence, the total bodily being is Transfigured by the Radiant Bliss of Consciousness, which is Transcendental Love.

Esoteric Knowledge Is Transcended
in the Seventh Stage of Life

Conventional mysticism communicates through metaphors of the Objective or Independent Creator Deity, the immortal soul, and the Spiritual Cosmos or Hierarchy of planes and heavens and powers. Thus, the language of mysticism is wedded to the religious or dualistic conception of God and soul, as well as the conception of a cosmic scheme, wherein the soul descends from God and, by ascending, returns to God.

But, truly, the secret key to the Wisdom concealed in mystical language is not religious philosophy nor any visionary or scientific description of the cosmos. The literal plane in which mystical activity takes place is not the cosmic world of soul travel but the ordinary body of Man. The key to mystical language and religious metaphor is not theology or cosmology but anatomy. All the religious and cosmological language of mysticism is metaphorical. And the metaphors are symbols for anatomical features of the higher functional structures of the human individual.

Those who enter deeply into the mystical dimension of experience soon discover that the cosmic design they expected to find in their inward path of ascent to God is in fact simply the design of their own anatomical or psycho-physical structures. Indeed, this is the secret divulged to initiates in mystical schools.

The world of ordinary men has traditionally been given only the exoteric instruction, wherein Man is described as a fleshy mortal with an immortal inner part. The exoteric instruction is essentially a moral and devotional teaching, offering salvation after death, when the mortal part falls away and the soul stands naked before the God above Nature.

But those who mature in self-discipline, moral sacrifice, and prayerful surrender are naturally drawn into a deeper consideration of the Condition of human existence. They enter into the inner path, the esoteric or mystical path. When they begin to enter the mystical path, they are given "secret teachings," or esoteric descriptions of the cosmic planes that will be experienced during the ascent to God. And such new initiates are also given instructions in the mystical attainment of inversion (or withdrawal of attention from the outward movement of the sense organs)—in the form of higher methods of prayer, yoga, and so forth.

However, the instructions given to new initiates into the mystical or inner path are themselves only metaphors for experiential revelations that will develop as the inner practices develop toward maturity. Therefore, only the most mature devotee both experiences and understands the secret of mystical religion and cosmology. Mystical knowledge is knowledge of the body-mind of Man, not the material and knowable universe outside the body-mind of Man.

In the Way that I Teach, devotees are led directly to the bodily or total psycho-physical consideration of the mystical instructions that have been given to initiates since ancient times. Devotees in this Way do not merely pass from exoteric to esoteric levels of experience and understanding. They also mature beyond the limits of esotericism, into the Transcendental Disposition of true Enlightenment, wherein the entire body-mind is Translated into the Radiant Transcendental Consciousness.

Brain Mysticism and the
Radiant Personality of Love

The ancient mystics were seeking to attain a "divine" and "imperishable" body. The Way was a psycho-physical discipline, represented by the "caduceus," the ancient heraldic and medical staff or wand of power and authority, symbol of the spinal cord and the brain core, or the central nervous system. The head, or "ajna chakra," epitomized by the thalamus (with its two parts or "petals") and the single pole of the pineal body, shines in the midst of the "winged" cerebrum (which is the "sahasrar," epitomized by the lateral ventricles and the corona radiata). The central or cerebrospinal nervous system, when in a state of release from the ascending (sensory) and descending (motor) or bipolar motions of the autonomic nervous system (symbolized by two intertwined serpents), resonates as a single Current in the brain core. There the Current of Transcendental Life-Light that Pervades all forms Radiates in the midst of the two lateral ventricles, which are likened to the two wings of a bird or angel. (The cerebrospinal core of the body-mind, when permitted to transcend, to master, or simply to witness the gross movements of the autonomic nervous system, is the vehicle of the "astral body" or subtle mind, capable of psychic flight, dreamlike tours, or intuitive reflections of all realms of experience within and without the individual. Thus, the universal inner mechanism, or caduceus, has also been traditionally and fancifully symbolized by winged angels and otherwise identified with superior beings, such as Krishna, Jesus, or Gautama,[5] or states of experience that are subtler than the gross physical.)

At the center is white brightness. Surrounding it is a blue sphere. And the vision is rounded with a golden yellow light. Sounds also surround and permeate the place, in an ascending scale, from deep humming vibrations at the medulla to tiny flute-like sounds in the upper extremities of the temporal lobe.[6]

Is this Heaven? Or is it simply the body in its primary mode, wherein the play of awareness and the senses begins, and where the heart may remain at rest, undisturbed, attuned to the Current of Life? The answer should now be obvious to your thinking mind, but you must also submit to it bodily, by literal inspection and growth into the states of contemplation. Mere mentalizing about the limitations or the excellences of mystical vision is itself the sign of a state below or less than mystical vision, habitually fixed in the lower mental and grosser bodily states.

5. Gautama (the "Buddha" or "Enlightened One") has become, with Jesus and Krishna, one of the great archetypal Divine Teachers of Man on Earth. Living and Teaching in India from 563 to 483 B.C., he gathered around him a brotherhood of followers to whom he Taught the "quenching" of desire and the Realization of Truth prior to all the impermanent and transitory conditions of life and mind. The original "Sangha" or community of practitioners grew and split into the factions that today comprise Buddhism, which has more adherents than any other religion on Earth.

6. Those who are seriously interested in a full elaboration of the esoteric anatomy of human evolution and self-transcendence should see *The Enlightenment of the Whole Body*, which is the principal source text of the Teaching of Da Free John.

Therefore, enter the Way and ascend to contemplation in the brain core. Then trace the movement of attention back to the heart. Then awaken at last beyond all the limits of the body-mind into Transcendental Identification with the Radiant Current and Consciousness in which the body-mind is floating. Only then will the Life-Current penetrate beyond the brain core and even the brain itself, to Shine in Transcendental Glory as Bliss, Love, and the very Being of Consciousness. Only This is Enlightenment. All the rest is mere experience, the puny occupation of Narcissus, or the body-mind itself, intent on the survival of its own illusions of independence and the endless enumeration of differentiated objects, never surrendered, never floated in the Real, never transcended, the Bliss of the Eternal never Realized.

I am at war with the lingering childhood of Man in the midst of our dreadful and universal preoccupation with Man himself. For it is only when Man is surrendered in the Transcendental Reality that he can grow up into his own higher consciousness, and only then may he truly and finally Intuit his Identity with what is prior to Man, which is the Transcendental Reality itself.

The human individual is nothing more than a poor and temporary modification of Light, appearing to surround and emanate from a central core of Light. In Truth, he is unnecessary, not even an emanation, but only a conventional appearance, without a Transcendental Cause. Therefore, Man is called to God, to self-transcendence, wherein the illusory body-mind is rested in its Transcendental Identity. Then he is not only Liberated from himself and his world, but even while he seems to live his actions Demonstrate only the Radiant Personality of Love.

Enlightenment is the Ecstatic Realization of literal and prior Identification with the Radiant Transcendental Consciousness in which the body-mind is floating. Enlightenment is not an experience, not a state of the personal body-mind in itself, but the Transcendental Condition of Existence, in which there is no difference, no other, no self, no mind, no body, and no world. Therefore, paradoxically, the conventions of experience—of difference, other, self, mind, body, and world—are known only in that Consciousness. They are arising only in that Radiant Life. They are communicating only that Personality of Love.

The Person of Existence

"Self-Realization" (or deep abidance in the essential inner Self) is not ultimate Liberation. "God-Realization" (or Ecstatic inherence in the Radiant Transcendental Being, in Whom the world and all beings are arising) is the only ultimate Liberation. It is only when the essential Self of the body-mind Realizes its inherence in the Transcendental and Universal Divine Self that there is the Awakening of perfect God-Realization.

179

It is truly said that the Great Happiness is in the Realization of the identity between the essential inner Self and the Supreme Divine Self. Therefore, some preach attachment to the essential inner Self—because of the conventional presumption that the essential inner Self is itself (in and as itself) identical to the Divine Being. But those who actually Realize the Divine Self do not do so merely by abiding in and as the essential inner Self. Rather, they <u>Realize</u> that the only Truth of the essential inner Self is its inherence in (and <u>therefore</u> identity with) the Divine Self. That is, they Transcend the independent disposition of the essential inner Self through Ecstasy, by Realizing the universal inherence of all phenomena, all beings, and the essential inner self in the Radiant Transcendental Divine Being— the Person of all that exists.

Beyond Self-Realization

The essential inner being or Self of the human individual inheres in the Transcendental Divine Being. But that Self is not <u>in itself</u> identical to God. Self-Realization alone is not God-Realization. Rather, the Realization of the Self must provide the basis for the Ecstatic Affirmation by the Self of its own inherence in the Divine. Self-Realization must become Ecstasy, or else it is only another deluded enclosure like the mind or the body or the conventions of objective experience in the world.

Therefore, the advocates of inwardness—whether they propose a mysticism of the mind-psyche or of the essential and unqualified inner being—must Awaken to Ecstasy, or Ecstatic Inherence in the Living One, the Divine Person, the Radiant Transcendental Being in Whom the world and the body and the mind and the independent inner being seem to arise.

180

Bodily Enlightenment

Enlightenment, or the truly religious and spiritual Salvation or Liberation of Man, is a matter of literal bodily transfiguration by the Transcendental Light or Life-Radiance that pervades the world and the body-mind of Man. That bodily Enlightenment does not occur as a result of any manipulative bodily culture, but as a result of ego-death, or the transcendence of the inner being (the mind). Therefore, when self-transcending love fulfills itself beyond all fear, all holding on to the psyche, or all possession by the self of independent consciousness, then the ultimate stage of human life begins—wherein the body at last dissolves in the Light of the world.

All forms of bodily dissolution (or death) prior to mind-death are simply instances of apparent separation of mind and body, leading to conventional rebirth, or the continuation of the illusions of independent subjective experience. And all fulfillment of the mind, or the independent subjective being, is only a distraction from the true Self, the Divine Personality or Identity, which is Realized when the mind is transcended.

Only when the mind or inner self dissolves, finally and beyond all the effects of fear, so that the body-only expresses the Ecstasy of Love-Communion with the Light of Life, are we Awakened to the Transcendental Truth. It is an incomparable Realization, and very few human beings have as yet come to this tacit, obvious, and direct consummation of the human cycle of existence.

The Secret of Spiritual Liberation

All experience is conditional (or dependent on temporary relations), psycho-physical (or subjective and "internal" as well as formal or functional and "external"), and self-defining (or tending to define and limit an "experiencer"). There is no form of experience that does not demonstrate these three qualities. And there is no entity or being (whether a god, or a human being, or a lower vital entity) that is not entirely a specimen of the conditional, psycho-physical, and self-defining process of experience.

All experience (whether high or low, subtle or gross) creates and reinforces the illusory, independent, separative, self-defending, and fearful "I" conception—unless the entire affair of experience is transcended. And experience, or "I," is transcended only in the instant of ecstatic intuition of the Transcendental Reality, the Matrix within which all phenomena, all beings, and all experiences are arising. When there is simple or native abiding in undifferentiated unity with the Radiant Transcendental Being (of which all conditions, beings, and experiences are only superficial, spontaneous or uncaused, and unnecessary or nonbinding modifications) then the "I" of experience, the limited psycho-physical self, and the entire phenomenal and experiential "Realm of Nature" are Transfigured and Outshined by the Radiant Love-Bliss of the Eternal Divine.

Man is a composite of three primary dimensions of functional experience. In the lower functional range of the body-mind, the human individual is an expression of elemental forces. He is, in the hierarchical strata of his lower body-mind, a process involving the various states of "matter" (expressed as earthy mass, or solid elements, watery or liquid elements, fiery or heat-producing chemical elements, and airy or gaseous elements) in playful combination with an etheric or pervasive energy field. The "lower coil" of the human body-mind is, therefore, a composite elemental or vital entity, and his "mind" or "psyche" is of an unconscious or subconscious nature.

In the higher functional range of the body-mind, the human individual is an expression of superterrestrial (or higher psychic), cosmic (or mental-conceptual), and supercosmic (or superconscious) forces. He is, in his higher body-mind, a process of perception, conception, creative intention (or will), and subtle illumination (or sublime awareness of the ultimate unity of "mind" and "matter"). The "upper coil" of the human body-mind is functionally senior to the "lower coil." The "upper coil" (associated with the higher brain functions and the central nervous system in general) commonly acts via the processes of the conscious mind (in the form of lower or elemental and etheric perception, conception, and intention) to control or participate in the common or objective experiences of ordinary living. And it is this "waking experience" (or the "lower coil" phenomena, associated with the sympathetic and parasympathetic divisions of the autonomic nervous system) that provides the conventional model for the popular understanding of human existence. However, the "upper coil" of the human body-mind may, when its higher evolutionary mechanisms are stimulated (usually by esoteric mystical disciplines, which involve conscious surrender to higher or subtle energy influences), enter into planes of phenomenal experience that are superconscious, or apparently independent of functional relations with the waking self (the "lower coil," or the gross physical being, coupled with the lower or Earth-bound psychic and mental aspects of the "upper coil," or the ordinary conscious being).

Because of the capacity of the higher or superconscious aspect of the human individual to function independent of apparent association with the lower mental, vital, and elemental aspects of the body-mind, efforts have been made since ancient times to exploit this capacity as a means of escaping from the mortal limitations of lower psycho-physical experience. (There is even a capacity for the psychic and etheric aspects of the lower functional being of Man to separate from apparent or fixed association with the purely physical or elemental body, and this capacity has also been exploited by various societies and individuals since ancient times.) Whenever the effort is made to dissociate the higher or superconscious aspect of Man from lower mental and gross psychic, vital, and elemental associations, the process is traditionally called religion or spirituality, and any direct influence over the lower mental and gross psychic, vital, and elemental being by the superconscious being is traditionally called a religious, spiritual, or even Divine influence. And whenever the effort is made to dissociate the lower mental, gross psychic, and vital (or etheric) aspect of Man from the elemental-physical body (or to control the elemental-physical body by releasing it to the influence of the subconscious and unconscious levels of mind) the process is traditionally called psychism, spiritualism, or magic.

Even so, all experience, whether of a superconscious, conscious, subconscious, or unconscious variety, is conditional, psycho-physical (or functionally organized in both internal, or subjective, and formal, or bodily, terms, whether the "body" is subtle or gross in nature), and, therefore, also self-defining. It is only in the third primary functional dimension of Man that there is the possibility for Realizing the Transcendental Ecstasy of unqualified unity with the Divine Reality or Real Condition of the limited psycho-physical self. That third primary functional dimension of Man is the root of self-consciousness, at the origin of attention and conventional association with the various states of mind and body (or "matter," whether in subtle or gross form).

The root of self-consciousness, of attention, and of the "I" conception is not within the realm of the "upper coil" (or central nervous system) of the body-mind, nor is it within the realm of the "lower coil" (or autonomic nervous system). It is in the region of the heart (not the brain or the solar plexus), on the right side, associated with the "pacemaker" (or sinoatrial node). The root of attention and of the psycho-physically defined personality or "I" may, in the profoundly intuitive depth of true and most radical spiritual practice, be discovered to be associated with the region of the right side of the heart. And when the process of experience, or "I" conception, is thoroughly understood, the root of attention in the heart is penetrated. Once this intuitive penetration occurs, there is tacit or native Liberation from the conditional, psycho-physical, and self-defining power of all experience.

The ultimate Destiny of Man is self-transcendence, or the ecstatic transcendence of experience. Man, or the human body-mind (high and low), is a limit. He is arising mysteriously within the Infinite Radiance that is God. Man, or a human lifetime, is to be experienced, understood, and ultimately transcended. Any exploitation of the experiential capacity of Man in himself is necessarily deluding, self-binding, and productive of fear, sorrow, anger, and bewilderment.

Therefore, we are obliged to self-mastery and self-transcendence, and even the higher evolutionary (or traditionally "magical," "intellectual," "religious," and "spiritual") mechanisms of our human experience must be transcended at last. The entire nervous system and the total body-mind of Man must be transcended. All the states of psyche and of "matter" are nothing more than signals of self-arising and the futile struggle toward everlastingly unchanging self-survival and perfect self-fulfillment. But if we transcend our own psycho-physical self-limit and thereby enjoy tacit unity with the Radiant Transcendental Being, then we will also Realize that even the planes of experiential phenomena and apparently limited beings are always floating in the All-Pervading Love-Radiance or Transcendental Bliss of the Eternal Divine Being. Such is the final stage of our human drama. In that Event, the world and the total body-mind become Radiant with the Fullness of Love-Bliss, and soon even the physical body and the material world are Transfigured and Outshined by the Radiance that was first intuited at the heart.

Each functional level of Man belongs to a particular level or stratum in the hierarchical structure of the phenomenal Realm of Nature. Each of the structural levels or dimensions of human functioning and human consciousness is dependently related to the universal scheme of conditions within the structural level of Nature to which it bears a likeness. And each such functional element of human structure and consciousness is destined, within its own framework of time, to lose its separated identity through eventual dissolution into its own particular level in the scheme of Nature. (Thus, for example, the gross physical or solid elemental body arises as a dependent and temporary condition within the gross elemental dimension or level of the Realm of Nature. The continued existence of the gross physical body is utterly dependent upon the state of conditions within the elemental dimension, and, in any case, the gross physical body will eventually dissolve within its own plane of time and space, thus losing its individual identity through disintegration and transformation in the universal scheme of elements.)

Even so, each and every part of Man and of the total Realm of Nature is always arising as a spontaneous and nonbinding or free modification of the Radiant Transcendental Being. Each and every part of Man is always already pervaded by the ultimate Reality, Life, Light, Truth, Condition, and Identity that may be Realized at the heart and via the heart's Ecstasy, which is self-transcending love-surrender, or radical intuition of the Identity or Real Condition of the body-mind, the world, and all experience.

The point of this analysis is not that we are born into a fixed dilemma or an inherently evil domain. The motive that is native to Man is not escape but surrender, love, intuitive union, or radical unity with the Transcendental or Native Condition that is at the Root— and which is the Source, Sustainer, Help, and Perfect Destiny of all worlds and beings. We are obliged to Love's Wisdom, not the ego's stealth. We need not pursue the strategic escape from experience, but we are inherently obliged to understand the total process of experience itself. Such understanding is expressed in the naturally self-transcending mood of love, or the intuitive and spontaneous sacrifice of the self-position.

185

The Ecstasy that arises naturally from right intuitive understanding is the only Wisdom of Man. The spontaneous or nonproblematic surrender of the psycho-physical or experiential self is the only Freedom. Radical and prior Unity with the Radiant Transcendental Being is the only Way of Happiness under any and all of the temporary conditions of experience.

The Body Is the Way to Life

Neither the body nor the mind is the Principle of human existence. The Radiant Life-Energy that pervades the body-mind and the World-Process is the Principle of human existence.

But the total body of Man is the Way to Life. The Way of Life is the Way of the body, prior to dilemma, knowledge, inwardness, experience, or power over experience.

The mind is never more than a reflection of Life, or a point of view toward Life. Only the body is Life. Only the body is intimate with Life most directly, without the mediation of any form of mind.

Worldly self-indulgence sacrifices intelligence in order to glorify the body for a moment. But this strategy kills the body and permits neither illumination of the mind nor bodily transcendence of the mind.

Mysticism sacrifices the body in order to glorify the mind forever. But this strategy is deluded by the inner self, the fantasies of the mind, and the glamor of the body's subtle parts. And neither body nor mind is immortalized by timeless illusions.

Therefore, the true Way for Man is to grow by self-transcending Love-Communion with the Living Reality, expressed through all natural bodily relations and supported by intuitive mental clarity. In this Way, the mind or interior self becomes the first sacrifice. And then the total body becomes the final, unblemished, and single sacrifice, Transfigured in the Bliss of unqualified Life.

The Body Is the True Mind

Ego-death, or radical self-transcendence, is the transcendence of the mind by the body (via the body's primal unity with the Radiant Transcendental Life-Consciousness that pervades the body and the entire World-Process).

However, ego-death does not in principle involve the loss of mental ability. Rather, it is a matter of bodily transcendence of the mind as an alternative or separate reality and self. Therefore, it is a matter of the whole bodily (or total psycho-physical) presumption and assertion of unity with the Radiant Energy and Transcendental Consciousness that is the ultimate Reality of Man and the World-Process.

The Love-Sacrifice of the Whole Body

Both body and mind must be transcended, Transfigured, and at last Dissolved in the Radiant Transcendental Life-Consciousness.

187

The body cannot be transcended in the mind. The body, like the mind, can only be transcended in the Radiant Transcendental Life-Consciousness.

First, the mind, or the illusion of a separate inner being and self, must be transcended through Love-Communion with the Radiant Transcendental Life-Consciousness. Then the whole body, or the unified psycho-physical being, free of its obsessive association with a separate inner or mental-psychic being, must be transcended, Transfigured, and ultimately Dissolved or Translated into the same Radiant Transcendental Life-Consciousness, and through perfection of the same process of self-transcending Love-Communion.

In the ultimate stage of the human or spiritual Process of Man, it is not a matter of existence as the body itself (in itself, separate from Consciousness or Life). Rather, it is a matter of direct bodily (or total psycho-physical) surrender into the Radiant Transcendental Life-Consciousness—prior to the presumed separation of the body from all other objects, or of the mind from the body, or of the Transcendental Consciousness from the Radiant Energy of Life.

Body, Mind, Death, and Life

Mind and body are mutually dependent. They arise as a dynamic play of nearly simultaneous opposites, and, as long as the pair exists, each constantly affects the other. Neither is more "real" than the other, except that the body, not the mind, is the first and the last to appear.

The mind is a reflection of the body, but it may also function in a manner senior to the body—by monitoring bodily processes and events, or by initiating changes via the will, creative imagination, intellectual and self-critical intelligence, or deep psychic motivation.

The body is a reflection of the mind and of energies subtler than the elemental or gross physical body. But the body is also senior to the mind, since simple, formal, or manifest bodily existence is the primary conditional circumstance of personal consciousness.

188

The body-mind is thus a dynamic unity. However, it is not, because of that unity, merely mortal. Both body and mind have their grosser and their subtler aspects. Matter is energy. Thought arises on the basis of a deep psyche that is pure energy. And the physical body is a mysterious and momentary phase of an ongoing process of eternal energy, or light.

Therefore, the individual body-mind is a dynamic play of changes that passes from birth to death. However, the body-mind also survives gross physical death. Personal psycho-physical existence continues in subtler realms of energy after gross physical death, and, thus, the body-mind continues to evolve and change in a dynamic pattern after gross physical death.

After gross physical death, the subtle psycho-physical being continues to function in subtler energy realms, until it either passes permanently beyond the gross physical realm or else reincarnates in the gross physical realm itself. Personal experience thus develops or evolves through adaptation to various levels of the psycho-physical dynamics, in cycles of birth, change, apparent death, and renewal. The play of individual psycho-physical existence is a kind of evolutionary schooling in the ultimate or Divine Law of growth via self-transcendence, until absolute Unity with the Divine Reality is realized, and an immortal or eternal Existence is enjoyed in the absolute Domain of the Living God (or Perfect Light of Life).

However, neither body nor mind is independent or immortal. All forms of body and mind are temporary and changing. No experience is permanent, and no experience is, in itself, God or Truth. Only the Living Reality is God and Truth, and the body-mind must always be surrendered into that Living Reality.

The root of the psycho-physical being of Man is in the region of the heart. It is an atom of consciousness and energy, which emanates as all kinds of psychic, mental, emotional, and physical states. The atom of the heart pervades the total body-mind with Life-Energy and extends into the body-mind as attention (or the base-consciousness of the body-mind).

Thus, during any lifetime of personal existence in gross physical form, the body-mind is supported by the energy and attention generated from the region of the heart. And after gross bodily death (and the death of the brain-mind) the atomic being functions in a body and realm of subtler energy, with attention transferred to a subtler dimension of mind.

189

But the atom of the heart is always moving toward the Truth of Life. Lifetimes of experience are gradually transcended through the Ecstasy of Love, which releases the atomic being into the Domain of unqualified Energy and perfect Consciousness. Therefore, the Work of Man is self-transcendence, or Ecstasy. We grow by loving surrender of body and mind (or all the subject-object conditions of experience) into the selfless and objectless sublimity of Life. And we are brought by these means to a Divine Destiny, which exceeds all that Man is structured to achieve, and even all that the gross physical universe is structured to provide.

This is the experience to which all mankind attests. This is the profundity, the paradoxical Wisdom to which all knowers are bound at the heart. And no lesser knowledge or worldly power will at last deny this Happiness to Man.

Only Life Overcomes Death

Death does not happen to Life. Only that which is merely touched and enlivened by Life can die (or seem to become Lifeless). But that which is Alive is deathless and never threatened. The being in Whom Man inheres is Life. And Life is only conserved and increased by the process of changes, or transformations. Life always persists, even after change and death.

Therefore, the idea that we are all going to die is simply false. It is a false, self-frustrating, and deluding presumption. "I" inheres in Life—and to believe otherwise is to embrace fear, separation, unlove, and all the philosophy that presumes death, rather than Life, to be the Principle of Existence. The idea that "I" can, will, or must die is a false belief, even a deadly act, founded on the failure to fully observe, consider, and understand our experience. When true understanding arises, there is only the natural and positive presumption of Life, which inherently transcends experience, change, and death through the Transfiguring and Transforming Power of Love-Surrender.

190

The Living Divine Being is not merely outside us and thus separate from our essential being. Nor is the Living Divine Being merely within us and thus separate from the body and the world. Rather, we wholly inhere in the Living Divine Being.

Therefore, the Way of Life is neither a matter of extroversion nor of introversion, but it is a matter of conversion, or self-transcending Love-Communion with the Infinitely Radiant and Eternally Living Divine Being. The Practice is feeling-surrender of body, mind, and attention—directly and via every kind of right or appropriate action—to the point or degree of Ecstasy, or Radiant Fullness of Life, beyond doubt and sorrow and fear.

Only Life overcomes death. Therefore, surrender to the Life-Principle and presume only Life to be our Situation.

True religion is not about safety, or the salvation of the individual from naked confrontation with suffering and pleasure and death and love.

True religion is about the difficult evolution and ultimate transcendence of the individual, and mankind, and Man.

Therefore, we must awaken from our self-protecting illusions of religious safety, and we must surrender to the Current of Life in which the body and the mind are swimming forever.

There is no "Holy Substitute" for Man.

There is no "representative" sacrifice.

There is no true alternative to awakened consciousness and unqualified love in the case of each individual.

Every one of us is the necessary sacrifice of God.

Da Free John

CHAPTER SIX

The Secret Identity
of the Holy Spirit of God

A Prophetic Criticism
of Great Religions

The religious consciousness of Western Man is trapped within an archaic structure of myths, dogmas, and social conflicts that no longer serve the true religious and spiritual process of true Man. These myths are largely Christian, Judeo-Christian, and broadly Semitic in origin, and they are held in place by the large-scale cultural, political, and economic dominance of the ancient religions of the Middle East, including Christianity, Judaism, and Islam.

The dominance of specifically Christian cults, myths, and dogmas is especially apparent in Europe and America. And if the dominance of Judaism and Islam is less apparent in Europe and America, the power of these ancient cults is certainly apparent throughout the Middle East (with clear, practical effect on the rest of the world).

Man himself cannot awaken to his evolutionary spiritual Destiny until the spell of mythological and self-possessed thinking is broken. And the future whole bodily culture of Man, in which East and West will realize a new cultural Synthesis, cannot take place until all the old religions are surrendered to the higher Principle or Truth that is the ultimate Master of religion.

We tend to think of "religion" as a benign influence on individual thought and behavior, and this is indeed the case when the higher aspects of religious consciousness begin to inform the thought and behavior of any individual. But religion is only rarely found to be an influence of such a kind. Very few individuals become truly creative personalities, mystics, saints, or even reliably good men or women as a result of religious associations.

Religion is, in general, an exoteric cultic phenomenon that controls the thought and behavior of individuals through external and psychologically manipulative techniques. And the principal religious phenomenon that is common in the world is not true or free religious consciousness and benign behavioral habits on the part of individuals. The principal phenomenon of religion is the institutional "Church," or all the central and centralizing institutions that contain and otherwise manipulate broad and massive segments of the human population.

The "Church" (or the primary institution within any religious tradition) is religion, insofar as religion basically affects the world at large. And large-scale institutional religion is not primarily a benign power in the world. We have only to look at the cultural and political conflicts in Europe and the Middle East to see how the immense institutions of ancient religion have now become, for the most part, contentious, absolutist, and the sources of petty social conflicts. And the problem is made extreme by the immensity of these institutions, each of which controls millions of people.

What is more, the power of the great traditional religious institutions is, for the most part, a worldly power. That is, these institutions are actually political and broadly social agencies that manipulate the political, social, and economic motivations of the citizens of all Western nations, as well as the nations of the Middle East, and much of Africa and South America. (The nations of Asia are, for the most part, controlled by secular political institutions, which tend to exclude not only religious institutions but also every kind of religious consciousness, and this pattern of secularization has also begun to spread to other areas of the world that have traditionally been under the powerful influence of ancient Middle Eastern religious institutions.)

In the popular media of our day, small non-establishment religious cults tend to be the target of hostile commentaries. But such groups are, in most cases, basically oriented toward the development of a higher or more universal spiritual and religious consciousness. It is the broadly based and worldly domain of established institutional religion that represents the more direct and practical threat to human development and to the communication of the Truth of Life.

And why is it that religious institutions, which seem to be founded on higher human and cultural persuasions, ultimately become the primary basis of social conflict and even personal neurosis? The reason is that religious institutions are obliged to deal with masses of immature and unevolved people who have very little will or capacity for the evolutionary and practical cultural exercise of higher religious or spiritual consciousness. As a result, the institutions of the "Church" develop much like institutions of "State" under the same conditions of universal human irresponsibility.

Thus, any institutional "Church" tends, except during periods of renewal by living and prophetic Adepts, to become more and more dogmatic, and eventually it becomes irrevocably associated with fixed ideas that, in one way or another, deny the religious authenticity or religious completeness of people who belong to other religious institutions or cultures. The "Church," like any other mortal or threatened entity in the world, tends to become more and more centered in itself and devoted to its own survival.

Conventional religious institutions learn how to survive by serving and manipulating a massive membership that is largely incapable of true and practical religious responsibility. This is done by minimizing the true religious demand for literal and personal conversion of mind and action, and replacing that difficult religious demand with the "easier" and more secular demand for mere allegiance to systems of myth, belief, ritual, and dogma. Thus, the condition for membership in most large institutions of religion is allegiance to fixed ideas and other outward or superficial signs of belonging to the "cult," whereas true religious practice is founded on conversion of the total being to the Living Divine Reality and the acceptance of behavioral disciplines that make one at the very least an outwardly moral and personally benign or restrained character.

Institutional religions of course recommend certain moral attitudes, but the practice of moral restraints is, except for a few extreme criminal acts, not made a condition of membership. And morality tends to be associated with archaic, neurotic, and petty sexual and social taboos, rather than with the obligations of love, service, and compassion. Likewise, most religious institutions today have abandoned even all ancient recommendations relative to personal disciplines of a healthful dietary nature—such as the obligation to avoid meat or other killed food, or impure manufactured food, or toxic stimulants, and so forth. And the esoteric, evolutionary, and universal spiritual teachings that are the only ultimate significance of religion have been almost totally abandoned and even lost by the great "Churches."

In the conventional affair of popular religion, the communication of difficult religious demands and also of esoteric spiritual understanding and practice is avoided, because conventional religious institutions are trying to survive by acquiring and maintaining massive memberships. Thus, religion is promoted and sold by hyped appeals to the nondiscriminating mind of "Everyman." But true religion is a superior human impulse, founded in self-criticism and profound psycho-physical conversion or change. Thus, over time, only false and merely exoteric or popular "religious" inventions are communicated by so-called "great religions." And, at last, the esoteric Truth and practice of universal religion is not only eliminated as the core of conventional religious instruction, but the survival pressures of dogmatic Churchism make such Truth and practice unacceptable and even damnable. Thus, over time, great "Churches" tend in fact to become the enemies of ultimate religious Truth. This was the situation that confronted Jesus, and it was and is the situation confronted by all true religious prophets and spiritual Adepts.

Since actual and mature religious practice has been generally replaced by outward adherence to false or deluding exoteric beliefs and superficial behavioral modifications, the true esoteric core of religion has lost its use within the great traditional cults that exist in our time. The whole affair of traditional religious institutions has become dangerous nonsense, because such religious institutions long ago abandoned the practice of making true religious and esoteric participation a condition of "Church" membership. If the demand for authentic participation had been continued, the institutions of religion that we now call "great" would have remained small esoteric communities (if they survived at all). Therefore, the "Churches" chose to survive, and they adapted to the world (rather than demand that the world change itself).

True religion is a universal, evolutionary, and self-transcending psycho-physical motivation of Man. However, at the present stage in human history, only relatively few individuals in any generation are able to make that gesture. Mankind is simply, in its great numbers, not yet ready or willing to adapt to the higher moral, spiritual, and evolutionary culture of Man. Therefore, until the races of humanity begin more generally to respond to the prophetic Teaching of true Adepts, religious "cultism" (or religious culture) in its true form must <u>necessarily</u> remain relatively small in its institutional dimensions. This is because an authentic religious institution must be devoted entirely to the communication of ultimate religious Truth and the relentless demand for higher human transformation—and only relatively few people are interested in that message! An authentic religious institution must, because of its inherent nature, remain more or less outside (or superior to) the stream of daily secular or worldly "culture." And, until mankind in general is able to become truly religious, religion must remain largely prophetic in its function. That is, religion must accept the role of critic in the world and not become like the world in order to become powerful and great in the world. No other role than this prophetic one is possible for authentic religion at this stage in the history of Man. Otherwise, what is truly religious is compromised and ultimately abandoned in the process of the mass institutionalization of popular religion.

When religious movements practice their critical prophetic role, they tend to be attacked by the reactions of worldly people. Thus, true religious leaders and true religious institutions or movements tend to suffer and become victimized to one or another degree by the factions that exist in the popular culture of the time and by the hypocritical attacks of foolish people, who suffer from the lack of the mental power of discrimination. (False leaders and movements may also come under attack, but not because they are bereft of allegiance to the esoteric Truth of Life. Rather, it is generally because of some more obvious human failing, or some conflict with the conventional values of ordinary society.) We find unjustified religious persecution in the case of Jesus and the early followers of Jesus, and also in the

197

case of Moses and certain generations of the Jews, as well as Mohammed and his early converts. But the "Churches" of Jesus and Moses and Mohammed went on to achieve worldly dominion by serving and adapting to the conventional mass culture of future generations. Thus, in our time, the factions of ancient official "Church" power are among those influences that serve and thrive upon the irresponsible subhumanity of Man and even dogmatically prevent the true religious awakening of Man.

The prophets who initiated the so-called "great religions" were made to suffer the official or popular displeasure of their day. The "Churches" that grew up on the foundation of those prophets survived and grew in power by gradually accommodating the very influences that true religion and every true prophet must criticize. Therefore, true religious cultism always arises as a critical voice, not only in relation to the worldly domain of popular and secular society, but also in relation to the wide culture of hypocritical, immature, and unspiritual religious institutions.

Beyond the Outer
or Public Cult of Jesus

But the time will come—indeed, this is the hour—when true worshippers will know they must worship God, the Creator or Father of the world, in Spirit and in Truth. God is seeking for those who will worship God. And God is Spirit, or the Breath of Life. Therefore, if it is God we would worship, we must worship by surrendering into the Life-Spirit, and our worship must be founded in right understanding, or Truth.

(Da Free John's expository translation of the words of Jesus of Nazareth, as recorded in the New Testament, *the Gospel of John the Beloved, chapter 4, verses 23 and 24.)*

J
ohn, known as the Beloved, and, presumably, also as the Elder, was apparently the principal disciple or devotee of Jesus of Nazareth. His primacy was essentially within the "inner circle" of mature converts (to whom the secrets of the esoteric or higher spiritual worship of the Living God were communicated). We may presume, from the indications in John's gospel, that he was also intended to be the principal spiritual successor of Jesus within the "inner circle." That is, the full esoteric spiritual Teaching as well as the initiatory (Spirit-baptizing) functions of Jesus were apparently transmitted to John, and all that John thus possessed was intended to be transmitted through him, within the "inner circle" or esoteric community that responded to the spiritual Teaching of Jesus. (Jesus himself had been the principal disciple or devotee of John the Baptist, and Jesus, therefore, succeeded John the Baptist, after the latter's death.)

Some investigators have offered evidence that Jesus of Nazareth may not have been an actual historical figure.[1] And the same may be true of John the Baptist, John the Beloved, and others. Certainly, if these figures actually lived, they may have been significantly different from the exoteric myths and archetypes described in the *New Testament*.

But there is a sufficient integrity to the documents of the *New Testament* that they may fruitfully be considered as if historical events and persons informed the writings that have come down to us. (And this in fact is how the writings of the *New Testament*, and especially of John the Beloved, will be treated in this essay.) Such relics as the "Shroud of Turin"[2] appear to support the claims of historicity (while perhaps calling for a new interpretation of that history). And, in any case, the *New Testament* writings—even though they may ultimately fail as an historical basis for exoteric

---

1. For documentation of the unorthodox historical considerations of Jesus suggested in this essay, see the Bibliography at the end of *The Enlightenment of the Whole Body*.

2. Allegedly the shroud or burial cloth in which Jesus was buried, it is now preserved in Turin, Italy. The shroud bears the "negative" image of a man's body, apparently imprinted on the cloth by a combination of intense body heat and related chemical activity. (The "negative" displays a "positive" likeness when reversed by photography.) Certain kinds of evidence on the shroud appear to support the theory that Jesus was not dead when placed in the tomb. (See the Bibliography at the end of *The Enlightenment of the Whole Body* for literature related to the Shroud of Turin.)

religion—certainly do provide interesting examples of ancient esoteric mystical philosophy and practice.

The *New Testament* is designed to appear as a single, coherent account of the life and total Teaching of Jesus and his disciples, or apostles. However, modern scholarship has begun to demonstrate that the *New Testament* is a strategically collected and edited conglomeration of many examples of oral and written material from the early centuries following (as well as preceding and including) the period of Jesus' presumably historical ministry. The *New Testament* is essentially an exoteric or outer and public manual of instruction. And it was created by the exoteric public cult of Jesus that became the official Church of the Roman Empire.

What I am indicating here is that the historical Christian Church (in its various sects) was and is essentially an exoteric or publicly oriented institution. And it intentionally limited its communications to exoteric matters when it first designed and established the *New Testament* as the basis of all of its instructions. In and by that process, the esoteric Teaching and practice was separated from the official institution, and it was gradually and completely lost.

However, we may find aspects of the "inner circle" Teaching described in certain texts of the *New Testament*, particularly the gospel and the letters of John the Beloved. And it was only that "inner circle" Teaching and practice that represented the full Teaching of Jesus and his school. The outer, public Teaching of Jesus and his followers was not much different from that of the other exoteric religious sects of the Middle East (such as Judaism) at the time of Jesus. And that public Teaching was essentially directed toward the winning of converts, who would later be "baptized" and instructed in the nonpublic setting of the "inner circle."

In the writings attributed to John the Beloved, we find aspects of the Teaching of the "inner circle," spoken more or less clearly. Thus, the Teaching of John the Beloved survives as testimony to the actual Teaching and practice of Jesus within his "inner circle" of converts. And if one approaches that literature from the point of view of higher spiritual understanding, gotten through awakened practice outside the outer cultism of exoteric religion, then the Teaching of John the Beloved can be rightly interpreted or understood.

200

Throughout my lifetime, I have entered into the deepest and most profound spiritual labor, and thus I have uncovered the various dimensions of esoteric realization that pertain to the native psycho-physical structure of Man. I speak as one who has lived the presumption and practice of esoteric Communion with the Living Reality or Divine Source of Man and the world. I have considered all that I have experienced and realized, and I have compared all of it to every kind of historical evidence relative to Jesus and the tradition that developed in relation to him. On the basis of all of this, I have come to the point of intuitive certainty about the essential experience and esoteric Teaching that was shared by Jesus, and John the Beloved, and the inner or initiated community that surrounded them.

The religion of Jesus and John the Beloved was essentially a proclamation of release from the negative burdens of life in this world through ecstatic or self-transcending union with the Living God. The Way of that union began with conversion from abstract belief in the "God of our fathers," or the "God of the Holy Book." Jesus and John the Beloved preached that there must be conversion from mere and idolatrous belief in an idea of God. Jesus and John the Beloved preached liberation from the exoteric Idol of God as a Being who is apart from Man and the world of Man—a God who created everything and imposed an order on everything, and thus obliged Man and all other creatures to live by various kinds of objective moral rules and natural laws in order to survive and succeed during life and after death. The Way of ecstatic union proclaimed by Jesus and John the Beloved was the ecstatic or self-transcending Way of Life, rather than the formal, legalistic, or self-fulfilling way of exoteric knowledge and conformity. And that ecstatic Way began with psycho-physical conversion, from Lifeless abstractions of the mind and to the Living God, the Truth of Man and the world.

John's gospel Teaches that the "Living God" is "Spirit." That is, God is eternally Present as the All-Pervading Life-Power, with which, therefore, every living being may Commune directly. In fact, the Living God is so intimate with Man that the word "Pneuma" or "Life-Breath" or "Spirit" is used by John the Beloved to describe God. And God is said to be identical to the Spirit, or the Living Energy that pervades the world, and that pervades the nervous system of Man, and that every one of us can contact via the bodily process of breathing and feeling. Indeed, John says not only that Jesus Taught that God is the Living Spirit (rather than the idea of God as abstracted Creator), but that he Taught that the Way to worship God is to worship in the Spirit. That is, Jesus Taught a method of worship that involved ecstatic bodily Communion with the Life-Power via breathing and feeling, based on Truth (or an awakened and secret understanding of the Divine Reality).

202

John the Beloved always wrote or spoke as an intimate devotee of a Spiritual Master. That is, he was communicating about the Way of true worship, or ecstatic bodily Communion with the Living God, but he always acknowledged his own Spiritual Master (who initiated him into the practice of esoteric Communion with the Living Spirit) as if his Master were identical to the Spirit and thus to God. This is a habit of acknowledgment that is typical of all oriental esoteric societies. It represents a profound acknowledgment and appreciation of the mechanism of initiation, guidance, and ecstatic participation enjoyed in the unique spiritual and esoteric relationship of the devotee and his or her Spiritual Master.

No heresy or delusion is contained in this manner of acknowledgment, unless, as has been the case with the exoteric Christian Church that survived the time of Jesus and John the Beloved, the language becomes exoteric and exclusive. That is, if the language of the ecstatic acknowledgment of a Spiritual Master by his true devotees is inherited by a nominal or exoteric cult, that individual tends to become exclusively identified with the Divine Reality. The result of this is that the Living God ceases to be the principle of experience and practice, but abstracted ideas or beliefs and symbolic personalities become, again, the idolatrous basis of the religion. And the religion, or cult, then ceases to understand itself as one of many possible traditional communities involved in esoteric worship. Instead, the cult tends to see and communicate itself as the only community that possesses the Truth.

This has precisely been the case with the Christian churches, most of which have become exclusive cults of Jesus, and most of which have lost both their esoteric foundation and their ability to see the Divine Truth in the Spirit-Worship of all esoteric traditions. And the Christian religion, as well as all other exclusive exoteric and even esoteric traditions, must again be re-awakened and transformed by the esoteric Teaching of Truth.

To continue in this description of the Teaching of Jesus and John the Beloved—they both proclaimed the Way of ecstatic union with the Living God, or Spirit. Jesus, as the Spiritual Master of John, was identified with the Spirit, or God, since he had given John not only the Teaching of Truth but the Spirit-Power itself, through baptism (or esoteric initiation into the Way of Life).

The "Spirit-Power of baptism" is an esoteric process wherein the Life-Current in the body-mind (and, principally, the central nervous system) of the human individual is stimulated to a point of profound intensity and turned about in its basic polarization or tendency. Thus, the Life-Current is felt to press inwards and upwards, via the spine, and towards the crown (or brain core) of the body-mind. The effect of Spirit-baptism was an experience of bodily conversion to a subjective movement of Life-Energy, away from the "flesh" (the "senses," or the plane of vital desires in the autonomic nervous sytem). As a result of such baptism, the various classical mystical phenomena arose, and this entire procedure was called, by Jesus and John the Beloved, "to be born again, via the Spirit."

The "born again" phenomenon proclaimed by modern Christian enthusiasts is merely a superficial mental and emotional conversion toward surrender into belief and dependency on the person Jesus, who is presumed still to be mysteriously present as a universal God-Man. But the "born again" phenomenon initiated by Jesus and John the Beloved was an esoteric procedure, involving mystical experience and literal transformations in the cycle of the Life-Current in the human body-mind. It was a process communicated only to serious converts—those who had already accepted responsibility for the personal and moral discipline of their daily lives. (In contrast, the "born again" phenomenon of exoteric Christian cultism is a conversion of mind and emotion upon which the convert is only then presumed to be capable of true personal and moral responsibility.)

In the writings of John the Beloved (consisting, according to tradition, of one gospel and three letters) "Jesus" is the name or code word for the Spirit of God. He was also the person who was John's Spiritual Master, and he was the historical figure who was the ongoing symbol of the Way in John's religious community. But, in the writings of John the Beloved, "Jesus" is primarily to be understood to be the Life-Principle—the "Living Word" or "Spirit" of God.

As the initiator or baptizer of others, Jesus was also the "Savior" of sinners. (The fourth chapter of John's gospel says that Jesus did not baptize, but had his disciples do it instead. This refers only to the first baptism—the water or cleansing baptism of repentance and forgiveness for turning away from the Divine Life-Spirit of God. After that conversion had matured into practical personal and moral responsibility, Jesus himself might then perform the baptism of the Holy Spirit, or initiation into the esotericism of ecstatic prayer and surrender into the higher mind via the Life-Current within the human body.) As one who enjoyed the ecstasy of union with the Spirit of God, Jesus, the Spiritual Master of John the Beloved, was—as are all others who share in his secret—the "Son of God." But "Jesus" is primarily to be understood to be the "Living Word" or "Spirit of God" personified (or represented by a human Adept or Agent).

Therefore, if the writings of John the Beloved are read as a Teaching about ecstatic bodily union with the Life-Principle, or the "Spirit of God," and if "Jesus" is understood as the representative person, symbol, and name of that Spirit and the Way of Communion with that Spirit, then those writings can be rightly understood. And only then do they represent a true and universal religious inspiration.

The broad tradition of evidence, including evidence presented by non-Christian sources and investigators, generally indicates that Jesus was an historical personality and that he survived the crucifixion bodily. (That he was an historical personality is somewhat in doubt, but there is no doubt that he survived the crucifixion bodily!) The *New Testament* is based on the claim that Jesus survived the crucifixion bodily, and the "Shroud of Turin," which is a remarkable relic, also confirms this. The means of his survival are not made clear in any of the gospels. There is evidence that he may have been forced into a coma on the cross and so was taken down before he had died. According to some theories, he later was restored to health and met secretly with at least some members of his "inner circle," including John the Beloved. Then he simply left Israel, perhaps in order both to flee from those who would kill him and to continue to work as Teacher and Baptizer elsewhere. There are indications that he may have continued his work among the scattered Jews in the Orient. And there is evidence that he may have settled in India, with his disciple Thomas, and that he died and was buried in Kashmir.

In any case, John the Beloved and the other initiates and intimate disciples of Jesus all went in various directions after Jesus' departure. Through their preaching, they developed unique communities, each founded on various kinds of emphasis, both exoteric and esoteric, and each expressing the special cultural background of the individual who founded the community as well as the cultural background of the members of the community itself. In the decades and centuries that followed the lifetimes of the original disciples, various literary documents were produced from the oral and written traditions of the various communities that were created by Jesus' disciples and by various converts and mystics, such as Paul,[3] who became associated with the cult of Jesus after Jesus' crucifixion, resurrection, and secret departure from Israel.

The claims of Jesus' "ascension into heaven" are themselves merely symbolic and exoteric statements that veil the esoteric secrets of bodily worship of the internally ascending Life-Current, and such exoteric stories also served to account for Jesus' absence from the public scene after the crucifixion and resurrection. If we understand that Jesus was simply the honored symbol for the Living Divine Spirit (or Life-Principle) and also the Way whereby every individual may worship or Commune with that Spirit in Truth (and so become a "Son of God"), then we can understand how the symbolic or exoteric descriptions of his "ascension to heaven" developed. (Whereas, to believe that Jesus somehow bodily rose into the clouds and out into the starry heavens not only is to propose a naive cosmology, but it is like believing that the Last Supper, or the holy and symbolic feast of the "body and blood," was actually a cannibalistic orgy.)

3. According to the *New Testament* Paul (A.D. 0-5 to 67 or 68) was one of the principal apostles of the new religion that was formed around the life and Teachings of Jesus. Paul was not a personal disciple of Jesus, nor did he ever meet him personally. After Jesus' death, Paul was a persecutor in the growing Christian movement, until he was converted by an overwhelming mystical experience, which he interpreted to be the spiritual Light, Presence, and Voice of the Ascended Jesus. From that time until his death he was one of the most energetic of the apostles, journeying throughout most of the Mediterranean coastal lands and the Middle East to preach the new "gospel" of Jesus the Christ. He was imprisoned many times, was nearly assassinated by hostile Jews, and, legend has it, was finally beheaded during the persecutions of the Christians by Nero, Emperor of Rome.

When the official councils of the Christian Church were convened by the Roman State to create the foundation of Christianity as the official State religion, the beliefs of Paul, relative to Jesus' personal and ultimately superphysical survival of death, became the dogmas of the Church.

The idea of Jesus' ascension is simply an exoteric or symbolic expression of the esoteric mystical experience of the ascension of the Spirit (or Life-Current) from the lower body to the brain core, whereby various kinds of mystical illumination and bliss are experienced. Thus, Jesus' fate is identified with mystical ascension of attention to the bodily or internal and mental Place of God above. And that same fate was mystically reproduced in the experience of all initiates within the "inner circle" of Jesus and John the Beloved (and, presumably, within the "inner circle" of at least some of the other disciples or apostles).

The method of entering into Communion with the Spirit of God in the company of Jesus or John the Beloved was to receive the second baptism (the baptism of "fire," or second birth via the Holy Spirit). That baptism, along with certain esoteric instructions, made it possible for the individual to "worship in Spirit," through surrender of body, emotion, and mind into the internal Life-Current. After the first baptism, or water baptism (the ritual of purification), a period of personal and moral testing followed. The convert who "kept the faith" and showed it in the form of personal and moral disciplines was eventually given the initiatory touch (baptism or anointing) of the Master (or one of the empowered disciples), usually during a secret meeting within the "inner circle" of initiates and disciples.

This same procedure may be observed even today in esoteric communities all over the world. It involves first the development of various psycho-physical changes in the case of an Adept, so that the Life-Current in him is made to function in an intensely magnetic fashion, polarized, in the central nervous system, toe to crown, rather than crown to toe. When this occurs, the Adept becomes fit to initiate others into the same process, and he does so through touch, or by looking into the person's eyes, or through the medium of speech (including the giving of a secret "Word," "Name," or magical formula to be repeated in prayerful meditation), or by merely thinking about the person (or regarding him in silence). Indeed, even to come into close proximity to such an Adept, or a group of people initiated by an Adept, may produce psycho-physical changes in one who does so. (A case in point is the woman who is said to have been healed merely by touching the garment of Jesus.)

It may be presumed that Spirit-baptized initiates were also taught esoteric methods of evocatory or invocatory prayer, as well as other contemplative exercises. And the name "Jesus" as well as the names "Abba" ("Father") and "Amen" were likely also intoned or otherwise used as a mystical means of entering into bodily Communion with the Spirit within the "inner circle" of Jesus, John the Beloved, and the others. The esoteric sacrificial feast of Jesus' "body and blood" was also practiced as a kind of common meal among the initiates, and it signified the act of taking on the Way of Jesus, which is the Way of self-surrender, love, and spiritual dependence on the Living God.

John the Beloved (or the Elder) apparently survived the longest of all of the original members of Jesus' intimate circle who remained in Israel after Jesus' departure. Perhaps for this reason his writings contain the most direct expression of the esotericism of his tradition—since all other early Christian writings seem to have reflected only or mainly the exotericism of the earliest public work of the disciples. John apparently survived long enough to communicate beyond the earliest period and in geographical areas where an esoteric Teaching was less threatened by hostile exoteric cults as well as hostile political cults. John also appears to have been inherently of a more innocent and mystical mind, and less interested in adapting or proclaiming his message to a hostile and immature public.

It was said of John that he would survive until Jesus came again. And so he did. He survived until old age, and fully demonstrated in himself and in his own "inner circle" of devotees that Jesus was simply the Spirit, and that the Spirit remained Alive even after Jesus had departed from the scene. It may also be presumed that John's own devotees realized the Spirit was still Alive for their benefit after John's own death.

I have written this special treatment of the exoteric and eso-teric cults of Jesus because the Christian tradition currently predominate in the Western world. I wanted to clarify the difference between exoteric, archaic, and ultimately childish (or superficial) beginner's beliefs and the true and even ancient esotericism that belongs to the higher Wisdom-Culture of mankind. The same consideration I have brought to the Christian tradition could and should be brought to any and all other popular exoteric cults of religion. We must do this, or else we cannot go beyond the childhood of Man. And we must also exceed the adolescent reluctance of Man (in the form of scientific materialism or any other kind of superficial intellectual point of view) to yield beyond objective knowledge and into ecstasy, or self-transcending Communion with the Living Reality.

208

John the Beloved may also be heard to speak to the rational scientific mind of our age, if we read and rightly interpret the beginning of the Gospel:

> *At the Origin of everything is the Creative Spirit, the Intelligent Life-Principle, the All-Pervading Matrix of the total world. And the Living Spirit-Breath of God is always united with very God, the Radiant Transcendental Consciousness, the true Heart of the world and the Truth of all beings. Indeed, the Spirit is God, for God is the Creative Life-Principle, the Eternally Free Transcendental Reality in Whom all beings and things arise and float and change and pass out of sight.*
>
> *All things and beings come to exist through the Agency of the Eternal Life-Principle, and not otherwise. And whatever or whoever exists because of the Living Spirit is indeed Alive—because everything and everyone is presently and eternally Sustained through surrender into that Living Spirit.*
>
> *The Life-Breath that sustains Man is also the Light that can show him the Way through the darkness and blindness of the world. That Light is now and always has been shining in the world and even in the body and mind of Man, and no darkness has ever quenched it.*
>
> *(Da Free John's expository translation of chapter 1, verses 1-5, of the Gospel of John the Beloved)*

The Good Principles of Jesus

Jesus apparently renewed, for his time, an ancient psycho-physical conception of the nature of the realm or world in which we appear. The mood of ordinary experience conceives the Principles of this world to be separation, negative results, and death. Jesus communicated the view that the Principles of this world are prior Unity with God, renunciation and forgiveness as a means of purification, and an individually conscious Life that is ever changing but never destroyed.

The significance of his entire life is the argument of this communication. He argued that we should accept these "good" Principles, which make those men good who believe or accept them, rather than accept the conventional and "evil" Principles, which only make all who believe or accept them into fearful, deluded, and wretched beings.

Jesus represents only the argument, the conviction, and the confession of this good assumption of Good Principles. He does not represent any independent historical Act that makes it unnecessary for any one else to accept and be responsible for these Principles. In other words, the Principles of our Life are Good, but these Good Principles are only as effective in our own case as the degree of our acceptance and responsibility relative to them.

All who accept these Principles must be wise and intelligent and humble, since their goodness, or identity with the Good Principles of Life, is gradual, or a process that matures and grows forever. Their Enlightenment is always instant—whenever their presumption of the Good and True is Real—but their lives are forever, and forever transformed by whatever they believe, accept, or presume.

Jesus Was a Sacrifice, Not a Survivor

Jesus of Nazareth has become a universal archetypal figure in the minds of all mankind. But he has thereby become more a part of conventional mind and meaning than a servant of the Real.

Unfortunately, he has become identified with personal or egoic survival rather than perfect sacrifice of self, mind, life, emotion, and body.

Paul the Apostle said that if Jesus did not survive his death, then belief in him and his Teaching is fruitless. Therefore, the bodily and personal survival of Jesus became the traditional foundation of Christian belief and practice. But Paul's conception is false. The Truth and the Law of sacrifice are not verified by or dependent upon the knowable survival or immortality of any man, including Jesus. The Truth of the Teaching of Jesus, itself an extension of the Teaching of the ancients, did not at all depend on his survival, or, more specifically, knowledge, on the part of others, of his survival. If it did depend on his personal or conventional soul-survival of death, or the knowledge of such on the part of others, he could not have taught anything of ultimate significance during his lifetime, and all Teaching before his time would have been inherently false. But Jesus himself specifically denied both possibilities.

The Teaching of Jesus is essentially the ancient Teaching of the Way of Sacrifice. He, like others, taught that the sacrifice that is essential is not cultic or external to the individual, but it is necessarily a moral and personal sacrifice made through love. It is the sacrifice of all that is oneself, and all that one possesses, into forms of loving and compassionate participation with others, and into the absolute Mystery of the Reality and Divine Person wherein we all arise and change and ultimately disappear. Therefore, the proof of his Teaching is not in the independent or knowable survival of anything or anyone, but in the enlightened, free, and moral happiness of those who live the sacrifice while alive and even at death.

We cannot cling to the survival of anyone, or even ourselves. This clinging has for centuries agonized would-be believers, who tried to be certain of the survival of Jesus and themselves. Truly, Jesus did not survive in the independent form that persisted while he lived, nor does anyone possess certain knowledge of the history of Jesus after his death. All reports are simply expressions of the mystical presumptions and archetypal mental structures of those who make the reports. And neither will we survive the process of universal dissolution everywhere displayed. Jesus sacrificed himself. He gave himself up in loving service to others and in ultimate love to Real God. All who do this become what they meditate upon. They are

Translated beyond this self or independent body-mind into a hidden Destiny in the Mystery or Intensity that includes and precedes all beings, things, and worlds.

The Christian Idol

The popular Myth of Jesus is an Idol of mass religion. It was created by the exoteric Christian Church, when it moved to legitimize itself in the eyes of the secular State of Rome. That Idol is worshipped by popular belief, and many have been and continue to be deluded and oppressed by the Cult of that Idol.

Like every Idol, the Myth of Jesus contains a secret about Man himself. But that secret is locked away in the features of the Image men worship. Men worship Jesus as an exclusive human embodiment of God because they are unwilling or unable to accept the kind of responsibility for themselves that Jesus accepted for himself.

Jesus did not teach the worship of himself as an Idol of God or a Substitute for the responsibility of each man for his own religious and spiritual sacrifice. And even if he did, it would be our responsibility to liberate ourselves from that Doctrine.

The popular Myth of Jesus is founded on archaic cosmological archetypes. Jesus is believed to have come down from Heaven (or the sky of stars above the Earth) and become a blood sacrifice (in the ancient style of cults that ritually killed animals and men), and then he is supposed to have risen up into the sky again—back to Heaven. The man Jesus is popularly believed to be God, the Creator of the Universe, and his death is glorified as a necessary Cosmic Event that somehow makes it unnecessary for any believer to suffer permanent mortal death.

All of this, and more, may have made some kind of imaginative, street-level sense in the days of the Roman Empire, but it is nothing more than benighted silliness in the last quarter of the twentieth century. And, in any case, none of this Idolatry was the teaching or the intention of Jesus or any of the other great spiritual Adepts of the world. All of the mythological idolization of Jesus was the creation of the exoteric and popular cultism of the early Christian Church. And the time has come for the world to renounce this nonsense—even if the Christian Church itself is yet unwilling to renounce its obnoxious absolutist claim on all of humanity.

The Myth and the Idol of Jesus have nothing to do with true religion or the spiritual responsibility of Man—as I have tried to explain in these essays and in many other writings. And it is time we stopped glorifying the martyrdom of Jesus. Even though it seems possible that he personally survived the crucifixion and went on to continue his work outside Israel, the popular belief is that he died on the cross. And the persecution and attempted assassination of Jesus by the hypocritical religious cultists of his time was not in any sense good for mankind. It was a grave misfortune, and a prime example of the stupid, unillumined, and aggressive mentality that still characterizes the popular or mass level of subhuman existence. The world would have profited much more if Jesus had been able to work openly and live to a remarkable old age as a great prophetic Teacher of Israel. In that case, the true esoteric foundation of religion might have begun to become the basis of human culture two thousand years ago. And, at the very least, mankind could have avoided the long tour of domination by yet another impenetrable Idol of the mind.

The idea that the martyrdom of Jesus was the literal and final Sacrifice of God is a perversion of the Truth. The true sacrifice of Jesus occurred while he was still alive. That sacrifice was of an esoteric spiritual nature, and it is of no inherent value to any other human being, unless that individual will duplicate that same sacrifice in the processes of his own body-mind.

Why do we persist in a retarded and negatively cultic understanding of religion? The Truth is plain—and it has been plainly preached and demonstrated, not only by Jesus, but by many Adepts in every epoch of human history. But the Idol of Jesus persists—because it is one of the great archetypal alternatives to authentic personal religious or spiritual responsibility. It is time for mankind to awaken to Wisdom and to the understanding of Jesus in Truth. Then perhaps some benefit will have come to us at last from that ancient outrage performed in Jerusalem.

Beyond the Hidden
Teachings of Jesus

A talk by Da Free John

I

D A FREE JOHN: The teaching of Jesus is both exoteric, or public and outward, and esoteric, or hidden and spiritual. In our consideration of Jesus, we must first of all differentiate the exoteric or public teaching that Jesus himself represented from the exoteric or public teaching of the Christian tradition that succeeded him. In general, the exoteric teaching of the Christian Church is based on a cultic, liturgical or ritualistic, and mythbound relationship to Jesus, who is proclaimed to be exclusively identical with the Creator-God of the Semitic tradition. The Jesus of exoteric Christianity is useful to Man only after his supposed death on the cross and his legendary resurrection and ascension. The essence of the traditional exoteric teaching of Christianity is that we can realize a personal relationship to this legendary Jesus, the exclusive God who will "save" us from a life of suffering, although we may not realize the same relationship to God that Jesus realized.

The exoteric teaching that Jesus himself actually offered was quite different from the cultic dogma that survived him. He taught that we must be free of cultic religious illusions and moral reluctance. He was willing to be of service as Spiritual Master to individuals, but not in the cultic form promoted by the Church in the centuries after his death. If the only relevant Jesus is the Jesus who has died for our sins and gone to heaven, then he could not have taught anything useful during his lifetime. Of what service was he, then, to somebody to whom he talked while he was alive, but who died before Jesus was supposedly "ascended to the Father"? Does it follow that the individual did not hear his teaching and did not have contact with the Presence of God? Clearly, there is no truth to such logic. Thus, the "ascended Messiah" exotericism of the Christian tradition is nonsense.

The exoteric teaching of Jesus during his lifetime was true, however. It was essentially a moral teaching that clarified the centuries-old Hebrew tradition of behavioral laws and ritualistic obligations. Jesus communicated a single moral disposition that obliged everyone to transcend mere adherence to the ancient, external legalisms and, instead of observing rituals, to sacrifice themselves in the midst of the daily circumstances of life. Since ancient times, the way of sacrifice has been the essential way of human integration with God. The orthodox, cultic sacrifices of the ancient days were ritualistic and superficial—one murdered a pigeon or a goat, performed a ritual or a prescribed liturgy, walked around a holy place, sang hymns, and so forth. Even today such ritual sacrifices are common to religious practices. Jesus, like the other Adepts who appeared before and after him, communicated the principle behind such ritual sacrifices, which is the sacrifice of self, the sacrifice of Man through and in the form of the individual human being. The ritual of any sacrifice is only the instrument, while also the evidence, of the individual's integration with the Living Divine Reality. The primary sacrifice is the sacrifice of the individual himself, not of something other than himself.

This teaching of sacrifice is the essential and true exoteric religion that has been communicated since ancient times. Jesus found a way to integrate it creatively with the lives of his contemporaries. He taught people that they themselves were obliged to be a sacrifice, through love and self-release, through ecstasy, through letting go, through abandoning rigid reactivity and self-possession when confronted with the circumstances of life.

True religious teachings oblige people to personal as well as moral disciplines at the exoteric or foundation level of practice. As the cultic falsification of Jesus' point of view has proceeded over time, however, the personal disciplines have largely been abandoned, and even the moral obligations have been weakened. Today, the essence of mainstream Christianity is that we may be "saved" through "faith," or belief in a cultic personal association with Jesus. We are not thus obliged to the full degree of self-transcending personal and moral responsibility, since Jesus supposedly will save us from the "wages" of our sins. Thus, the true exoteric teaching of Jesus has been diluted by the false exotericism of the cult that followed him. Jesus himself primarily obliged people to a life of personal and moral sacrifice, whereby they could transcend cultic limitations and personal pettiness in the midst of the ordinary conditions of living.

Jesus' teaching is summarized in the Great Commandment "Love the Lord thy God with all your heart, and with all your soul, and with all your mind; and love your neighbor as yourself." How that all-absorbing, God-Realizing love was to be accomplished was communicated in the "inner circle," through esoteric or secret, higher, and mystical teaching, but the God-Realizing process included and began with one's life in the world, among one's neighbors, in intimate cultural relationship to others. One was obliged to be a sacrifice in the management of intimate community, daily work, diet, and health. One's sexuality was to be managed through concentration, through relational love-commitment in marriage. One's relationship to others was to be managed from the point of view of moral sacrifice, the life of loving and compassionate service, the abandonment of petty legalisms in favor of wholehearted love relations, community relations, mutual agreements, and unreserved help.

These disciplines that were the foundation of the way of life that Jesus communicated are only a preparatory phase of true religious life. Yet in Jesus' time, as today, it was immensely difficult to bring people to change their orientation from reactive self-possession to self-transcending relationship with the Living God and all other beings. Even the simple personal and moral disciplines were more than most people could conceive of and accept as the appropriate burden of a religious life. Many of them spent the rest of their lives struggling with that ordinary doctrine. Likewise, the leaders of the official cults of that time and place had so much difficulty with the implications of this natural teaching that they contemplated means to defame and ultimately destroy Jesus. To live simply and directly in the personal and moral disposition Jesus recommended would have negated the dependence of the people on all of the cultic laws and temple practices by which the priests maintained their wealth and their control over the mass population. Jesus was too revolutionary for ordinary childish people as well as for the parentlike priests who were their "shepherds." Therefore, the way of life he communicated in public was very upsetting and threatening to the official cults of his time.

This is how Jesus managed his exoteric and esoteric levels of instruction: As his disciples traveled and communicated the radical, moral point of view, they looked for those who were most prepared to accept, in relatively simple and human fashion, the personal and moral responsibilities of this way of life. The disciples were instructed to look for the most devotional, the most responsive and responsible, individuals. When they discovered such men and women, they did not initiate them into the esoteric teaching immediately, but they did bring them into closer proximity to the esoteric core of Jesus' work. The *New Testament* describes several occasions when Jesus and the disciples spent time in the homes of followers. Here and there they found an individual who was physically, psychologically, morally, and emotionally capable of the full esoteric way of life, which included higher psycho-physical disciplines and adaptation in addition to the personal and moral disciplines of the exoteric teaching.

Thus, those who were prepared were initiated into an esoteric order or circle around Jesus. These were the people with whom he did not limit his speech to parables and lessons of moral transformation. These people were given the mystical, bodily secrets of the "Kingdom of God," the secrets of how to become the Sons and Daughters of God—in other words, how to be pervaded by the Divine Life-Current and "lifted up" and transformed.

Jesus was not the Messiah that the Jews had expected. He had no intention to be a political figure and to purify Israel of the Roman rule. Thus, it is true that he was not and is not the traditionally expected Messiah of the Jews. He was a different kind of person altogether. He denied being the worldly Messiah that his contemporaries sought: "My Kingdom is not of this world." All during his ministry he avoided any obligation to worldly power, to be warlike and politically active. He gave all his attention to the reawakening of a moral way of life in the world, the transformation of the relationships between individuals, the regeneration of the relationship between the individual and the Living Divine, and restoration of the Law of sacrifice—not the sacrifice of pigeons sold in the hallways around the temple, but the moral and spiritual love-sacrifice of the individual himself in his relationship to others and to the Living Spirit that is God.

Jesus' exoteric teaching is quite different from the exoteric teaching of the institutional Church of conventional Christianity. Nor is the conventional Christian Church the bearer of the esoteric teaching of Jesus. That secret teaching was lost in the social circumstances of the early centuries after Jesus' death. It did not disappear immediately, but it disappeared fairly quickly. A fragment of a letter that was written in the second century after Jesus by a man named Clement of Alexandria[4] indicates that the writer knows something about the esoteric tradition among Jesus' followers, but it is obvious from the tone of the letter that the higher esoteric tradition had already disappeared by Clement's own time. He is a wise old man of the Christian tradition, and he knows something about this esoteric matter, but it is already in the past. He writes about the way it was in the past.

Thus, within the first 150 years or so after Jesus' disappearance from Israel, the esoteric aspect of his teaching disappeared. By the time the Church councils were created to formalize the cult and its dogma and to exalt the teaching of Paul as the official point of view of the Church, the esotericism of Jesus had long since ceased to be practiced. Finally, it was completely, officially, and dogmatically eliminated. Certain aspects of the exoteric moral and personal disciplines of life recommended by Jesus remain in the Church, but they are not its fundamental focus, nor are they obligatory in any fundamental sense. The essential focus of the cult of the Christian Church is the believer's "saving" relationship to Jesus as an exclusive and mythbound manifestation of God. Only the greatest saints of the Christian tradition have broken through the exoteric limits of orthodox Christianity to develop an illumined, mystical, or transcendental and ecstatic relationship with God or Christ as Living Spirit—and they have often been brutally persecuted by the authorities of the conventional Church.

In the literature of Jesus' time, very little survives of the esotericism of his work. Only some suggestion of it is revealed to a careful reading of the *New Testament*, and related documents, such as the fragment of the letter by Clement of Alexandria. But, elsewhere on the Earth, there still remains the esoteric tradition of which Jesus, in his time, was simply a representative. He only applied the understanding and the techniques of higher adaptation, prayerful meditation, psychic awakening, and spiritual growth as they already

4. An analysis of the authenticity and significance of this letter as well as the story of its discovery by Morton Smith are presented in *The Secret Gospel: The Discovery and Interpretation of the Secret Gospel According to Mark,* by Morton Smith (New York: Harper & Row, 1973).

appeared in the esoteric cultures of the ancient world, and he communicated or interpreted these through the traditional law, archetypes, and mythology of his contemporaries in Israel.

The conventional cultic and exoteric interpretation of the life and person of Jesus considers him to be an exclusive manifestation of God, representing a history, a way of life, and a destiny that no one else can enjoy or duplicate, and thus for which no one else can be responsible. Such was absolutely not the point of view of Jesus himself. He communicated a way of life for which each individual must be as responsible as Jesus was in his own case. His teaching relieved people of conventional exoteric religious cultism, and it led true "hearers" into a life of spiritual sacrifice of self, including the higher, esoteric or evolutionary practice of ecstatic prayer (or meditation on the Life-Principle via concentration in the brain) and an esoteric spiritual interpretation of the Hebrew tradition. He essentially communicated the point of view of sacrifice, as a total human activity that fulfills the Law and is the essence of the Way of Truth, and his teaching was directed to the personal, moral, and higher psycho-physical experience of Love-Communion with the Life-Principle, the Living Spirit that is God.

I have criticized the cultic Christian revision of Jesus' life and work, since it forgets and even anathematizes his real work and totally misinterprets the significance of his spiritual influence. At another level, however, my criticism must also be directed at the inverted, self-divided, world-denying, soul-glorifying orientation of the ancient oriental mystical traditions as a whole—since much of the "inner circle" Teaching of Jesus was an extension of that ancient "gnosticism" of "Heaven-seeking" via internal mystical techniques. Ultimately, the esoteric idols of mysticism must be overcome, just as must the exoteric and public idols of analytical intellectualism. Mysticism, like science, is another way of "knowing about." It is simply an arcane method for acquiring certain kinds of knowledge.

On the one hand, the ancients presumed they were knowing about and participating in the total universe with their mystical, inward methods. This was true only to a modest degree, limited by the mechanics of reflection and symbol (as in all cases of mere knowledge). On the other hand, they thought, and rightly so, that they were viewing the inner side of Man. That is, in fact, fundamentally and exactly what they were doing. They were viewing the interior, subtler aspect of the body and the subtler aspects of the brain-mind. However, they generally attributed an independent reality to what they viewed within.

The two most prominent doctrines of traditional oriental mysticism were that inner visions were direct experiences of the cosmos beyond Earth, and that the inner being, mind, or soul of Man is not only distinct and therefore separable from the physical body— but that the fulfillment of human existence is the conscious separation of the mind or soul from the physical body and the Earth. Therefore, mystical practitioners, including the "inner circle" of Jesus, commonly believed that by stimulating these inward phenomena they could temporarily (and even finally) escape the Earth, the human body, and ordinary existence. (And this "gnostic" or more or less ascetic mystical ideal was contrary to the exoteric and world-affirming doctrines of the "establishment" Judaism of Jesus' time, just as it runs contrary to the world-affirming or worldly point of view of exoteric Christianity and of modern societies in general.)

The ultimate presumption of conventional mysticism is not, in its traditional formulation, simply or patently true. Mystical experience and mystical language are rightly understood only if they are accepted as forms of paradox—a special way of intuiting and surrendering to the Eternal Divine Mystery, rather than an experience that is itself taken to be God. Most of the phenomena that are experienced inwardly are not truly cosmic (arising outside the personal sphere of the body-mind), and neither are they separable from the physical body. They are, in most instances, expressions of the individual psyche, determined by the conventions of the human nervous system. They are native to the body of Man. They depend on the physical or elemental structures of the human body and brain-mind. They are not truly separate from the physical or superior to it. They do not represent another or alternative reality that one can cling to and thereby abandon the physical.

In any case, experiences are not Truth. And, although we may learn and grow by experience, experiences do not in themselves liberate us into the Transcendental Reality or Realm of the Absolute Divine. Only the Life-Principle itself, which is the Matrix of all experiences, is the Truth. And, therefore, the ultimate liberation of Man is not in knowledge or experience, but only in self-transcending and total psycho-physical surrender into the ultimate Domain of the

Life-Principle (which we contact directly via the central nervous system, and which is senior to every aspect of mind and body).

The Truth is not within. However, from the point of view of the ancient and traditional mystics, the Truth is indeed within. The esoteric initiates of Jesus were themselves essentially traditional mystics, involved with the mystical and magical phenomena of the "kundalini."[5] They used the language and symbols of their own time and place, but the process they engaged was essentially that of the "kundalini," or the internal Life-Current in the central nervous system, rising from the "flesh," from the realm of the senses, from the lowest point or base of the body, to the brain core and the "heaven" of inwardness.

This mystical and magical absorption of attention in the Life-Current certainly does belong to the developing stages and practical expressions of the esotericism of the ultimate Way of Truth. But the phenomena that are experienced through the method of ascending inwardness are not the liberating Truth, they are not the very Divine, they are not the very Realm of God. They are simply inner phenomena, inner knowledge, subtler aspects of the human body-mind itself. The liberating Truth is in the Realization that "I" am not within this body. "I" am the body. And the total bodily (or psycho-physical) being inheres in the Living Transcendental Divine Being. It is only when we are relieved of the subjective being, when we are released from the illusion of mind as a separable reality, when we are released from the illusion of mind as an independent soul, or the illusion of mind as another territory, another dimension of ourselves that can be taken away from this body and separated from this world—it is only when we are relieved of the entire inward search, the selfward tendency, the self-divided solution, that the radical and whole bodily confession of Truth can begin.

5. The "kundalini," or "serpent power," traditionally viewed, is that aspect of the internal current of bodily energy that is awakened from a dormant state at the base of the spine, and ascends the spinal line to the crown. That is, the process of the "kundalini," or mystical ascent, essentially involves the inversion of attention, so that the nerve energy in the autonomic nervous system withdraws (from the realm of the "flesh" or the "senses") and is experienced more or less exclusively in the "heavenly" terms of the central nervous system (the spinal cord and brain). The path of "kundalini," or internal energy, is the basis of all religious mysticism, and the process produces a range of extraordinary psycho-physical phenomena that are symbolized and otherwise described in many of the exoteric and esoteric religious literatures of the world.

220

Therefore, if we study and understand Jesus rightly and in Truth, we must transcend the sectarian limitations of the historical Cult of Jesus (or Christianity). Thus, we will necessarily enter into the esoteric domain of religious, mystical, and magical religion, which is communicated in traditions all over the world. But at last we will exceed the conventional limitations of the esoteric mysticism of "soul-development." Such a course is necessarily implied in the worship of God in Spirit and in Truth. And since such worship was apparently recommended by Jesus himself, we can assume that his highest Teaching embraced this very Realization, exceeding the outer and the inner cults of Man.

221

II

The notion that Jesus died <u>for</u> our sins (rather than because of them, or merely as part of the natural chaos of the subhuman world) is based on the Hebrew ritualism of the *Old Testament* and the ancient cults of "blood sacrifice." Just as the idea of Jesus' "ascent into Heaven" does not really coincide with the cosmology that we know to be true from our present knowledge (but actually coincides with the traditional mystical symbolism of internal ascent), similarly, the ancient rites of "blood sacrifice," of which Jesus' death is traditionally supposed to be the highest example, are not really understandable in the conventional terms of modern daily life.

If we are to find some value, or likeness to Truth, in the biblical idea of sin, we must examine what "sin" is in any case. The dreadfully dark word "sin" is a version of an ancient expression which simply means "to miss the mark." To miss a mark, as when missing a target with a bow and arrow, is to be eccentric, off the center. Thus, to "sin" is to turn one's attention away from the Center or Heart of Existence. It is to be unattached to God, turned away from God, deflected from God, turned elsewhere than to God. It is to worship principles that are not God. It is to be attached to experiences, to self, to the body-mind, rather than to the Divine Life-Principle or Transcendental Consciousness.

The *New Testament* proclaims that all sins are forgivable— except one, which is the "sin against the Holy Spirit." But the idea of a special act that is a sin against the Holy Spirit is only a kind of play on words. All sin is turning away from the Living God, the Life-Principle, or the Holy Spirit. Then what is not the ultimate sin? What is the only activity that is "forgiven" (or permitted to find God)? It is to meet the mark, or to worship the Living God—not with conventional ritualism or cultic belief, but through Love-Communion, through feeling and breathing, through the total, cultural, and ecstatic or self-transcending process that is most intimately associated with one's very existence and with all one's relationships. One cannot, therefore, avoid committing the unforgivable sin by means of any ordinary behavioral aversion, since all sins are the same—all sins are a matter of turning away from the Life-Spirit, or the Living Divine. All sins are equally and absolutely "unforgivable." Therefore, not only must all sins be forgiven, but sin itself (or the "sin against the Holy Spirit") must be forgiven, or else there is no forgiveness (or no intimacy with God). To be "forgiven" for one's sin is to be released from the consequences of sin, but, above all, it is to be released from the tendency, activity, and consciousness that is sin. "Forgiveness of sin" is to be released from eccentricity and returned to the "mark." To be "forgiven" is to be converted, or turned about in one's attention. It is to be released from reactive and self-possessed (or Narcissistic) obsession and returned to self-transcending Love-Communion with the Life-Principle, the Holy Spirit, the Living God. Therefore, if we will only accept the Teaching of Truth in our understanding and turn body and mind from self-possession to God-Communion, we are "forgiven," or released from "sin," by virtue of that conversion.

Thus, it should be clear that the process of human liberation in Truth has nothing whatsoever to do with any cultic ritual of "blood sacrifice," even the "blood sacrifice" that Jesus supposedly performed by being nailed to a cross. Such an idea is cultic and ritualistic nonsense—exactly the kind of religious nonsense that Jesus himself preached against. Jesus and his disciples preached conversion to the Living God, not to the "God of our fathers," not to the God of cultic belief, not to the God of priestly ritualism, not to the God of liturgies and literal or vicarious and symbolic "blood sacrifices." Everyone must make the true and bloodless sacrifice of conversion to the Life-Principle. Everyone must be "forgiven." Everyone must turn away

222

from "sin." Everyone must submit to the living "cross," the central nervous system, which obliges all knowledge and all desire to submit to Life. In other words, everyone must enter into heartfelt bodily Communion with the Living God.

This is the single and entire message of the *New Testament*. There is no other true message there, or in any other religious tradition. That is it. The question is, what are we going to do about it? We can spend the rest of our lives studying the *New Testament* and all the superficially complicated content of biblical faith, but true religion still depends fundamentally on this matter of personal and total psycho-physical conversion to the Life-Principle, and the assumption of a truly spiritual Way of Life, or a practical habit of existence that always (or via all our human functions) Communes with the Spirit.

223

I once functioned as chaplain in a mental hospital. On at least two occasions I gave a sermon on the passage in the *New Testament* that describes the sin against the Holy Spirit as the only unforgivable sin. People who are insane are often obsessed with the idea that they have committed the one sin that cannot be forgiven. When I preached the first sermon on this matter, I presumed—but I did not have to presume—I noticed that everybody there was completely insane! I very quickly had to become responsible to serve people who had not one whit of attention left over from their mechanical, self-possesssed, inward life, their turning away. They were devoted sinners! They were not communing with God; they were not open-eyed, clear, conscious, full of attention. They were distracted in themselves. They were obsessively missing the mark, moment to moment. Their breath was irregular, their bodies were all out of harmony, they were self-possessed, dark, demonic egos. They were like any ordinary person, except that they were an exaggeration of the ordinary state.

It was the perfect place to preach, a perfect setting, and the ultimate place to preach that particular sermon. The people in the audience were doing exactly the thing that I was talking about. The only imperfection in the circumstance was that no one in the audience was capable of "hearing" me and understanding what I was saying! I was obliged to give this sermon, but they could all do whatever they pleased while I gave it. They were generally expected to remain confined to the room, but, apart from this basic obligation, very few demands were placed on them. Thus, their "sinning" was totally obvious.

The usual man functions, he talks to you, he often seems reasonable and intelligent. Even so, he is also mad, because he is utterly and fearfully involved with himself. He is creating the fake reality, the subjective world of self, exactly as were the mental patients to whom I preached. Like a madman, the usual man or woman is completely involved with the repetitive ritual of obsessive interpretations and misinterpretations, and the chronic contraction of his or her own body from the obvious and Radiant Reality of the Living Person, the Divine and Transcendental Truth of Man.

The people in the mental hospital were simply a kind of cartoon version of humanity. While I gave this sermon, which seemed to me basically insightful, they were aggressively busy with themselves, shouting, playing with their noses and their genitals, and rehearsing their bizarre emotional rituals. They were all totally out of relationship to their environment and to me and to all the other people in the room. Each one of them was like a planet in a separate universe, with no relationship to any other planets and universes. The "audience" reeled with this tremendous movement, like a great ocean. As I look out at you who listen to me today, I see a relatively orderly gathering. But the audience of mental patients was not orderly at all. All the heads and bodies were moving constantly. Each person was a heap of gestures and a chaos of noises and silences, acting in an eternal moment that is without relationship to anyone or anything else.

They were the perfect example of "sinners." In that eternal and absolute moment of self-involvement they were eternally and absolutely "unforgiven." The teaching and the fate of Jesus made no difference to them. They were unforgiven because they would not be converted in their attention. They would not, in other words, cease to sin. They would not turn from self to Life. They would not return their attention to the Absolute and All-Pervading Reality. They maintained their attention on and in themselves to the point of madness, the "black hole" of egoic implosion. Most people have not reached that point. Most people are neurotic and deluded, but they are conventionally sane. They function within the same ritual order that most other people acknowledge to be "reality." Still, everyone is a "sinner," exactly as every madman who came to watch me preach.

All of this is perhaps not quite so obvious to the Sunday morning preacher. When he confronts his dreadfully sane congregation, it may not seem obvious to him that every one present is sinning at that very moment. It is not really obvious to the preacher that he himself is also sinning via the ritual of all his thoughts and acts. He and his congregation have their Jesus, and this makes them orderly, but they have no awareness of the sinless life of ecstatic conversion to the Living Truth! Their attention is on themselves, they are full of concerns, and, together, they believe in the ritual nonsense of ordinary religion, in order to alleviate the critical anxiety of ordinary fear. They are not awakened to true "faith," which is literal God-Communion—perhaps because they have not yet experienced and recognized the stark reality of their own madness, their own sinfulness.

The deadly tendency of my own body-mind has always appeared as stark to me as the tendency I could see among the madmen in the mental hospital. The Life-negative and self-meditating tendency of this human mechanism has always been obvious to me. From the beginning of my life, I have been dealing with this literal matter of "sin." However, to the usual man or woman, asleep with all the anchormen of the TV news, the reality and effect of "sin" is not obvious. To the usual man, "sin" is merely conventionally "illicit" behavior, such as stealing, or alcoholism, or sexual intercourse, or even enjoyment itself! A false idea of "sin" only contributes to our fundamental insanity and "sinfulness." "Sin" is not merely or even at all a form of behavior that may be socially inappropriate in a white Christian suburb of puritan America. "Sin" is an anti-spiritual gesture. It is the Life-negative gesture of self-possession. It is the contraction of body and psyche from the Life-Principle. It is self-attention and self-division. It is recoil from Ecstasy, toward the inward obsessiveness of the defined and separative self.

We are all struggling with this chronic gesture of reactive contraction, of psycho-physical recoil, of fear, of self-possession, of self-division, of turning attention away from the Life-Principle and toward all the idols of egoic experience. Such idolatry is the chronically negative substance of everyone's life, even of the highest of lives. It is even part of the substance of the life of Jesus. (This realization should not shock us. In his ecstasy, Jesus was identical to the Spirit that is God, but in his natural state, he was a devotee of God, a mystic, and a man of his own time. Therefore, Jesus himself declares, in the *New Testament*, that it is not Man that is "Good"—even if he is Jesus—but only God is "Good," and it is to God that every man and woman must be surrendered.)

Even so, in the context of his own moment of time, Jesus was not an idolator. He angrily denounced the idolatrous trends of his day. He was part of the movement in that epoch of ancient history in which all the "great religions" were developed. In that epoch, the cultural movement of mankind was focused on the realization of the awakening of the undifferentiated psyche to a position of moral and mystical self-consciousness. All the religions of that time existed for that purpose. Thus, they were true in their time. Nevertheless, the concrete mysticism of the ancient cults, including the "inner circle" of Jesus, represents only a moment or an early stage in the ultimate drama of human transformation.

There is a kind of worship of idols in the form of mystical experiences, just as there is in the common idolatry of the scientific and religious worship of the powers of Nature and all the cultic and secular frenzy over the Gods we make from words. Once we pass beyond the limits of our own body-mind, and, therefore, of the ancient concept of mind, we can see that even the mystical realization preached by the ancient esoteric cults is, as much as any other form of idolatry, to be transcended as we mature in Divine Communion. What is offered as the absolute Realization of Truth from the point of view of the ancient mysticism is simply a more highly evolved aspect of human knowledge and experience. But the Truth is a matter of absolute self-transcendence. The Truth is not Realized by the confinement of attention to any form of experience at all, but only by the release of attention, and all the gestures of attention, into the Living Divine Reality.

Therefore, the Truth is the Life-Principle itself, and the Realization of Truth is never Absolute, since the Living Truth must necessarily be Realized in every newly arising moment of existence. The Realization of Truth is an endless Process of constant transcendence of self (and of the functional limits of Man) through psycho-physical surrender into the Life-Principle. Man himself will have become evolutionary rubble long before the experientially reflected Light of God-Realization even begins to produce an intimate glimmer of the Wonder that is yet to be born at Infinity.

Jesus Is Life

The historical person of Jesus is now beyond the ordinary reach of mankind. He has gone on to fulfill his own evolutionary destiny in the realm of Nature. Only the Living God, or the Transcendental Reality to which Jesus pointed with his entire life and Teaching, remains for us to embrace in love.

We must surrender to the Life-Principle, the Living God, the Holy Spirit, the Radiant Self of all beings, Who is the Truth, the Way, and the Destiny of Man. If you like, you can name that Living Reality "Jesus," or the "Christ," but do not threaten and deny the rights of those who name that same Principle by other names. Every religion is simply an historical intuition of the One and Only Life-Principle. Therefore, people in other traditions than the Christian tradition name that same Reality by other names, such as Yahweh, Allah, Krishna, the Atman, Brahman, Om, the Buddha, Nirvana, or the Tao. And it is time for us to see beyond the names we have given to Life. It is time we surrender ourselves bodily to the Life-Principle and accept compassionate and loving responsibility for the Wisdom and welfare of all mankind.

"Jesus," or the "Christ," is simply a traditional name or archetypal symbol for the Life-Principle—and, therefore, in the symbolic or archetypal sense, "Jesus" is "God."

And the universal Life-Current pervades the body of Man via the central nervous system. Therefore, the central nervous system is the "Mountain of God," the "Tree of the World," the "Savior of the World," the Living "Crucifix," the Spiritual "Law," the Way, the Truth, and the Life of Man. And "Jesus" is a traditional name or symbol for the central nervous system in its direct Communion with the Life-Principle—or Man in his wholeness, crucified, or sacrificed to the Living Spirit.

The Life-Principle manifests as the mind and the body—or the "higher" and "lower" parts of Man. But neither mind nor body is the Truth and the ultimate resort of Man. Only the Life-Principle itself is the Way, the Truth, and the Life of Man.

The Way of Life is not found in the mind itself or in the body itself, but only in the transcendence of the total body-mind through Love-Communion with the Life-Principle. Therefore, the Way of Life is to be founded on the heart of Man, since mind and body spring from the Center, or the Life-Spirit of Love, which is at the heart of Man.

228

The Great Commandment of "Jesus" is to love, trust, or surrender to God, Who is the Life-Principle. We are obliged by the Law of Life, to which the central nervous system and the heart of Man are eternally bound. Each of us must Awaken to his own positive and total functional connection to the Life-Principle. And then each of us must love, or Radiate Life to all others, to the same absolute degree that we are all given Life, or love, in and as ourselves.

Therefore, since we are given absolute Life, we must consent to be absolute Life in all our relationships. And, since we are only love, we must consent to transcend all psycho-physical limits in the exercise of love, or unqualified Life-Radiance.

The Enlightenment of Man Is in His Bodily Commitment to Life

Man is mortal, and also immortal. The individual apparently lives and dies, but his existence is not threatened. His psycho-physical form passes through cycles of birth, and change, and death, but each cycle is followed by another, so that all the evolutionary lessons may be learned. This is the understanding that enlightens our perception of Man.

But unenlightened men and women do not perceive or understand the paradox of Man and the immortality of the cycles of mortality. Therefore, the usual individual is full of self and fear, and he constantly seeks to protect himself against ultimate and apparently absolute threats to his survival. And, because of his self-possessed search for immunity from frustration, pain, and death, the human individual fails to surrender to the full cycle of his own existence.

Therefore, unenlightened Man lives recoiled from his own bodily destiny. Indeed, he lives recoiled from the Principle in which the body is arising. That Principle is the All-Pervading Radiant Life and Transcendental Consciousness that is the very Condition and Self of all beings.

Unenlightened Man is recoiled from surrender as the body and into the Life-Principle. He is self-possessed, recoiled from Life and even all relationships. He is, unwittingly and even unconsciously, the enemy of the body, and all relationships, and Life itself. He is Narcissus, the separated one, the mind-bearer.

Thus, the human world remains tormented and chaotic, unable to make peace or love. And there is a deep disposition of fear in us that resists the bodily confession of Life. Therefore, human beauty and vitality are always tending to be destroyed, by the fear of bodily death and the inability to surrender bodily to Life.

The civilizations of mankind have to date embraced cultural principles that reflect the universal fear of death and all the self-possessed, self-protective, and separative strategies of conventional consciousness. In the East, the revolt against the body has produced the more or less ascetic ideals of mystical other-worldliness. In the West, that same revolt has produced the ideals of victorious manipulation of the natural realm. In both cases, the revolt and struggle against material and bodily existence is the root of all cultural adaptation. Man revolts against mortality by negatively manipulating his own body and the natural or material realm. Thus, he either separates himself from the body and the world by resorting to the illusory independence of the inner self or mind, or else he dominates the body and the world with an unillumined will to power through knowledge and conventional self-fulfillment.

Even the traditional culture of the West, with its seemingly indomitable will to embrace the worldly play of Nature, has associated itself historically with the ultimately other-worldly cult of Christianity. And no matter how hard Western man tries to "humanize" the religion and person of Jesus, the more or less ascetic, other-worldly, mystical, self-effacing, and body-denying core of that religion remains to complicate the typically self-protecting and world-exploiting tendency of Western-born individuals.

Thus, the West has historically demonstrated an inherently self-divided, self-destructive, and Life-denying disposition by embracing a religious ideal that is, at the root, oriental, or Eastern and ultimately world-renouncing in its character. And conventional religion, in both the East and the West, has thus provided the historical basis or justification for negative cultural programs that recoil from the bodily Life-Principle.

Even so, the Life-Principle is enshrined in the idealisms of Christianity, and Judaism, and Islam, and even certain dimensions of Hinduism, Buddhism, and other oriental religious cultures. It is simply that the implications of the truly human relationship to the Life-Principle have not been consciously acknowledged or implemented in the broad cultural programs of the traditional East or the traditional West. Thus, conventional religious culture or idealism tends to be associated with certain positive moral values (such as truthfulness, honesty, non-stealing, non-killing, and so forth), but traditional religious culture is also always associated with an ultimately negative evaluation of bodily existence and the existence of Man within the realm of Nature. As a result, religious acculturation, East and West, always carries with it taboos against bodily pleasure, sexual intensity, and even the will to live a long and healthful life.

The time has come to transcend our ancient acculturation to the bodily negative recoil from Life. We must transcend the ancient religions and the ancient cultural taboos. We must be enlightened in our understanding of the paradox of human mortality and immortality. Therefore, we must embrace Life bodily and surrender into bodily Communion with the Living Reality. We must throw away all of our bodily negative, anti-sexual, anti-Life adaptations. We must realize a truly regenerative bodily love of Life. It is not that we are to become libertines, but neither are we to become ascetics. We must surrender bodily to Life, via all our actions. We must transcend mortal fear and all of its false religious and social dogmas. We must allow Life to regenerate us in every part, and we must yield to the evolutionary plan and pattern that is hidden in the body and in the play of Nature, and which is not at all contained in the mind (since the mind is only a reflection of previous experience and previous or chronic limitations of knowledge, perception, and presumption). We must transcend ourselves through ecstatic, mind-transcending, bodily love of Life, or direct and whole bodily Communion with the Living God. Only by doing all of this can Man move beyond the present impasse of worldwide conflict and subhuman idealism.

We are at the dead end of the ancient ways, and we are suffering from the inability to move fully into our right, human, and immortal destiny. Only an enlightened and liberated understanding of our old cultural and subhuman presumptions will permit us to yield to Life bodily, in love, and so move on in the Way of God.

I attest to this with every cell of my body. I affirm it with all my heart. I plead with you to consider it fully and resort to a new Way of Life.

231

The Practical Necessity of Wisdom

Experience and knowledge are forms of our conventional or ordinary self-fulfillment. They are not, in general, to be avoided, since they belong to the appropriate stages of our developmental growth. However, we must likewise grow in the more primary sense—in wisdom, love, or spiritual maturity.

     Experience and knowledge, in themselves, contribute to our sense of independence, and they effectively separate us from the processes, relations, beings, or objects by which they are generated. But wisdom, love, or spiritual awakening establishes us again in sublime continuity with all beings, things, processes, and their Single Mystery.

Da Free John

CHAPTER SEVEN

What Is Wisdom?

True Detachment

The pleasure-happiness of living depends on the maintenance of many psycho-physical conditions. If those conditions change or disappear, we react, suffer, struggle, and soon become bewildered until death. Therefore, existence as dependence on the conditions of pleasure-happiness is itself a trap, a torment, and an inevitable failure. We must Awaken to the Wisdom of self-transcending God-Communion and thus transform our participation in the play of experience. In that case, we will presume the disposition of service, surrender, love, tolerance, and transcendence of the effects of experience, while fulfilling the role or conventional obligation to which we are suited or led.

Even so, as we continue to live in the mode of ecstatic God-Communion (or inherence in the Radiant Transcendental Being) we will become more and more profoundly free of the mechanics, motives, and effects of experience. Thus, as the devotee matures he becomes more and more detached and sublimely indifferent to the psycho-physical patterns of experience. And such true detachment or sublime indifference is not the result of mere reactive emotional dissociation, nor is it chronically and outwardly demonstrated as rigid and loveless coolness. Rather, it is a happy and ultimate expression of

Ecstatic Inherence in God and the dissolution of the unenlightened link to the body-mind that enforces the relentless cycle of self-defining, self-limiting, and self-frustrating psycho-physical events. Such indifference is essentially a quality of freedom, not of world-rejection. Indeed, such "indifferent freedom" is, paradoxically, the root of the most creative impulses toward the loving service of the living world of beings.

234

Pleasure and Pain

I t is a natural tendency of embodied adaptation to seek pleasur-able experiences and avoid painful experiences. The Way of Life is a Process wherein both pleasurable and painful experiences (or the natural tendencies and destinies of embodied existence) are transcended, even while association with the round of pleasures and pains yet persists. And that Process is not itself a matter of the strategic avoidance of pleasurable or painful experiences, but it is a matter of the recognition of every moment's experience as a transparent, superficial, or nonbinding modification of the Radiant Transcendental Being.

The Transcendence of Negativity and Unlove

W hen we experience the world in and of itself, we inevi-tably find justification for recoil, negativity, despair, and degenerative self-exploitation. The roots of both asceticism and a faithless ordinary life are in this confrontation with the bare facts of experiential existence. But even if the self-contraction is justified by the conventions of mortal experience, it is immediately undermined by intuitive Realization of the Condition of the world and all experience.

The problem is that our attention tends to be fixed on the world or experience in itself—as a bare fact of awareness. We must resort to a deeper or more direct and intuitive awareness of arising phenomena. The world of experiential fact may appear to be threatening and ultimately futile (and self-contraction is itself nothing more than a reflection or emotional imitation of that appearance), but we are always already in a Condition that transcends mere experience. We are always already or priorly in a transcendental (or experience-transcending and self-transcending) relationship to the factual conventions of experience. That is to say, whatever the limiting facts of present experience, we are primarily and priorly related not to experience but to the Condition in which all experience is arising.

235

We may tend to recoil from the world of experience and toward the self, but that tendency is, in effect, not merely a rejection of experience but a rejection of the Condition in which experience (or the world and the self) inheres. Thus, if that Condition itself (rather than experience in itself) becomes the primary focus of awareness, then the world is transcended and the tendency of recoil is transcended. And, in this manner, the quality of the individual being ceases to be self-bound and becomes one of ecstasy and love.

We are rightly related to the world and all beings only if we are able to transcend the habit of recoil from the world and all beings. Therefore, we are obliged—as a Law of our born existence—to remain awake to the Living Radiance or Mysterious Reality that pervades all phenomena and lives every individual being. Then, as a matter of moment to moment practice, we must transcend that habit of emotional and general psycho-physical recoil from events and - others by intuitively Remembering the Radiant One that is alive as the world and that lives as every being in the world. In this manner, we will find an emotional, mental, and physical cure in every moment of experience. By constantly Remembering and surrendering into the Radiant Reality or Condition or God of the world, we will naturally transcend the specific, limiting, and frequently negative quality of experiences, other beings, and events. Therefore, by such self-transcending or ecstatic Remembrance and surrender we will abide as free attention and love in the world.

All our dissociative emotion relative to experience and other human beings and the world itself is cured by moment to moment resort to the intuitive base of existence, wherein we directly confront the Living Condition or Radiant Transcendental Being wherein all conditions and beings arise and inhere. Thus, by such intuitive Remembrance and ecstatic surrender we become capable of love, or self-transcending and Life-positive participation in the events and encounters of a lifetime. It is neither necessary nor appropriate to love the world in and for itself—or other beings in and for themselves. The qualities of the world and other beings are generally forms of limitation and they are often profoundly negative. But the link between each of us and the world (as well as all other beings) is our native or prior love of the Radiant Condition in which the world and every being are arising, changing, and passing beyond our grasp. Thus, in each moment, we must Realize the One Who is Alive as the conditions and encounters of the present moment, and in every moment of such Realization (or ecstatic Remembrance) we will remain free in love, or free feeling-attention, relative to whatever aspect of the world or other beings is presently before us. And by remaining thus Life-positive, free, and feeling in our response to the world and to others, we will be able to participate creatively in the school of this world. Then, whatever arises in any moment, we will remain happy in the single eternal Encounter that is our only ultimate Destiny.

What Is Wisdom?

Experience limits, defines, and compresses the being. Experience is a contraction of the body-mind. Experience is a limiting condition on the being. Experience is a contraction or suppression of the being. Therefore, all experience is a form of stress, or psycho-physical tension.

For this reason, the longer we live, or the more experience we accumulate, the more our behavior tends to become an effort to relieve ourselves of stressful tension. Therefore, the usual individual degenerates over time, because of the effects of stressful and self-indulgent habits that represent attempts to be relieved of stress.

But all our action to relieve stress in this realm of psycho-physical experience is nothing other than an effort to relieve ourselves of experience itself. We deceive ourselves if we presume that one or another complex condition is binding us with suppressive stress. <u>All</u> our experience is a binding or self-limiting force. This is not a merely negative fact. It is a presumption by which all wisdom is generated.

If we presume that particular experiences are the basic cause of stress, then our lives will become bound either to the suffering of those experiences or else to patterns of effort that are themselves stressful and degenerative but that seek release or escape from the conditions or experiences that we originally presumed to be the causes of our suffering. In either case, the body-mind is corrupted by the confrontation with stressful experiences.

Therefore, we must understand experience itself, or else we will never be truly free. And if we observe and understand experience, we see that stress, tension, the sense of suppression, or a limiting compressive force on the being is <u>always</u> an essential component of every moment of psycho-physical experience. There is no experience that can be attained that is inherently free of the limiting conditional force that we identify as painful stress. We may pursue and attain an experience that temporarily distracts us from some present condition of painful stress, but in another moment the very experience that was first felt as relief becomes a limitation.

What wisdom shines in this understanding? Simply this: The confrontation with experience is <u>inherently</u> binding, self-limiting, or stress-inducing, and this indicates that the process wherein we realize freedom is not in the realm or pursuit of experience itself but in the dimension of the transcendence of experience.

True wisdom implies a self-transcending participation in the conditions of experience. The native motive of self-transcendence is the law revealed to us by experience itself. Experience and knowledge are not the basic purpose of our existence. Rather, we are mysteriously involved in a process of conditional experience in which we are inherently and constantly obliged either to transcend ourselves or be corrupted and destroyed.

Those who will not establish themselves in the wisdom or true intelligence of the being are obliged to suffer their lifetime of experience, bound to the conditional self-limits of their circumstances, and otherwise striving for release through desperate programs of degenerative self-indulgence and all the fitful politics whereby human beings seek to dominate and perfect their circumstances in the Realm of Nature. But if true wisdom awakens, then our commitment ceases to be directed merely to experience itself, but to the process of self-transcendence (or moment to moment liberation from experiential confinement) in the midst of the arising play of conditional experience.

238

Once we are awakened to the wisdom of a self-transcending or ecstatic practice in relationship to the process of experience, then we gradually cease to indulge the automaticities of stress, self-indulgence, and exaggerated efforts to know and to accomplish and to be overwhelmingly powerful in the world. We do not, however, turn upon ourselves and away from the relational patterns of experience. Rather, we simply feel through and beyond the stress of events—we recognize the component of self-binding contraction in every moment of experience and transcend that compressive force in direct relaxation of the patterns arising in the body-mind.

This wisdom is the intuitive essence of spiritual practice, which transcends all attachment to experiential conditions of body, emotion, mind, and psyche. The process in practice must be realized as a complete culture of existence, and that culture or Way of Life is learned by testing and instruction in the Company and the community of the Wise.

Stress Chemistry and Whole Bodily Enlightenment

A talk by Da Free John

I   239

DA FREE JOHN: We live under stress, in a subhuman culture whose populace is completely confused even in the
most elemental levels of existence. We are all involved in an animal-
like struggle for survival, without much intelligence even at the level
of the verbal mind. Such a circumstance tends to stimulate a chemical
profusion in the body that enables it to function and survive under
stress, but that chemical design does not allow the higher psychic and
subtle centers of the body-mind to awaken. On the contrary, this
stress chemistry triggers the degenerative processes of aging as well
as all other forms of bodily degeneration, and this same stress
chemistry is generally empty of the profound genetic signals that can
trigger the higher evolutionary functions of Man.

In response to the stress of the usual worldly life, practitioners
of traditional mysticism and yoga found ways to evolve into the
consciousness of the higher states of mind, particularly those
awakened in the right hemisphere of the brain. These practitioners
commonly went out into the wilderness and used esoteric "tricks,"
such as fasting, prayer, and techniques of brain-stimulating
meditation, to encourage the body not only to stop producing the
chemistry of stress, anger, sexual desire, and fear, but to start
producing another and superior kind of chemistry. They were thus
able to awaken certain aspects of the brain that will be naturally and
commonly awake only in the future evolutionary stages of mankind.

Until we have created a human order that is fundamentally
free of mutual threat, it will not be common for people to live in a
truly awakened and peaceful state, not only of mind, but of body (or
the total body-mind). The body-mind must receive the signals that
the stressful world has been overcome, that we need not fear, that we

presently have a peaceful human society, not a society full of bombs and benighted craziness. The evolutionary mechanism of the bodily being is programmed to awaken its next higher centers of function only when the chronic problems of its lower functional centers have been solved and when the being can live without chronically creating degenerative stress chemistry. You can perhaps make yourself more comfortable by becoming free of some of the anxiety of your ordinary daily life, but you cannot thus become so peaceful that the right hemisphere of the brain and the higher evolutionary mechanisms of the body-mind as a whole are stimulated. To enter into your higher human destiny, you must be altogether "cured" in your deep psychic heart.

240

Basically, the human race is yet functioning within the realm of the threatened existence of beings who are eaten by other beings. We stressfully and chronically ·continue to animate the urge to reproduce, because we feel that everybody is in danger of being eaten! We feel, bodily, that everyone is prey to someone else. In fact, we continually witness the drama of hunter and prey all over the world. Listen to the daily news! People are being killed all over the Earth every day—simply murdered in weird personal and social or political conflicts. Such a dreadful circumstance is a natural part of the unevolved and lower state of Man. Everybody asks, "Why are we doing this?" But no broad social and political agency has come up with any reason to stop doing it! We could just as easily change our circumstances. Why don't we just change them then? It is because the animal still lives in our hormones, you see. Our bodily chemistry is yet stimulating us to live like the vital-elemental creature. Thus, we must have conflicts and opponents. We must eat and be devoured ourselves.

Certainly, we would like the quality of our existence to be different. But people in general are not yet moving toward anything significantly different. Thus, the would-be human world is yet a lower-adapted, subhuman world. Perhaps some people are more highly evolved—people who can live an apparently moral, ecstatic, or spiritually devoted life—but they are not common. Most people are fixed in their adaptation to living under stress, and they do not know enough to create human and spiritual sanctuary for themselves.

To create a human sanctuary for higher adaptation and the ultimate transcendence of Man is a true urge, even the primal human urge. We inherently desire a human and natural environment in which we can live without the chronic production of stress chemistry. We want to be cured at the heart of our mind and thereby transformed bodily. And we know, deeply, psychically, that we cannot realize that transformation until we can create a culture in which people can live without degenerative stress. Thus, sanctuary, or spiritual community, is the motive in Man that contains the genetic secret of the next stage in human evolution.

241

We do not live a life of love and blissfulness and peace and harmony, in which the basic requirements of ordinary physical and social life are mutually granted. Yet, such is the state of evolution or adaptation that mankind must enjoy in order to experience spiritual and bodily bliss both significantly and continuously. And it will not be natural or common for people in general to exist in such a condition, until the human world is profoundly changed in a very practical way.

This consideration of chronic stress, or confinement to lower adaptation, is not simply a negative criticism of the way we tend to live; it is also, unfortunately, a description of the way most of us must live at the present time. We must be stressful, politically and socially, to protect the world and our own lives and families and communities from the profoundly chaotic madness of this subhuman global society. We are all struggling. We all have our eyes on what happens in the daily world, in the news. Thus, we cannot exist in anything like a blissful condition all the time—and, truly, except in the case of profoundly creative spiritual practice, we cannot enjoy the higher bliss of Man even some of the time.

Because we believe that we are not easily surviving, that we are indeed under constant mortal threat, we die early. We think it is extraordinary to live to the age of seventy or eighty. Our expected life span is better than it was even a few decades ago, but, even so, our lifetime is no time at all. And we live under stress the whole time! Very little tends to be accomplished in such a span. Therefore, we are always dropping the body and having to begin again. You must find the ways to overcome the stresses of lower adaptation, to transform the chemistry of the body-mind literally, so that you can live your daily life without personal, social, cultural, and chemical stress. Such a life is not possible for a group of people until they manage to create sanctuary with one another—a mutually protected, stable, basically unthreatened way of life.

"We are threatened!" is the message of the news. It reminds us of our chronic situation. The theatre of the news is all about people who are threatening one another, either with terrible violence or with just plain social nastiness, exploiting one another to death. We constantly reinforce loveless society in our associations with one another. We teach each other and we pass on to our children all the techniques for living as a stressful personality. We believe bodily, stressfully, that our life cannot, even should not, be long, that it is not good to be alive in the body, that we are only supposed to go elsewhere. We have all these ideas that are Life-negative in bodily terms, but the ultimate way of Enlightenment is to become Life-positive in bodily terms, which is just the reverse of what we are tending to do. Human beings are living way down at the bottom of their evolutionary potential. Nevertheless, if you can personally, and with a few others, grasp the higher realities of the mechanisms in which you live, then you can practice a Way of life that stimulates and develops those higher factors. You must have sanctuary, a relatively protected world, in which to do that, because, if you are going to rise above the civilization of the daily news, you must live in a way that is superior to the way that people in general tend to live.

II

DA FREE JOHN: How, then, will you come to that point of feeling totally without anxiety, without fear, without any of the ordinary mortal consciousness in the midst of your daily life? How will you transcend that fear so that you can truly develop the mystical and ultimate spiritual phenomena that I have described, and that are effects of the stimulation of the right side of the brain and the deep totality of the body-mind? You can have a taste of those phenomena through suspension of attention in the lower psycho-physical centers while you are still under stress. But you cannot generate such phenomena to the point that they become the principal forms of your consciousness until you overcome the lower evolutionary dimension of the body-mind, which is oriented to a life of physical distress and the struggle to survive bodily without higher consciousness. You cannot rest naturally in a higher realm of consciousness until you are able to manage the stresses of your daily life—including the stress of feeling that you are mortal, that perhaps when you die you are just plain dead. Until you enjoy a greater consciousness, you can never be certain about the matter of your death, you see.

When we first become involved in the possibility of spiritual life, we tend to want to "turn within," because, physically, we are under stress. The first dimension of higher human realization is indeed mental, subtle, subjective, astral; it is realized to be "within" in a certain sense. But there is a higher or greater level of Realization, or true Enlightenment. Such is whole bodily Enlightenment, in which the mind is transcended and the body is realized to be simply Energy and Consciousness.

Can you feel that the body is only free energy right now? You can feel a tension, an urge to want to hold something in at your heart. But that is just your stress, you see, your reluctance to relax, your suppression of radiance, of love, of profuse happiness. Let that contraction go, and you will feel the whole body radiate. The body is energy. An aspect of it appears to be solid, but it is only a certain frequency of vibration. There exist many higher and many lower vibrations of the being. Beyond a certain point in this great spectrum of vibrations we lose the visibility of God, we lose track of the depth of Infinity, because our physical stress attunes us only to this limited vibration of apparent matter. But if we relax the stress, then we can feel that energy and the physical body are the same.

The question is, how do you learn to persist as energy all the time? You must develop the capacity to stimulate the blissful sensation that the right side of the brain feels in its conventional transcendence of the physical dimension of existence. Why should you not exist with such good feeling? Why should not that bliss be what human life is all about? You certainly should be in at least such a state, but you must learn how to adapt to it physically. The body must naturally produce the higher chemistry of blissful radiance.

The play of energy that appears in our daily world is a play on the threat of death. The ordinary games of energy force the body to retain a subhuman level of chemical awareness, the lower-adapting chemistry that is expressed in the left side of the brain. The right side of the brain remains, for the most part, negative, inert, not consciously active. Thus, until you learn how to transcend the stress of this world, you cannot seem to be blissful without using some artificial and degenerative means. Even yoga, mysticism, and all the rest of the methodology of esoteric self-effort are just as artificial to the body as drugs. They are simply ways of "tricking" or deliberately stimulating parts of the brain-mind. The only difference between taking a drug and performing yogic disciplines is that the blissful bodily and psychic state attained through yoga is realized through the native capacity of the body-mind itself. Thus, such bliss can eventually become natural and permanent, making all effort obsolete.

244

At present, however, you do not know how to function in the world and to be blissful at the same time. You are distracted from bliss by stressful attitudes and games of survival. Your creative being is asleep—not only mentally, but also physically. You can still feel yourself tightening up your chest and solar plexus, can't you? You have learned to live with that constriction. What do you think that constriction is doing? It is turning off the more subtle chemistry and turning on the gross chemistry that keeps you fastened in stressful survival games, such as chronic sex obsession. What do you think generates this intense sex drive? A hormonal signal in the body constantly urges you to reproduce, because human bodily life is so profoundly threatened. In other words, stress chemistry keeps us profoundly attached to sex. That stress chemistry maintains the urge of the body to reproduce without fail, independent of our consciousness or intention, and that chemistry is being stimulated all the time.

Truly human sexuality is not a matter of tolerating the constant stress of sexual desiring and anxiety. Truly human sexuality is a matter of coming to the point bodily, not just sexually, but altogether, of not living under the Life-negative emotional stress of the erotic. Eroticism is an expression of threatened or Life-negative bodily chemistry. Erotic fascination stimulates our reproductive drive and thus our stress-reinforcing chemistry. Eroticism is related to the chronic and stressful urge to orgasm, which is an expression of bodily chemistry that is vitally important for producing children, but that does not enlighten you. Therefore, you must create another chemistry, higher or more subtle than the one that moves you to orgasm, in order for the body to become blissful. Only when the Life-

Current is inverted, or polarized toe to crown, rather than crown to toe (as in the degenerative display of conventional orgasm), is the higher-adapting activity of the brain stimulated. Therefore, if you keep the chronic emotional and physical stress of sex in your life, then you are always working against the benign transformation that must ultimately be initiated in the higher brain. Sex and emotion must become free of stress, but very few in the modern world show the signs of living without emotional-sexual stress. Our entire lives tend to be expressions of such emotional-sexual stress—not only in the problems we have in our actual personal sexual intimacy, but in the stressfulness of being promiscuously and constantly driven by emotional reactivity and sexual obsession or mere sexual desire itself.

Besides sex, there is also the stressful chemistry of digestion and the entire obsessive ritual of food—the threat that you will not get enough to eat, that you will not be fed, that you will not be permitted to breathe, that you will be snuffed out. There is the stress of all the games of worldly life—of money, food, and sex. This stressful, threatened consciousness is the frenzy in which you always tend to function. You cannot afford to be blissful. That is the truth of it. That is what this evolutionary trigger in the brain is revealing to you under stress. You may feel good for a moment now and then, but you have not learned how to adapt to the point of enjoying the highest level of feeling in the body-mind and at the same time functioning effectively and sanely in ordinary life. There are too many things that you must take into account in your daily life. You must be under stress. You must protect yourself. Survival is your impulse. That is the reason you feel depressed, and that is the reason you are struggling for life. And you will continue struggling until you have conquered the game of the world at this ordinary level of money, food, and sex.

Presently, most people can enjoy a relatively blissful condition of experience only in extreme circumstances, such as when under the influence of an intoxicating stimulant or some profound outward success. But if you were literally dying at this moment, you would become a mystic so fast it would amaze you. That is what happens, you see. That is what death involves: the passing of attention upwards via the sensory currents into the right hemisphere of the brain, and then into the separable astral being, the subtle body of manifest energy. This mechanism is the source of all those experiences that people report when they have been clinically dead for a period of time and have then come back to physical consciousness and the downward-outward motor impulses of the left hemisphere of the brain. The extraordinary experiences reported in such cases are basically phenomena of the right hemisphere of the brain, where the sensory currents are collected upwardly and inwardly, permitting temporary identification with the astral or subtle dimension of the body-mind without yet requiring permanent dissociation from the physical body. Even so, once ordinary physical consciousness resumes, the suddenly awakened higher consciousness generally goes to sleep again, just as we forget to dream once we awaken to the gross physical world. Therefore, people who have "died" and then revived report this remarkable experience they once had—they usually talk about it for the rest of their lives—but they generally never have anything like the same experience again, until they actually die. At death, then, this profound change in the brain-mind occurs, and it throws the being into the astral body, or "star body." However, yet possessing the accumulated tendencies toward the stressful experience of lower adaptation, the subtle individual is eventually reborn, reassociated with this vital-elemental plane of possibility. Thus, we continue to be reborn under stress until we evolve beyond this realm of experience.

The whole affair of birth and experience and death is primarily a matter of the evolutionary physiological transformation of the body. It is not principally an affair of the soul, or the inwardly conscious being, separate from the body. The soul is the body at this moment. When you lose this body, you will immediately attain another one of some kind. You always have a body, until you dissolve in God. The body, not the soul apart from the body, is the mechanism of evolution. The soul simply becomes more and more conscious and ecstatic via various kinds of embodiment. The soul is gradually transformed, eventually becoming Radiant to Infinity. The soul acquires all the faculties of God through ecstatic surrender, and it acquires a more and more Divine body. Such a Divine body is a body of Light, created from the transformation of the physical into Light, or Radiant Consciousness. That transformation is like an atomic explosion. It is not a matter of abandoning the physical, but of disintegrating the physical through the identification of the physical (or "matter") with Energy and Consciousness. Such disintegration or dissolution of the body-mind in Transcendental Light and Consciousness is the secret of Enlightenment.

How are you going to become aligned to that ultimate process? In order to realize the degree of freedom from fear that it requires, you must conquer the little fear that is causing stress in your daily life. Like everyone else, you are afraid of death, and you are obsessed with food and sex and every kind of self-fulfillment. You are aligned only to the physical level of survival, so you do not have the bodily sensation and subtlety necessary for higher consciousness. You cannot become Divinely intoxicated, you cannot become Enlightened, until you can simply live a happy, ordinary, human life, free of these obsessions—the fear obsession, the food obsession, the sex obsession. Therefore, we must transcend our subhuman adaptation to food and sex as stressful mechanisms of survival. We must signal the body that it need not constantly gorge itself nor reproduce in thousands or in millions in order for the species to survive. The body must feel that it is alive with Divine Life itself, with basically no inherent problems, or obstructions to Life. That is why it is also important that we learn all about health and longevity. We must turn off the stress mechanisms that are threatened by death. We must overcome the fear of death.

All of this means that you must simply let death happen. Now you feel the threat of death in every moment. If you yield to it, you will find the body acting differently. At some time you will also literally and physically die, but you must die in every moment, as it is said in all the Scriptures. Death must happen in every moment, for me and for everyone. It is not that you must try to work on your fear of death. In that case you conceive yourself to be other than your fear. Do not work on the fear of death. Simply die. You are presently threatened. You have the fear already. You are already reacting to the possibility of death. Thus, you need only yield, even bodily, and relax beyond fear. That yielding in the body signals the physical being that it is unqualifiedly alive, and so the body will begin to function at a higher evolutionary level. To surrender in every moment, even to the degree of permitting death, is thus the highest of the traditional spiritual disciplines. It is self-transcendence, ecstatic love of the Living God, Divine Communion. We must constantly fall into Life without resistance to death. In such surrender we do not stressfully overcome fear or even wonder or think about death.

III

248

D A FREE JOHN: We must discover all the ways whereby we can minimize and eliminate the stress factors in the body's chemistry. Our spiritual task must be understood in just these physiological terms. You must understand that the processes involved in the ultimate affair of esoteric religion and spirituality are fundamentally a physiological, biological, and evolutionary matter. True religious life is not devoted to all the cosmological and mythological nonsense through which popular religion is communicated in the world in general. Religion is a psycho-physical matter, fundamentally.

As a human being, you are always basically dealing with the structures of your own body-mind, your brain, your nervous system. Therefore, whatever you call religion should be examined in terms of what it does to your brain, your nervous system, your emotional state, and your body itself. Religion is a specific activity which, if it is actually practiced, transforms you into a benign personality. If you are not in this moment a benign personality, you are not practicing religion. You are only consoling yourself in some conventional fashion. If you are not becoming a more radiant, loving, benign, happy person, you are not practicing religion. If you are not bringing order to your life, if you are not becoming tranquil and more capable of existing in a higher, pleasurable state, then you are not practicing religion, because religion is about literally transforming the body-mind in the process of love-surrender to the Living Divine.

Therefore, we must judge our religion in psycho-physiological terms, in factual terms, real, actual, living, human terms. That is how you tell the difference between true teachers or prophets or practitioners and mere believers. What is their quality of existence? What do they do? If you see people practicing some religious path and they look happy, and they are healthy, and they are sane, and they are also intelligent, and their experience is real and also extraordinary, then naturally they are attractive and there is value in listening to them and talking to them. They must be doing something appropriate at some level if they are in such a good state. But if you see a group of crazy fanatical people, who call themselves true believers but who have no clarity, no humanity, no love, no ability to inspect and transcend themselves, then you can know that, whatever they are doing, they are not practicing anything more profound than mechanically feeling their own insides or mumbling the usual belief in the Myth of Jesus. They are performing a very modest physiological trick with their religion, whereas we must associate with people who are performing extraordinary physiological tricks with their religion!

249

Anatomists can now identify many of the key physiological factors in this affair of converting the degenerative pattern of stress chemistry into the regenerative, transformative, blissful chemistry of spiritual ecstasy. For instance, the thymus gland, in the upper center of the chest, is directly related to the subtle or astral heart, or what has traditionally been called the "heart chakra."[1] The thymus gland is a primary key to the whole body's response to stress. If the thymus is weak and contracted, we feel a physical contraction in the heart and the solar plexus, even throughout the entire body, and we are afraid. The depressed thymus gland secretes a chemical message that triggers all the rest of the glands of the body into a Life-negative, contractive pattern. It triggers the total body to react to stress, to attempt to survive, to reproduce endlessly, to struggle for food, to

---

1. The "heart chakra" is the "spiritual heart" described in mystical traditions throughout the world. "Chakra" literally means "wheel" or "circle." The term refers to the internal centers of the body-mind, commonly symbolized as lotus flowers, through which the awakened life-force flows, producing various phenomena in life, body, and consciousness. The chakras are associated with but not exclusively identical to the various ganglia of the nervous system, and the various endocrine glands of the body and brain.

In *The Enlightenment of the Whole Body* (pages 406-407) Da Free John describes the "heart chakra" or "middle heart" as follows:

The middle section of the physical heart corresponds to the general realm of functions in the midsection of the body—including the physical heart itself, and the lungs—or the blood circulating and breathing cycles. In itself, the middle section of the heart is the "anahata chakra," the wheel of the psyche. It also corresponds to the creative dimension of life and consciousness, associated with the sex organs (and the "swadhishthana chakra"), the hands, and the brain core (or "ajna chakra").

The middle section of the heart lies directly behind the median of the chest. And the state of consciousness associated with the middle section of the heart is the "dreaming" state, including both the subconscious mind (associated with the emotional-sexual functions, below the heart), and the superconscious mind (associated with the superconscious functions in the brain core). It is the realm of dreams and subtle visions, or subtle knowledge, both low and high in the scale of Nature. This state of consciousness is felt to be associated with the central region of the heart, because it is actually associated with the middle section of the heart.

continue to kill, and to animate the distress of all the rest of our vital and elemental motives.

This stress mechanism in the heart equips us with negative, reactive emotions. Conventionally, therefore, we associate the heart with emotion. Heart-stress triggers the limbic system—the structures in the brain concerned with emotion and visceral responses—and the other mechanisms of the brain core that relate to stress. Then the body itself receives all the signals that call for stressful reactions. Thus, under stress, we are always ready with anger for self-defense and attack, lust for reproduction, and cravings of all kinds, and we are continually subject to sorrow and fear and guilt and shame.

Since all of this is so, the thymus gland must become the generative center of a new and Life-positive response to the conditions of existence. You must get your heart to function differently. You must awaken to the fourth or psychically awakened stage of life,[2] wherein the heart or deep psyche is naturally free of the reactive patterns that cause the stress-signalling biochemical secretions of the thymus gland and all the other parts of the endocrine system. You must realize the disposition of the heart that is in its native state, free of the chronic tendency toward reactive

---

2. In *The Enlightenment of the Whole Body* (page 403), Da Free John describes the fourth stage of life as follows:

In the fourth stage of life, the purpose of adaptation is to gain positive control over the unconscious and lower subconscious motivations that create the conventional patterns and phases of gross physical and mental (or psychological) behavior, desire, emotion, thought, and will. Thus, the processes in the fourth stage of life purify, harmonize, and positively transform the fixed, self-possessed, and self-divided behavioral patterns of the unconscious and lower subconscious dimensions of the body-mind.

The means of this evolutionary procedure are spiritual. That is, the extended body-mind (controlled by the autonomic nervous system and the unconscious and lower subconscious tendencies of the bodily being) is consciously submitted to the Transcendental Reality and made to be obedient to the Law of sacrifice, or love, in the pattern of all relationships.

The submission of the body-mind to the Transcendental Reality, or the Divine Person, is a matter of aligning the gross body-mind (or active feeling-attention) to the All-Pervading Life-Current, which is directly communicated to the central or cerebrospinal nervous system. Thus, in the fourth stage of life, the fixed association of the Radiant Transcendental Consciousness with the extended body-mind, the unconscious and lower subconscious mind, the superficial conscious mind, and the dual or dynamic patterns of the autonomic nervous system is transcended. The Radiant Transcendental Consciousness, communicated via the cerebrospinal nervous system, is permitted to Master, purify, harmonize, and positively transform the gross dimension or lower coil of the human body-mind.

The fourth stage of life is the true and critical beginning of fully human and spiritual life. It is the beginning of literal functional and psychic submission of the extended body-mind to its own root-processes and its Transcendental Source or Divine Condition.

emotions. Then you can live in the Life-positive emotion of love, or natural, whole bodily radiance. You accomplish or realize this transformation in the fourth stage of life, so that you can then enter into the fifth stage of life equipped with a higher chemical advantage that stimulates bodily blissfulness, interior or astral forms of perception, psychic capabilities, extrasensory perception, and the like.

We must adapt and evolve in our yogic and mystical use of the right hemisphere of the brain, as well as in our verbal-conceptual use of the left hemisphere. But we must ultimately evolve beyond Man. Thus, we have to do more than evolve mystically, you see. We must realize the Energy itself of which we are now composed. We must release ourselves into the Condition of Energy. We must transform even the physical body into Light, through surrender, through relaxation into and beyond fear, into and beyond the threat of non-existence. We must be Enlightened bodily. The final stage of Enlightenment is the Translation of the body into pure Energy, or the Realization that the body is identical to Infinite Energy, fundamental Energy, the White Energy, the Transparent Energy, the Radiant Form that is identical to Consciousness itself, the Living God. We are destined to Realize and thus become Translated into that very Identity. We are more and more profoundly transformed in the midst of the process that leads toward Radiant Transfiguration and Translation, and in the ultimate moment of literal bodily Translation into Light we become perfectly identified with the Absolute Energy of the Room, the Domain, the Transcendental Being, the Divine Person in Whom the entire manifest universe is appearing.

What destiny lies beyond that? It is beyond comprehension. We realize so much that is extraordinary long before such Bodily Translation. Therefore, so much of what you may now imagine to be Enlightenment is really just a moment on the Way. The explosion that occurs when the physical body is Translated into Light is larger than the universe. No single individual may attain such Translation while alive without destroying the universe. Therefore, the attainment is secret, a matter of esoteric Realization in a state of Transfigured Bliss. The devotee in the final stage of Enlightenment is a Paradox in the Realm of Nature. He is exploded, and yet everything appears to continue.

251

QUESTIONER: Does this consideration relate to the present level of our understanding of nuclear energy—nuclear bombs and atomic fission?

DA FREE JOHN: Yes. The splitting of the atom is an expression of the law involved in Bodily Translation, or the Translation of matter into energy. The considerations of natural science have not yet understood the human implications of nuclear processes, and mankind has not yet adapted psychically to the level of understanding implicit in the practical theories of modern physics. We have not developed a real human, cultural and bodily sensitivity to the atom and its potential, and so it is frightening, you see. Truly, however, the explosion of the atom is our own future. We must split the atom in our own person. Man, in the form of every individual, must enter into the space of the atom, even as now we enter bodily into the outer space where Earth and all the stars are mysteriously moving.

If each of us could exist at a level of energy equivalent to that of an atomic explosion, we would be altogether different people! Now we are all short-lived, like five-watt light bulbs. The wind comes up and we collapse. We are wasting time in the unconscious recycling of ourselves from life to life, instead of deciding to opt for what is true of us and creatively determining a life in which we can live the Enlightened existence of both the mind and the body. Those who are involved in spiritual techniques of one or another kind are generally looking toward the enlightenment of the mind. The traditions of that search and its techniques are very old. But the most ancient spiritual tradition is the one that leads to Bodily Enlightenment, which is beyond ordinary psychic comprehension and beyond the next higher stage of psychic and mystical evolution. The possibilities we represent are immense.

The body is the last principle, and it is also the vehicle, of the entire process. All of the levels of Enlightenment are realized bodily in some fundamental sense. The bodily being is even now identical to Light, but it seems to be present in a state in which it is not yet awake and functioning as Light. It is still differentiated from Light in its apparent existence as "matter." Thus, the urge in us, based on what we are fundamentally, or atomically, is to transcend the differentiation of the self, of the mind, and of the body from Light. This is Realized through direct and radical psycho-physical

Translation of all that we seem to be into the Realm of Perfect Light. All limits must be transcended. We must die completely, but we must die into the Light, not away from Light into the unconsciousness of ordinary bodily death. We must give ourselves up to the Life-Principle from the deep psyche or heart.

The Condition of Dissolution in Light is a latent disposition in our own nervous system, in our own endocrine system. It is potential in every part of the body. All the cells are ultimately moving toward Illumination and Translation. We must cooperate with that native disposition of the body, of the cells. If the cells are put to another task, then we postpone true Enlightenment. Therefore, we must stop living under stress. We can feel a little yogic or mystical energy for a moment, but we cannot enjoy it continuously, we cannot be alive, until we awaken to the Divine Radiance of Life. We must create the conditions wherein to realize such Energy and Consciousness. Now we are wasting our potential in fretting, wasting our lives in stress. We are doing nothing but getting older. Even if we are staying essentially healthy, we are still just getting older. In other words, we are not evolving. But if we are ever to Realize the Ultimate Divine Enlightenment that is our true Destiny, then we must change our lives, evolve, and become capable of the Translation of the very body into the Light beyond all knowing.

253

Action without Stress or Concern

Intense physical endeavor tends to be generated and accompanied by internal stress. The secret of free action, then, is to transcend the component of stress, or internal contraction and concern, in the midst of every activity. Thus, the devotee of the Living God abides constantly in the attitude of heartfelt Divine Communion and relational surrender while engaging whole-heartedly and energetically in every form of appropriate activity.

Transcendence of Attention Is Ecstasy

254

Ecstasy is in the transcendence of attention, or the transcendence of the conventional or binding implications of experience or relational conditions. The gesture of attention establishes both the primary sense of relationship and the primary presumption of independent subjectivity (or the implied self that perceives or conceives the objects of attention). The independent self (the subject of attention) becomes the binding post of individual existence once fear and frustration motivate the mechanism of recoil in the midst of experience. In that event, the objects and relations of experience (or attention) become secondary to the subject, and the complex patterns of subjectivity and recoil from the patterns of relationship begin to be established.

The Way of Life is founded upon ecstasy, or transcendence of the separative or independent self and its habits of recoil, contraction, or the avoidance of relationship. Therefore, the Way of Life is founded upon that insight or sympathy which natively transcends the simple gesture of attention, whereby both "self" and "object" arise as basic and opposing conceptions, or primary and simultaneous modifications of the prior, unconditional, Divine Self.

God-Realization Is the Transcendence of Experience

The processes of conventional religious mysticism and esoteric yoga can ultimately be analyzed and reduced to a conditional psycho-physical description. Such processes belong entirely to the egoic realm of the manifest body-mind. They do not lead to God, nor are they inherently spiritual (or Spirit-Realizing), since God, or the Divine Spirit, is Transcendental and Absolute. Truly, the extraordinary phenomena of conventional religious mysticism and esoteric yoga belong to the realm of higher human evolution within the Cosmic Sphere or Realm of the Machine of Nature, not to the Realm of God-Realization. (Such phenomena are not to be strategically prevented or indiscriminately avoided, since human growth is appropriate to our form of birth, but they must be critically understood, and we must discriminate between the persuasions and paths of conventional religious mysticism, or esoteric yoga, and the Wisdom or Way of Transcendental God-Realization.)

The Transcendental Way of God-Realization is neither evolutionary nor self-fulfilling. It is founded on the intuition or native motive of Ecstasy, or self-transcendence. It is a matter of the easeful and heartfelt surrender of body and mind, or all the conditions of experience, in every moment. The practice transcends all the experiential and evolutionary significance or content of even our most extraordinary sensations, perceptions, and conceptions. And those who are devoted to such practice transcend all the senses of physical and mental (or psychic) self-existence. They Realize that we are not souls born into the body-mind—we do not inhere in our psycho-physical conditions—but we Inhere or Eternally Abide as undifferentiated Bliss in the Infinite Transcendental Radiance of the Divine Being.

True Wisdom is the capacity for perfect madness. Therefore, only the practice of love has the capacity to keep the Wise sane. And only they can love who have been set free of every humorless intent by the intuition of Infinite Life.

Da Free John

CHAPTER EIGHT

The Transcendental Vision

The Ultimate Truth
of All Religions

True religious "faith" is simply the awakened intuition of the Living Spirit of God.

The secret of religious faith, or the Spiritual Realization of the Living God, is not any logical or illogical belief, nor any strategy of mystical self-manipulation, nor any knowledge about the interior or the exterior domain of Man. Rather, the secret of the awakening of the intuition of the Living God is simply to be <u>present</u> when the Revelation of the Living God is made.

But the Revelation of the Living God is not a final or once-and-for-all historical event. The Revelation of the Living God is taking place in every moment, to everyone, and everywhere in space.

The Living God is simply and eternally Present. The Living God is Self-Revealing, or always Shown. The problem is that human individuals are not themselves always or profoundly <u>present</u> to the Living Reality. Human individuals are commonly involved in a chaos of self-conscious motives and self-possessed distractions. Therefore, if we fail to be intuitively and directly present to the moment to moment Revelation of the Living God, we will also fail to be truly religious or Spiritual in our understanding of human existence and our participation in the higher Way of Man.

God is eternally moved to be Present to the world and every being, because God is not other than the Living Spirit, the All-Pervading Current of Life and the very Consciousness in which all manifest conditions and all beings are arising, changing, and passing beyond all worldly knowing. Therefore, Man is obliged to be constantly present to the Presence of the Living God. And the Way in which we may be present to the Divine Presence is the whole bodily Way of heartfelt, mind-transcending, and direct and breathing bodily Communion with the Radiant Current of Life, Love, and Transcendental Consciousness.

Such is the eternal, true, mature, and esoteric religion of Man. And all temporal, specific, or historical revelations of this Truth, via the words and experiential conceptions of any individuals whatsoever, are only inspirational and more or less reliable guides to our own present religious and Spiritual practice of Transcendental God-Communion.

Where Is Space, a Thought, a Person, or a Thing?

God is not within us. (But we are within God.) God is not identical to our independent subjectivity, nor is God found by means of the mysticism of our egoic and separative inwardness.

Neither is God outside us. (But we tend to presume we are separate and independent from God.) God is not a separate Self, an Other Being, Elsewhere, arbitrarily manipulating the robot beings who live and die in the Realm of Nature. Nor is God found by any knowledge or any self-fulfilling efforts in the play of our outward experience.

God is the One in Whom we and the total world inhere. God is the Transcendental Being in Whom the entire Realm of Nature is constantly and mysteriously arising, changing, and passing away. And

God is found only in Transcendental Ecstasy, or the constant practice of heartfelt surrender of body and mind into the dependent position and self-yielding mood of simple and easeful inherence in the Infinitely Radiant Transcendental Being.

Everything, Everyone, Anything, Anyone, Something, Someone, Nothing, and No one all appear in the Absolute Perfect Fullness of the Radiant Transcendental Being.

The Person of Love

The entire world, visible and invisible, gross and subtle, is the Body of God, and even one's own body inheres in That Body.

All that we can have in mind inheres in the Mind of God, and the very Being of God is That in which one's own essential being inheres.

No matter what one may do, there is no accumulation of changes in this world that would make a Paradise, since the possibilities of suffering and death would always be greater and more powerful than the summary of any moment's tentative pleasure.

No matter what one may come to experience and know about the internal and external domains of awareness, there is no possible accumulation of experience or knowledge that could exceed or overwhelm the Unanswerable Mystery of the Fact of Existence.

No matter how deeply one may enter into the Current of one's own inner being, there is no greater Bliss or Joy than the Ecstasy of surrender into the Radiant Transcendental Being or Person wherein the world, and the body, and all relations, and the mind, and the inner being are arising.

Whatever the world, or experience, or existence may seem to be, that seeming is merely a state or presumption that is determined and conditioned and limited by the body-mind.

However much of many, or other, or mine, or fear, or sorrow, or doubt, or anger, or desire, or separation of me appears—all of it is nothing more than an apparent condition of the body-mind in itself.

But the body-mind is only a convention of experience, a temporary condition in space-time, whereas the body-mind and space-time always inhere in the Radiant Divine Being.

Therefore, we must not permit ourselves to be disheartened by the world, or by physical mortality, or by experience, or by knowledge, or by thought, or even by the emptiness of our internal seclusion. The total psycho-physical being must remain Awake in the Feeling-Remembrance of the Eternally Present Divine Being.

The emotion of the being is the Principle that makes a priesthood of mankind. The Radiance of the heart is the Means of a great and constant and ultimately perfect Sacrifice. The fire of constant Remembrance of the Living One, in Whom the world and the body-mind of every being inhere, provides the Altar of our Sacrifice. Surrender the world, the body, all conditions and relations, every experience, all thoughts and every part of mind, and even the deep seclusion of the inner being into the Radiant Universal Transcendental Divine Being, the Only Existing One.

Such Remembrance, or Love-Sacrifice of the independence of all conditions of the being, is free of every trace of dilemma and self-bound strategy. There is no game in God, no awful demand for clever victory in the world or in the inward domain. The eyes may remain open, and the body may move about, but it is always a matter of simple, direct, ecstatic Love-Communion with the Blissful Person of Love, Who is Alive as the world, Active as the body, Conscious as the mind, and Existing as the inner being of every being.

The Universal Plan of Experience and the Ultimate Event of Liberation

The world is a Machine of experience—of beginnings, changes, endings, and beginnings again.

Every being arises as a consciousness of experience and becomes automatically involved in the Pattern.

Every being is ultimately deathless and constantly reawakens to the levels of experience to which it feels attached or attracted.

Every being, therefore, has the potential for a countless number of lifetimes—or epochs of experience.

Lifetimes arise spontaneously and for countless aeons (as long as the sphere of experience to which the being is attached continues to arise). Therefore, experience of all possibilities is a mechanical inevitability, until there is Awakening to the Condition beyond or prior to conditional experience.

Experience arises for its own sake, and there are countless realms of variously combined possibilities. However, experience is a limiting force, a self-defining power, a Machine of destinies. Therefore, there is no ultimate Happiness, Joy, or Bliss possible in the realms of conditional experience.

The inherent frustration of Happiness, Joy, or Bliss in the realms of conditional experience is the only force within the realms of experience that is greater than the motive of experience itself. It is the recognition of this inherent frustration that begins to Awaken the being to the Transcendental Reality that is the Source-Basis or Condition of all conditional experience. Therefore, recognition of the inherent and profound frustration of Happiness, Joy, and Bliss that we all are suffering is the basis of Wisdom and the ultimate Realization of Happiness, Joy, and Bliss.

Every being inevitably continues to experience lifetimes of conditional and self-binding experience until there is the recognition of the inherent frustration of Happiness, Joy, and Bliss in the process of conditional experience. When this recognition becomes profound, there is the Awakening to the Transcendental or Divine Condition in which all conditional experience is arising—and this Awakening Realizes Wisdom, Happiness, Joy, and Bliss.

When any being Awakens to the Wisdom, Happiness, Joy, and Bliss of inherence in the Transcendental Divine (the Condition of conditions), the mechanical association with the Machine of experience is released. Therefore, beings are constantly reborn to the conditions of their experiential attachment, and they go on and on in the experience of mechanical destinies, only more or less aware of the profundity of their inherent frustration, until they recognize that frustration, Awaken from their mechanical associations, and Realize the Wisdom, Happiness, Joy, and Bliss of inherence in the Transcendental Divine Being. In that Event, they are as if sifted out of the conditional worlds, and they are moved by Ecstasy into the Radiant Eternal Domain of the Transcendental Divine Being, prior to all association with experiential limitations.

Those who are not thus Awakened are seen to play out their frustrated adventures in the chaos of destinies always present in any dimension of the world. But those who recognize the inherent frustration involved in any such adventure see the profundity, inevitability, and universality of suffering in the conditional world. They continue to fulfill the pattern of activity and experience which is appropriate to their circumstances of existence, but their orientation is no longer to experience itself or to the self-being itself. Rather, they live and act in a spirit of self-transcending surrender, Ecstasy, or Love-Communion with the Radiant Transcendental Divine Being. Therefore, their days pass in the midst of the conventions of activity and awareness in the world, but they are more and more profoundly Transfigured by the Wisdom, Happiness, Joy, and Bliss of God-Communion. Finally, they cease to be born to attention in the realms of conditional experience. They are Outshined, and the world is Outshined, by the Radiant Being of God.

The Dream of Changes

All experience is "karma" or results. All experience follows mechanically from the total pattern of previous conditional motions. The future is as fixed and knowable as the past—except that it can, at least to some degree, be modified by self-transcending activity (on the part of single individuals or groups of individuals).

When this becomes obvious, there is a turnabout in the conscious being, an awakening by surprise. The dream of changes ceases to be the principle and motive of existence. Rather, the transcendence of the process of experience becomes the Way intuited in the midst of this cycle of events.

The Structure and Evolutionary Destiny of Man

Man, and thus the human individual, is actually a composite of three dimensions of Light.

The most obvious dimension is the physical being, which <u>seems</u> to be "material" and not made of Light at all. Its root center or primary seat of association with the Life-Principle is in the great vital region between the solar plexus and the perineum.

The second dimension of Man is subtler than the physical. It is the astral or "star body" (or body-mind), which interpenetrates and surrounds the physical being with biophysical energy, and which we identify as the "psyche" of individual existence. This second dimension of Man survives the physical death of the individual, but it is also the primary principle of illusion, which is the sense of independent subjectivity. (Its root center or primary seat of association with the Life-Principle is in the brain.)

The "star body" seems to be composed of energy and consciousness, and thus it seems to be more like Light than does the physical body. Therefore, this inner being or "soul" is the traditional resort or refuge of conventional religion and of all who seek release from the mortal threats that are the natural companions of physical existence. But the "star body" (or psyche) is neither immortal nor free nor truly independent or self-contained. It is simply the conventional, inward, and temporary solution to mortal fear.

The "star body" has the capacity (like the mind) to take on any form. But as long as the association between the "star body" and physical body (or "earth body") remains, the "star body" is expressed as a field of biophysical energy that pervades and conforms to the basic shape of the physical body, and also extends beyond the physical body as an "aura" of personal radiance that has the ultimate capacity to enjoy direct telepathic association with all beings and events in the biophysical universe.

The "star body" separates from the physical body at death (and it may also do so, temporarily and partially, on certain occasions within the physical lifetime, such as during sleep or dreams, or during

263

the phenomenon called the out-of-body experience, or OOBE). But the "star body" is not inherently free of existence in physical bodily form. Physical death is, like an out-of-body experience during the lifetime of physical embodiment, only a temporary and partial separation between the "star body" and the physical body. In the after-death states (which are psychic states within the personal bio-energetic field, or "star body") the previous physical embodiment is basically duplicated, including its states of mind and its emotional tendencies. And, eventually, another physical embodiment follows (or, in the case of egos that are highly developed in the psychic dimension, future embodiment may take place in subtler but also temporary realms of manifest existence, to evolve beyond the limits of the independent personal psyche).

Therefore, the "star body" must be <u>understood</u> to be simply an extension or subtler dimension of physical embodiment. It is in play, or dynamic union, with the physical body, and, although the "star body" (or mind) may be manipulated to cause changes in the physical (and also to <u>seem</u> to escape the physical), the existence of the limited personal psyche (or apparently independent mind and self) is priorly determined by the fact of physical embodiment. Thus, the physical body is ultimately senior to the "star body" at the level of the original determination of egoic existence (or existence as a limited independent self, presently embodied in one or another form or degree of manifest Light).

The "star body," or independent mind, must constantly be surrendered to the seniority of the principle of the body (in whatever form or degree of Light the body is presently expressed). This is the Law that we must perceive within the dynamic incident of our born existence.

The mind must acknowledge the principle of the irreducible simultaneity of psyche (or mind) and body—or the irreducible unity of the body-mind. The mind is not <u>other</u> than the body. The mind is not <u>within</u> the body. The mind is simply the subtler version of the <u>total</u> or simultaneous body-mind. The "mind" is itself a body-mind. It is psyche, but it is also a body made of energy (just as the physical body is truly a form of energy, or Light). The "star body" is simply a subtler dimension of the natural or physically expressed body-mind. Thus, the "star body" survives physical death, but it must also be understood to be in simultaneous or irreducible unity with the physical body during the physical lifetime. There is simply the body-mind in the midst of any moment of experience. And both body and mind are expressions of a common or single root, which is the nervous system. Just so, the nervous system itself is rooted in the third dimension of Man, which is the Radiant Transcendental Life-Principle or Transcendental Life-Consciousness.

The mind is only an illusory extension of the independent existence (or self) implied by the body. Therefore, unless the mind acknowledges its dependence on the body for its sense of independent existence, the mind (or independent self) will tend to be embraced as the senior and independent principle of existence, evolution, and even Truth. But the secret of the mind is the body. And the mind cannot be free unless it surrenders its independent selfhood to the body, so that the body itself (and the principle of independent selfhood) may be transcended in the Transcendental Life-Principle.

The third dimension of Man is senior to the physical body, the "star body," and even all embodiment, or all deluded identification with limited independent existence, mind, and form. The third dimension of Man is free, immortal, eternal, and Transcendental, or Divine. It is the true Self or Identity of Man and of every human individual. It is the Radiant Life-Principle and Transcendental Consciousness in which both the psyche (the mind, or "star body") and the physical body are presently arising. It is the Transcendental Heart, the Life-Principle itself, and its psycho-physical root (or origin of association with the body-mind) is in the heart of Man.

Human existence is an evolutionary trial, or growth lesson, in which the individual must first adapt to physical existence, or the physically and bodily defined self. After complex physical adaptation is achieved, the individual is obliged to adapt to the various functional levels of vital energy, emotion, and mind (both lower and higher). This second level of adaptation requires the development of the various higher functional capabilities that are native to the structures of the autonomic nervous system and the central nervous system (especially the brain).

Thus, the evolutionary trial (which may go on for many lifetimes or rebirths in human form) is projected on a progressive scale, beginning with the gross dimension of the physical body, and extending into the various subtler dimensions of the physical body, the nervous system, the brain, and the psyche. And at some point in that process the individual awakens to the experiential knowledge that the psyche is actually a subtle and separable body-mind, made of subtle energy and subtle states of consciousness. Even so, that discovery is not the highest reach of Man, nor does it signify the ultimate liberation and fulfillment of individual existence.

266

The "star body" (or psyche) is intimately associated with the autonomic nervous system and the central nervous system. However, it is not the ultimate or highest dimension of existence to which the central nervous system and the autonomic nervous system are connected. The Transcendental Light, or the Radiant Life-Principle and Transcendental Self, is the true Identity of Man. And the human individual is not free or fulfilled except in ecstatic surrender into the very Condition of that Transcendental Identity. Therefore, the ultimate stage of human evolutionary growth is Realized only when the "star body," or the apparently independent inner self and mind, is itself transcended through love of the Living Truth, or self-transcending submission to the Life-Principle and Transcendental Identity that is the Truth and Condition of the total body-mind of Man. (Only when the independent and limited self, mind, or psyche is first transcended through surrender to the Life-Principle may the physical body, or the original tendency to limited consciousness and limited embodiment, also be transcended through surrender to the same Life-Principle.)

The process of the ultimate evolutionary test of Man involves both intuitive transcendence of the <u>subjective</u> being (or mind) and total <u>physical</u> surrender to the Radiant Transcendental Life-Principle via all of one's actions and relations. In this manner, the Living Identity, the Light itself, that eternally transcends the limited body-mind, may be Realized prior to the physical body, the limits of the nervous system, and all the experiential states of independent self and mind. And, in the process, even the physical body itself, along with the mind, is Transfigured or Infused with the Life-Light of the Divine Self. Thus, at last Man is transcended in his own ultimate Identity. And when the Radiant Self or Heart of Man is Realized as Life, Light, Consciousness, and Love prior to the limited body and mind of Man, then a Free Destiny begins in the Radiant Domain that is just beyond the plane of the material universe (or Chaos) itself.

Those who are extraordinary or somewhat more evolved in the scale of Man look forward to material and psychic adventures in space-time, to be attained via manipulation of the physical body and the nervous system and the psyche (or "star body") of Man. And such is indeed a superior destiny to that which is the presently common experience of humanity. Indeed, even those who transcend Man in their Transcendental Realization of the Living Truth may naturally migrate into the more highly evolved worlds of the space-time continuum before they pass forever into the Transcendental Domain or Light. But the true Man and the Spiritual Master of Man are constantly turned toward the Living Truth itself, through ecstatic love. Therefore, those who embrace the Truth become Radiant even in the worlds. And they, at last, reach beyond the worlds to the Radiant Domain of Eternal Life.

267

The Composite Structure of Man and the Esoteric Process of God-Realization

The five "koshas" or functional sheaths that are traditionally said to compose the human individual correspond to (and yet also, in their subtler aspects, transcend and exist independent of) the basic structures of the nervous system and brain. The "annamaya kosha" or food sheath corresponds to the motor or outer-directed current of the body (or the primary impulse associated with the sympathetic nervous system), "pingala nadi," related to sheer physicality and the right side of the extended body. The "pranamaya kosha" or life sheath corresponds to the sensory or inner-directed current of the body (or the primary impulse associated with the parasympathetic nervous system), "ida nadi," related to basic internal physical energies and the left side of the extended body. The "manomaya kosha" or mental sheath (particularly associated with the outer-directed or body-motivating aspects of the mental processes) corresponds to the left hemisphere of the brain. And the "vijnanamaya kosha," the intellect sheath or process of essential knowing and intuitive comprehension, corresponds to the right hemisphere of the brain.

The fifth sheath, "anandamaya kosha" or the bliss sheath of essential self-consciousness, is expressed as the central Life-Current ("sushumna nadi"), which is extended from the base of the body to the crown, and which is epitomized at the heart, although it pervades the total body-mind. It is the limited self-identity or basic consciousness, identical to the Universal Life-Current of Radiant Transcendental Being, but cognized via identification with the individual body-mind.

The esoteric spiritual process involves first the transcendence by the self-identity (or "anandamaya kosha") of the four extended functional sheaths that compose the manifest body-mind—then the self-identity Awakens to its Identity or Condition in Divine Truth, transcending the limited self-identity and body-mind. The entire process is one in which the Central Being and Life-Current progressively Awakens within the very conditions of the body-mind or limited self, and thereby gradually Outshines the limited self-conception and Transfigures and Transforms the functional body-mind as a whole. In the ultimate stage of the process, the limited self (or "anandamaya kosha") is utterly transcended in the Realization of the Divine Condition of Transcendental Being. And the extended body-mind, rooted in the Divine Self or Transcendental Identity, is itself continued as a Play of that same Identity, or the Radiant Light and Life-Current of the Universal Divine Being.

Therefore, the ultimate destiny of apparently limited beings is the self-transcending Realization of the Transcendental Being, which in turn and by degrees Transfigures and Transforms the manifest individual (or all manifest individuals and the total world) into the Play of Light, the Divine Domain, the Translated World of God.

CHRIST=mc²

A talk by Da Free John

I

DA FREE JOHN: Scientists tend to be as obsessed with self as any other human beings. And, in the trend of their own traditional philosophy, they represent the same barbaric mentality as those who are, in the manner of the streets, more obviously committed to fleshly mortality. Scientists, too, seem to want to reduce existence to physical, elemental terms. They are obsessed with "matter" and death and cause-and-effect relations. Consider, for example, the now popular theory that the universe was caused by a giant explosion, the "Big Bang." This theory has been confirmed by a great deal of physical evidence, and thus it has become the generally accepted view of how our universe appeared. This cosmology, like the physical laws considered by Newton,[1] will probably always remain true on some level of experience, even though the paradox of such a view may become more apparent in the future. Somehow, the idea of the universe as a one-dimensional or strictly material event that suddenly begins and ends is basic to the popular and traditional understanding of "civilized" Man.

269

Physicists are currently considering the implications of the paradoxical fact that the physical universe is apparently not eternal but began with an explosion. They are also confronting the unavoidable conclusion that everything that preceded the "Big Bang" can no longer be discovered and known. In other words, scientists cannot in this case find the ultimate material cause they are seeking, because any facts or information that existed prior to the explosion that created the material universe have been totally obliterated or transformed beyond recognition by that explosion.

You can understand how this reasoning offends the conventional scientific mind, which is disposed to a total understanding of the physical universe in terms of the material

---

1. Sir Isaac Newton (A.D. 1642-1727) was an English mathematician, physicist, and philosopher. He is best known for his formulation of a strictly mechanical model of the universe based on his laws of motion and gravity. These laws describe the cause-and-effect interactions of simply observed phenomena in Nature—such as the legendary apple that fell from a tree onto Newton's head, awakening him to an explanation of gravitational pull between objects. His laws of motion described the movements of material particles in absolute, unchanging space and absolute time conceived as unconnected to the material world. He stated that any object set in motion will remain in motion unless and until it encounters another object, and that every action (cause) in Nature has an equal and opposite reaction (effect).

Under normal circumstances of observation Newton's laws seem to describe adequately the linear interactions of objects in space and time. But more sophisticated observations made during the last part of the nineteenth century began to reveal inconsistencies in Newton's laws. These irregularities were explained in the theories of special and general relativity formulated by Albert Einstein. (See footnotes 2, 3, and 5 following.)

sequences of cause and effect. Our scientists cannot fulfill their passionate elemental urge to thoroughly know about the physical universe. Because everything that existed prior to the moment of the "Big Bang" was destroyed in the process, they cannot seek beyond it for physical evidence, it appears. Even more, some scientists have gone so far as to consider that the fact of the "Big Bang" is compatible with popular religious conceptions of the origin of the universe, such as that described in the *Old Testament* book of Genesis. Such a view proposes a necessary link between popular religion and popular science, or at least a point where science reaches the limit of knowledge and must either be silent or defer to the archaic poetry of exoteric religious conception.

The philosophical alternative to ultimate scientific knowledge proposed by popular theorists would seem to be either never to be able to know or else somehow to become religious in the manner of downtown, middle-class churchism. But true religion is a greater conception than any that such theorists conceive. They are still talking about the creation myths of the *Old Testament* as if those descriptions were originally intended to be an historical record of fact (rather than a cultic device, containing both esoteric and exoteric religious instruction). The *Old Testament* and other such popular Scriptures were originally intended to communicate many dimensions of esoteric and exoteric meaning (although "civilized" people continually approach the ancient holy writings as simplistic and literal descriptions of the one-dimensional or material world of modern conception), but true religion is even a greater conception than that offered by the ancient books of Jews and Christians. We must therefore conceive of religion, both true and ancient, in greater terms than the popular mind conceives. Within the framework of great and true esoteric religious and spiritual consideration there is ample room for our sufficient and comprehensive understanding of the physical universe, including the "Big Bang" and all the other illusions of "matter."

Nevertheless, truly to understand the universe of our experience is not a matter of tracing the pattern of material events back to some absolute original physical Event or material Cause. There may not be such an Event or Cause in any case. If we trace the one-dimensional chain of material events (or apparent effects of causes) back far enough, even if we could discover what existed before

270

the "Big Bang," there still may be no End to apparent effects and causes. But if we accept the factuality and the implications of the "Big Bang" itself, it does seem that, at least with the ordinary, mental equipment of Man, we will never be able to go beyond a certain point, and so our prideful presumption of attaining complete knowledge about (and thus superiority over) the universe in which we are appearing will, we must admit, inevitably be frustrated. Today's scientists may be busy discovering all kinds of things, but they are, by virtue of this consideration, beginning to realize that they are all something like plumbers now, you see. They are no longer in the business of discovering and disseminating ultimate knowledge, and so their priesthood is in doubt.

271

But let us consider whether a truly illuminating understanding is possible for us. Perhaps there is a conceptual link between the highest considerations of scientific inquiry and the highest considerations of true and universal religious and spiritual Realization. Consider this: While the present configuration of "matter," or the apparently material universe, can be perceived as an effect of a chain of material causes originating with the "Big Bang" (and what presumably was the case even before it), the material universe itself and as a whole can also be considered in every present moment to be the expression of a dimension of existence that is subtler and greater than the material universe itself. Therefore, we may also perceive and conceive the physical universe to be arising within and in some sense as the effect of another dimension that is hierarchically senior to it and yet perhaps otherwise invisible or inconceivable from the materialistic point of view of the conventional and one-dimensional position of perception and conception. In fact, I am certain that we must realize just such a perception and conception of the universe in order to have an authentic science and an authentically human culture. And the formula $E=mc^2$ is perhaps best understood as a specimen of the very conception I am suggesting.[2]

2. $E=mc^2$ is the mathematical equation formulated by Albert Einstein in 1905 to express the ultimate equivalence of matter and energy. "E" stands for energy, "m" for mass or quantity of matter, and "c²" for the speed of light (186,000 miles per second) multiplied by itself. This formula shows that the amount of energy represented by any given material object can be determined by multiplying its mass by the speed of light squared. Thus, the formula represents the actual conversion of matter into energy. This conversion takes place in the nuclear reactions

When its true implications are taken into account, Einstein's[3] equation of energy and matter (expressed in the formula $E=mc^2$) represents the possibility of a multidimensional interpretation of the total universe, in which the so-called "material" universe is realized to be a paradoxical entity or process.

The conventional philosophy of pre-Einsteinian physics considers the material universe in the very primitive terms of the medieval mind (against which science was supposed to have rebelled). If we would approach the "matter" of the universe as honest physicists, as scientists who are truly sensitive to the higher physics of things, we would realize that the "material" universe is energy, that it is light, that all "material" events are an expression of another dimension than what we call "matter," that "matter" is itself energy, that it behaves as energy, that "matter," and the universe, and, therefore, Man and every individual being, are, each and all, a paradoxical manifestation of infinite Energy and Being, and that the struggle to trace the chain of material causes and effects back to and even beyond the "Big Bang" is a very naive and unillumined approach to understanding the universe of our experience and contemplation. It is the multidimensional understanding in the present that is significant. $E=mc^2$ is the modern left-brained or verbal-analytical expression of that multidimensional thinking—a way of entering into the realization that the physical universe is a paradox of light. Thus, we must understand that the universe of our experience is not merely a sequence of physical events and a material effect of the past. The "material" universe is a present expression of light. Matter is light; matter, or the total Realm of Nature, emanates presently from the Matrix of Light.

---

that produce light-energy in all stars and in man-made atomic or nuclear weapons.

In the following pages of this talk Da Free John discusses this equation and its ultimate spiritual implications for Man.

3. Albert Einstein (A.D. 1879-1955) is considered one of the greatest scientific geniuses of human history. His discoveries in theoretical physics revolutionized modern man's understanding of the nature and structure of the universe. Born in West Germany, Einstein brought forth many of his radical contributions to theoretical physics in 1905, the same year he earned his doctorate degree. He was awarded a Nobel Prize for his work in 1921. Einstein emigrated to the United States in the early 1930s, as the Nazis were coming to power in Germany, and he spent the rest of his life working to unify the radical new laws of physics.

The obsession with one-dimensional cause-and-effect relations and the materialistic ideal of tracing the configuration of the present moment back to the "Big Bang" or some other material Cause are motivations founded in the barbaric—or at least archaic!—mechanical principles of Newtonian physics and the medieval dreams of Aristotelian[4] philosophy and not at all in the ecstatic and liberating Realization of the paradoxical Reality in which the total World and Man are appearing. The formula $E=mc^2$ and the theories of "relativity,"[5] on the other hand, are expressions of the intuition that the universe is an awesome paradox (not a cause-and-effect simplicity), and that the present conditions as well as the ultimate Condition of the apparent universe (analyzed by our senses) are never more than partially revealed to the lower-adapted conventional mentality of unevolved Man. Just so, one of the ultimate consequences of this paradoxical conception is the conviction that "matter" is <u>now</u> energy, an expression of energy, a process of energy. To realize perfect identification with that subtle force that is light itself, material forms must be converted, that is true, but even now, as whatever form it appears to be, "matter" is itself a form of light-energy. And, likewise, when Man begins to awaken to this conviction in his own case, he thereby enters into a Process of more and more perfect identity with Energy, or ultimate Translation into the Infinite Domain of Light.

273

4. Aristotle (383-323 B.C.) was one of the most eminent philosophers, logicians, and scientists in the history of Western thought. He established a scheme for systematic logical thought based on the philosophical insights of Socrates and Plato and his own observation and classification of the phenomena of Nature. To Aristotle every interaction in Nature or in the mind of Man could be logically known and explained via precisely defined rules of cause and effect and linear logic. In his approach (which came to characterize Western thought and, specifically, Western science) there is no possibility for paradox or inexplicable mystery.

5. The theories of "relativity," as originally presented by Albert Einstein and developed by many physicists during the course of this century, propose the relative rather than absolute character of motion, velocity, mass, and other principal factors in the physics of Nature and the interdependence of matter, time, and space as a four-dimensional continuum.
Einstein proposed the *special theory of relativity*, which is concerned principally with electromagnetic phenomena and the dynamics of their activity in time and space, and the *general theory of relativity*, which is principally concerned with the concept of gravitation and the equality of gravitational mass and inertial mass. He and many others refined these theories over the years and sought to develop a *unified field theory* that would account for all the paradoxical properties and interactions of all known phenomena of the universe.

QUESTIONER: Einstein once said that there is enough energy in just striking a match to lift off a mountain.

DA FREE JOHN: The amount of energy manifested or radiated by even the smallest piece of matter, if we were to convert it into light-energy, would be tremendous. "$E=mc^2$" means that the amount of energy that any piece of so-called "matter" represents, and into which it could be directly converted, is the amount of its mass (whatever measure you use to determine how much mass this chunk represents) multiplied by the square of the speed of light (that is, the speed of light multiplied by itself). In other words, if the physical universe is converted into radiant energy, we must all enter into a domain of energy that is many times greater than the physical universe itself. The physical universe, therefore, is actually a speck floating in a Realm of Light-Energy that is neither visible nor comprehensible to Man in his subhuman, unevolved, and un-Enlightened state. Well! That is exactly the spiritual conception of existence, you see, except that true or spiritual existence encompasses far more than mere energies, even more than higher physical energies, and even more than the mere light of higher psychic consciousness. The entire psycho-physical universe, including you as you now appear, is a superficial, unnecessary, and free or nonbinding expression or apparent modification of the Absolute, All-Pervading, Radiant Divine Consciousness. This is the fundamental Realization: Every thing is merely a transparent modification of Consciousness, of the Radiant Love-Energy or Transcendental Bliss-Light that is literally All-Pervading Transcendental Consciousness.

Einstein felt some religious implication in what he was understanding about the physical universe, but he was not a practitioner of true or esoteric religion. He was not a practicing devotee. He did not observe the human body-mind with the same intensity with which he observed the rest of the physical (or, really, psycho-physical) universe. Thus, he did not discover any higher personal implications in his scientific findings than the humanistic urge to be a good and intellectually serious man in the world. He did not enter truly into a higher religious consideration, involving the actual transformation of his own body-mind into light, but such is the obvious implication of his formula $E=mc^2$, if you are thinking clearly. What is true of the physical universe and the total world is also true

274

of this human psycho-physical being. Energy is our condition already. The body-mind comes out of energy, as does the entire world. And all of this and us must ultimately and will inevitably return to the Realization of prior identification with energy and with the Radiant Transcendental Consciousness that is the Light and Truth and Self of the world.

Einstein's scientific considerations are basically a repetition of ancient esoteric and paradoxical descriptions of the universe. His work has legitimized, in the mathematical, scientific terms of the twentieth century, a certain level of higher consideration about material existence. We have, in both the popular and academic areas of our industrial societies, accepted the general and technical implications of this very sophisticated and elaborate understanding of the elemental world, but we have not realized what that understanding implies about the world and about Man altogether. We are still suffering the cultural limitations upon which our scientific civilization has always been based. Scientists continue merely to think and doubt and exploit the worldly powers of their own enterprise, and they have not yet supported the creation of a total human culture based on the implications of their own discoveries to date. "E=mc²" actually and exactly means the same thing to us today, to our nervous systems, to the individual body-mind or being, that "Christ is risen from the dead" meant 2,000 years ago. "E=mc²" is exactly what "Christ is risen from the dead" means. E=mc² is good news! It proclaims that matter is energy—that the body-mind of every human being can be Realized to be energy, or light.

What does this communication mean in human terms? It means that you are energy. However you may be described altogether, you are not "matter." Matter is dead stuff, a dead end, a solid and separate and only mortal thing. But "matter" does not exist in any case! There is no such thing as "matter," in itself and distinct from light, or energy, or mind, or psyche, or ego, or God. It is not that there is no such thing as our apparent experience here, but all of it is energy, or a temporary form of light. There are many more subtle aspects of light than we see in our subhuman manner, and the entire manifest cosmos, including the body-mind of Man, is a spectrum of energy. Therefore, human beings must become acculturated to living as energy, or spirit-force, instead of struggling in the barbaric mentality of the "flesh." And we must develop a culture of men and

275

women who are being light instead of merely being "matter" and that dark, simple, dreadfully mortal thing that "matter" implies. We must create a culture out of our identification, at this moment, with light, or energy, or the "Holy Spirit" that is Life and that is Alive as every thing and every being.

"E=mc²" is the principal contribution of theoretical physics to date. It is the premier archetypal scientific discovery of the twentieth century. We are just beginning to realize its cultural implications, and those cultural implications are vast. The idea legitimized by the formula $E=mc^2$ is the greatest scientific discovery of our time, because it has the most archetypal force. Yet, it is not new. The same idea has been part of the great tradition of esoteric spiritual society since the most ancient times. This formula is simply the modern scientific form or statement of the ancient Wisdom of Life. Because this formulated idea was developed within the domain of science, it has been legitimized by argument and demonstration within the acceptable framework of what is conceived to be knowledge in our time. $E=mc^2$ signifies that all matter is simply a form of energy. Therefore, there is no such thing as "matter." The fundamental conception of our existence and the state of our knowledge at the present time is that we and every thing are energy.

But who acts as if energy is the actual state of our existence? People are, in general, still living as if "matter" is the ultimate state of all existence. The masses of humanity, including their intellectual and political leaders, are living in an archaic state of mind and culture. Thus, there are many positive cultural implications in the archetypal formula or re-discovery communicated by Einstein. "E=mc²," like "Christ is risen from the dead," is not made of words, but of archetypal symbols, or pure significance. It is the way the ancient good news is communicated in the terms of twentieth century logic. "Christ is risen from the dead" and "E=mc²" are the same truth stated in the terms of two different epochs of human understanding. Yet, nearly everybody pretends that there is a vast difference between "Christ is risen from the dead" and "E=mc²."

Intellectual and dogmatic pretenses have generated a sophomoric debate between science and religion, as if they communicate two different kinds of information. In truth, popular or exoteric religion and conventional or exoteric science represent two specialized points of view toward the same information. Science represents the analytical point of view, the separate consciousness, the mood of doubt, always analyzing what it sees, not involved in what it is perceiving, or always trying to eliminate itself from such involvement. Such a point of view has some practical application, obviously, but it also has its own inherent limits. Religion fundamentally represents the point of view of unity with everything, rather than analytical separation. It expresses the right-brained mystical and intuitive consideration, rather than the left-brained or verbal consideration. At some point we must come to realize the hierarchical relationship beween these two points of view. We must understand that the mood of unity is the highest or most fundamental point of view, and therefore the most essential cultural orientation. Thus, humanity must devote itself to true religion, to spirituality in its truest, most esoteric sense.

A greater, even more primary archetypal discovery than $E=mc^2$ is also concealed in the "native state" of religion. The reason that higher truth is yet <u>hidden</u> is that the only religion people commonly know about is essentially a banal, poetic, fixed-mindedness. Popular religion is not a living inspiration full of Transcendental Wisdom, and esoteric religion is ultimately comprehensible only to Adepts. "$E=mc^2$" is transcended by the Truth greater than "Christ is risen from the dead," greater than the fact that "matter" is a species of light, utterly capable of direct translation into light. It is certainly true that "matter" is light, but the Truth of existence is greater than that. Yes, the Realization of Truth does include a literal transformation wherein the body is Realized and demonstrated to be light (as it is popularly believed to have been the case with Jesus of Nazareth). Spiritual growth is indeed a matter of Man's entering into the Domain of Energy. It involves the repolarizing of the energy of the body (or nervous system) from toe to crown, while also maintaining the capacity to express that current of energy from the crown to the toe, and thus to live the full circle of the human structure in peace. But the ultimate Realization is a Transcendental Awakening into the Domain in which even light, or space, or change, or energy, or "matter," or the body, or Nature itself, which is essentially the play of light, are all arising.

What is the Condition or ultimate Domain in which light exists? What is the Condition in which Nature exists? We tend to think of Nature in the archaic terms of material processes. But we now also presume that $E=mc^2$, that Nature is <u>only</u> light or energy. What, then, is the Condition or "Place" in which light-energy is arising? The Realization of that Condition is the ultimate religious, esoteric, and spiritual discovery. Truly, energy is arising in the Transcendental, Absolute, and Perfect Domain that is Consciousness. Consciousness is Absolute, Infinite, Radiant Bliss—Undifferentiated and All-Pervading. It is that Condition in which light and "matter" and "mind" and all of us are arising. It is that Condition which is called "God," even by those who have no direct Realization of the Truth. The play of energy, or light, is, therefore, also God. And the human body-mind is full of light, or the Energy of Life. Indeed, Man is only light, or Life, even bodily. And the body of Man is to be Realized as nothing but Radiant Consciousness, or Love, which is the Self that is God.

Thus, we are always already established in a Divine Paradox. That is how we must understand the entire Realm of Nature. We should not despair of understanding the universe simply because we cannot go beyond the "Big Bang" in tracing the material chain of causes and effects. We may be deprived, at least as Man, of a certain inspection of the mechanics of great material processes—or we may not. Perhaps everything can be intuited. If we can enter into the domain of the psyche, the higher mind, or the consciousness of light-energy in its subtler aspects, perhaps we can then discover even the causative processes of material existence that existed previous to the "Big Bang" and that are otherwise unavailable to inspection by bodily or gross physical investigation by Man. Like the higher Wisdom or Truth itself, this intuitive capacity is also hidden in religion. It is simply not considered or utilized by the current scientific establishment and our conventions of knowing.

The conception of $E=mc^2$ is arising in the Transcendental Depth that is Consciousness, just as are the self-idea and the subjective consciousness of the individual. The subjective or egoic self or body-mind is realized in the seventh or perfect stage of life to be not other than energy. It is not merely self-contained or objectively experienced bliss, but it is ecstasy, or a Realization founded on self-transcendence, or the perfect sacrifice of the body-mind of the individual. It is Love, Energy, Radiance, and Absolute Consciousness. Everything is Realized to be simply the modification of that One Self and Reality Who is Absolute Consciousness and Absolute Energy,

Undifferentiated, Transcendental, and All-Pervading. That is God and the Truth of the individual self. That One may be Realized to be one's very Self in ecstasy, when one transcends the subjective or psycho-physical self-reference and enters into God-Consciousness truly. That One may also be felt in relationship, Pervading all experience. And that One may be felt as a Divine Personality, great beyond ordinary conception, but nonetheless a Person, not mere energy (like the rays of the sun), but Consciousness (like the sun itself), Alive, Pervading all, Transcending all, Existing as all.

279

Presently, in the cause-and-effect terms of time and space, you cannot go beyond the "Big Bang" to account for yourself. You can, however, enter into consideration of the super-dimensional realm in which "matter" truly exists. That is an altogether different consideration of physics. What is the Condition in which light arises? When that Condition can be conceptually presumed through mathematical and technological consideration of phenomena, then those who are presently bound to the subhuman limits of popular scientific conceptions may realize a much higher cultural stage of human life. That cultural realization will bridge the gap between religion and science, and, ultimately, between esoteric and exoteric knowledge. It must be presumed, deeply in the psyche, that matter is a form of energy, a modification of light. But we must also see that light, energy, change, arises within the Infinite Radiance of Transcendental Consciousness. And what that means is that matter (and, therefore, the human body) likewise arises in Consciousness, since matter can be rightly conceived only as a modification of light. This higher and practical consideration must be brought into the scientific realm of physics, so that the spiritual consideration of Truth can begin to be understood in its fullest sense. This is an exalted consideration. It is not a street-level salvation "gospel." It is available to ordinary people if they will be converted to true and esoteric spiritual practice, but the origin and the fulfillment of the consideration itself is founded in a most high and ultimate Realization that exceeds all the limits of the body-mind of Man.

The analytical description of the universe in which current scientific formulas like $E=mc^2$ are appearing should begin to be accepted and legitimized within the greater framework of spiritual understanding that I have proposed. How can we legitimize this conception? How do we bring true religion and esoteric spirituality out of the closet—or, really, the cultural concentration camp to which they have been relegated by all the barbaric and absolutist propaganda of scientific materialism? Religion is the cultural idiot of the modern world, while science is the TV hero of all the News, but the traditional and current popular state of science and the materialistic culture it promotes does not permit a fully illumined or enlightened or peaceful, happy life. The higher and spiritual implications of revolutionary contemporary physics must be understood relative to Man, to the individual. Our scientists must therefore move the frontiers of science from theoretical physics to biophysics. What is the significance of $E=mc^2$ for the human body-mind? How do we promote and establish cultural ideals that enable all men and women to function and grow as light or energy rather than as lifeless matter?

We must presume, based even on our present understanding and application of theoretical physics, that matter is energy. Then what about our understanding and application of biochemistry, biophysics, human anatomy, human life, human culture? What will we do when we take the discovery of the relationship between matter and energy seriously? How do we make medicine out of the understanding that the human body is energy? How do we practice ordinary diet, sexuality, and social relations on that basis? How do we bring the higher knowledge of physics and spiritual esotericism into the daily practice of ordinary people? And then, how do we also bring mankind into the greater conception and ultimate Realization of the Transcendental and Divine Consciousness, in which matter, energy, and light are appearing? If you are serious about such questions, then I suggest you study all of the literature I have written for just such a one as yourself. Then choose what you will do.

The Divine understanding of the universe, with all of its paradoxes and mysteries, must be restored to Man. Human beings must be allowed the greater and truly human culture of self-transcendence in God-Communion, wherein they may also enjoy the benefits of cooperative life, peaceful human existence, perhaps even some technological sophistication—since there is nothing inherently evil about technology—or even whatever simplicity a person may choose if he or she prefers to be very simple about the ordinary affair of material existence. Every person must be permitted the higher understanding and free spiritual practice of Life, even if he or she chooses to live a lifetime in relative seclusion, or within the Sanctuary of an autonomous religious community, rather than in the broad popular environment of mass politics and all the casual births and deaths of subhuman acculturation.

II

281

DA FREE JOHN: Can you conceive of the madness of such a universe as this? First <u>nothing</u>—and then all <u>this</u>, this apparent world, seemingly mechanical, in which every individual element or entity is, in itself, mortal, a world that seems to afford no opportunity for any individual to know anything about what is beyond and prior to his or her own actual, physical form or process. What an absurdity to appear out of nothing! Why should anything appear at all? Why should such a joke appear out of nothing? Where has all of this happened?

All of this seems to me to be very important for us to consider to the point of certainty and self-surrender. The intensity of our understanding of these matters will most definitely determine the quality of our lives. And how do you intend to get to the foundation of this wondering?

If the universe is simply mad, and if there is no way to understand it, no way even to feel back beyond the appearance of your own nervous system and body, any more than you can feel back beyond the "Big Bang" and discover how the universe came to exist— if that is the nature of existence, you see, then there are at least two basic ways whereby you can respond: Either you can become so serious that you seem not to take anything seriously at all (and so just burn yourself out, destroying yourself in self-indulgence or whatever chaos you want to use to distract yourself) or, with equal seriousness, you can approach life as the conventional Buddhists do!

The classical or exoteric type of Buddhist (who should be distinguished from the esoteric or higher type of "Buddhist," examples of which have appeared, for instance, among the Adepts of Tibet[6]) is responding to the same conception of the universe as the

6. In this essay Da Free John distinguishes among the various dimensions of Buddhist philosophy and Realization and criticizes those that are less than Transcendental—just as, in

person who burns himself out. He has exactly the same motivation! The person who burns himself out does so because he cannot handle the "truth" that he seems to have discovered. The usual Buddhist, however, although convinced of the same "truth," does not take up the way of self-indulgence; in his intellectual view, that is only another form of suffering. Instead, he yields all the tension in his being. He just gives up all hold on himself. He becomes less and less subject to the stress of living, and he ultimately renounces all motivation, so that he is neither threatened nor threatening. He becomes so free of reactive stress that he is no longer struggling with his inevitable mortality. Thus, he conquers the awesome facts of Nature by giving up all striving in the midst of a mortal life.

If you were to come to this conclusion—that you are mortal, that the universe is essentially chaotic, that in any case you cannot <u>know</u> beyond your own nervous system, that you cannot find out the actual nature of your situation—if all that were to become your own conviction, I do not see how you could take the world unseriously enough to quietly play out an orderly and productive ordinary life, except perhaps to the degree that you were simply frightened. And, of course, such fear is an important element of life for most of us. People are essentially desperate. They do live lives of "quiet desperation." They have discovered, at least in their superficial reflections and feelings, that they are mortal and hopeless, that they cannot know anything ultimately and are not congratulated by the universe. And

---

the earlier chapters, he analyzes and criticizes the traditions of Christianity. However, he has also aligned his Teaching directly to the highest philosophical traditions of Buddhism, as well as to the highest or most perfect Realization of Adepts in all traditions.

The Adept, in the Buddhist tradition or in any other tradition, may criticize any of the secondary or conventional aspects of any or all existing traditions—indeed, such criticism is one of the primary functions or services Adepts perform for the sake of mankind. Thus, Da Free John criticizes various aspects of the traditions of the Way conceived or inspired by Gautama and views others favorably, while still recognizing the Transcendental Realization of Gautama.

Da Free John speaks sympathetically about many aspects of Buddhism in general while criticizing what belongs to conventional path-consciousness, orientalism, and cultic asceticism. The Teaching of Da Free John is aligned to the highest expression of the Transcendental Realization found in the literature of Buddhism, e.g., the *Lankavatara Sutra*, the *Diamond Sutra*, the *Platform Sutra*, and to the Realization of Adepts such as Nagarjuna, the Sixth Patriarch, Padmasambhava, Marpa, Milarepa, and many others.

For further discussion, please see Da Free John's source text on the ultimate philosophy and practice of this Way, *The Lion Sutra: Radical Wisdom and the Seventh Stage of Life.*

they are afraid, because they know that they can suffer terribly, so they neither burn themselves out nor yield to their mortality by giving up to the point of the Buddhists' passivity, or nonresistance to change and death.

Gautama, called the Buddha, did not believe in striving toward heaven worlds. There is no traditional command in classical or original Buddhism to make efforts to succeed in mystical matters. Gautama simply ceased to be disturbed by the mortal facts of suffering. By craving experience and entering into the whole affair of experience, including psychic as well as physical phenomena, he found that experience itself is deluding. Experience makes us feel as if we are involved in some great importance, whereas if we really observe ourselves, we will see that in a very few years we will start getting terribly ill, and eventually we will die, losing every thing and every one in the process. Gautama's point of view was very desperate, in that sense. He saw clearly that we can have riches and visions and all kinds of material "blessings," but these things all become ridiculous when we remember that we are mortal. Gautama's ultimate philosophical mood of nonreaction was based on the observation of his present and inevitable mortality, not on the idea of eventual immortality. He simply came to the point of yielding, of nonresistance. He could accept the view that bodily life and everything that we can have in mind is temporary and mortal, but he also realized that this life could pass without being disturbing. While alive, he engaged in no disturbing efforts to fulfill motivations and desires. He became desireless through insight into desire.

Gautama did not create any program for going to heaven or for existing forever in any objective form. Yet, the older Indian tradition of the immortal soul, of higher or heavenly worlds, and of reincarnation or transmigration is also associated with Gautama's patterns of thought and presumption. Such traditional lore, whether fanciful or factual, does not seem to fit very well with Gautama's particularly fatalistic observation of the facts of Nature. That is why so much of traditional religious Buddhism is really based on accretions of popular nonsense, such as developed over time in the case of all ancient exoteric religious traditions. The glorious heavenly images of the Buddha that have appeared within the later traditions of Buddhism have nothing to do with the original root of inspired intuition that awakened in Gautama himself.

283

The root of exoteric Buddhism is a desperate or fatalistic observation of the facts of Nature, which justifies the conceptual understanding that you are mortal—not that you are an immortal soul, not that there are great cosmic possibilities, but, simply and only, that you are mortal. Once this principle is accepted, anything great that may come into your experience has to be understood from that point of view, or you will be deluded by it. Thus, any great desire, when satisfied, can delude you, by making you forget your actual situation. The more involved you become with experience, the more you crave experience; and the more you crave experience, the more you want to continue to exist, and, therefore, the more you fear death. Gautama's approach was to enjoy insight into this matter, to presume with absolute clarity simply that "I" am mortal. That was the great insight. It was not a metaphysical idea of some sort. It was a process of awakening to mortality and allowing the sheer fact of mortality to overwhelm him, so that he could be liberated from the game of fulfilling all the psycho-physical forms of mortal possibility.

We also see a variation on the mood of this fatalistic insight in our contemporary scientific, technological culture. We are all tending to be possessed by a conception of our life and world and destiny that is based exclusively on the observation of the material and mortal facts of Nature, such as the "Big Bang" of the birth of the physical universe, beyond which we cannot know. When we presume that we are merely and only mortal, we also begin logically to presume other things—for instance, we may observe (and negatively interpret) that much of what are considered religious, mystical, and other-worldly phenomena are simply expressions of the internal, subjective, and self-generated profusion of the brain and the total nervous system. How then can we avoid having to yield to the extremes of fatalistic self-abandonment (rather than ecstatic, self-transcending, Life-positive, loving, and relational intent) through either degenerative self-indulgence or else passive giving up in nonresistance to the mutability of the world? How can we avoid the conventional methods of either passive Buddhism or nihilistic libertinism in the face of our maturing observation of the world?

To enjoy spiritual insight means that one has realized what is truly Transcendental, not what is merely psychic and attractive and apparently non-physical. So much of ordinary yoga and mysticism merely distracts people with internal objects that are hyped to them as spiritual, soul-like, immortal, and even Divine phenomena. But internal objects are, in themselves, nothing more than reflections of the changes occurring in our own nervous systems and the self-centered expansions of our own bodies and minds. People imagine themselves to be spiritual because they are involved in yoga, mysticism, poetic religious beliefs, and the like, but, truly, they are, in the midst of their subjective fascinations, no more spiritual (or surrendered to the "Spirit" that contains, pervades, and transcends the psycho-physical self) than a typical Buddhist monk, or an atheistic nuclear physicist, or a self-indulgent man on the street. Such people are simply focusing their attention on subtler aspects of the manifest self, the mutable psycho-physical being, whereas real spirituality involves direct and ecstatic (or self-transcending) Communion with the Transcendental Reality. Mystics, yogis, ascetics, libertines, even ordinary religious people are merely playing with their own nervous systems, their own bodies and minds. They have not yet begun to associate with the Living Divine Personality through the self-sacrifice that is love.

How can you realize the Transcendental Spiritual Reality—not merely your psyche, your nervous system, your internal subjectivity, but the Divine and Transcendental Reality that is prior to you, that is prior to the event of your birth, that will continue after your death, and that is so intimately associated with you that it is you? How can you discover this Transcendental Reality that is to be Realized at the very point where your own consciousness originates, and that is greater than the manifest identity of your own psycho-physical mechanism? How can you transcend the limits of your own body-mind? How can you penetrate the deluding power of your own experience? If you observe Nature clearly, you will see, as Gautama did, that your experience itself can be accounted for entirely within the limits of a mortal psycho-physical description. How, then, will you escape the apparently nihilistic paths either of burning yourself out by exploiting experience or of analyzing yourself and yielding all cravings to the point of the annihilation of experience?

The Way of Life, or the Living Truth, is to enter into active self-sacrifice, or ecstasy, toward or into the Radiant Transcendental Person, Reality, or Self, rather than to exercise either the exploitation or the passive yielding of our own body-mind. This is the principle of true and esoteric religious life. The body-mind must be able to function in and as such God-Communion at all times. Therefore, we are inherently obliged to learn all about the functional capacities of our own body-mind, and we grow by stages, eventually comprehending and mastering even the highest psychic and superconscious aspects of ourselves. But we must always, in every present moment, return to the fundamental and ecstatic action that I have described, and that is generated from the root of the heart, the essential root-consciousness of the psyche, the epitome of the entire body-mind. True religious practice is always to enter directly into sacrifice of the total body-mind to the Transcendental Reality, through self-transcending love, or ecstasy. That is the fundamental practice—not to enter into exploitation of the body-mind in any experiential way, active or passive, but to learn all about what is merely the body-mind so that you can surrender all of it ever more profoundly (while neither exploiting nor prohibiting any of it). At some stage in such heart-practice you may think you are surrendering quite profoundly, since you will have come to enjoy great mystical and psychic powers in the Realm of Nature, but you will again realize that that into which you have been surrendering is merely another part of yourself, your own psycho-physical being. Then you must surrender beyond even that into the Absolute, Living, Radiant Consciousness that is the Reality and Truth and God and Self of all.

In this great spiritual process you Realize that the Divine Reality is not only Transcendental Consciousness but also All-Pervading and Radiant Force or Love-Energy. That Force is conducted within the great Realm of Nature by all the circuitries within your body-mind and by those greater circuitries within which exist your body-mind, all its relations, and even the totality of the manifest universe. That great Life-Current can be felt or intuited directly as the Universal, All-Pervading, and Absolute Being, and It can also be felt constantly in all the specific exchanges of our experience. We can be confined or contracted upon ourselves in the midst of all of that, or we can be open, radiant, expanded, free of our reactivity, our lovelessness, our fatalistic nihilism, our self-possession.

You must transcend your emotional problem, your physical problem, your sexual problem, your mental problem, your psychic problem. You must transcend all the usual and uncommon problems of unillumined Man, through the heartfelt sympathy of the total body-mind with That in which it inheres, That in which it is arising,

286

That on which it depends absolutely. Live in the intuitive ecstasy of that devotion, that feeling that radiates freely from the heart. It is feeling, it is an emotional matter, breathed, felt bodily, granted by Divine Grace. Abiding in that practice, we depend upon and are given the spiritual Revelation that transcends the body-mind. This Revelation is not accounted for in the conventionally ascetic and Life-denying point of view of classical exoteric Buddhism, nor in the mind-worshipping other-worldliness of conventional religious and mystical esotericism (East or West), nor in the self-centered, nihilistic, and Life-degrading point of view of the burnt-out man on the streets, nor in the frightened mediocrity and subhuman ordinariness of the mass populations surviving anywhere in the world.

All who profess religious or spiritual aspirations must understand the Life-negative and nihilistic tendency in themselves. It is not a spiritual tendency. It is in fact an extension of worldly reactivity, the worldly tendencies of the usual man. It is not based on the Transcendental Realization of Life. It is based on the presumption of certain obvious material facts in Nature that support a nihilistic view of life. It is based on the illusion of "matter" and despair in the face of death.

The truly religious and spiritual Way also does not involve strategic development of the great soul within, or presuming that your inner being, if only it can be separated from the body, is a great, immortal individual. Rather, true spiritual understanding involves the recognition of all experience, even the most glorious mystical raptures of the inner "soul," as a limit upon the Infinite Expanse of the heart's natively ecstatic feeling. Even so, such recognition is not nihilistic and "matter-renouncing." Rather, it is founded on ecstatic and radical intuition of the Paradox that even the body is Consciousness, Light, Energy, Bliss, Love, and Transcendental Radiance, prior to all the seriousness of self and world. Such recognition occurs within the Condition of God-Communion, Transcendental Ecstasy, the truly spiritual state of awareness Awakened by the Grace of the Living God. The limited being is naturally moved to give itself up to what is truly Great. And, therefore, only what is Great is ultimately Realized to exist, whatever may arise as experience.

Religion must be founded upon the Living Truth. However, the so-called "great world religions" are, in their exclusive and exoteric forms, not founded on devotion to the highest and universal spiritual Truth. We have just considered classical or exoteric Buddhism, and we should understand that it is not, at its root, founded on a truly spiritual realization of life. It is founded on a serious or even desperate interpretation of certain observations about the mortal physics of Nature. Other religions, such as Christianity and popular Hinduism, which are founded on the doctrine of the inner soul and the idea of God as a separate Creator, are in fact based on illusions of the nervous system, or the internal, subjective, and apparently non-physical aspect of the body-mind, as well as the illusion of "matter." Thus, the real spiritual Revelation is still essentially hidden within if not absent from the so-called great religions (although it has been at least implied by the demonstrative lives of great Adepts, among whom, paradoxically, we should include Gautama, Jesus, Krishna, and countless others). But the spiritual Truth of the Living Reality must be the foundation and essential Revelation and core of practice of any true religion. If any religious or spiritual way is true, then it necessarily involves the disposition of ecstatic self-release into the Living Divine Personality that is the Condition and Self of all beings and worlds.

However, the mere verbal recommendation of such a disposition sounds like a conventional, downtown religious message. Therefore, you must enter into the thorough and total psycho-physical consideration of spiritual Truth, and you must come to understand the whole affair of your life, of religion, of emotion, and of consciousness before you can truly become the devotee of the Living Personality of God. Otherwise, to consider devoting yourelf to God is nothing more than a superficial religious idea. You must be truly "serious" (and, therefore, profoundly and intensely free or "humorous") about this consideration, because you must discriminate between your own limited experience and the ecstatic intuition of the Transcendental Divine Reality. Otherwise, you will never find your way out of the maze of conventional awareness. You must find the spiritual Reality—the Living Spirit, Person, and Self. You must be devoted to the Truth that includes and transcends you. Therefore, you must thoroughly investigate, consider, and inquire into your actual circumstance, your born-situation, your fundamental existence, the whole event of your experience. And, ultimately, you must come to the certain understanding that your entire existence is only summarized in ecstatic love of the Living God. You must become committed to a life of active, practical, and esoteric devotion to God. There is no other way to live and be happy and peaceful and sane.

The Ultimate Vision

The idea of a solid or objective world of "matter" and "one shot" mortality is an archaic and even "Victorian" concept that survives to this day in popular pseudo-scientific descriptions of the world and of human existence. But the now firmly established modern scientific conception that applies to <u>all</u> events (whether "material" or "mental") is that all phenomena and all beings are actually temporary states of atomic energy, or light. And energy, or light itself, is an eternally continuous process of transformation. Form always changes, but energy is always conserved. Therefore, individual beings, experiences, and worlds themselves are, each and all, only temporary events, or moments of the everlasting play of energy. But since all phenomena are changing and passing into new forms or states of <u>energy</u>, all beings, human or otherwise, since they are only energy itself, will also be conserved forever, although forever in new forms.

This conception of the world and of human existence is modern and also ancient. The ancient sages comprehended the world as permutations of energy and saw that a human lifetime is only a single event in a beginningless and endless procession of transformations (or births and deaths in all the subtle and gross or high and low realms of phenomenal possibility). Some interpreted the factuality of eternal survival to be the ultimate Truth. These were the religious mystics, yogis, and magicians, who became enamored of experience and perpetual devotion to self-existence. Others, such as the classical Buddhists, were psychologically disposed to interpret the endlessness of factual survival negatively, as inherently a matter of suffering, since living beings appeared only to be constantly changing and dying and being born again, sometimes rising up and sometimes falling again, under the perpetual force of mechanical necessity. Even since ancient times, those of a superficial and unillumined mind have been possessed by the self-indulgent and world-resisting fear of mortality, while others, being more profoundly informed by experience, have been consoled by factual immortality, and still others have been determined to bring a factual and final end to the perpetual cycles of mechanical and self-centered experience. But what is the Truth? What is the Realization that transcends both positive and negative concerns for mortality and immortality?

The Truth that must ultimately be Realized is spontaneously Awakened when the body-mind and the world and all experience become suddenly "transparent" to the fundamental consciousness. This "transparency" is not generally or necessarily associated with a visual experience. Rather, it is at first a matter of ego-death, or the establishment of natural identification with the deepest or "native" position of ordinary consciousness. Then the "eyes" of intuition must open. That is, the state of the atomic energies that compose or define the body-mind, and the world, and all experience, must become obvious.

It is like having one's visual awareness suddenly established in the plane of the atom. Then, instead of viewing the body-mind, and the world, and all experience as "objective" or solid phenomena that cannot be penetrated by consciousness, there is the sudden awareness that all phenomena are made of transparent fields of apparent "particles" of energy that are suspended in "space" and moving about in mysterious and ever-changing associations with one another. Thus, even the empirical "self," the total body-mind, is viewed or understood as a transparent field of suspended particles or vortexes of energy. The body-mind is mostly "space," and none of its suspended particles seem to touch one another, but only to move relative to one another as if controlled by invisible flows of pervasive magnetic or electronic energy. And the difference between the particles that compose the body-mind and those that compose the world "outside" is not any longer profound. Only certain magnetic or electronic influences make the difference between the form of the body-mind and that of the world, but the space between the particles of the body-mind and the space between the particles of the world are the same continuous or absolute space.

Once this "vision" or intuitive understanding is Awakened, the idea of a solid and separate self, or a solid body that somehow materially creates or contains consciousness, is instantly (or inherently) dissolved. Only the absence of "transparency" (or self-transcendence) creates or implies the illusion of a limited consciousness necessarily bound to a fixed physical entity. In fact, consciousness is limited only to the degree it identifies with the solid personal appearance of the body-mind, the world, and the conventions of psycho-physical experience. The deeper the personal consciousness enters into its psycho-physical situation, the more its perceptions and conceptions project beyond the limited self into psychically expanded space-time phenomena. And when there is intuitive penetration of the total body-mind, the solid or objective world, and all the limits of experience, it is Realized that consciousness is Infinite.

291

The internal or personal consciousness is actually identical to the Infinite Space in which the particles of atoms that compose all phenomena are suspended. When the illusion of the atom itself is penetrated, so that the Mystery of Transcendental Space becomes obvious to consciousness, then the ego-conception is Released, and only Transcendental Consciousness becomes obvious in the Radiant Transparent Infinity of energy motions. This obvious Transparency is Liberation and God-Realization.

When this Liberated Realization occurs, the "problem" of manifest existence dissolves and all necessity is transcended. The changing conventions of psycho-physical existence may remain, but they are not any longer viewed as a problem to be overcome. There is simply Radiance, Love, Humor, Happiness, Delight, Wisdom, Strength, Freedom, and the capacity to Serve the world of living beings with the Transfiguring Power of Divine Truth.

Original Light

The conventions of our sense experience habituate us to the idea that light is always generated from a defined source, specific locus, or point in space. It is this presumption that permits us to perceive and conceive of defined or differentiated objects, space between objects, relative degrees of illumination, and also shadows.

But, truly, all space, all locations, all objects are equally pervaded by true, original, or fundamental Light, Universal Energy, or Transcendental Radiance. If we consider the nature of perception and cognition within that Light, which is omnidirectional or Infinite, then we realize that no objects, no degrees of light, no shadows, no differences can be found therein. Just so, if we Realize Ecstasy, or perfect inherence in the Transcendental Light wherein all objects or conventions of difference appear, then we transcend all differences, all states of body, mind, space, time, self, and relations.

292

True Ecstasy in the Living Divine Reality is self-transcending inherence in the selfless, mindless, bodiless, worldless Infinity of Radiance, Bliss, or Love. The literal Divine, the Radiant Reality that is only Obvious and not to be identified with any independently subjective or objective states, is Infinite Light, the condition of all conditions or permutations of light-energy. We must enter into the Presumption of that Condition via our native transcendence of the conventions of psycho-physical experience. Then that same Light will Transfigure and Transform us in every part, until there is not the slightest difference between us and that uninterrupted Glory.

Body-Mind and Space-Time

Just as the body exists in space, the mind exists in time. The body-mind, therefore, exists in space-time, and it demonstrates all of the paradoxes of space-time phenomena.

The mind, through association with the body, enjoys the modes of movement or change in space. The body, through association with the mind, enjoys the modes of movement or change in time. But the body-mind inheres in the Divine Being or Infinitely Radiant Self. Therefore, the Being Who is the Self of the body-mind always transcends time, space, and space-time, or all the phenomena and paradoxes of experience.

All conditions in time may be conceived or inspected in the mind's permutations. All space may be perceived or visited in the body's mutations or planes of manifestation. All space-time may be known in the states of the body-mind, if the body-mind is surrendered in Transcendental Ecstasy (or inherence in the Infinitely Radiant Being).

Time and Ecstasy

All time exists simultaneously. Therefore, all events are fixed and knowable in advance as well as during and after the fact of their apparent "happening."

Even so, the knowledge of any event depends on our ability to enter into the plane or moment of that event. Therefore, knowledge of events outside of conventional memory and perception depends on our ability to transcend the body-mind in its present space-time state, configuration, or definition. And true knowledge of what is not contained in the present space-time limits of our experience depends on self-surrender, deep consciousness, ecstasy or self-transcendence, and resort to Ignorance, or that Condition of Being that transcends all past and present knowledge. In fact, then, the same requirements exist as a condition of perfect memory, foreknowledge, and total knowledge that exist as the Ultimate Condition of Transcendental Ecstasy or God-Realization. Such is the Paradox or Equation of Reality. The same Condition pertains at Zero, Everything, and Anything.

The Hole in the Universe Is in the Heart of Man

The mind does not exist in space. The mind exists only in time. But the mind arises in the Transcendental Being or Consciousness, which is prior to time.

The body does not exist in time. The body exists only in space. But the body arises in Infinite Energy, which is prior to space.

The body-mind, or the individual and apparently independent psycho-physical being (the ego or "I"), exists only as a temporary and dependent pattern within the space-time continuum, or the Vast and Multi-Dimensional Realm of Nature. But the Truth, Condition, or Real Identity of the body-mind and the entire Realm of Nature is the Infinitely Radiant Transcendental Being.

If "I" try to find some Great Consolation within the body-mind or anywhere else within the Realm of Nature, "I" am confounded and disheartened. All experience is self-limited. All my parts are always changing, disappearing. Every part of the whole is temporary, threatened. There is no Immortal in me. "I" myself am always only changing, passing, no matter what my state of experience. "I" can find no hope in the Realm of Nature. "I" find no consolation in any contemplation of myself, however deep or high "I" look. All "I" can find is myself by self-knowledge, and "I" am only changes changing. What hope is there in all my loving and pleasuring, creating and growing, experiencing and repeating? The principle that is "I," the body-mind, the idea and experience of personal or independent psycho-physical existence, is only changing, passing through countless mortal theatres of experience and repetition.

Therefore, the principle that is "I" is unable to provide a basis for any Great Consolation or Immortal Happiness.

But when "I" is understood, when personal existence is intuitively re-cognized and Realized to be arising within the Infinite Radiance of Transcendental Being, then there is only Happiness, whatever experience arises as the body-mind. When "I" is spontaneously penetrated and Released into Ecstasy, or Identification with the Real Condition of all beings and all phenomenal dimensions of the Realm of Nature, then there is Liberation from all the implications of psycho-physical existence and experience.

Therefore, only tacit Identification with the Radiant Transcendental Being provides the Basis in Truth from which "I" and the Realm of Nature can be understood.

There is a Great Hole in the Realm of Nature, and It stands in the heart of the body-mind, at the root of the awareness that is "I." This Hole must be found by intuitive insight, once "I" have become disheartened by the fake hopefulness of all experience.

When "I" Realize the Transcendental Identity, then fear leaves the body-mind, and Humor is restored.

When "I" Realize the Transcendental Identity of every one that is loved and every thing that is desired, then sorrow leaves the body-mind, and Happiness is restored.

When "I" Realize the Transcendental Condition of all phenomena, all experiences, and all dimensions or worlds in the Realm of Nature, then anger leaves the body-mind, and Love is restored.

So be it.

The Ultimate Mystery of Consciousness

All the predicates added on to the "I" sense in the form of both experiences (high and low) and thought-conceptions (great and small) are in fact forms of relation-avoidance, self-contraction, or "I"-modification. When that entire process is understood and transcended, "I" is Realized not as an inward, independent, separate, or separated subject or center of experience and thought but as the Unconditionally Radiant Transcendental Being in or of which even the entire Realm of Nature (internal, or conventionally "subjective," and external, or conventionally "objective") is arising as a spontaneous modification that is eternally unnecessary and without binding power.

The Way of that Realization is not at all a matter of conventional inwardness nor of outward self-exploitation. It is a matter of Ecstasy, self-transcendence, or transcendence of the conventions of thought and phenomenal experience. And Ecstasy is associated with processes of intuitive understanding, or self-criticism in response to the argument of Truth, as well as heartfelt whole bodily (or total psycho-physical) surrender into the Radiant Transcendental Presence and Being Who is the Divine Master and Condition of all beings and worlds.

The Way of Ecstasy is expressed as Liberation from the

subjective or psychological dilemma of physical and psychic self-limitation, and, on the basis of that Liberation, the apparent individual, and mankind, and all beings, and the total universe or world of light, will be Transfigured, forever Transformed, and ultimately Translated in and into the Radiant Domain of the Infinite Free Blissful Love-Great Divine.

Therefore, the "I" sense (or simple Consciousness) is not only or merely the conventional basis of our experiential existence. It is the basis of our Destiny altogether. We may submit to the conditions of experience (all mental, emotional, and physical predications of the basic "I" sense), and so become endlessly distracted by the positive and negative extremes of experiential and conceptual possibility, or we may Realize the Condition indicated by the simple "I" sense (prior to all the limitations of the "I" sense that are determined by predication, or conventional association with psycho-physical conditions), and thus transcend the dilemma of self-limitation.

Ecstasy is the Realization of the Truth or Transcendental Condition of the "I" sense (or simple, mere Consciousness) through transcendence of "I" as the ego, the conventionally presumed subject of experience. It is to Realize the "I" sense (or simple Consciousness, prior to the thought "I") as Unconditional or Transcendental Being, the Condition of which all experience is only a nonbinding (or egoless) modification.

The thought "I" is the ego, the conceived subject of experience. But the simple Consciousness is prior to experience, prior to the independent ego-self, prior to body and mind, such that body and mind (or all psycho-physical conditions) are only spontaneous modifications or permutations of that very Consciousness, which is Itself never limited or bound by any experiential or conceptual phenomenon—except that It may presume Itself to be limited, separate or independent, and depressed to the degree that It identifies Itself merely as the bodily and inner "I," the subject of experience, the "entity" upon which all concepts and experiences are conventionally predicated.

Therefore, we must Awaken from the conventions of our independent subjective mode of "being" and enter into the Transcendental Realization of our own Consciousness (Which is Itself not merely the conventional "I" of mental and physical self-conception, but even the very Life or Light or Spirit in which the mind and the body and the phenomenal world are presently arising). In that case we will be literally Enlightened, or Transfigured, body _and_ mind, by that same Life-Light or Blissfully Radiant Spirit-Being, and we will be physically, morally, and psychically Transformed, even to the ultimate degree of perfect Translation of the apparent self and the apparent world into the Radiant Domain or Infinite Divine Being that is the Mystery of our Consciousness.

297

The Two Moments of Enlightenment

There is no "ego."
There is no "matter."
The "ego," or the independent self, is a presumption in or of the mind, based on the conventional psycho-physical self-reference.

And "matter," or the independence of the body and all other apparent forms, is likewise a presumption in or of the mind, also based on the conventional psycho-physical self-reference.

Once insight awakens relative to the conventional psycho-physical self-reference and it is Realized to be itself only a condition of (or contraction of, or superimposition upon, or modification of) the native Being-Energy wherein all conceptions, presumptions, perceptions, and sensations arise—then "ego" (or independent self) and "matter" (or the independence of forms) become transparent in the Unconditional Being-Energy (or Radiant Transcendental Consciousness) that is always already the Condition of "I" and all the "forms" that arise as experience.

This Realization is the first, primary, or foundation Moment (or level) of Enlightenment.

When this Realization begins to be both profound and stable under all experiential conditions, then the Transcendental Being begins to Radiate or Shine in Excess of conditions themselves. That is, the primary Realization of the Real Condition of the body-mind and all experience is ultimately Demonstrated as the Outshining or Bliss-Transfiguration of psycho-physical phenomena by the Radiant

Transcendental Being, the Living Divine.

The Blissful Excess of Radiant Being, or Love, is the ultimate or Perfect Moment (or level) of Enlightenment. And that Process of Transfiguration gradually produces all the possible forms of Transformation of experience, including all possibilities within and beyond a single human lifetime, culminating in eventual Translation into That in which all phenomenal changes always already inhere.

The Presumption of God-Realization

Realization Transfigures. Transformation and Translation depend on moment to moment Practice of Realization (not merely on the fact that a profound moment of Realization can be remembered to have occurred in the past).

Realization is the first great Event, and it is profoundly difficult for it to be established as a tacit Presumption that is senior to the deluding arguments of conventional experience. Even so, once this Presumption is Awake, it is necessary and also difficult to Practice or Abide in the Realized Presumption under all conditions and in all states.

The Awakening of Realization is the sometimes conscious or intentional Occupation of the first great cycle of our lives. The Practice of Realization (or Ecstasy, or self-transcending God-Communion) is the necessarily conscious or presumed Occupation of the second or ultimate great cycle of our lives.

When the Body Is Full of Light

Mindless embodiment.
Consciousness without inwardness.
Thus it becomes obvious.

Every object is only Light, the Energy of Consciousness.
Even so, there is no mind.
Only this stark embodiment, without inwardness.

First transcend the mind, not the body.
Inwardness is flight from Life and Love.
Only the body is Full of Consciousness.

Therefore, be the body-only, feeling into Life.
Surrender the mind into Love, until the body dissolves in Light.
Dare this Ecstasy, and never be made thoughtful by birth and
experience and death.

The Perfect Teachers of Man are the Transcendental Adepts. They appear in various times and places, to Awaken all individual beings to the Living Divine and to create a renewal of truly human and spiritual culture. They unanimously declare and confess that only the Living God, the Eternally Radiant Divine Being in whom all beings and things arise and inhere, is the Truth and Ever-Present Savior of Man. The Adepts come and go. They Serve and Incarnate the One who is always already here.

Da Free John

CHAPTER NINE

The Western Way

The Western Way
of Bodily Self-Sacrifice

I

The conventional and traditional Eastern or oriental ideal or path is a specific design for attention in the body-mind. It is characteristically oriented toward mind, or the subtle subjective realm of the interior self. And this orientation itself is a direct result of a basic disposition of recoil from the bodily self, its relations, and its world. (Even the Buddhist schools, which reject the notion that there is an ultimate concrete or substantial and eternal inner self, retain the fundamental disposition of recoil from the bodily self and its relations. The body, or even the total body-mind and its experiences is interpreted negatively, as suffering. Even the Mahayana ideal of accepting birth as compassionate service to all beings in order to awaken and enlighten them is based on this negative interpretation rather than on bodily positive enlightenment.)

The conventional and traditional Western or occidental ideal or path is not inherently founded upon or disposed toward ultimate spiritual enlightenment or even a positive philosophical interpretation of the body-mind and the world. Rather, it is oriented toward bodily existence in the world simply because it conceives of individual existence only in the basic terms of matter, body, and outer-directed bodily motivation through desire and will. The Western orientation, or the typical orientation of "worldly" people and industrial societies, tends to be precisely that which is criticized and avoided in the Eastern path. Just so, the Eastern orientation and tendency toward inversion is criticized in the Western path (wherein recoil from this world seems to reflect an attitude of fear, loss of nerve, weakness, and abandonment of responsibility or duty, as well as a refusal of the basic or given pleasures of existence).

The Way of Life, which I have Realized, and which I propose, is founded upon equanimity, or prior transcendence of any and all conceptions of a dilemma or inherent problem of existence. Likewise, it is founded upon transcendence of the mood of recoil from bodily existence, or preference for confinement to the mental, psychic, or non-bodily illusion of self. I call the Way that I Teach the "Western Way," because it is free of the disposition of recoil or subjective inversion, and also because it is (not merely or conventionally but positively) oriented toward (or, rather, as) the body and its relations. However, the Western Way (in contrast with the conventional Western or occidental path) is altogether a spiritual process. It is positively oriented toward the evolutionary spiritual growth of human existence, but its disposition and practice are oriented toward Ecstasy, the spiritual sacrifice of the total psycho-physical self, or self-transcending Love-Communion with the Radiant Transcendental Being, the Divine Person, Who is the Identity and Condition of all beings and conditions. The Way that I Teach is characterized by the practice of love-surrender, as the whole bodily being (or total and single psycho-physical self), in all relations, to the degree of Ecstasy, or Transfiguration and Transformation by the Radiant Transcendental Being (even to the point of Translation or Emergence, wherein the present body-mind is forgotten or Outshined by the Radiant Divine).

This Western Way that I propose is a new and radical conception of human existence, practice, and destiny. It is supported by many aspects of both the Eastern and the Western traditions, but it is also critical in its interpretation of those traditions. The Western Way is a spiritual Way of Life—oriented entirely toward the All-

Pervading Transcendental Divine. However, it is founded upon present Communion with the Divine, not any search for or progressive attainment of such Communion. Just so, it is based on constantly reawakened understanding and transcendence of the habit of recoil from manifest and bodily relations (which recoil produces the typically oriental tendency to embrace a process of reductive inversion toward bodiless and even mindless subjectivity). Rather, the Western Way is established in the vision or presumption of the human self as a psycho-physical unity. The actual self is the total body-mind (not merely the inward part—called mind, psyche, soul, or essential Self). And the Way of Life is a matter of surrender of the total body-mind—or whole bodily worship of the All-Pervading, Total, and Transcendental Divine—to the degree of Transfigured Ecstasy.

The Western Way is not fulfilled in self-knowledge (or the experience of internal states, mental quiescence, psychic stimulation, soul visions, or essential Self-Consciousness). The Western Way is fulfilled only in Ecstasy, or self-surrender to the degree of self-transcendence. And the self that is to be surrendered is the actual and total psycho-physical self, or body-mind. The process involves constant transcendence of the habits of recoil, inversion, and the illusion of confinement to an independent internal self.

II

The condition that is our suffering (and which is, therefore, to be transcended) is not a fixed, objective, or subjective "thing" that is the self or ego. Rather, the conditon that is our suffering is the habitual <u>action</u> of self-possession. The action of recoil toward self (whether bodily or internal) is always a form of contraction, or withdrawal from the universal pattern of relations. That action ultimately leads to disintegration of experience, possession by illusions of mind, reduction of phenomena to Chaos, and, finally, reduction of the dynamic self to Zero.

I have engaged the conventional patterns of both Eastern and Western experience. I have explored the internal and the external dimensions of our human possibilities. And I have been Awakened from confinement to the problems, reactions, illusions, and limitations of our yet self-divided and unevolved humanity. I have Awakened from the separate motions of East and West, and this Awakening established me in the true Equanimity and Unity of the body-mind, so that I have become moved as a single sacrifice in Love.

304

The "I" that is each one of us is not merely a mysterious internal self. The self or "I" is indeed mysterious—since we do not ultimately know what it is—but it must be understood to be not other than the total, obvious, and dynamic body-mind. "I" is the body, or the total body-mind process (whatever that is, altogether and ultimately).

If "I" recoil from born experience and thus turn upon myself like Narcissus, the body-mind contracts. In that process, discomfort or dis-ease arises. The natural equanimity of the body-mind is lost in self-consciousness. A conception of dilemma arises, so that thereafter it is always as if I am motivated by some yet unspoken problem and toward some yet unrealized solution, happiness, or release. Then I no longer conceive of myself in dependent relationship with a universal Unity of relations. I am constantly disturbed by my own search for a unity of my own parts. I begin to feel homesick for the vision of unity, equilibrium, harmony, integrity, beauty, peace, happiness, pleasure, delight, and joy. In body and mind I am tempted by brief and separate illusions of what I seek, but my constant experience is deeply one of dreadful chaos, confusion, disharmony, division, fear, sorrow, anger, guilt, remorse, and torment. And the deeper I enter into the domain of self, the more profoundly I suffer a vision of everything and "I" reduced to Zero, Emptiness, and Changeless Disturbances without the slightest trace of Meaning or Love.

But it has been given to me to Awaken from this terrible Script. And the Way of Life for Man has been clarified in my heart. This dreadful destiny of recoil and self-possession must be transcended. Every tradition of Narcissus must be overlooked. We must be reestablished in the native equanimity of fearless birth. This is the Secret: We are a Universal Divine Incarnation.

Every moment of recoil from the arising experience of our birth is a recoil from Ecstatic Unity with the Radiant Transcendental Being. The Law is this: "I" must surrender or Love as the total self (the total body-mind) into and through all relations to the point of Ecstasy, wherein the total body-mind (relieved of recoil, contraction, and self-possession) is Transfigured and Transformed by the Radiance or Light that pervades the total world. And this process of self-sacrifice, or self-surrender in God to the point of Ecstasy, ultimately Outshines the experiential body-mind (or Translates it into the Radiant Divine Domain).

To recoil and contract upon the body-mind is to move away from the Ecstatic Vision of Unity and Realized Bliss. It is to rush toward Chaos, Illusion, and the Zero of self-suppression. The Way of Life is not at all a matter of recoil, contraction, and suppression or division of body, emotion, mind, or self. Rather, it is a matter of love-surrender as the total self or body-mind to the degree of self-transcendence, or Ecstatic Emergence into the Light and Delight of the Spiritual Divine.

Those who advocate the traditional ideal of soul culture, or inversion toward psychic states to the exclusion of physical states, base their enterprise on the observation that we die—and, therefore, they accept only the ideal of adaptation to that which survives bodily death (which is called mind, soul, or essential Self). It is true that death is not a terminal event. Only an aspect of the total being is discarded in death. However, I have observed that merely to die is not sufficient to become Free, Happy, or Enlightened.

In order to properly evaluate the processes of birth and death we must transcend the tendency to recoil from mortal experience, change, and death. Then we can observe that the Law and Purpose of our existence is not merely to become identified with that part of the self that immediately survives death. That part of us that immediately survives death is not itself our ultimate Condition or Destiny. That inner part of the self that observes the phenomena of body and mind is not to be identified as the total self, nor do we Realize Enlightenment or Divine Truth merely by a meditative contemplation that sees and hears and otherwise experiences the internal structures of the body-mind. The Law and Purpose of our existence is Incarnation, or birth as the total psycho-physical self, until that self is thoroughly Transcended, Transfigured, and Transformed through self-sacrifice or Love-Communion with the Living or Spiritual Divine.

It is not merely some inward or subtle part of us that survives death. To be sure, it is only that subtler part that immediately survives physical death, but that subtler part is only partial. It is not inherently

Enlightened or Completed, and it does not permanently remain independent of embodiment. The subtler self is structured so that it inevitably returns to embodiment, or the pattern of Incarnation and Ecstasy, somewhere on Earth or in the Universal Realm of Nature. Therefore, truly, it is not merely a mind or subtle self that survives death. If the total cycle is considered, we must say that a total psycho-physical self survives the death of every psycho-physical self—until Translation, or Emergence into the Transcendental Divine Domain.

306

We are reborn again and again. We are fitted to an endless cycle or circle of manifestation. We may recoil from this process, but in doing so we contract the self, forcing it into self-suppressing patterns of chaos, illusion, or exclusion. Recoil and self-possession, which imitate the appearance of death, are in fact negations of Life. Only transcendence of recoil and self-contraction (and thus of fear, suffering, and nothingness) is the Way of Life. We will inevitably return to states of body-mind until the total body-mind or psycho-physical self is Translated into Light.

Therefore, only God-Love is the true practice of Man—not self-protection, self-possession, and all the desperate and self-deluding acts of Narcissus. We must thoroughly understand our born circumstance and our ultimate Purpose or Destiny. We must Worship the Living Divine Person in Spirit and in Truth. We must, therefore, Worship God bodily—through love-surrender as the total and inherently single or undivided psycho-physical self. We must transcend the self (or body-mind) through love, or expansion beyond self-contraction, rather than submit to self-possession, self-division, and self-negation. We must enter into the natural Equanimity of Ecstasy in God. Therefore, instead of recoiling from the pattern of relations and into the illusions of self, we must surrender directly into the Radiant Transcendental Being and depend on Divine Blessing, Help, and Grace.

The Great Principle of Life-Practice

The usual Man is Narcissus, the self-possessed, the eternal adolescent. He is contracted upon himself at the heart. His willfulness is automatic, unconscious, bereft of the feeling-intelligence. Therefore, he is weak-willed, unable to transcend himself through continuous growth, higher adaptation, and Ecstasy, or Enlightened self-surrender.

The usual Man is a problem. He is self-divided. All his alternatives contradict one another. He is always at war with the parts of his own experience. He is contracted upon the various functions of his own body-mind. He is in shock, suddenly existing as himself alone, unable to discover the Truth of his own Origin, Help, and Condition.

The problem of the usual Man is emotional dissociation. The body-mind or psycho-physical being that is the usual Man is automatically tending to contract upon itself, to be differentiated from all experiential phenomena, to possess and fill its emptiness with the objects of all experience, to protect itself with all knowledge, to separate itself from the mysterious emotional demand of all relations and events.

The strategy of the usual Man is the avoidance of relationship, the avoidance of free emotional association with all beings and events. Each function of the human body-mind is tending toward emotional dissociation from experience. And the root-effort in all forms of psycho-physical dissociation is emotional and total psycho-physical contraction from the All-Pervading Life-Principle, the Living Being that is the Truth and Transcendental Condition of the body-mind and the world itself.

The usual Man is mysteriously committed to self-possessed emotional dissociation from the Universal Life-Energy, and, therefore, from all experience—since all experiences, events, relations, and beings are arising as spontaneous manifestations or modifications of the Universal Life-Energy, the Radiance or Light that is the Matrix and Destiny of all forms of appearance and "matter." The heart of the usual Man, or the emotional-psychic root-being of the unawakened individual, is chronically disturbed, contracted upon itself, dissociated from the Universal Life-Principle that is its own Condition, Help, and Origin. Therefore, the body-mind or total psycho-physical being that expresses the heart of the usual Man is chronically disturbed, contracted upon itself, dissociated from all experience, all phenomena, all events, all relations, all beings, and even from the fulfillment of its own functional existence.

308

The Salvation or Happiness of Man is in emotional conversion, or the conversion of the heart from the automaticities of self-possession to the conscious Realization of Ecstasy, or self-transcending Love-Communion with the Universal Principle or Being that is Life. Such emotional conversion is awakened through constant study and hearing of the Teaching of Truth and constant seeing or intuiting of the Living Divine Presence in the Company of the God-Realized Man and the Community of devotees of the Living God.

Our fundamental responsibility is literal and deep psychic Love of the Presence of Life. We must surrender to Life in order to be full of Life. The Life-Current is the "Holy Spirit," the Divine Effulgence or Grace whereby we may be Transfigured and made One with the Living and Eternal Divine Reality. But we may be thus Transformed only if we transcend all emotional contraction upon the self and, instead, Radiate as Love of the Life-Principle or Living Person that is God. It is emotional conversion to Life that heals our dis-ease. And one who is thus converted will naturally extend his enjoyment of freely-circulating Life into disciplines that prevent toxemia and degenerative abuse of the structural body-mind.

Right emotional submission to the Life-Principle in every moment permits transcendence of enervating emotional and general psycho-physical contractions. And right emotional submission to the Life-Principle in every moment is the basic form of spiritual or religious practice. It is Ecstasy, or Radiant release and transcendence of the self-contraction or ego-obsession that separates us from Life, or the Grace and Person and Condition of the Living God.

My Analysis of Man

The typical esoteric analysis of human existence that is found in the classic mystical and yogic traditions of India is as follows: The soul (or essential self) is different from the body and exists independent of mental and physical states. Observe that no matter what arises as a state of body or mind, whether during waking, dreaming, or sleeping consciousness, <u>you</u> are the <u>witness</u> of it. Therefore, awaken to the presumption of existence as soul or essential self, free by virtue of being independent of body and mind. Likewise, just as the soul or essential self exists within the body-mind, the Infinite Transcendental Divine Reality exists within the soul. Enter into independence as the essential being, and worship or surrender to the Divine within it.

The problem with this analysis—which is a technique of salvation, or liberation of the soul from this world—is that it is a strategy, not merely or simply a direct intuition of the Truth. The entire consideration and process is an expression of an intention that, from the beginning, is primarily concerned with experience as a problem to be escaped—this rather than the expression of a mood that is awakened to the Reality or Truth that is obvious even in the moment of experience.

There is an awakening and a process that develops on the basis of simple and direct consideration of experience. That is the consideration that I have called the Way of Divine Ignorance, or the Western Way. It too is liberating, but it is not strategic in nature. Therefore, it is not to be identified with the analysis or technique that arises in the oriental mode. Nor is it a species of the preference for separation from the experience of body-mind or the effort of exclusive inversion toward inwardness.

The analysis of human existence that naturally arises in the consideration of this Western Way is quite the opposite of the classic oriental or Eastern analysis. In the oriental analysis, the soul or essential self is conceived to be within and separate from the body-mind. In my analysis, the body-mind is conceived to be within (or an inherent modification of) the soul or total self. Just so, in the oriental analysis, the Divine or Transcendental Reality is conceived to be within the soul or self. In my analysis, the total self is conceived to be within (or an inherent modification of) the Transcendental Divine Reality.

Of course, variations on the classic oriental analysis of human experience can be found in the many traditions of the East. Some seem to have a more positive view of psycho-physical experience, or at least a sense that such experience is not to be merely cut off. Others do not have a notion of the Divine within the soul or essential self, but they consider the essential self to be the Transcendental Reality (or Self). But all typically oriental paths are tied in one fashion or another to the preference for strategic inversion, or an orientation which is based in the prior sense of psycho-physical existence as a problem to be solved.

My analysis begins only after the problem or the problem-consciousness is itself overcome in the direct understanding of our experiential position—which is not inherently one of knowledge, dilemma, or doubt, but one of Ignorance, always already and totally free of the binding power of experience in limitation. My analysis does not seek strategic separation of soul or essential self from its empirical conditions. Rather, my analysis proceeds from an understanding of the prior freedom of existence even under the conditions of the body-mind.

The Western Way is, therefore, not a conventional technique of salvation (or liberation from inherent bondage). The Western Way is simply the Way of Life, or the process of Man as Man is.

We exist in Ignorance under the conditions of a universal pattern of psycho-physical conditions, or spontaneous modifications of the Transcendental Reality (in which the total self inheres). Once this is understood, the process of human existence becomes one of equanimity and ecstasy, or self-transcendence within a progressive school or ordeal of Life-positive adaptation and growth.

The Ritual of Incarnation

The meaning or purpose of individual human existence is not evident in the bare fact of birth and experience. Rather, the meaning and purpose of individual human existence is Man, or the ultimate ritual of Incarnation.

311

The test of human existence is in our confrontation with frustration and fear. We are not born merely to exist and to experience. We are not born for our own sake. We are born in God and for the purposes of God, Who is the Living One, the Radiant Being in Whom all beings and things are arising and changing. We are born to transcend ourselves in ecstatic Love-Communion with the Present Divine.

Those who are overcome by frustration and fear recoil or turn back upon themselves, and they are moved to exploit existence for their own sake and to experience for its own sake. Such individuals embrace the usual paths—oriental and occidental. They either become inverted upon their own subjective selves, and thus struggle to escape the body, this world, and the Present Divine in the search for higher or less threatening planes of experience—or else they become extroverted through all the patterns of self-indulgence in the evident scheme of mechanical or "material" Nature. But neither of those paths is true to Man, since both are done in reaction to the Present Play of God, and each is done for the sake of self rather than for the sake of God.

The Way of Life is demonstrated only in the truly human "ritual" of Incarnation, or total psycho-physical surrender to the Present God. The Way of Life is a matter of Ecstasy, or self-transcendence in Love-Communion with the Living Being, the Universal Identity. The Way of Life is demonstrated in the transcendence of frustration, fear, self-possession, and the self-defining or separative power of experience. The Way of Life is demonstrated in freedom from the motive to avoid the relational conditions into which we are born, and in freedom from the tendency to recoil from the mood of ecstatic inherence in the Living Divine. The Way of Life is demonstrated in freedom from all the conditions of attention. The Paradox of the Way of Life is that it depends upon the transcendence of mere experiential attention, whereas it is demonstrated as the Transfigured Incarnation of the Radiant Being, or of Love.

We must surrender to and into the Present God. God is not elsewhere in relation to us now. God is always Present, Alive as all beings, Manifest as the total world. Our obligation is not to invert and go elsewhere to God, nor to extrovert and exploit ourselves in the self-possessed or anti-ecstatic mood that presumes God to be absent or non-existent. Our obligation is to Awaken beyond our selves, beyond the phenomena of body and mind, into That in which body and mind inhere. When we are thus Awakened, our lives become the Incarnation Ritual of Man, whereby only God is evident and only God is the Process of the present and the future. That Way of Life is not bound to this world or any other world, nor to any form of attention in body or mind. Rather, the Way of Life is Ecstatic, God-Made, Free, Radiant, and always already Happy.

Divine Incarnation and the Traditional Method of Death

Traditional esoteric meditation systems are based on duplication of the pattern of death (or "return"), expressed via methods of inversion, withdrawal of attention and energy from the autonomic or peripheral nervous system, exclusive concentration of attention in the central nervous system and the brain, and so forth. Such practices are exercises based on prior emotional, philosophical, and psychic recoil (or revulsion) from the relational pattern of psycho-physical existence and experience. But once the processes of inversion, meditation, or "return" have become complete—to the point of a Transcendental Awakening or Enlightenment, the motive of revulsive recoil from the relational or dependent patterns of experience is itself transcended in newly discovered Spiritual Happiness. Therefore, from the point of view of Enlightenment (rather than the point of view of suffering which provokes the conventional and inverted search for Enlightenment), the "great path of return," or meditation in the likeness of dying, is unnecessary.

The Way that I Teach is founded on the presumption of Enlightenment, rather than on the presumption of suffering which provokes the search for Enlightenment. The Way that I Teach is a Process wherein the Work of Enlightenment determines the practice. My Argument, my Work, and my Presence or Company among those who come to me all serve the Awakening of the presumption of Enlightenment, so that the individual may live and practice in the ecstatic disposition of Transfigured Equanimity rather than the egoic dilemma or self-possessed disposition of fear and entrapment. Therefore, even though initial adaptation to the practice of the Way develops many characteristics of interior attention, the primary and ultimate force and attitude of the practice is not based on a duplication of the exclusive and inverted pattern of death (or the abandonment of body and mind). The ultimate practice of the Way is Radiant, founded on Ecstasy, or priorly Enlightened Equanimity, which spontaneously and inherently Transfigures and Transforms the body-mind and the world of its relations with the Brightness of the Divine Life-Power. Therefore, the practice of the Way that I Teach is based on self-transcending Ecstasy, or present God-Communion, and that practice is expressed via a duplication of the process of birth, or the Radiant Incarnation of God, rather than on death, or the idea of return to God.

Practice of the Way that I Teach Shines via Love, or relational Happiness, free of doubt and separative recoil or contraction of body, emotion, and mind (or attention). The Way does not develop on the basis of self-possessed seeking into the subjective or interior dimension (although the evidence of the deep psyche is not strategically suppressed). Rather, the Way develops on the basis of prior freedom from bondage to the subjective position (or the idea of an independent internal self).

The Way that I Teach is based on the presumption of the Fullness, Onliness, Oneness, and Universal Presence of the Divine Being, Who is the Identity of all beings, and in Whom all phenomena arise as nonbinding modifications of Its own Radiant Consciousness. Therefore, the problematic, internal, independent, and separative self, enclosed and limited by the body-mind, is utterly absent from the presumptions on which practice of the Way is based. There is no internal, finite, separate, and independent self. That is only an illusion we conceive on the basis of our fearful recoil from the experience into which we are Mysteriously born. But if we Awaken to the Living God, the Radiant Self and Universal Body of all, then we are drawn into Ecstasy, or fearless God-Communion, in which the subjective illusions of the body-mind are transcended in the Intuition of a Single, Infinite, Radiant Field of Being, Which includes all beings and things and processes and events, and in Which there are no "consequences" for birth, change, and death, but there is only the Eternal Humor of Love, Transcendence, Bliss, Wisdom, and Happiness.

314

The Living One is always already Present, Alive, Inviting us to Ecstatic Remembrance and Freedom in Divine Communion. The Living One Transfigures or Outshines us in every moment we Remember and Surrender into the Divine Condition, prior to the self-recoil. The Living One is God, the "Expected One" Who is always already here, the Eternal Master Who is Shown directly to Man in the Incarnate Adept and Duplicated in the Happiness of all True Devotees.

Idols

No thought or figure or any perception arising in the mind is, in itself, God. No thing, no body, no moment or place, in itself, is God. Rather, every moment, place, thing, body, or state of mind inheres in God. Whatever arises should be recognized in God, not idolized as God. Then all conditions become Reminders that draw us into the ecstatic presumption of the Mysterious Presence of the Living One.

A Transcendental Adept or true Spiritual Master is a Transparent Reminder of the Living One, a Guide to Ecstatic Remembrance of the One in Whom all conditions arise and change and pass away. Such an Adept is not to be made into the Idol of a Cult, as if God were exclusively contained in the objective person and subjective beliefs of a particular sect. Rather, right relationship to an Adept Spiritual Master takes the form of free ecstatic surrender to the Living Divine based on recognition of the Living One in the

Revelation of Freedom, Happiness, Love, Wisdom, Help, and Radiant Power that Shines in the Company of the Adept. Right relationship to a true Spiritual Master is the most fundamental basis of the universal process that is true religion, and there is no basis for "religious differences" at the level of actual practice and Realization.

The Ultimate Instruction

The *Bhagavad Gita*[1] can ultimately (and rightly) be read as a consideration of the spiritual intuition whereby we may pass from the sixth into the seventh stage of life (or <u>from</u> the practices and experiences of the first six stages of life <u>to</u> the ecstatic disposition or Way represented by the seventh stage of life). The *Bhagavad Gita* is a book about how the body-mind and the atomic soul (the "Atman" or Self of the body-mind) may be transcended via ecstatic surrender into the Infinite Divine Soul (the "Paramatman" or Self of the total Cosmos of beings and worlds).

Thus, "Arjuna" ultimately represents the atomic soul at the level of Self-Realization, or the mood wherein the being desires undisturbed repose in itself, to the exclusion of the Play of Man in the

---

1. The *Bhagavad Gita* (literally, "Divine Song") is one of the most revered Scriptures of the Hindus, and a religious text of universal appeal and profound esoteric significance. Vyasa (Krishna Draipayana) is traditionally presumed to be the author, and it was written perhaps as early as the 5th century B.C. (but with its roots in the oral tradition of even more ancient days). Most scholars agree that it may have been revised and expanded considerably over the years.

The *Gita* is a portion of the great ancient epic and spiritual allegory, the *Mahabharata* which is the story of a great fratricidal struggle between two royal families in northern India some 4,000 years ago. It is the purported dialogue between the God-Man Krishna and his devotee Arjuna, Commander-in-Chief of the army of the Pandavas, for whom Krishna serves as Charioteer. Arjuna, faced with the prospect of having to kill friends and cousins in an imminent battle, wishes to shirk his duty as a warrior. Krishna refuses to allow him such self-indulgence. He engages Arjuna in a Teaching conversation that continues for seven hundred verses and presents a philosophical summation of the Nature of God as the Supreme Self, a critical exposition of the many ways of esoteric spiritual practice, and a declaration of the supremacy of the Way of devotional Communion with the Supreme Divine Person in the Form of the living Divine Master—in this case, Krishna himself. His entire spiritual Teaching to Arjuna is summarized in his instruction for the forthcoming battle: "Remember Me, and fight."

Realm of Nature. "Krishna" represents the Divine Soul or Transcendental Being, wherein <u>both</u> the Realm of Nature, including the body-mind of Man, and the Atman, the Self or atomic individual soul, are arising.

Therefore, Krishna first describes to Arjuna (for the sake of the reader, who is presumed to represent any possible level of soul-evolution, up to the sixth stage, or inner Self-Realization) the various processes of self-transcending discipline that ultimately permit perfect discrimination between the inner Self (which is the Transcendental Essence of individual existence) and all phenomenal conditions of the body-mind. Then, at last, Krishna reveals the Secret of the Liberation even of the inner Self in the Universal Divine Self.

Arjuna, representing the stage of inner Self-Realization, is shown to be in doubt, even despair, and tormented by the "problem" that world-consciousness (or psycho-physical awareness in the Realm of Nature) presents to the soul that desires to rest in itself. He represents the inherent dilemma of the sixth stage of life. Krishna explains the entire philosophy and practice that leads up to the superior and yet not Liberated state of Arjuna. But Arjuna's doubt or dilemma is dissolved only when he is distracted from himself (or the world-excluding mood of inward Self-Realization) by the Revelation of That which transcends the Atman. Only when the inner Self (or the soul exclusive of psycho-physical conditions and objects) is Awakened to the Revelation of its own Divine Source (which is also the ultimate Source of all psycho-physical conditions and objects—or the Realm of Nature) is it Liberated into Happiness.

Therefore, Krishna, the Divine Person or Transcendental Being, Reveals that the ultimate inward Self is not the Truth—nor is that Realization equal to ultimate Liberation and Happiness. The soul itself (or the inner Self Itself) must surrender totally to the Remembrance of the Being which is not merely within Man but within which Man and the entire Realm of Nature are arising. The Truth is not the being within the body-mind but the Being in which both the inner being and the total world of experience inhere.

The Instruction of the Divine Person is that Happiness is not to be found in exclusive devotion to one's own deepest being for its own sake. Rather, Happiness is found in ecstatic surrender of the deep being and all its psycho-physical expressions to the Transcendental, Infinite, Radiant, All-Pervading Divine Person. It is the constant <u>presumption</u> of utter relationship to the Divine Being (to the point of inherence) that Krishna prescribes as the ultimate Way of Life. And that Way of Life, it is promised, not only permits transcendence of the limitations of the body-mind (and the conditions of this world) while we are yet alive, but it permits the soul (once it has matured to the degree of Perfectly Transfigured Ecstasy) to pass out of this world (even the entire conditional Realm of Nature, or the "material universe") at death, and thence to pass into the deathless and Divine Realm of Eternal Life or Eternal Inherence in the Divine Bliss.

Krishna's ultimate Instruction is: "Remember Me. Yield your attention to Me through love in every moment, and serve Me in love as all beings, through every kind of harmonious and right activity, under all conditions." This is the ultimate Teaching of the Perfect Adept. It is given by Krishna in the *Bhagavad Gita*, by Jesus in the *New Testament,* and under many other Names in the Holy Books of all religious traditions that are rooted in the Work of Transcendental Adepts or true Spiritual Masters. Such Instruction implies constant adherence to ecstatic or self-transcending disciplines of action and attention until all limitations are Outshined by the Unqualified Bliss of the Radiant Divine.

The Ultimate Instruction and Revelation given through Divine Adepts is a Way of Ecstatic Happiness, whereby the "school" of this world may be gracefully accomplished and a Perfect Destiny generated through right <u>esoteric</u> sacrifice, or love. That Instruction also includes ordinary or exoteric grades of demand, including physical and moral disciplines as well as emotional, mental, and higher psychic stages of development. But the highest grade of this Instruction is a purely esoteric or Transcendental Revelation, which is finally understood only in the Event of Self-Realization (or the profound Realization of the sixth stage of life).

The inward or central Self of the body, the senses, the emotions, the mind, and the higher psyche must be perfectly Realized, and then even that deep Self must surrender into the Universal Self of the total Cosmos of beings, things, and processes. Such a Way of Life is not the same as the popular exoteric religious idea of the need for the creature to depend on the Creator, for such dependency is not an inherently ecstatic or self-transcending practice. (The conventional dependence of the creature on the Creator involves unenlightened identification of the creature-being with the conditions of the body-mind and similar identification of the Creator-Being with the phenomenal Realm of Nature, whereas both the inner Self and the Divine Self are always in a Condition of Transcendental Equilibrium, even under the apparent conditions of experience in the Realm of Nature. And there is no Freedom for Man in Nature unless the inner Self is Awakened from its presumed bondage to the body-mind and also from its illusions of independence from the Universal Transcendental Divine Being.) Therefore, the "creature" must transcend both the body-mind and the universe (or the total Realm of Nature). And such transcendence or Ecstasy is Realized only through Love-Communion with the Universal Divine Person, the Living One, the Divine Master, the Source of all, Who is in all, transcending all, living and breathing and loving all, and eternally Free. The Way of Life so considered involves growth to maturity in the sixth stage of life and perfect Transfiguration in the seventh stage of life.

318

The Gospel of Krishna and Jesus

I

*The "Supreme Secret" of the **Bhagavad Gita***

The original cultural context of the *Bhagavad Gita* was one founded on the idea of "dharma." Every aspect of human life and action was, in ancient India, founded on the idea of a "dharma," or a right and prescribed form of association and action leading toward right, benign, lawful, positive, and pleasurable results. And "dharmas" or actions in general were conceived to belong to one or the other of two classes: those that would produce good results in this world and lifetime (as well as the next) and those that would lead away from the plane of such results and toward the highest or most perfect Realization of God. Krishna, the Supreme Lord, Savior or

Liberator, and Teacher in the *Bhagavad Gita,* speaks of all the various "dharmas," both worldly and ascetic, and instructs us that any or all of them may be performed—even should be performed (according to our station in life)—but He explains that all "dharmas" or actions should be performed without attachment to the motive represented by the result that naturally follows. Thus, Krishna admonishes us: Do what is right and necessary in your station of life, but do not be attached to the results of what you do.

319

The first seventeen chapters of the *Bhagavad Gita* are devoted essentially to the enumeration of "dharmas" and the paradoxical (and seemingly difficult) admonition not to avoid them but also not to be attached to what results from them. It is only in the eighteenth and final chapter that the "Supreme Secret" is told. And that "Secret" is the Teaching that makes it possible to act rightly and at the same time remain free of the motivation to attain pleasurable results for their own sake.

The *Bhagavad Gita* does not merely recommend either active or psychological detachment from pleasurable experiences and results of action. Rather, it recommends an orientation in the moment of action (since action itself need not and even cannot be avoided) that permits one to live as if free of "karma" (or the results of action) even though one still performs actions that naturally lead to worldly results. The ascetic path of performing only those "dharmas" that lead away from worldly results and only toward Divine results is not recommended as the appropriate path for everyone (although it is not denied as an appropriate path for those whose station or circumstance and qualities make it suitable). But the path of worldly "dharmas" is reinterpreted and oriented toward God-Realization. The method is not ascetic detachment from association with action and result. Rather, the method recommended in the *Bhagavad Gita* is right or appropriate action, including non-avoidance of the results— but the orientation in every moment is to be the one of service and whole-hearted surrender of feeling-attention to the Transcendental Divine Being.

Throughout the *Bhagavad Gita* the "Secret" of devotion to the Divine Person and Being (or Ultimate Identity and Power) is suggested as the key to Liberation and Happiness. But in chapter eighteen the Supreme Doctrine is most explicitly and summarily expressed. In verse sixty-six the essence of the Divine Message of the

320

Supreme Master is proclaimed: Abandon and release the point of view of all conventional "dharmas" (or the various kinds of lawful action anciently prescribed for the different classes of humanity, and which naturally produce the auspicious results for which they were designed, such as control of body and mind, mystical ascent to subtler planes of experience, health and well-being in this gross plane of experience, family and social relations, property and wealth, power and fame, and even righteous victory over enemy powers and daemonic individuals who aggressively oppose the "dharmic" way of life and its harmonizing social influence), and embrace only the point of view of My "Dharma" (which can and should be applied as the Principle of all lawful and appropriate actions, and which naturally produces the Most Auspicious Result of Transcendental Absorption in the Divine Being and Liberation from all the binding results of action and experience in this world). Do what is right, appropriate, and necessary, but do not do anything for its own sake or merely for the sake of its conventional and self-fulfilling reward. Do whatever is right, appropriate, and necessary, but do it as literal service to Me, as heartfelt surrender to Me, as Remembrance of Me, as Communion with Me—and by this means you will constantly Realize Me and ultimately come to Me.

The *Bhagavad Gita*, in its setting, represents a philosophical solution to the problem posed by the obligation to act in the world according to one's station (which obligation was spelled out in clearly detailed "dharmas" according to the class of one's birth in ancient Indian society) and the desire to escape the world and fly to the Divine Domain. Therefore, action (including the apparent "actor," or the total body-mind) is reinterpreted as a sacrifice to God rather than as a means toward ends for their own sake—and action as sacrifice is further interpreted as ecstatic or self-transcending surrender into the Divine Person and Identity. Those who renounced conventional "dharmas" and accepted this "Dharma" were thus promised the same ultimate "Reward" (which is God-Realization or Liberation in God) that ascetics pursue by renouncing action itself.

The "Message" of the *Bhagavad Gita* remains spiritually relevant even outside the "dharma"-regulated social system of ancient and traditional India. Salvation or Liberation from the destiny of suffering, self-confinement, and separation from the Transcendental Bliss of the Ultimate Divine Reality is neither a matter of strategic self-service and self-indulgence (or "hedonism") nor strategic self-suppression (or "asceticism"). Rather, it is a matter of constant Ecstasy, moment to moment God-Communion, or self-surrendering and self-transcending Love-Communion with the Living, All-Pervading, Transcendental Divine Being.

321

II

The "Good News" of the New Testament

The cultural context in which Jesus of Nazareth and the foundation culture of the *New Testament* originally appeared was the ancient sacred social order of the Jews. That sacred social order was founded as a complex of "laws," or actions prescribed by the sacred tradition as being right, auspicious, and fruitful. The sacred social order of the ancient Jews, founded on the system of "laws," was, within its own domain, much like the sacred social order of the ancient Hindus, founded on the system of "dharmas." The concept or point of view of life according to the "laws" of ancient Israel is the primary notion to which the criticism of Jesus is directed in the *New Testament*, just as the concept or point of view of life according to the "dharmas" of the ancient Hindus is the primary notion to which the criticism of Krishna is directed in the *Bhagavad Gita*. And the Gospel ("Good News") of Jesus (who is the "Christ" or Supreme Lord, Savior or Liberator, and Teacher in the *New Testament,* just as Krishna is in the *Bhagavad Gita*) is essentially identical to the "Supreme Secret" of Krishna.

In the Teaching of Jesus, as in that of Krishna, the principle of "law" (or "dharma") is replaced by the Principle of Divine Communion (or absolute surrender of body and mind, from the heart, in Communion with the Divine Being and Master of all beings, through the engagement of all right, necessary, and appropriate actions as service to the Lord of all, Who is presumed to be Transcendental, All-Pervading, and also manifest in and through all other beings and all circumstances). The "law" only produces results for the independent self, and thus it is self-binding and tending toward loveless or non-ecstatic self-possession. But Divine Communion is Truth, Happiness, and Liberation (or Salvation). Thus, the "law" is not replaced (right, appropriate, and even sacredly prescribed action in all relationships is still enjoined by Jesus), but the idea or point of view of action for its own sake is replaced by the Idea or point of view of action as Communion with God.

322

Jesus is presumed, in the *New Testament*, to be a man in a Condition of total Union, Unity, and Identity with the Divine Being, just as Krishna is presumed to be in the *Bhagavad Gita*. Krishna "proves" or demonstrates His Divinity by showing His devotee, Arjuna, how all beings and things and dimensions of the cosmos reside in Him and depend on Him. Jesus "proves" or demonstrates His Divinity by restoring His own life after He was dead and by similar expressions of Spirit-Power. And, in the case of both Krishna and Jesus, the ecstatic or self-transcending devotional relationship to the Divine Master as the Eternal Person in Whom we inhere (or "live and move and have our being") is communicated to mankind as the Way and the Truth of Life, Liberation, and Salvation (whereby every such devotee will ultimately be drawn out of the maze of suffering and into the Kingdom or Ultimate Domain of God).

Jesus, in the *New Testament*, Reveals to His devotees that He is to be accepted simply as the Eternal Divine Being while He lives, and He declares that He is also to be presumed to return to a Mysterious Condition of absolute Identity with the Divine Being after He dies (or otherwise leaves this world and is seen no more in His human appearance). The self-sacrificing or ecstatic love-relationship to Him (Who is simply the Eternal Divine Being) is to be embraced as the Way, the Truth, and the very substance of Eternal Life or Happiness. He is to be Remembered in love in every moment, and served by every kind of appropriate (or loving, compassionate, self-transcending, and Life-positive or Spirit-positive) action. The self-based principle and point of view of the "letter" of the "laws" (or the "dharmas") prescribed for righteousness before God and good results in this world are to be relaxed and released, and the heart is to become centered in present God-Communion, so that the mind and every action will be transformed by the infusion of the Spirit of God.

Both Jesus and Krishna declare: Remember Me in every moment, in every action, and in all beings. Such "Remembrance" is not the same as calling a past acquaintance, now dead, to memory. Rather, Divine Remembrance is present Divine Communion. It is to Remember (or call oneself to the presumption) that the Lord, Master, and Divine Being of all beings is Eternally Present, Transcendental, All-Pervading, and Radiant.

Just so, we should not be righteously angered or even dismayed to discover that the same Truth, Doctrine, and Offering has been Communicated by two entirely different Teachers (or Traditions). Indeed, the same Truth, Doctrine, and Teaching has been legitimately made by many different Teachers, or Spiritual Masters, in many times and places in this world—and, happily, such Masters will always be a feature of human history. When such a Master speaks, it is not merely the man that speaks and says: I am God. It is the Realization of the man that speaks. And that Realization has not only been the Great Discovery and Destiny of a few. It has, since ancient times, been declared to be the Truth and Condition to be Realized equally by all—if they will enter into the Ecstasy of the Way of Divine Communion.

There is no true basis for Christian sectarianism or Hindu sectarianism. Indeed, all the "great religions" of the world are centered in the same Revelation. It is time we all awakened from our provincial religious presumptions and accepted all human cultures as our heritage. It is time we ceased to struggle to dominate one another with our sectarian "Revelations" and actually began to practice the right, appropriate, responsible, and Life-positive discipline of action in the Ecstatic Way, Truth, and Life (or Spirit) of God-Communion, which is the only means of the Salvation, Liberation, or Happiness of Man.

323

Krishna, Jesus,
and the Way of God-Communion

The *Srimad Bhagavatam* (which is also known as the *Bhagavata Purana*,[2] and which, along with the *Bhagavad Gita*, represents the basic Teachings of Krishna) contains the most ancient "oriental" idea: If you are not literally separated from (or absorbed away from) the body (and then the mind) before death, then at death the body (or the mind, if the body is already renounced) will determine the future (as reincarnation in a physical body or as temporary ascent to a subtle-mental realm). Therefore, Krishna advises that we turn away from the body and the mind while alive—and the Way He recommends is to surrender mind and body into the Transcendental Divine Being while immediately or gradually abandoning or withdrawing from overt physical and mental activities and relations.

As a consequence of this ancient "oriental" and even ascetic logic, the world, the body, and the mind have generally been interpreted in negative terms in the Hindu tradition. However, the world, the body, and the mind are not a threat to Divine Realization—they are only a threat to the independent ego-self (which depends on them, obsessively clings to them, and is separated from them by misfortune and death). It is only necessary to transcend the ego-self in the Divine Being, since the arising or non-arising of experiential conditions cannot undermine the Love-Bliss or Radiant Happiness of Ecstatic God-Realization. Therefore, an alternative to the ascetic or strategically world-denying Way is proposed in the *Srimad Bhagavatam*, the *Bhagavad Gita*, and other ancient Hindu texts. It is the Way of Ecstatic or self-transcending Love-Communion with the Transcendental Divine Being (or Person) via all kinds of

---

2. The *Bhagavata Purana*, or the *Srimad Bhagavatam*, is rightly esteemed as the most complete and authoritative exposition of ancient knowledge in the literature of the Hindu tradition of spirituality. Its roots are in ancient oral traditions, but it may have been put into writing between the fifth and tenth centuries A.D. The author is purported to be Vyasa. This "Purana" is the ultimate text of spiritual science, or the Way of the Devotional Sacrifice of Man into God. It extols the Virtues of the Divine Person, principally in the form of Krishna, and communicates the esoteric secrets of the Way in which we may Realize that One.

physical and mental actions and relations. This alternative Way does not require conventional renunciation (or strategic separation of the being from the world, the body, and the mind) but only right (lawful or appropriate) action and association done as direct service and surrender to the Divine Being. The Teaching of this alternative Way indicates that there are superior relations as well as superior or right actions. Thus, it is recommended that general association with other devotees is the optimum circumstance, and the unique devotional relationship to a God-Realized Spiritual Master is prescribed as the most profound and direct means of transformation toward Ecstasy.

The Teaching of Krishna is actually transmitted in two basic modes. The first is the ascetic mode, or the "Dharma" of intelligent renunciation of body and mind (since these are mortal, troublesome, and deluding). This "ascetic Dharma" involves strict limitation of one's bodily associations and obligations as well as profound inversion of mind toward the "inner Controller," which is ultimately Realized to inhere in the Single, Infinite, and Transcendental Divine Being. The second mode of Krishna's Teaching is one that could be called His "popular Dharma." And it does not involve strategic renunciation of bodily associations, nor even the specific esoteric techniques of mental inversion (including breath control, attention to subtle internal objects, and so forth). Rather, it is simply the Way of devotional Communion with the Divine Being, Who is conceived to Exist as the One Transcendental Reality, but Who is also to be Worshipped and Remembered by Name, in the form of the Spiritual Master, through stories about His activities in the world, through service to His devotees, through ceremonial worship, prayer, and loving internal meditation on simple images of His form and attributes, and so forth.

The "popular Dharma" of Krishna is not "easy" in the sense that it requires no discipline, but it is a Way that can be pursued without strategic avoidance of "natural" associations and activities. Therefore, it can be recommended to all, whereas the "ascetic Dharma" can be successfully embraced only by the relative few who are, by tendency, suited for it. Even so, the Way proposed by Krishna, whether in the form of the "ascetic Dharma" or the "popular Dharma," is always associated with a process of ultimate inversion or absorption, so that the body and mind will not determine the future of the devotee after death. The Ultimate Goal of the Way of Krishna is <u>always</u> absorption in the Transcendental Divine Being—to the exclusion of bodily and mental states of experience.

It is this devotion to the Transcendental Divine Being to the point of the exclusion of physical and mental awareness of this world (and even higher worlds) that most basically characterizes the ancient "oriental" Way of Liberation or Religious Salvation. It is the Way of Worship of the Divine as Source, even prior to the Divine as Creator and Creation.

In contrast to Krishna's "oriental" Teaching of the Way, we may consider Jesus' "occidental" Teaching of the Way. The *New Testament* is best understood as an extension of the religious culture of the *Old Testament,* or the tradition of the Hebrew people. The tradition of the Hebrews (or Jews) is, in comparison to the Hindu tradition, classically "occidental." The traditions of the Semites (including the followers of Islam) of the ancient Middle East are all profoundly committed to the idea of God as Creator (not the Transcendental Being prior to the Creator and Creation) and to a religious Way of Life based on the relationship between the individual (or communities of individuals) and the Creative Divine Being. Therefore, when Jesus speaks as Teacher within the Hebrew tradition, He naturally fits the mode of a spiritual philosopher in that tradition (even as Krishna belongs to the mode of philosophy natural to the Hindus). For this reason, just as Krishna may ultimately value the devotee who is a meditative ascetic (or at least one who acts only as a service to God and who thereby becomes meditatively or Transcendentally absorbed), Jesus seems to value the "good man" who receives every kind of fulfillment as a gift from God. However, Krishna does not value renunciation for its own sake, nor does Jesus value good works for their own sake. Both Krishna and Jesus value the <u>means</u> of the Way only because those means make possible the Realization of God (or the Transcendental Happiness that awakens in Spiritual Communion with the Divine Being).

Krishna is not ultimately committed to the "oriental" habit (or the method of renunciation and inversion), as His Teaching of the "popular Dharma" declares. (In the case of Arjuna, Krishna even demands acceptance of dutiful obligations in a spirit of inner renunciation rather than the ascetic mode of outer renunciation.) Just so, Jesus is not ultimately committed to the "occidental" mode of devotion to God for the sake of worldly blessings. (Even the historical

326

disregard of the mystical and gnostic esotericism of Jesus cannot hide the obviously mystical, ascetic, and even "oriental" quality of His personal habit of mind and body.) Both Krishna and Jesus are (or were) Teachers within religious and cultural traditions that are either relatively "oriental" or relatively "occidental"—but both Krishna and Jesus are primarily oriented not to an exclusive or one-sided cultural identity but to the Liberation or Salvation of mankind through direct and Ecstatic Love-Communion with the Divine Being.

Krishna may seem to propose a Way in which to escape the world, the body, and the mind—but actually He proposes a Way to Realize God. It is simply that He speaks within an "oriental" cultural context, in which it is presumed that, if God is Realized, the world, the body, and the mind are necessarily abandoned or escaped.

Just so, it may seem that Jesus proposes a Way in which to fulfill and even glorify the world, the body, and the mind—but actually He, like Krishna, proposes a Way to Realize God. It is simply that He speaks within an "occidental" context, in which it is presumed that if God is Realized, the world, the body, and the mind are helped, fulfilled, and ultimately glorified.

The "oriental" mode of the Teaching of Krishna may seem to propose that God be Realized in order to escape the world, the body, and the mind—but actually He proposes that God be Realized purely for the sake of that Realization itself. It is simply that the "oriental" concept of God-Realization implies ecstatic identification with the Transcendental Divine Being in itself, prior to any association with the worlds, bodies, or conditions of mind that emanate from or seem to be reflected upon the Divine Being.

Just so, the "occidental" mode of the Teaching of Jesus may seem to propose that God be Realized for the sake of the world, the body, and the mind—but actually He proposes that God be Realized purely for the sake of that Realization itself. It is simply that the "occidental" concept of God-Realization implies Ecstatic devotion to the Transcendental Divine Being within the context of the world, bodily relations, and all the states of mind that arise within and depend upon the Divine Being.

Therefore, both Krishna and Jesus, in the scriptural traditions in which they appear to us, propose a Way of Life in which the fundamental purpose is service, surrender, and Ecstatic or self-transcending devotion to the Transcendental Divine Being or Person in which all beings, worlds, bodies, and states of mind appear, change, and disappear. But each Teaches the Way basically from the point of view of either the "oriental" or the "occidental" context in which they appeared or within which the scriptural traditions of their Teachings have been transmitted.

But which Way is the true Way? Both are true within their cultural context—just as God may be considered to Exist both as the undifferentiated Transcendental Being and as the Creator, Sustainer, Destiny, All-Pervading Grace, and Ultimate Resort of the world, the body, and the mind.

However, in our time, very few individuals or cultures actually survive within the specific and independent context of either the "orient" or the "occident." And in the future the worldwide community of Man will likely cease to create the "oriental-occidental" cultural divisions that defined the ancient cultures and religions and modes of knowledge. Therefore, the God and Truth of Krishna and Jesus must be Realized as One God and Truth. And the Teaching that I propose to you in this time or age is the ancient Teaching of God-Realization, but I propose God-Realization to you both for its own sake and for the sake of the world, the body, the mind, and all beings. The Way that I Teach is not founded on the strategic position of either the "orient" or the "occident" relative to the world, the body, and the mind. Rather, it is founded simply on the direct matter of God-Realization. And if God is Realized prior to strategies either for or against the world, the body, and the mind, then the world, the body, and the mind will be Transfigured (and thereby fulfilled and ultimately glorified) by that Realization. Likewise, mankind and every devotee will, in time, discover that even the world, the body, and the mind are inherently Transcended and ultimately dissolved or Outshined by the Power of that same Realization.

Human existence is not rightly engaged as an ascetic effort toward separation from the world, the body, and the mind, nor is human existence rightly engaged as an effort toward fulfillment and glorification of the world, the body, and the mind. Human existence is rightly engaged only as self-transcending Communion with the Living Divine Person, Who is the Eternal Transcendental Being in which all beings, worlds, bodies, and states of mind arise, change, disappear, and always inhere, and Who also is Present as the Creative Purpose of every moment of the world, the body, and the mind (if these will only be surrendered and devoted to the One Who Lives them). We must confess our dependence upon and our inherence within the Divine Being. And that confession must exceed the notion of an inward "soul" or "essence" that is in contact with God. Our confession must be a total confession of the total being—it must be a total confession of body and mind, in which the "I" that surrenders is not merely <u>within</u> the body-mind but is actually surrendered <u>as</u> or via the body-mind. The Way of Life is not merely a matter of "oriental" introversion or of "occidental" extroversion. It is not a matter of either separating the being from the body-mind or of identifying the being exclusively with the limits of the body-mind. It is always a matter of the Blissful <u>Equanimity</u> of Divine Communion, whether one is personally relatively "ascetic" or relatively "worldly." It is always a matter of the moment to moment transcendence of the limits of experience, or the limits of the body-mind, through active as well as meditative surrender of body and mind in Ecstatic Love-Communion with the Living One.

329

The Way That I Teach

The Way that I Teach is the Way of surrender, or spontaneous and total psycho-physical Transfiguration. It is the radical Way of native, whole bodily, moment to moment surrender to the Radiant Principle that pervades the body-mind and the total world. It is the Way of the transcendence of the egoic adventure of attention, or the self-contraction that is itself attention. It is the Way of surrender of the psycho-physical attention that is the ego, or the reactive self-contraction in every moment. It is the Transcendental Way of the tacit Realization of God, Who is the Primal Life-Radiance and Essential Being of all. It is the Way that is founded upon direct, moment to moment, intuitive, emotional, and even bodily Realization that the Infinitely Radiant Being is the Principle of existence, rather than "matter," or the contracted self, who is the disturbed, self-divided being that is always seeking its own fulfillment through experience and acquired knowledge.

330

Traditionally, spiritual life is viewed as a progressive path of experience, a progression of stages of the return of attention (which is ultimately the same as the ego-contraction) to the Source, Condition, and Environment of Happiness. The Great Path of Return, in either its Eastern or its Western mode, is typically the adventure of the contracted or mortally threatened ego's search for God, for Truth, the Answer, the Source, the Creator, the Self, the Ultimate Principle, the Wonderful Reality, the Eternal Pleasure, or Happiness itself.

The difference between the Great Path of experience, or self-fulfillment, and Way that I Teach is the difference between attention, or egoic concentration in experience, and surrender, or self-transcendence in every moment of experience. The "Good News" of the Way that I Teach is that Truth is the all-pervading Foundation of experiential existence, and it is the Truth in this moment. Thus, in the case of the Way that I Teach, the individual lives on the basis of the always present surrender of the body-mind, or the state of experience and knowledge, into the always Present or Transcendental Life-Principle. The Way is founded on the Ecstatic or self-transcending Realization of God in every moment, rather than on the basis of the experiential dilemma and self-fulfilling motivations of the psycho-physical ego, which you usually consider to be the foundation of human existence and destiny. This Way of surrender, then, this Way of Divine Ignorance, or Radical Understanding, is the very Way of Life, which presupposes the Truth or self-transfiguring Happiness of God-Realization in every instant.

The Way that I Teach is not itself another path, separate from the progressive stages of human experience or growth and evolution. The Way that I Teach is the disposition of psycho-physical surrender to the Radiant Being, through which all inevitable experience may be transcended.

The Restoration of Laughter

All the objects of experience and all the kinds of knowledge imply and exploit the psycho-physical self (the composite ego or total "I"), and each moment of experience or knowledge defines or limits the ego (the functional experiencer or manifest knower) and turns or fastens it upon itself. Therefore, experience or knowledge of any kind <u>inherently</u> involves finite or separated egoic existence and functional or manifest self-confinement. And the continuous process of experiencing or knowing tends to produce or reinforce the defensive habit or reactive reflex of self-contraction, self-meditation, and self-possession.

331

There is no form of experience nor any kind or degree of knowledge that can produce release from the three-phase (or three-part) cycle of experience, knowledge, and self-confinement. As a result, the conventional core or essence or effect of all experience or knowledge is the mysterious sense of limitation, the mysterious feeling of separation, and the gnawing presumption of the lack of perfect knowledge. And the usual man, unaware of the fruitlessness of his own ultimate motivation, is inherently bound to a chronic sense of dilemma and to a life of seeking for release, completion, or "reunion" via consummate experience and ultimate or complete knowledge.

No amount of experience finally releases or dissolves the experiencer (the troubled ego), since all experience involves and reinforces the psycho-physical or manifest and composite self. And no amount of knowledge acquired through experience or through contemplation of experience dissolves the ego-sense, the sense of inherent limitation (selfness or self-contraction), the sense of unbridgeable separation (from all that is not oneself), and the growing presumption of the lack of perfect or complete knowledge (or the attainment of what is yet to be experienced and known). The reactive ego-contraction tends to remain at the root of all experience and all knowledge, and the total psycho-physical self is, therefore, constantly bound by the sense of craving for what is not yet attained.

That craving sense is only the <u>mood</u> or self-perception of the ego itself. That craving <u>is</u> the self. That eternal dissatisfaction <u>is</u> the

"I" within "me," and that is "me" altogether. Fear, sorrow, desire (or "lust"), and anger are "myself," since "I" am separate, alone, unfinished, incomplete, and threatened "forever." This fruitless adventure in search for ultimate satisfaction, union, and release is the necessary destiny of the relentless ego. "I" is Narcissus, the self-centered body-mind. "I" is inherently committed to the failure of its own search, to separation from all relations, beings, things, and events. The commitment or will to release via experience and knowledge is a sham. It is idol worship. It is nothing more than self-embrace. Its results are never more than frustration, tension, and bewilderment.

Therefore, experience or knowledge cannot satisfy or release the self from itself. Only self-transcendence is release from self. And, because the self is created, defined, and limited by the composite of psycho-physical experience and knowledge, the secret of self-transcendence is the native or inherent transcendence of all experience, all knowledge, all psycho-physical phenomena of every kind, high or low.

The Way to self-transcendence, or—since the self is simply the craving sense, mood, or center defined by experience and knowledge—the Way to transcendence of experience and knowledge, is not to be found in any manipulation of the psycho-physical being. It is not a matter of seeking to abandon experience, knowledge, thought, action, pleasure, pain, sex, food, breath, and so forth. Nor is self-transcendence itself identical to any absence of activity, or thought, and so forth. Quietude, or any suppression of the experiential or knowing body-mind is, in itself, a merely self-negating state, not a matter of self-transcendence.

The Way to self-transcendence is not to become the enemy of Life, or of human existence, or even of one's own manifest existence. To suppress the composite self or "I" is only to intensify the mood of the self, which is the primary sense of separation, limitation, and vulnerability.

Nor is the Way to self-transcendence a matter of the strategic embrace of one's own functional existence, to exploit, until death, the psycho-physical potential for experience and knowledge. The Way to self-transcendence is not a matter of embracing the world for one's own sake, or for the sake of experience and knowledge themselves, or for the sake of any conceived ideal, result, or ultimate end. All of that is an abusive passion, an unliberated craving, in which the primary effect of self-possession, anger, and despair is the only certain attainment.

There is no Way to self-transcendence, since all progress or change is only a modification of the self, or the continuation of confinement to separation, limitation, and the unsolvable dilemma of craving for union or release. The Way can only be a matter of self-transcendence. The Way must, in every moment, be actual and perfect self-transcendence, or else self-transcendence is never Realized.

Then what is the Way? Just as interest in the Way is founded upon insight into the necessary egoic-confinement that is the inherent result of psycho-physical experiencing and knowing, the actual process of the Way is also a matter of insight, or direct and immediate intuitive understanding, in every moment. Insight reveals the factuality of reactive self-confinement and the fruitlessness of the search for salvation, release, or perfect fulfillment. And radical insight is itself the very moment of self-transcendence.

And what is that radical insight that is itself self-transcendence, or release of the mood and motivated effort of self-confinement? It is the native Realization or Intuition that no matter what "I" may experience, or reflect, or know about the apparent realm or process of subjective and objective phenomena, "I" do not know what even a single thing is. "I" am inherently and eternally Ignorant. What is "I"? What is the world? What is energy or Life? Neither limited nor complete experience or knowledge could ever modify or dissolve the inherent Ignorance that is the fundamental Condition of the experiential and knowing psycho-physical self. By maintaining stressful or motivated interest in more and more experience and knowledge (or subjective reflection of the world of phenomena), "I" may postpone confrontation with the ultimate Fact and Consequence of inherent Ignorance. But this confrontation is both necessary and ultimate, and the Consequence of that confrontation is immediate and wholly Liberating.

Ignorance, or inherent non-confinement to any limitation, is always already the very and ultimate Condition of the body-mind, the manifest self, the composite "I." In any moment that this insight prevails, there is no self-confinement, no limitation created by the intrusion of any experience or form of knowledge. To abide in this insight or intuition of one's native Condition is to transcend all the forms of self-confinement, self-awareness, object-awareness, awareness of limitation, separation-awareness, and craving or seeking for release via more perfect or complete experience or knowledge. Even as all kinds of experience and knowledge arise, and even as the conventions of mindfulness of "I" (or the sense of limited experiential self-existence and the sense of separation from various levels of phenomena or knowledge) arise, if the intuition of Ignorance is Awakened in that moment, no limit is established, and the drama of the threatened self is inherently transcended.

Therefore, the Way that I Teach is the Way of Radical Understanding, or this Radical Intuition of Ignorance, which is the same as Divine Ecstasy (or self-transcending Love-Communion with the Radiant Transcendental All-Pervading and Only God). For those who Understand, there is only God. No experience, no knowledge, no object, no other, and no internal or subjective state ever binds the Divine Self, the Transcendental Heart, if there is "Remembrance" of God (or the Transcendental Condition prior to self-confinement) through radical Intuition of inherent Ignorance.

The Way is this: "Hear" (or understand) the criticism of the usual life of self-confinement and the torment of self-generated seeking. "See" (or surrender to the Living God) in the Company of the perfect or complete Adept, who abides always in Ecstasy, whatever arises. Awaken to the stable Intuition of self-transcending (or experience-transcending and knowledge-transcending) Ignorance through the Grace or Divine Presence that Radiates in the Good Company of the Adept (who is a Spiritual Master in the seventh stage of life). And, through that Intuition, Abide always in Ecstasy, constant Love-Communion, or inherent Identification with the Radiant Transcendental Being that is the Truth or Real Condition of "I" and "God" and "the World." In this manner, you will exist only in the Divine Condition or Transcendental Domain, but you will also inevitably fulfill whatever functional role is your temporary destiny as Man and beyond Man in the Realm of Nature.

This is the Wisdom that transcends all events, all the science, attainment, and failure of mind, all of culture and household consolation, all the dread or "News" of cosmic and downtown stress, all the terminal pleasures that penetrate silence, circumference, measure, probability, and death This is the Restoration of Laughter, the Revelation of the secret Cause, the beginning and the end of matter, light, and every kind of universe.

How to Begin to Practice the Way That I Teach

T hinking and bodily experiencing are the present-day common methods used to discover the <u>Truth</u>! Thinking (including both passive psychism, or revery, and active conceptualization) and bodily experiencing (or general psycho-physical confrontation with both gross and subtle phenomena) are the processes to which every individual immediately resorts in the midst of his inevitable doubt and anxiety. But doubt and anxiety are themselves states of mind and body (or body-mind)—indeed, it is mind and body that we doubt and are anxious about. The obvious limitations and implied mortality of the body-mind are reflected in us as the reactions of doubt (including the motive to find an "answer") and anxiety (or even fear, self-destructiveness, and habitual self-indulgence).

We must clearly observe this process and understand it (or release our obsessive grip on it) via intuitive insight. The search for Truth, or an "answer" that transcends or escapes the limitations of mind and body, <u>must fail</u>, because it is itself an exercise and an expression of mind and body. We must see that thinking and bodily experiencing are merely and simply limited conventions of our psycho-physical existence. Thinking and bodily experiencing are <u>inherently</u> limited. They are simply limited and mortal activities of a limited and mortal mechanism. It is our inevitable emotional confrontation with the factuality of mental limitation and physical mortality that generates the reaction of doubt and anxiety. And doubt and anxiety (or the composite and profound emotional sense of existence as a dilemma) are the trouble or motive that causes us to apply the body-mind to find an "answer," or experience an "escape."

The "Truth" that we seek (and sometimes claim to find) on the basis of our trouble is an invention of our own. The "Truth" that is proposed as an "answer" to the conceived dilemma of existence and that seems to represent an escape from the mortal limitations of the body-mind is itself nothing more than a state of the body-mind.

The actual Truth of our existence is simply the case. It is not an answer to a question. Indeed, any question (or emotional dilemma) must be an obstruction to the Realization (or clear and direct intuition) of what is always already the case. A disturbed and strategically active state of mind and body cannot discover the very Condition or Truth of the body-mind.

Thinking and bodily experiencing are natural and ordinary conventions of our form of psycho-physical existence. They are useful, practical, inevitable functions, with every kind of personal and social significance. However, the doubt, anxiety, seeking, and answering (or escaping) that arise on the basis of confrontation with the inherent limitations of the body-mind are an exaggeration, a distortion, and a binding superimposition that we add to the simple processes of thinking and bodily experiencing. Therefore, the search for Truth must be understood and transcended before the actual Truth can be Realized.

Thinking and bodily experiencing are not proper or useful instruments for actually Realizing the Truth of our existence. It must be clearly understood that thinking and bodily experiencing are merely limited conventions of an inherently limited and mortal body-mind. The search for an answer to the dilemma of mortal limitation, or an escape from mind and body via the exercise of mind (or thought and psyche) and body, is, and must be understood to be, simply evidence of an emotional problem or reactive contraction of the body-mind. The only foundation upon which the Truth can be Realized is the observation and <u>acceptance</u> of the limited and mortal nature of the body-mind (or the experiential ego-self).

It is necessary for us to transcend our dissociative emotional reaction to the inherent limitations of the body-mind and its experiences. This is the first truly human or humanizing stage of development. It is only on the basis of a body-mind that is free of the conception and motivation of existence as a dilemma that the actual Realization of Truth can be founded. It is not the problem-solving exercise of mind or psyche that Realizes the Truth, but only the relaxed openness or tacit suspension of mind, psyche, or attention itself permits that Realization. It is not the strategic exercise of the body, or the total body-mind, that Realizes the Truth of the body-mind, but only the relaxed openness or tacit suspension of all contraction, all knowledge (or "knowing about"), and all self-possession permits that Realization.

Therefore, the human individual must grow into an understanding of himself, such that the reactive programs of knowing and acting are transcended in a tacit Realization of the Transcendental Condition in which the body-mind is arising, floating, changing, and passing away. The actual or Realized Truth is not itself an answer to the emotional dilemma of our existence, since we must transcend that dilemma as a precondition for Realizing the Truth. And the Truth is not an escape from the limited mortality of the body-mind, since neither mind (or psyche) nor body is made immortal by the Realization of the Truth.

The Realization of the Truth is a matter of devotion or surrender of mind and body to the Condition on which they depend (and which is, therefore, the Truth of mind and body). When the mortal limitations of mind and body are accepted to the point of release of the reactive emotional contraction (or motivating dilemma) that aggravates the body-mind and obscures the Truth, then the habitual and obsessive activation of mind and body relaxes, and the Truth or Condition of the body-mind becomes tacitly obvious.

Therefore, the Way of Life or Truth is a sober enterprise that is founded upon the mature equanimity of the body-mind. That Way is not itself characterized by mental knowledge, mystical states of the psyche, or physical and mental strategies for attainment. Those who take up that Way must have first matured to a sensitive state of psycho-physical equanimity, or freedom from reactive and self-possessed programs of thinking and bodily experiencing that cause one always to seek the Truth rather than presently surrender to the obvious Truth. Only when such maturity or equanimity has stabilized the body-mind can actual practice of the Way begin. That practice is one of self-transcending Communion with the Transcendental Reality, or tacit surrender and release of mind and body on the basis of radical and present intuition of the All-Pervading Reality that contains self and mind and body and world. Once that Way begins, the psycho-physical self and the world are also progressively Transfigured and Transformed, even to the point of total Absorption in the Radiant Transcendental Being.

338

Many will read this and, having considered it, they will be moved to practice the Way itself. But such motivation is only the beginning. It is not the beginning of the Way, but it is the beginning of an approach to the Way. Actual practice of the Way must necessarily be preceded by a period of preparation, testing, and humanizing growth. That period is one of study, acculturation to a life of service and community cooperation, and practice of basic personal disciplines. Only through such preparation can the individual be established in the full and natural human disposition in which the Living Truth is both obvious and available to the body-mind.

Some imagine that the practices associated with preparation for the Way are themselves practice of the Way. People all over the world are involved in serious religious, intellectual, meditative, and social practices that they presume are expressions of a life devoted to Truth. But actually such programs, while they may be positive, right, and necessary, are only expressions of the basic education of mankind. The Great Work only begins when the Truth is Realized and the body-mind is released into a Transfigured devotion to the Living Divine Reality.

I acknowledge and accept the necessity for people to hear and respond to the Teaching of Truth, and then to take up a progressive practice of study, personal discipline, service, community cooperation, and formal religious activity (such as prayerful Remembrance of the Divine and various sacramental activities). But it must be understood that such is only preparation for ultimate practice, which is not a cultural program for the body-mind, but it is a practice in which the body-mind is constantly transcended (and, paradoxically, also transformed) in direct Realization of the Divine or Transcendental Condition of self and world.

Therefore, hear me and begin to grow again through study of the Way and gradual adaptation to truly human conditions of existence. Your practice will develop by stages, until mind and body are released of their self-possessed motives and reactive contractions, and a thoughtless sublimity will provide the "moment" or turning point for your ultimate life of practice. That "moment" is Enlightenment, or Perfect Ignorance, and it brings an end to the period of preparation, but it only begins the endless practice of the Way which inevitably follows.

So Be It

The Way of Life that I Teach is necessarily evolved in seven stages of adaptation and transcendence, each stage of which corresponds to a specific level in the hierarchy of psycho-physical structures in Man. Some rare individuals may, because of their unique characteristics, move fairly quickly and easily toward the higher or later phases of this necessary spiritual career, but most individuals, even though they may possibly fulfill all seven stages in their lifetime, must grow by degrees in a difficult but profound creative struggle, stage by stage, day by day.

The essential Truth is Realized even from the beginning of this progress by those who truly "hear" or understand the Teaching and directly "see" or intuit and surrender to the Spiritual Presence that is uniquely Communicated and Magnified in this world through the Agency of a Perfect or Completed Adept (who is a Spiritual Master fully Awakened in the seventh stage of life). But the process of living the Way is a matter of natural and right adaptation to the various structures of the human body-mind, and then, at the point of maturity in each stage of such adaptation, transcending all limitations represented by that particular level of structure or experience. Therefore, the Way of Life is a progressive sacrifice of the psycho-physical self, leading toward perfect Ecstasy, or self-transcendence. But the primary means of this sacrifice is also Ecstasy, or self-transcending Love-Communion with the Living Reality and Eternal Presence that is God, or the Transcendental Truth of Man and the world.

Many people presume to Know the Truth and to Teach the Way of Life, but very few such people have even accepted the necessity of the personal and moral disciplines that mark the beginning of the fourth stage of life. And even among those who demonstrate the signs of ordinary self-mastery (or submission of the lower physical, emotional, and mental functions to the Life-Principle, so that the lower body-mind demonstrates the regenerative conservation of Life-Energy), very few demonstrate the true heart of God-Love. Just so, even among those who attain a high degree of adaptation to the higher psychic, mental, and superconscious range of cosmic experience, very few transcend either the distracting egoic consolations offered by such phenomena or the nihilistic emptiness that arises when such phenomena, as well as the ordinary states of physical experience, are suspended in trance meditation. But even among those who transcend the consolations of the higher and the lower body-mind, and so pass through ego-death, or intuitive Awakening to the Transcendental Being or Self within which all minds and bodies are arising, very few also Awaken beyond the introverted tendency that excludes the world, or psycho-physical experience, from the Transcendental Consciousness.

Only those who truly Awaken in the seventh stage of life have fulfilled the Way of Life completely. They are open-eyed and free, addicted neither to the negation of the world (or the nihilistic emptiness of the body-mind) nor to the distracted and troubled embrace of the world itself (or interminable preoccupation with the numberless possibilities of mere experience, high or low). Only such individuals have Realized perfect Identity with the Transcendental Being (the Eternal Self), or perfect Unity between the body-mind and the All-Pervading and Transcendental Divine Radiance. Only such individuals have finally transcended the structural schism in the body-mind that divides experience into mutually exclusive categories, such as high and low, self and other, subjective and objective, mind and matter, life and death, East and West. Only such individuals are fully, finally, and perfectly established in that sacrifice of self in which all subjectivity (or self-possessed inwardness of mind and psyche) is already transcended in radical intuition of Eternal Identity with the Transcendental Self (or Divine Being), so that the Way has become simple, direct, and total bodily surrender into the All-Pervading Radiance wherein the world and the body-mind are always presently arising. Therefore, only in the Fullness of the seventh stage of life is Man transcended and also Transfigured by the Radiant Divine Being. So be it.

The Secret of Attention

Attention is the root of all experience of mind, body, and the body's relations. It is in the process of attention that we become habituated to the presumption of limitations. And attention itself arises directly, as the first element of all experience, from the essential being (which inheres in the Infinitely Radiant Transcendental Being).

If the intuition of the ecstatic inherence of the essential being in the Radiant Transcendental Being is forgotten in the play of attention (or experience), then the presumption of limits binds the being. From this forgetting there first arises the presumption of an independent, separate, and limited self, and attention seems to be projected from that separate self-center. From this there arises the total realm of subjectivity or mind, with its mechanical relationship to body and world.

Therefore, the key to both Enlightenment and suffering is the process or fact of attention itself.

The spiritual process or Way of Life is a development founded on insight and responsibility relative to attention (which is the root of experience, and which is also both rooted and expanded in the Radiant Transcendental Being). That process or Way begins, on the basis of intuition and insight, as a responsible redirection of attention into the Radiant Divine Being. (It is a matter of the surrender of the body and its relations into the Radiant Life-Principle while the attention, prior to the random subjective movement of perception, thought, and self-contraction, is directed to Invocation or Remembrance of the Divine Being.)

Attention may go to objects (mental or physical) or it may contract upon itself (thus producing the negative sense of separate self, doubt, limitation, frustration, and so forth). But the spiritual process or Way of Life is a matter of understanding and feeling and surrendering the body-mind and its root-attention into the Radiant All-Pervading Divine Being.

Over time this process develops into a profound re-cognition of the conditions of psycho-physical experience, so that the spiritual process in each moment becomes one of tacit re-cognition or transcendence of every act of attention (or attention itself). Then all conditions are directly Realized to be only modifications of the Radiant Divine or Transcendental Being and it is Realized that only that Radiant Being is the case. When this Realization becomes constant, the body-mind and the world of experience become Transfigured (seeming to the being to be as if transparent and utterly continuous with Infinitely Radiant Bliss). And such Transfiguration becomes the Liberated Life-Will, or Transformation of the body-mind and the world, until these are Outshined, or else the apparent being is Translated beyond the human domain.

342

Surrender to Life

The Transcendental Divine Reality is not Realized by avoiding the relational conditions of existence. That is, the Transcendental Divine Reality is not realized via the action of excluding phenomena (or changes) and concentrating on either noumena (mental or psychic and apparently non-corporeal phenomena) or on a motionless state of changelessness. Neither is the Transcendental Divine Reality Realized by exploiting, indulging, or submitting to phenomena, or change, or experiential and relational conditions in themselves. Rather, the Transcendental Divine Reality is natively Realized in every instant of intuitive or tacit non-contraction from (or non-exclusion of) phenomena, or change itself.

The Transcendental Divine Reality is not identical to gross events in themselves, nor to the subtle inward or mental phenomena behind gross events, nor is It a changeless or fixed State that persists separately and stands within or over against phenomena or change. The Transcendental Divine Reality is the Radiant Life-Principle, within which all phenomena or changes, both subtle and gross, are constantly arising as nonbinding modifications of Itself.

Therefore, the true Way is the Way of non-contraction, of non-exclusion, of intuitive surrender of the total body-mind to the Transcendental Divine Reality (or Life-Principle) via the total process of phenomena, or change itself. The true Way is the Way of

Radiance, Love, or God-Communion. It is to surrender to the Radiant Life-Principle while intuitively or tacitly re-cognizing every event as a superficial modification of the Transcendental Consciousness that is the Self of the Life-Principle.

Feeling, Breathing, and the Supreme Identity

343

G od is Spirit, or the Living Radiance in which the world and all beings are arising. God, or the Truth that is Reality, is the Light-Energy or Radiant Life Power in which every thing and every one arises, changes, disappears, and always inheres. As such, God is always accessible to living beings via the exercise of total psycho-physical surrender, expressed through the central process of whole bodily ecstasy, or self-transcending feeling and breathing.

God is Transcendental Being, with which the world and all beings are ultimately identical. As such, God is to be Realized in the total transcendence of psycho-physical experience, such that the essential or "inner" being (prior to identification with the self-defining limits of the body-mind) Awakens or Yields into the Supreme Condition of Infinite Transcendental Being.

God is the Truth of the world and all beings. The Way of Life in Truth is the Way of Divine Love-Communion, or feeling-surrender of the body-mind into the All-Pervading Life-Radiance with every breath. If this is done to the point of ecstasy, the body-mind or psycho-physical self swoons beyond the limiting force of its contractions and Awakens into its inherent identification with Transcendental Being. Then the body-mind and the world cease to be a dilemma or obstruction to Truth, Happiness, Bliss, and Freedom— and whatever arises as experience suddenly becomes a transparent force, a superficial modification of Radiant Transcendental Being. One who is thus Awake abides in native identification with Transcendental Being (prior to the psycho-physical or experiential self), and even the body-mind is constantly Transfigured by the Free Radiance or unobstructed Spirit that is naturally released to it in the Full Mood of Love.

The Principle of Transfiguration

"Transfiguration" is a matter of the conversion of attention to relational love, and it is expressed as the limitless en-Livening of the total body-mind, even to the point of bodily Translation (or the "Outshining" of psycho-physical phenomena by the Brightness or felt Radiance of Divine Being). It is distinct from the inverted processes of conventional meditation and inward self-discovery, since such processes involve the general withdrawal of attention and the Life-Principle from the world, the body, and at least the grosser levels of mind.

Transfiguration depends on psycho-physical Equanimity, rather than on problem-based and solution-oriented effort. It is a natural or native, essential, and spontaneous process which develops by Free Divine Grace and which is founded on the priorly free disposition of surrender, or inherence in the Radiant Transcendental and Eternally Living Being.

What I Mean

The "inner self" is not the ego, or "I." The total body-mind or experiential self is the ego, the "I" of "me" and "mine," Narcissus. And all suffering is egoity, or self-possession, the reflexive drama of Narcissus. All unhappiness is bondage to the body-mind. "I" is the psycho-physical urge, the complex destiny of repetitions, the eternal sameness of needs and fears, desires and aversions, expansions and withdrawals, entrances and exits, births and deaths.

Truth is the Condition prior to the adventure of the ego, prior to self-possession, prior to obsessive association with the body-mind. The Way of Truth is Ecstasy, self-transcendence, or transcendence of the experiential body-mind. The practice of Ecstasy is a matter of the surrender of the total body-mind via radical insight, or intuitive transcendence of all forms of recoil toward self, all forms of the avoidance of relationship, all forms of psycho-physical contraction, all forms of experience or differentiated attention. It is a matter of self-abandonment and self-forgetting in the Universal Field of Radiant Life-Energy and Transcendental Consciousness. It is acceptance of death to the point of Ecstasy, Unqualified Life, the vanishing of all experiential necessities, all subjective implications, all subject-object urges. It is Liberation from all forms of psycho-physical existence. It is Dissolution of the "soul," who is both the inner and the outer Man. It is Translation into the Divine Condition. It is to Swoon in the Transition to the Transcendental Domain of objectless Radiance, beyond all the worlds of the body-mind, whether they are high or low in the scale of Cosmic experience. It is to be Outshined by the Divine Truth or Radiant Condition of all the universes and all the selves that play and feed upon one another in the total Machine of Nature. It is to be Rescued through perfect identification with God. It is Surrender of self-defense. Therefore, it is the Surrender of everything that we mean by a "lifetime." It is Infinite Love.

The Search for Liberation and the Way of Prior Freedom

The Occupation of most human beings is the search to be fulfilled and liberated by experience and knowledge. But I was born already Free. Therefore, my Occupation has been to incarnate and yet remain Free, whereas others seek to become Free by escaping the real circumstances of incarnation.

I have understood the false need for self-fulfillment and liberation. I have been adapting and learning all the while, but I am Free. Therefore, I do not Teach the way of escape, or of distraction by experience, or of self-indulgence, or of knowledge and power. Every man and every woman must adapt to every part of Man in the World-Process, but I Teach the Way in which all of that may be done in Divine Freedom.

I do not Teach the way of mere fulfillment of lower and higher desires. I do not Teach the Way of mere liberation, or escape from the World-Process. I do not Teach the search for liberation, based on the dilemma of fear, unlove, and separation from Life. I Teach the Way of incarnate love, founded on prior Freedom and Communion with Life. I Teach understanding of the loveless dilemma that promotes the search for Freedom and Love and Life.

Others Teach the methods of liberation through one or another kind of fulfillment of Man. But I have transcended all escape and all fulfillment through the native Freedom in which I have been born. I have transcended the need for liberation, and all of my experience is a centerless Chaos of Joy. I Teach the Way of the body in love. I was born to incarnate. I am the Enemy of every illusion by which Man is betrayed.

346

The Way That I Teach, or the Principal Conception of Future Religion

The Way that I Teach is not founded on the ancient traditional ideal of the separation of the "soul" from the "body," or the idea of the cosmological separation between "Heaven" (or the "Kingdom of God") and "Earth," or the conventional conception of mind and body as distinct and independent functions that are separate or should be separated from one another. Such conceptions are founded on mere experience, without awakened insight, so that bodily processes and all so-called "external" and "material" processes are presumed to be expressions of a different realm of existence than mental, or so-called "internal" and "non-material," processes of the "psyche" or "soul."

The Way that I Teach is thoroughly founded on insight into the singularity of the "body-mind," or the presumption of an inherent and dynamic or cooperative unity between all experiential functions and processes. In this conception, "Man," or the individual "self," is understood to be a psycho-physical being, not a being with two antagonistic parts (one internal and one external) who is ill at ease in the worlds of his own experience.

However, this conception of the human being as a psycho-physical unity (and, likewise, of the "material" universe as a psycho-physical continuum) is not itself a materialistic conception. It is not that mind <u>and</u> body are material (and <u>therefore</u> a unity). Such is itself a conventional and suppressive materialistic conception, as bereft of insight as the ancient conception of the division of "Heaven" and "Earth," or the inherent and irreducible separateness of subjective and objective phenomena. Mind (or psyche) and body are a dynamic or cooperative process or play of two dimensions or aspects of a single being. The unity of psyche and body is not based on the materiality of both psyche and body, but on the equation of both psyche and body with the Universal Light-Energy, the All-Pervading, Transcendental Radiance that is the Matrix and Reality of all phenomena. Thus, both psyche and body (along with all other conditions or events) are to be understood, mutually related, constantly practiced, and surrendered as a single process that is ultimately identical to the Universal Life-Current, the Infinite Profusion of Light-Energy and Transcendental Being (or Consciousness) from which and in which all psycho-physical phenomena are always arising.

347

When we are devoted to our psycho-physical unity with the Radiant Transcendental Reality, then our human existence may be realized as a harmonious equation that is growing and evolving in Light and that is even presently identical to Light. And if our total psycho-physical existence becomes a harmonious and ecstatic sacrifice, yielded into Blissful Identity with the Reality or Radiant Being of Light, then the body-mind itself will be Transfigured and Transformed by Light, and we will be Translated, even bodily, into Light itself, which is the Radiant Consciousness or Love or Bliss that Contains and Creates and Sustains all worlds and all beings.

Such is the lately Revealed religious and truly spiritual Principle on which the future higher culture of Man must be founded.

The body, in its various forms, is the vehicle in which we may attain the experience of the numberless worlds. The human body is the vehicle of our experience of Earth. And the Transfigured body, Transformed beyond the shape of mere Man, will be the vehicle of our experience of all other planets, stars, places, spaces, times, and planes. The free Life-Energy we are structured to develop through surrender of mind and body to the Radiant Life-Principle will be the primary, necessary, and ultimate means of our migration beyond Earth and Man. And that same Energy is the Spiritual Body in which we Transcend even all the worlds of our evolutionary embodiment.

Da Free John

CHAPTER TEN

The Ultimate Passion of Man

The Evolution of Man
and the Sacrifice of the World

Man is only a brief design in the numberless evolutionary stages of the World. And the individual human being is only a moment, a specimen, a partial realization of Man. The individual is not made for his own sake, but to be a sacrifice toward Man—so that Man may fulfill his evolutionary destiny. And Man is not made for his own sake, but to be a sacrifice toward the ultimate evolutionary process of the World. And the World is not made for its own sake, but to be a sacrifice to the unqualified and eternal Divine.

If the design of Man is examined, he is revealed to be a composite of all previous creatures, environments, and experiences. His body below the brows is a machine of animals and elemental cycles. He is full-made of horses and crocodiles, honey bees and swans, sardines and earth forces, redwood and fruit palm, Amazon, Pacific, solar fire, Everest, weather of water and air, all the usual stars, and antique ocean mammals leaning away from Earth. He is not truly unique below the brows. He is, rather, a summation of all that came before him and everything that he already knows.

350

But Man is also a new stage in the event of time. His newness or uniqueness is hidden in the brain. His lower or vital brain, including his rudimentary speech and thought, is part of the summary and reflection of the past. But the middle range of his brain, beginning with the higher verbal or abstract mental functions, is the doorway to the future. And above the thinking and imaging function of the middle brain is the naked mass of yet unadapted purity, the higher brain, which Communes with Light. This higher brain is the structural cauldron of the present and future evolutionary changes of Man and what is beyond Man in the scheme of the World.

The individual is only a moment, and his structural adaptation of the whole body-mind to its potential above the brows is generally quite modest, if it occurs at all. Man, at any moment, is the summary of what has been. Therefore, the millions or billions of men and women who live and die in every generation may add a fraction of development to the destiny of Man. But the Teaching of Truth is also given to all, so that the principles of structural evolution may be grasped and fulfilled by at least a few in every generation. Thus, the realization of these few is also added to Man, and all future men and women may be raised up by such means.

The Spiritual Master is given the task of communicating the Laws of evolution and of sacrifice to his own generation, so that Man may be raised up in God. And the Spiritual Master himself advances the evolution of Man by a difficult process of personal psycho-physical transformation. But what he realizes cannot be added to Man until many representatives of mankind embrace the Way of Truth and submit to the process of transformation and sacrifice.

The individual is a sacrifice to God through Man. Man is a sacrifice to God through the World. The World is a sacrifice to God in every present moment. Therefore, all things and beings are a present, past, and future sacrifice toward a Condition that no one in time can appear to have Realized Perfectly—since everyone in the present summarizes the past, and a few, at best, demonstrate an Awakening to the future and ultimate Condition. But even the Spiritual Master generally appears to others in the bodily form of the present state of Man.

Even so, the radical Realization of the ultimate Destiny of the World is possible in the present and in the case of any individual who will give himself up to the Divine in Truth. This is also the Teaching and the Demonstration of the Spiritual Master. Most individuals are content to pursue an ordinary personal destiny, by exploiting what Man has already become. Such individuals live a basically subhuman life, and they add nothing new to Man. Others are not content unless they can exceed themselves. But unless they transcend the old creature and enter into the development of the higher brain, they do not exceed the present state of Man. Therefore, only a few individuals in every generation enter into the evolutionary module of the higher brain, through which the whole body is brightened in the universal Field of Light. Such individuals work changes in themselves by exploiting the potential of Man. But until what they do is also communicated and lived by greater numbers of individuals, even their experiment is not added to the Incarnation of Man.

Therefore, the Spiritual Master appears, to communicate the Way of the transcendence of self and the transcendence of the present stage of Man—so that mankind may more generally fulfill the higher trend of evolution, rather than fall back upon itself in regressive self-possession and exploitation of the elemental Man. However, the Spiritual Master is also full of Transcendental urgency. He also communicates to Man. He reminds Man that even Man is a moment, a process, grotesque when seen in himself. He reminds Man that his beauty and happiness are in his Ecstasy, his sacrifice toward what is yet to come and what is Perfect. He reminds Man that his true Destiny is not in his own evolutionary fulfillment, but in the fulfillment of the sacrifice of the whole World, which includes everything before and after Man, as well as Man himself.

Therefore, the Spiritual Master is most profoundly devoted to the Awakening of individuals and Man and the whole World to that Process of Sacrifice that transcends not only the past and present but also the future of all evolution of self, of Man, and of the World. His Teaching ultimately exceeds all evolutionary prescriptions. He moves his devotees through the structures of self, of Man, and of the World, until these devotees can be the Sacrifice of even the World itself. Therefore, his Teaching, his Demonstration, and the ultimate demonstration of his devotees is the one of Perfect Ecstasy, or the Sacrifice of self and Man and the World into the Condition that is Divine.

To such devotees, the Spiritual Master Communicates and Reveals himself in that Form which is beyond Man, and he also is

Revealed to be the Sacrifice of even that Form, beyond all consolations and attainments. This is what moves us to Love. And we may be the Liberation of self and Man and the World, if we will abandon all withholding, fear, and doubt—and if we will turn out from all subhuman, human, and superhuman self-possession into the Ecstasy of Worldlessness.

352

The Higher Culture of Man Depends on the Higher Nervous System of Man

The functions of the autonomic nervous system (traditionally called the "flesh," or the "realm of the senses") are enlivened by the universal Life-Current, but they are generally stimulated by the casual influence of ordinary or "natural" functional associations (since our attention tends to be fixed in the lower or grosser bodily processes). But if the Life-Current can be <u>directly</u> stimulated in the central nervous system (traditionally called the "soul" or, simply, the "psyche," or the "mind"), and then directed upwards and toward rather than downwards and away from the brain, the higher structural functions of the body and mind will be activated and permitted to grow by adaptation.

This process inevitably produces the immediate phenomena we recognize as the <u>mystical</u> states associated with religious and otherwise illumined consciousness. But if the process is made continuous over time, it produces the phenomena of the higher <u>evolutionary</u> development of the yet hidden structural potential of Man. These phenomena include higher mental (or brain-mind) development at the level of genius capacity in both the abilities of the right hemisphere of the brain (such as in the arts) and the abilities of the left hemisphere of the brain (such as in the sciences and other intellectual disciplines). There is also the potential development of higher physical abilities, such as superior health, longevity, natural healing power, and so forth. Likewise, higher psychic phenomena, usually called extrasensory abilities, develop—and they may enter into areas of psychic participation in the play of the universe beyond Earth, beyond the solar system, and even beyond the plane of material visibility. And there is also the ultimate potential that the body-mind of Man, in the case of both individuals and the species as a whole, can ultimately be transcended to the perfect degree, so that it is Translated out of the gross material plane altogether.

353

All the phenomena I have suggested or described here are not only possible—they have already been proven, in the experience of countless spiritual Adepts throughout human history. I myself am one in that line of experimenters, and I can attest to the actuality of mystical and evolutionary phenomena. Indeed, I am prepared to help others to realize and demonstrate these very same things, if they will consider the Truth and practice the higher cultural Way of adaptation to Life.

What is more, the processes I have suggested or described depend on the transference of human attention from exclusive orientation to the functional extremities of the lower body-mind, so that the realm of attention also naturally includes the functional extremities of the upper body-mind. And this total process depends on the granting of full and bodily feeling-attention to the universal All-Pervading Current of Life-Energy.

The higher evolutionary process has traditionally been served by individual understanding of the instructions of an Adept, and by individual acceptance of the guidance of an Adept during every stage of practice. And the Adept himself, by higher psycho-physical means, stimulates the central nervous system of others (both in itself and as a means of changing the mental and bodily being via the autonomic nervous system). This process is known in the traditions of religion as spiritual transmission. For these reasons, spiritual Adepts tended and still tend to accept disciples or devotees, and also to create a community or culture of such individuals. Such "cults," or communities of practice, have always been the necessary instruments of the higher adaptation of human individuals and, ultimately, of all mankind. The world should understand this and value it, rather than ignorantly work to suppress the appearance of the higher destiny of Man. The spiritual communities or true cults of spiritual practice are the higher servants of mankind, and it is time this whole affair became better known in the world, rather than remained hidden as a result of persecution, suppression, and popular stupidity.

This is a time when the traditionally esoteric Teachings and practices of religion can become the common basis of the higher evolutionary culture of Man. But it will occur only if the level of public intelligence is raised toward this possibility. Therefore, please listen to my argument and understand. Abandon what is false in the practice of human life, but embrace what is benign and true. And begin to support and serve the communication and implementation of the Way of Truth in your own life and that of the public in general.

Mysticism and Evolution

The earliest or most immediate effects of the stimulation of the higher or central nervous system of Man by the Universal Life-Current are personal, subjective, and mystical. For this reason, this process and its various natural phenomena have traditionally been maintained within the exclusive province of exoteric and esoteric religion.

However, the ultimate significance of this process is not merely as a means of individual salvation or release via internal or subjective experiences. Rather, the ultimate significance and value of this process is <u>evolutionary</u>, or an instrument of the growth, transformation, and self-transcendence of Man (and thus of mankind).

The earliest and most immediate effects of this process are subjective, internal, psychic, and mystical. Therefore, this process has traditionally been found attractive by those who desire release from this world via the inwardness of the human psyche. But all such experiences are deluding, unless properly understood, and, in any case, they represent nothing more than limited forms of <u>knowledge about</u> the experiential condition of Man.

The ultimate and long-term development of this process, as a cultural affair of humanity as a whole, is not merely mystical, personal, psychic, and associated with experiential knowledge. Rather, the ultimate and long-term development of this human cultural process is evolutionary and physical. That is, if this process is engaged with right understanding, and in devotion to the Paradox of the Living Reality rather than to the vagrant possibilities of personal and merely internal experience, knowledge, or release, then the subjective, intellectual, and mystical effects are transcended, and evolutionary transformations of the broadly cultural and literal physical conditions of Man (both individually and collectively) are increased.

355

In the evolutionary acculturation of mankind, the Radiance of the Living Reality pervades the total body-mind of Man, thus permitting growth and transformation, and, at last, even the translation of Man into the Radiant Domain of Love, Life, and Ecstatic Transcendental Consciousness that transcends the self, and the mind, and the body of every human individual and every group of human individuals.

The mystical and evolutionary processes of human development have been practiced and transmitted by various kinds or degrees of Adepts throughout human history. Certain founders of religion (such as Jesus and Gautama) were practicing Adepts of this kind. Other religious founders or leaders, such as Mohammed and Martin Luther, were not practicing Adepts, but they were inspired men of insight or prophetic urgency, whose personal activity was entirely within the domain of exoteric religion. But most practitioners or Adepts of the mystical and evolutionary science were active outside the realm of "Everyman," and they were known only within the esoteric "inner circles" of the religious and spiritual traditions.

Lesser Adepts are individuals who have enjoyed remarkable mystical experiences and attained a degree of Wisdom that is helpful or useful to individuals who are less developed than themselves. These lesser Adepts serve the awakening of idealism and functional discipline in ordinary people, and the level of experience to which they lead their followers is generally limited to mystical developments of the Life-Current in the autonomic nervous system and the central nervous system.

However, the highest Adepts serve the awakening of radical insight and responsibility in others, and they guide others through and beyond personal and subjective mysticism, into the domain of the evolutionary transformation and ultimate self-transcendence of Man. Therefore, the Work of the highest Adepts is fundamental to human culture as a whole. And the process developed by practitioners in the Company of such Adepts ultimately transcends both the autonomic and the central nervous systems of Man through perfect devotion to the Radiant All-Pervading Life-Current and Transcendental Consciousness that is the Truth of Man and the World.

356

Therefore, the value of the esoteric spiritual process is not mere subjective mystical experience. Traditional and, especially, oriental schools of mysticism tend to ascribe independent significance and reality to internal or subjective phenomena, so that mystical experiences become an end in themselves. But such experiences are only symptoms and early signs of the larger process, and they only signify and depend upon higher physical events in the structure of Man (particularly in the central nervous system and the organs of the brain core). Personal experiential mysticism, or internal self-watching, thus remains an appropriate preoccupation of human beings only in the period of transition or growth beyond confinement to the lower functions of the human body-mind. The true and ultimate value of the esoteric spiritual process is the evolutionary physical (or total psycho-physical) and cultural adaptation of the human body-mind (or total personality). And such evolutionary cultural and total physical (or psycho-physical) transformation becomes the prime interest only after we mature beyond fascination with internal or subjective mystical phenomena, higher or extraordinary kinds of knowledge, and all of the lower or conventional rituals of the ordinary physical, emotional, and mental experience of the subhuman "Everyman."

Once mankind has entered into the higher culture of human adaptation, the mystical and the evolutionary mechanics will be commonly experienced and understood. And then not only will the culture of Man be founded in higher Wisdom, but the Destiny of Man will be understood to be beyond Man, in the Ecstasy of ultimate self-transcendence and even the bodily or material Translation of Man and the material World into the Radiant Domain of Life.

The Five Evolutionary States
of True Man

The primary cultural enterprise of the West is scientific materialism, or the extroverted and aggressive technological exploitation of the body and the world of Man.

The primary cultural enterprise of the East is mystical transcendentalism, or the introverted and "other-worldly" exploitation of the mind and soul of Man.

Until now, these separate enterprises have been granted a kind of "holy" status—set apart from any fundamental criticism. Thus, West and East have been conventionally understood as irreducibly separate cultural enterprises that must constantly be distinguished and allowed to realize their independent destinies. But this conventional understanding is founded on the very logic that is forcing the present cultural and political conflicts in the world.

In fact, the separate cultures of West and East are products of the ancient self-divided state of Man in his evolutionary childhood and adolescence. And there is no hope for the evolutionary future of Man unless the self-divided conception of Man is overcome—along with all of the ancient cultural divisions.

If Man is understood as a whole, then he is seen in terms of the dynamic unity of the two divisions of the autonomic nervous system, which reflect the primal unity of the central nervous system and the universal Life-Current (or Light-Energy). And this understanding of Man must become the Principle whereby we criticize the personal and cultural divisions demonstrated by mankind.

From this point of view, we can see that the great cultural enterprise of the West is founded on the impulses and functional patterns of the verbal-analytical left hemisphere of the brain and the "extroverted" or sympathetic division of the autonomic nervous system. And the great cultural enterprise of the East, in contrast to the West, is founded on the symbolical and intuitive right hemisphere of the brain and the "introverted" or parasympathetic division of the autonomic nervous system.

The new great culture of the whole body of Man will and must be founded on transcendence of these divisions and their cultural limitations. Therefore, let us consider more of the psychology and physiology of personal and cultural self-division.

The human individual functions via a daily cycle of dramatic changes of state. That is, the conventional pattern of human experience involves a daily passage through three common states of experiential consciousness. These three states or conditions of experience are the waking state, the dreaming state, and the sleeping state.

Everyone generally passes through these states as a matter of necessity, or unavoidable psycho-physical urgency, in a regular pattern, more or less coordinated with the rhythmic daily cycle of sunlight. And yet we tend to think of our lives exclusively in terms of the waking state—as if dreaming and sleeping were secondary functional patterns that serve our general health but have no ultimate or real philosophical and personal significance. We tend to think that to "be alive" is to be in the waking state, whereas to dream or to sleep is to be in a state more like death, where the "self" (as both mind and body) is passive, threatened, vulnerable, undefinable, or even non-existent.

If we examine the human individual in the waking state, we discover that in this state, the urges and patterns of the sympathetic (or extroverted) division of the autonomic nervous system are generally dominant. And, therefore, it is our attachment to "self" as waking consciousness that accounts for our self-divided tendency to conceive of Man fundamentally as an extroverted and analytically thinking creature. Our attachment to the waking state causes an imbalance in our functional being. And that imbalance is demonstrated in our personal lives and in our cultural enterprises.

Men and women of both the West and the East suffer and react to the same self-dividing effect of attachment to the "self" as experience in the waking state. However, the Western or occidental individual generally tends to adapt this self-divided and self-possessed state of being to a different functional ideal than the Eastern or oriental individual.

The "self" in the waking state is tending to be self-divided, self-possessed, more or less extroverted (or oriented toward the play of bodily experience), possessed of a personal sense of "self" as a mortal physical being, and possessed as well by a sense of the world as a machine of irreducible material processes. The Western or "occidental" mode of response to this view of existence is to adapt to it and to try by persistent analysis and material effort to overcome all mortal limitations. However, the Eastern or "oriental" mode of response is to try to escape the game of existence as it appears from the conventional point of view of the waking state.

The "oriental" tendency is founded on a tacit sense that the body-mind of Man and the cycle of ordinary human experience contain an alternative experiential path to that which is revealed in the waking state. As I have tried to suggest, that alternative path is simply the parasympathetic division of the autonomic nervous system.

In the waking state, the sympathetic or "extroverted" division of the autonomic nervous system is dominant. But in the dreaming state the parasympathetic or "introverted" division of the autonomic nervous system is dominant. In the waking state, the verbal-analytical functions of the left hemisphere of the brain are dominant. But in the dreaming state the symbolical and holistic functions of the right hemisphere of the brain are dominant.

The conventions of the Western way of life exploit the extroverted or body-oriented motives of the sympathetic division of the autonomic nervous system, and the traditional Western mind functions predominantly in the verbal-analytical mode. Western man is Man exclusively in the waking state, without integration of consciousness with the dreaming and sleeping states. Just so, Eastern man is Man seeking to be exclusively in either the dreaming or the sleeping state, without full or even partial integration with the waking state.

The alternative personal and cultural path that has been developed in oriental cultures since ancient times is the path of inwardness, or the inversion of consciousness via the mechanisms of the parasympathetic division of the autonomic nervous system. That is, the oriental method is generally a matter of either mystical or intuitive inversion—or escape from the limiting association of consciousness with the mortal limitations of the conventional waking state.

The method typical of oriental mysticism (and, indeed, of all traditional mystical paths of religion, wherever they arise) always involves the inversion of attention—turning attention away from the bodily senses and away from the verbal mind. The process involves various psycho-physical techniques for switching the attention from the psycho-physical circuit of the descending and outgoing motor impulses that move from the brain to the bodily outlets of the senses, directing attention instead toward the ascending and ingoing sensory impulses that move from the sense terminals to the brain core. When this is done successfully, the body and the ordinary thinking mind are quieted, and the interior mind of dream, creative imagination, and psychic perception beyond the bodily limits of the individual tends to awaken, producing various kinds of subjective, mystical, and higher psychic experiences (ultimately including telepathic association with all of the conditions in the space-time continuum).

The goal of oriental mysticism is release from bodily limits and projection of attention into states of mind and psyche that are at least relatively free of conventional physical limitations. The result is a view or understanding of existence that is quite the opposite of the conventional Western or occidental view. It is a magical consciousness, driven by an impulse toward singularity, or absorption of mind and attention in nondualistic bliss.

The oriental path itself has two primary divisions. Oriental idealism pursues a condition of consciousness that is either mystical (or primarily visionary) or intuitive (or primarily associated with nondualistic absorption of mind or attention). This division (which may also represent two stages in a single process, ultimately leading to nondualistic absorption) is due to the unique psycho-physical anatomy of Man. Once attention is turned from the sympathetic (or extroverted) circuit to the parasympathetic (or introverted) circuit, the psychic and higher physical phenomena of mysticism appear. However, once attention passes fully back to the brain core, the primal Life-Current in the central nervous system is contacted. Therefore, mystical consciousness is ultimately followed by transcendence of the mystical mind in the primal intuition of the universal Life-Consciousness.

Our experience of the dreaming process is an expression of the relaxation of outer or extroverted attention (or relaxation of the verbal-analytical mental process in the left hemisphere of the brain and the outgoing motor process in the sympathetic division of the autonomic nervous system) followed by the inversion of attention, primarily toward the visually oriented mental centers of the right hemisphere of the brain (via the sensory circuit of the parasympathetic division of the autonomic nervous system). The process by which mystical consciousness is developed is precisely the same process by which everyone enters into dreams—except that the mystic engages in a conscious exercise of this mechanism and exploits its potential to the highest degree.

However, just as we may pass from dreaming to sleeping, we may also pass from mystical states of consciousness to an apparently mindless and even bodiless state of "pure consciousness." This phenomenon is described in the oriental literature of esoteric spirituality as "liberation," "nirvana" (or the realization of the "quenching" of the principle of desire), "nirvikalpa samadhi" (a samadhi, or trance state, without the conception of form), the "realization of the Atman" (or true Self), or the "realization of Brahman" (the Absolute Consciousness). However, the process by which this intuitive state of self-transcendence is attained is precisely the same process by which everyone enters into the deep sleep state—except that the oriental seeker of intuitive self-transcendence enters into this state without the loss of conscious awareness. (In ordinary sleep, the individual is bereft of the awareness of states of mind and body, and so he feels "unconscious," but in the state of intuitive self-transcendence via inward absorption, the consciousness remains intact, free of mental and bodily associations.)

The mechanism of deep sleep is associated with the shut-down of attention in both the right and the left hemispheres of the higher brain. In deep sleep, the brain yields into the central Life-Current that pervades the central nervous system. Therefore, in the oriental process of internalized self-transcendence, it is the Life-Current in the central nervous system that occupies and absorbs attention, and, thus, the attention appears to have no functional locus (except that some relationship may intuitively or tacitly be felt to exist between the upper right side of the heart and the Transcendental Consciousness in the Life-Current).

Thus, the oriental path is described and followed in terms of mysticism and/or intuitive and inverted self-transcendence. And the mechanism of this process is the same one that everyone experiences during states of dreaming and sleeping.

We may say, then, that oriental culture and Eastern man are founded on the solution to the problem of the mortal "self" by means of the exclusive exploitation of the inverted consciousness otherwise displayed in the processes of dreaming and sleeping. And occidental culture and Western man are founded on the solution to the problem of the mortal "self" by means of the exclusive exploitation of the extroverted consciousness otherwise displayed in the processes of the waking state itself.

The problem inherent in this whole affair is that there are two solutions, and these are mutually exclusive. Traditionally, you must choose (or be born into) one or the other way of life. But, in our time of worldwide communication and blending of cultures, we are all confronted by both possibilities. Therefore, since both options confront all of us, we are no longer truly capable of the now provincial attitude of either Eastern or Western man. Instead, we are all disturbed by the absence of absolutes, and the paradox of our possibilities is overwhelmingly clear. As a result, the simple pursuit of either an Eastern or a Western program of life has a quality of absurdity about it that no one but the most culturally provincial individual can deny.

Therefore, we are being obliged to transcend the exclusive Eastern and Western programs of ancient and traditional culture. We are being obliged altogether to transcend the self-possessed and self-divided mode of existence—in order to realize a new and whole bodily synthesis of ecstatic personal and collective culture.

Just as more "creative" or more fully integrated individuals are able to function within the mental realms of both the right and left hemispheres of the brain, and to realize a harmony of well-being in both divisions of the autonomic nervous system, all human individuals must be acculturated toward more and more inclusive and insightful levels of functioning—in the waking state and in all other states. Every conventional state (waking, dreaming, or sleeping) has its appropriate moment, and every part of the body-mind must contribute to a truly human or integrated consciousness in the waking state. The true waking state is awake whole bodily, in a harmony, and also in every aspect of the brain-mind and the higher psyche. And unless we thus perfect our adaptation to the waking state, we will only seem awake—whereas we will be asleep in our deep psychic and intuitive being, or else at war with bodily existence via an irrational preference for the disembodied symbols of our own imagination.

The culture of the whole body and whole brain is infinitely superior to the culture of aggressive extroversion and the culture of conventional religious inwardness. The true Man is a spiritual being,

362

yielded in his total body-mind to the Living Reality that contains and pervades the World-Process. The other-worldly, body-denying, anti-sexual, anti-intellectual mysticism of the exclusively oriental man is a heresy in the whole body of true Man. Likewise, the exclusively verbal and analytical mind, with its materialistic pride of bodily power and its deep psychic impoverishment, is the heresy of exclusively Western man.

The whole Man lives in a fourth state, a unity with the Transcendental Life-Consciousness that includes and also transcends the waking, dreaming, and sleeping states. The whole Man transcends and also includes every aspect of his own body-mind. He lives and grows through self-transcending adaptation (of his own functional possibilities) to the universal Life-Current. At last, he enters into a fifth state, in which mind and body are both Transfigured and ultimately Dissolved in the Radiant Bliss of the Transcendental Reality, which is expressed as the Light of Love, projected from the heart (or the center, free "soul," and true Self of the body-mind) and the central nervous system (or the vehicle of the subtle "astral" body-mind at the core of the physical body-mind). (And this Process of true death, or bodily Transfiguration and Translation, is the mechanism in the World-Process whereby individual existence as Man is transcended, and individual or higher conscious existence in more highly evolved worlds or planets, or even in the Transcendental Realm, is begun.)

The Divine Physics of Evolution

A talk by Da Free John

D A FREE JOHN: This great affair that I am describing is absolutely uncommon. It has hardly ever transpired in anyone's case in the whole history of the human world. What I am describing is a process that belongs to the further evolution of humanity. At best it belongs to thousands, millions, billions of years in the future for the race as a whole. At present almost all human beings persist in an infantile moment in the evolution of existence, a moment that has nothing whatever to do with the ultimate Truth. Modern men and women are still dependent, violent, self-possessed, still seeking consolations in the realm of changes. So people should not imagine for a moment that the Way of Truth is an easy matter, that they can simply listen to this argument and thereby enter the ultimate Realization. This Way is the work of evolution, the work of the universe itself. It is the obligation or Law of eternal Existence that we are considering, and that the true relationship to the Spiritual Master generates and regenerates.

The human Spiritual Master is an agent to the advantage of those in like form. When one enters into right relationship with a Spiritual Master, changes happen in the literal physics of one's existence. It is not just a matter of ideas. I am talking about transformations at the level of energy, at the level of the higher light of physics, at the level of mind beyond the physical limitations that people now presume, at the level of the absolute Speed of ultimate Light. The transforming process is enacted in devotees, duplicated in them in and through that Living Company. It is not a matter of conceptual symbolisms or emotional attachment to some extraordinary person. It is real physics. And it is to the advantage of people when someone among them has gone through the whole cycle of Transformation, because they can then make use of the Offering of that Process, that Company.

Spiritual life has nothing to do with the childishness that people tend to dramatize in the relationship to the Spiritual Master. I criticize that childish or dependent approach more directly than most people. Others are merely petulant about it, in the self-righteous mood of adolescence. But there are real reasons why both the childish and adolescent approaches to the Spiritual Master are forms of destructive nonsense and must be overcome. However, the mature, sacrifical relationship to the Spiritual Master is itself absolutely Lawful and necessary. Those who object to that relationship might as well object to the relationship between the Earth and the sun.

Most people are willing to sacrifice things, but not themselves. They are willing to pay cash, in other words, for a quick salvation. This is an ancient ritual of worship, but it is false and futile. True worship is the sacrifice of your own bodily being in Truth, in the living and Transforming Company of the Spiritual Master. People absolutely resist that sacrifice. The reason they resist it is that they know nothing about it. They are subhuman in their present level of adaptation. Sacrifice represents another stage of evolution for them. They are presently incapable of it in their actual, literal, psycho-physical condition. They must be drawn out of that condition, led out into another state of existence. And it is as far to go from where they are now to the ultimate Divine Realization as it is for the amoeba in the primal mud of the Earth to become a human being. Everything about them, even the body, must change radically.

There is a profound difference between the condition of the usual man or woman and the Condition of the Awakened individual. It is an inconceivable leap in evolution. But there is a real process for it, and there is Help for it: the mature, devotional relationship to the Awakened Spiritual Master. In other words, there is something in the physics of the universe that makes it possible for a single or random individual to pass through the entire affair of Transformation in God, and then to bring others into the sphere of his existence, so that they may duplicate his Condition and be drawn into that entire and ultimate evolutionary cycle. Therefore, the relationship to the Spiritual Master is the primary function of spiritual life.

What must take place, if spiritual life is to be true, is not just a change in your mind, an inner awakening, a good feeling about everything. Spiritual processes do not occur in the subjective nonsense that people associate with religion—all this vicarious belief and vicarious salvation—as if real Awakening were just a matter of asking some silly questions or going to a few lectures for the weekend! That is not Enlightenment. Enlightenment is a literal change of the whole body. When you have acquired the human form, the literal change that must occur in the body is not really so much in its outward appearance, because you already have the necessary structure. But the changes that must occur are literal, psycho-physical changes, just as literal as if you were to acquire more legs and arms, except that the most dramatic changes occur in dimensions different from the outward shape of the body. Certainly changes occur in the flesh and the elemental structures of the body, but the changes do not really alter its outward shape. The change is as literal as evolving from a dinosaur to a human being, and it is as dramatic as that, but it principally occurs at more subtle levels of the physics of the bodily being. There are literal changes in the nervous system, literal changes in the chemistry of the body, literal changes in the structural functioning of the brain.

You cannot realize such a change in a weekend. Such a change is a living process, a matter of growth. But it can be quickened and intensified through right practice, through real moral or sacrificial discipline, through the Company of the Spiritual Master. In that Company, the Condition of the higher physics is Communicated to the individual, in such a way that it brings about a radical Transformation in the disposition of the body-mind, and then magnifies the effectiveness of that disposition many times, so that the whole process can take place even in a single lifetime. That process can at least be dramatically advanced in one lifetime, if not completely fulfilled.

I have described the full esoteric progression of this remarkable Transformation in *The Enlightenment of the Whole Body*. This description is not based merely on an intellectual synthesis of things I have read and thought. The whole path is my literal experience—not only the complete moral preparation, but also the awakenings of energy, including the full kundalini process, the elaboration of subtle sounds and lights via the awakening of the brain centers, all the great archetypal visions, everything. I have had all the classic yogic experiences, from the muladhar, or the lowest terminal of the bodily being at the perineum, to the upper reaches of the mind in the brain core. Eventually, it became evident that the "muladhar to sahasrar[1] game" (or, really, the raising of attention from the muladhar to the ajna center,[2] with contemplation of the "sky of mind" in the direction of the sahasrar), whether played through the grosser, extended bodily processes of the kundalini awakening, or through the higher path of the awakening of the brain centers through meditations on subtle light and sound, is not the Way of Truth. It became evident that the Realization of Truth is perfect sacrifice from the heart, not only of the lower or gross level of existence, but also of the whole subtle or higher mental elaboration of experience and function. Thus, in my case, ultimately there was

1. The sahasrar is the highest center of Life-Energy and the terminal goal of the yogi. It is associated with the crown of the head, the upper brain, and higher mind.

2. The brain core or subtle yogic center between and behind the eyebrows, which governs the dynamic mind, will, vision, audition, imagination, etc.

perfect Realization of the Heart of Consciousness, or Self-Realization, which is an Awakening beyond the limits of the inward soul, into unqualified God-Realization.

That one person has had all these extraordinary experiences and also enjoys this Unconditional Awakening as his constant Condition is a great opportunity for all others. His Realization and Teaching bring all these matters into a clear unity, so that the whole affair of our existence can be approached rightly. The Realization of the perfect Intensity of Truth has continued as my very Existence. It was not and could not have been a passing experience. And the Power of it is available for the Transformation of others, if people will enter into right relationship with me.

If you move into such a relationship, the Process begins to duplicate itself in your case. It is not as if you are a robot that is being transformed through the effect of some computer—no, it is a living and human relationship. But it is not like the conventional doctor-patient or mommy-daddy-baby games. Irresponsible people cannot enter into it. You must be responsible for yourself at the human level, and in a profoundly uncommon way. You must live the ordinary discipline yourself. You yourself must be love under all ordinary, daily conditions. You must make a moral change in your life. There is no way whereby you can be relieved of this necessity, and nobody can do it for you. But all of that ordinary personal and moral responsibility simply prepares you for the right relationship to the Spiritual Agency made available by the Divine through the Spiritual Master. Such a one is your unique advantage, because he is present in the same bodily form as you—manifest in this same physical condition, with the same nervous system, the same kind of brain. But in him all of these things are raised to an absolute level of functioning, so that entering into contact or Communion with that individual brings changes even at the level of the psycho-physical body which you bring into relationship with him.

The abstract Deity cannot serve in you in that way, you see, because the physics of this Process must be directly present, and the human Demonstration of the Process must be present, in a form that can do its Work in your case. That Work is the purpose of the Spiritual Master, because he represents a state of the ultimate physics of things that is your potential but not your actuality at the present time. The abstract Divine and the potential powers of the universe are just as true as the Spiritual Master, but they are not organized (except in the case of the Spiritual Master) for the sake of the immediate transformation of human beings. If people enter into right relationship with the Spiritual Master, then they themselves begin to realize the same transformations. Then, at the end of the Spiritual Master's life (or when he finally retires from personal contact with others), his devotees will have gone through sufficient Transformation that the Community of devotees can become the extended mechanism or Agent of his Function. That Community Agency does the work of the Divine Power in the future. But there must be a long period of literal Transformation of devotees before the same Agency can be transferred to them, or to their unique Form, which is the Community.

Until such devotees exist, there is only the Agency of the Spiritual Master. The Spiritual Master is the Awakened Servant of Man. He serves to regenerate the moral Teaching of Truth and to resurrect the great Culture of Compassion and Wisdom among men. That is a secondary aspect of his service to men and women, an emanation of his Realization and Ultimate Function. His True and Ultimate Function is to instigate the superphysics of literal God-Realization among true devotees. If there is no duplication of that superphysical Process, there can be no true continuation of the Teaching, except in verbal form, because there can be no living Agency. So how would the Process take place in the future? Perhaps, as in the past, people could resort to the pieces of it that men of experience represent. People can always experience a little mysticism, a little psychism, a little internal energy, a little insight. But when the Total Representation of Divine Realization is demonstrated in the literal human form of one individual, people must make use of it. It is an advantage that is unique in human time.

Lower, Middle, and Highest

The lowest order of humanity does not understand even the lowest kinds of functional experience. Therefore, they remain bound to the mechanical repetition of unillumined events.

The middling range of uncommon and extraordinary humanity is founded on a critical understanding of the lowest kinds of functional experience. Therefore, such individuals serve as parental or superior guides and instructors, leading mankind toward higher possibilities. But these individuals, whom we acknowledge as great mystics, saints, and creative or intuitive geniuses, do not thoroughly understand the high and highest kinds of functional experience. Therefore, such individuals remain bound to mechanical contemplation of the luminous events of the higher mind and body of Man.

369

The highest human type is represented by those yet rare individuals who are established in critical and intuitive understanding of all human experience, both low and high in the structural scale of human possibility. Therefore, such individuals have understood, and thus transcended, even their own highest possible experience. Such individuals represent the ultimate Destiny of Man, which is Ecstasy, Divine Love, or the transcendence of the psycho-physical limit that is Man himself.

When Man is transcended in the Living Truth, then all knowledge and all experience yield to Life, and both body and mind Dissolve in the Thrill of Divinity.

Nature and God

Nature is a Transformer, a Play on God, Who is the Only Living One. In the Realm of Nature, beings appear to be born, changed, and destroyed at last, but the Principle and Condition of their existence is also the Principle and Condition upon which the Realm of Nature itself is dependently set. The Realm of Nature does not give us existence, nor can all its changes and endings negate our existence. We must surrender to the Living One and Awaken to the presumption of unqualified existence as our very Condition. Then we will transcend our born selves, our changes, and all the endings in store for us. In our Ecstasy, we will be Present in the Play of Changes as the Living One, the Master of Nature, free of all fear and despair. Then we will be Happy, and we will also manifest or serve the Will whereby Nature itself is ultimately Purposed toward the Good and Happiness of all beings.

The Universe Is a Laughing Matter

A talk by Da Free John

I

DA FREE JOHN: Shall we talk some more about evolution? Some scientists today believe there is evidence that the genetic material from which human beings developed migrated to Earth from other planets. Do you think this is a possibility? Where <u>did</u> we come from? What are we doing here? We do not seem to have evolved directly from the ape, if at all, if we accept the latest evidence—although current scientific thinking vacillates between accepting Man's evolution from the ape and regarding Man as a special intervention into the scheme of evolution. You are all human beings—what do you think? Where did you come from?

As an ape, you would have had to do a lot of evolving to become Man, and the conventional evolutionary scale does not describe much in the interval between apes and men. Truly you cannot become Man merely by adapting as an animal. Human beings possess functions that animals do not possess, but we human beings ourselves have not yet adapted to or evolved those functions. Not only did we not create them by adaptation—they are still latent in us!

Where did these higher or latent human functions come from, then? No animal created them. No animal approximates the full development of the brain of Man. Therefore, we did not acquire the higher brain centers from the lower creatures. Certain mechanisms of the human being can be found in animals, and we can see our relationship to the genetic series of the world. But the unique element that is in Man is not the product of adaptation. Furthermore, what is truly unique about Man is even now unused by human beings. We have yet to adapt and evolve toward what is <u>already</u> in us!

Can you account for Man within the scheme of natural selection and the adaptation of lower creatures? You absolutely cannot. What exactly is going on, then? What is evolving as Man? If lower creatures are not evolving as Man, then something senior to the human race is trying to take birth. We have yet to adapt to the functions we have been given, the higher functions of the human brain, which are new in the scheme of life on Earth. Since the human race began, only a few remarkable individuals have awakened to these higher capabilities. Over time, however, the laws by which these functions may be developed—and which extraordinary individuals have demonstrated in their own lives—may become known to many people who can apply them toward the evolution of Man.

371

QUESTIONER: You often speak of our urge toward self-enclosure or death, but it must also be true that we possess an equivalent urge toward life, or this higher process you are describing. Otherwise, if we felt only our mortality, we probably would not continue to live.

DA FREE JOHN: Yes. In the deep psyche you are awake. What is more, the body is not your personal representative. The human body, your body, is the genetic representative of all the functions and capabilities of the species that is Man, not merely those qualities that you, in your limited adaptation, are willing or able to manifest at the present time. Thus, it is not only your personal awakening to the Truth that moves you bodily to live and to evolve. The genetic impulse inherent in the body is more profound than any personal strength or weakness. We are the pawns or servants of the genetic motive. Man is working through us. The "Man motive" is our controller.

Therefore, we are not controlled by what is less than we are in the scale of evolution except to the degree that we are confused by existence and recoiled from Life. When we discover the Truth of our existence, when we therefore become Life-positive, then we are obliged by that insight to adapt to what is inherent in us as Man but that we have not yet acknowledged in our personal existence. When you can laugh at the animal in yourself, when you can laugh at your present vitally obsessed state and transcend it then you can be responsible for your habits of living and for your moral, relational existence, and you can begin to adapt bodily to the Process of Life. It is then that evolution begins.

The powers of knowledge in the world today, however, are not so Life-positive. They are possessed by a negative view of life and the world. The problem is not that the priesthood of science is simply materialistic, as all ordinary men are. The problem is that this priesthood does not account for anything beyond the world as it seems to be. As a result, and despite the best work of our sciences, we still do not understand our situation as human beings. We are limited by our presumed knowledge, which has been given to us by our religions and our sciences. We naturally assume that something of the scientific dogma of evolution is true, but even so we cannot account for Man in terms of what apparently preceded him in the scale of evolution.

To account for Man we must look into the future, to something that is more or greater than Man. Just as the wilderness of Nature is the realm in which animals adapt, so the realm of the higher conscious individual is the wilderness of Man. The higher functions of the body-mind are our wilderness. The ordinary world of survival, of the lower bodily functions of food, sex, and relationships, is the domain we should already have mastered. It is our "civilization," the part of our existence to which we must already have brought order. The truly human epoch begins when we bring order to the scheme of our daily existence in the world. Only then are we free to wander in the wilderness of the higher functions and of our true existence.

The consideration of the higher evolutionary growth of Man rightly belongs to the tradition of esoteric religion and spirituality. However, the true consideration of Man and his relationship to the world and to God has been locked away, obscured by the mumbo-jumbo of metaphorical religious philosophy and exoteric dogma. True religious and spiritual teachings essentially describe the evolutionary and transcendental destiny of the human species. Thus, the visions and symbolic descriptions of the traditional mystics describe not God but the psycho-physiological structures of our own body-mind. We must demythologize mysticism through our own experience of the higher processes of the evolution of Man. We must understand that the principle of mystical experience is also the principle of gross bodily experience. That principle is the Radiant Life-Current that pervades and surrounds and gives Life to the body-mind and all beings, and in which the entire universe is arising, changing, floating, and disappearing.

In the midst of this consideration, however, you must realize that we are still talking only about conditions of Man, conditions of our own nervous system and brain. These higher centers seem marvelous to us, and so we locate them in the realms of the cosmos beyond Man and Earth. Hallucinogenic drugs also can give us an experience of expanded consciousness (although the content of drug experiences is far exceeded by the content of mystical experiences of the highest type). The states of consciousness produced by mystical awareness and hallucinogens seem, in either case, to be generated in a space beyond body and mind, and so we make judgments about the total universe based on these experiences. But, after all, they are developments of the brain, not of the cosmos. We are still only investigating ourselves.

What is truly marvelous is not realized within the realm of our experience. We can experience only the realm of Man. What is marvelous is not even symbolized in our consciousness. It is beyond ourselves—beyond what is latent within this nervous system, this brain, this genetic structure, beyond all that we can investigate. What is truly marvelous is not even contacted in our higher mysticism, which still contacts "me," the structures of Man. Although mysticism contacts the higher centers of the brain, nevertheless the skull is still the foundation and signature of our sky. The brain is our vehicle, our compartment, our limit. Thus, when you have finished exceeding yourself and going higher and higher in your being, you find that you must reach beyond the body-mind, beyond knowledge, beyond the universe of matter. Once you make that transcendental gesture, you cannot know what our destiny will be. You must simply take the gamble!

That toward which we are evolving is present in us as an urge, not as a vision. Enlightenment is an urge, not an answer. It is the process by which we realize what is marvelous, what no one has ever envisioned or suggested. It has only been felt to be necessary! Somehow the entire expanse of everything is sitting in a Room somewhere. To break out of the pattern of the arising world and become identical to its transcendental Principle is to enter that Room—whatever it is. The Transcendental Domain is beyond comprehension. It has nothing to do with our memory, our repetitions, or our possible knowledge. We may acquire knowledge about the workings of the entire universe, all the galaxies and the totality of manifestation, and still not realize the marvelous. The Domain toward which we have the ultimate urge to go does not stop short of the marvelous. Thus, there is nothing to say about what is beyond the ultimate stage of the evolution of Man. You can linger in that stage or you can cross over. When you will do this is immaterial. It is a laughing matter!

374

II

D A FREE JOHN: The essence of humor is repetition. To make a joke is to mimic and repeat what is ordinary. Comics are constantly talking about what happens to everybody else and imitating what everybody else does, but they are not actually doing what everybody else does. They are repeating it. What is funny is to see what we do repeated, to be permitted to laugh about it.

What is humor? If we can discover what it is bodily, then we will have discovered the key to humor, because humor is a bodily matter. Laughter is the signal of humor, the sign of getting a joke. We tend to associate laughter with good feelings. We presume, therefore, that laughter is purely pleasurable. But I have considered the origin of laughter bodily, and I have observed that we laugh when we are tickled. Yet when we tickle somebody, we are aware that although nothing is funny, we have stimulated precisely the reaction that we bring to something that is funny. The key to humor, therefore, is to create laughter or to stimulate the reaction to being tickled.

You know very well that, although you laugh when you are tickled, being tickled is not entirely pleasurable. Laughter is your defense against that not-quite-pleasurable contact. Joking is likewise a defense against contact with the world, an escape from the realities of ordinary life. Thus, although humor or joking is a form of our play, its origin is in the pleasure-pain reaction of laughing when being tickled.

This is why conventional joking or humor is not simply funny. It is a way of dealing with pain, a repetition of things that are painful but that are presented to us to create a reaction of pleasure. That pleasurable reaction, however, is a reaction to pain. Our conventional joking or humor is a way to feel pleasure in the face of pain, but it is not real humor.

Real humor is a spiritual matter. It transcends even laughter, because it transcends the pain of existence. Real humor is not associated with pain, and, therefore, it is not in general associated with laughter or any other apparent mood. Through true humor we transcend the seriousness of events by suddenly awakening to their Divine Condition. Suddenly, for a moment, we glimpse the non-necessity of everything, the humor of everything, the non-threateningness of everything. Thus, true humor comes with Enlightenment, or the transcendence of all conditions of experience, both pleasurable and painful.

Until we are Enlightened and truly humorous, we use laughter or joking, our worldly humor, to escape from pain. We are not really happy when we are merely laughing. We are addicted to joking and laughing, just as we are addicted to orgasm. Both conventional laughter and conventional orgasm are forms of reactive defense, ways of feeling good in the midst of pain.

True or free laughter is a product of real humor, humor that is associated with the body and even with ordinary events. But the reason that an enlightened and humorous being laughs is not mere pain. It is recognition. I, for instance, am not amused merely by repetitions. This laughter arises spontaneously in the instant I transcend what I see repeated. However, one can be just as full of humor without laughing. One who is truly humorous, who transcends all the events of ordinary life in every moment, can appear to be in any mood, but his or her humor, or enjoyment of the Divine Condition, is obvious.

You must be able to find the humor, the joke, in all the events that you now take so seriously. To become capable of laughing at life—and even at the whole matter of evolution—is to be able always to awaken pleasurable feeling in yourself even though you have been born. You must be able to be full of pleasure even though you may tend to react to the events of your ordinary life.

At the present time, you see, you are very serious about many things, so serious that you laugh only at clowns. You do not see that, like the clown, you too are repetitious, that you are doing everything again. You do not do anything new—you do everything again. Everything you do is an "again." Practically nothing is new. If something new appears in your life, it is new for only a fraction of a second, because the instant you realize it is pleasurable, you start repeating it! You rarely feel in relationship to anything because you are too busy repeating everything. That is clowning!

376

Therefore, you must engage your repeating of life consciously. Then you can be mocked. Then you have become a laughing matter and you are free. Then evolution and even the body are a laughing matter. Then you realize true laughter as bodily dissolution. The Spiritual Master's laughter is one of his vague attempts to blow himself to smithereens! True laughter is shattering.

Unless you transcend yourself, you repeat yourself, and repetition without enlightenment is karma, or bondage to fixed destiny. If we simply realized this moment completely and fully, there would be no bondage, but we tend to repeat this moment and hold on to it. We do not live this moment in the Infinity of Life. We live it for its own sake, and we hold on to it desperately, afraid to lose the pleasure and consolation it offers. Out of fear we repeat everything. We even repeat the things we choose not to repeat, by avoiding them. Thus, we are karma-laden, burdened by the urge to repetition. But to the Enlightened man or woman karma is a joke. You too must see that your own limited life of tendency is funny. You must become truly humorous about your life. You must transcend the repetition that is your present way of life by entering into delight and becoming a laughing matter.

Presently you are afraid to experience anything directly— simply because you are afraid, not because you truly are afraid of experiencing anything directly. You are turned away from experience. You are recoiling upon yourself. You are full of fear. You are protecting yourself. Laughter and all the other things to which you are addicted are the methods you use to protect yourself, ways of trying to trigger the emotion, the bodily sense, the clarity of feeling good under stress. You must go beyond that game of repeating pleasurable moments. You must have humor about all the things you are presently taking so seriously. The first step toward spiritualizing your existence is to become humorous about the ordinary things of life, and therefore free. Transcend the animal, therefore, and become truly human.

Laughter is the root of transfiguration, and the tickle is the original urge to God-Realization. Pain and death, which are the root stimuli of the tickle, are the origins of the motive to be free. But most people are not urgent enough in that motive. At some point they stop growing. They adapt just enough to console themselves in their fear and they do not grow any more. They do nothing for the rest of their lives except to repeat themselves. I have seen a great deal of the world, and it seems to be repeating itself. It is even beginning to repeat itself everywhere in multiples, like an image in a hall of mirrors! More and more of the same thing is happening all of the time. Have you observed this? I feel somewhat in the mood of the old monks and ascetics who left the world having finally gotten that joke. I really am possessed by the realization that the world is immovable in its karma. Paradoxically, that realization, like death, is one of the goads to real, creative life.

QUESTIONER: The possibility of saving the world is a goad to your Teaching Work?

DA FREE JOHN: Yes, and the impossibility of saving the world creates laughter. There is the urge to Enlighten every being, and then there comes the realization that it is impossible to do. That is the joke. The impossibility makes a joke of spiritual Teaching. Spiritual Teaching is a primal urge, like sex, you see, but it is bound to be laughed at. It must become a laughing matter so that the Teacher can go on to something else.

This Teaching is also a kind of joke, an expression of my sense of humor. I am a clown, don't you see? I do everything for the sake of good humor. You are able to see the Brightness of God only through responding properly to his fool—in other words, by getting the "jokes" of the Teaching of the Adept, by transcending the world in his Company. If you do not laugh at God's fool, then you do not see God. The way to God is through God's fool, God's clown, one who has already transcended the world.

Thus, I am here to make a mockery of the universe, to demonstrate that the universe is a laughing matter, so that you will transcend it. I am here to tell the ultimate jokes—all seven of them. There are seven eternal jokes, which are not revealed in words—they are not quips or one-liners, but whole pieces of existence, or stages of life. The seven stages of life are the seven original jokes. They too are the fool of God. When you transcend them by fulfilling them, then you are able to see the wonderment of God. When you have fulfilled the Teaching of Truth, then you get the joke of human existence.

378

Living the stages of life, though a profound and necessary gesture, is ultimately foolishness. The seven stages are stages of laughter, each of which must, in its turn, become a great laugh to you. You must be able to feel total pleasure in the face of each stage of experience before you can go on to complete the next stage. In your present level of realization, however, you have not yet laughed at any of the stages of life. You are still burdened by them, still carrying them around, still being tested by them. You are not yet laughing at God's fool. You yourself will become God's fool as you incarnate and laugh at each of the stages of life. Even the seventh stage of life, you will see, is a colossal lot of foolishness. The only way to move through the seventh stage is to laugh your head off. The seventh stage of life must become a laughing matter, along with all the rest of your body and all its stages of growth. You must get the seventh joke, which is the body itself, the last laugh. That joke is eternal and its Humor is infinite Bliss.

It is not what we find out about the Universe that matters. What matters is our moment to moment emotional relationship to the Universe and to the Condition in which the Universe is always suddenly arising.

The only living and true religion in any society and in any historical epoch is the effort of the individual to surrender to the radical intuition of Truth and to be transformed by the Radiant Transcendental Love-Energy that moves the world.

Da Free John

CHAPTER ELEVEN

Beyond Doubt

The Urgency of the Teaching

A talk by Da Free John

D A FREE JOHN: If you want to learn about Truth when Truth has become corrupted, then go to an Adept. Go to one who has Realized the Truth. Go to one who has already fulfilled the process completely. If you live in a moment in time when there is no Enlightened Tradition, when all the cults are corrupt, you can be certain that somewhere on Earth an Adept is alive. Such a person appears under exactly those conditions, when Truth is no longer visible in the cults, and when religions have become so corrupted by history and fetishism that they are about to become extinct.

The religious traditions in our time are about to be smothered by a mechanistic, political, and scientific world view, only because the cults are in doubt. They have held on to their fetishes so tenaciously that they have lost their association with the Living God. They do not even know the Living God anymore. Most people who belong to conventional churches, religions, and spiritual societies have no unqualified connection with the Living Reality. There is no true devotion in them, and, therefore, no Realization. Their association with God is only words and hopefulness. Therefore, they do not represent a living force in the world. They have nothing to offer that is Alive. Only the Adepts, who are God-Realized, through whom the living Power of God manifests, can make a difference in human time. Such individuals are the instruments for the acculturation of humanity.

Periodically, such individuals must appear, and they must be influential. There is a notion that Adepts should be hiding in caves in the wilderness. This is not true. If the Adepts do not speak, the only voice that will be heard is that of ordinary people who are not God-Realized. The Adepts are the Sources of spiritual life. Such individuals must therefore enter into the stream of society, to purify the culture and reestablish the process of God-Realization. If they do not speak and become influential, there is no hope at all for humanity.

We exist in a moment in time when the cults are universally corrupted. Thus, it is a time for Adepts and true devotees to reappear if there is to be any hope for the future of human beings. We are about to be swallowed up in anti-cultism, anti-Godism, anti-religion, anti-spirituality. The impetus or force behind this movement against the true culture of Man, which is a God-Realizing culture, is largely the reaction to cultism. The cults, which should be a means for establishing people in a right relationship to the Living God, have become frozen in their idolatry, fixed in their association with their historical peculiarities and limitations, and they do not represent a window to the Living God anymore. They represent a piece of mind frozen in the form of words and imagery and histories of all kinds.

Intelligent people cannot find God in such a mass of idiocy, so quite naturally they look for satisfaction elsewhere. Thus, people are preoccupied with all kinds of political and scientific idealism, as if politics and scientific and technological progress were the Way of Truth. They are absolutely not the Way of Truth. They never have been the Way of Truth. They are no more the Way of Truth than sex or any other satisfaction or fulfillment of function. None of that is the Way of Truth at all. It is the ordinary impulse of the ego, glamorizing itself by great enterprises.

If this trend toward political and scientific obsession is to be broken, some light must be brought to the whole affair of spiritual and religious understanding. The conventional, exoteric cults must be purified. They must give up their primacy. Their legitimacy must come into doubt. Then the Teaching of Adepts, the Sources of Truth, will again become available, and the Living Reality will again become obvious, obliging human beings to a different way of life than the ego proposes.

If not, the world will be overwhelmed. It is almost inevitable now that it will be overwhelmed in any case. The world, even the Realm of Nature as a whole, is founded on a righteous Principle. Therefore, the world will be purified, without a doubt. The Force of the Divine pervades everything, and, therefore, It also purifies everything in one way or another. If human beings, while they have the benign capacity to enter into God-Communion, will not do so, but instead create a corrupt culture, a subhuman order, then the purification will not occur within the ordinary and benign course of natural processes. It is then no longer a matter of some Adept's saying a holy word or speaking the Truth whereupon everybody changes his or her approach to life. It would be good if as many as possible could hear the universal Teaching of Truth and respond to it. But if the Teaching alone is not sufficient, then great upheavals necessarily occur. That is how the righteous Law works. It is not just that we pay our dues for past activity. A righteous Principle is positively at work, constantly to purify and to reestablish order.

Thus, there are periods of great negative upheaval in the world, including natural disasters, wars, and conflicts of all kinds. On the one hand, during these periods, the world pays its dues for failing to live by the Law. On the other hand, these times of upheaval are the evidence of a continuous process of purification. They are themselves a demonstration of the Law. At the end of these periods, the Law is reestablished in righteousness.

It is very likely that we are entering into such a time of upheaval, because of the extent of the failure of human culture. There is simply no light abroad in the world today. There is nothing but corruption, nothing but the failure to accept the Way of God. There is absolutely no sign of the Way of Truth, except in rare instances of individuals and small groups of people. The Truth is essentially hidden and secondary. There is a long history of corruption in every area of human life, and the entire social structure of the world is devoted to subhuman ends and forms of self-indulgence. There are no signs of an imminent Golden Age in the disposition or condition of humanity at large. Rather, the signs are of the necessity for a great purification, a great reestablishment of order, a righteous readjustment of the whole world.

The View That Must Be Tested

The waking world is not a "place," a fixed shape, but a sizeless realm, an undefinable dimension, just as the condition or region into which you enter in dreams is an undefinable realm. The world of our experience is not fixed, like a moon or any object, but it is fluid, like space or light. It is operative as a play of possibility, rather than fixed mechanical destiny. And its conditions in every moment arise not merely according to physical laws, but according to psycho-physical laws. The universe in which Earth appears is a psycho-physical system (psycho-spatial and psycho-temporal), not a mere physical or material one. The same world or realm, in other of its aspects, is seen in dreams and sleeping too. This view is ancient and must be tested. It is native to man and makes him wonder, fear, seek, and hide.

Every human individual represents only a limited realization of the psycho-physical scheme of appearances. The more psychic or conscious he becomes, the more he sees the world as a Psychic or Conscious Process. It is not only the man who is a psycho-physical process. His world is also. Free life begins only when we begin to operate from this profound premise. This thesis is itself the most significant consideration of Man. To enter into the Truth of our condition we must enter into psychic, heartfelt relationship with the world. Then we see not only the body of the world, but its mind also, its subjective or subtle places, and its degrees of self.

But when even this soulful knowing shows itself to be suffering, then Enjoyment is awake, prior to the birth of worlds, and beings, and you that contemplates the Mystery. The waking world is a psycho-physical realm. Everything appears, then, as in dreams, in correspondence with the tendencies, high and low, which are the individual. When this becomes clear, one ceases to identify with preferences, judgments, perceptions, reactions, experiences, forms of knowing, or the pursuit of strategies, high or low, since it is all illusory, changing, and held in place by these very actions. When you awaken, you are no longer concerned about the dream world, since it is all phantoms, created in a moment by tendencies that are the real creators of every circumstance of dreams. Just so, when this waking world is seen truly, it becomes clear that the phantoms of its appearance are endless, appearing out of a formless depth, and that true responsibility is relative to the forces of one's own apparent psycho-physical activity, which creates the theatre and calls up all that is good or bad. The realm itself is not to be valued or rejected in terms of any of its content. The realm cannot even be defined. Where do you dream? Where is a place? Rather, one's own action, one's very self must be seen as a contraction from the Condition of Radiance, or Love, in which the very world is floating. There must be awakening to that Condition which is prior to the Play. Such is the only real responsibility. The rest is the destiny of complication. When the true Condition is realized, the reality of all distractions, of self, of action, of world, of God apart, is undone. There is no necessity to the dream, but there is apparent persistence of the dream. See it truly and abide in the Presence and Radiance that is Real. That Communion is truly awake, even as the dream conventions remain, since it notices nothing, but abides as itself, whatever arises.

We appear in this waking world by the very same process by which we appear in dreams. And the solid waking world is, when seen in Truth, no more real, necessary, fixed, significant, or true than any random dream place. When this begins to become even a little obvious, a process of awakening has begun, similar to waking in the morning from your dreams. When you begin to suspect yourself a little, then you begin to become distracted by another and formless dimension, much as the sleeper begins to sense his bed cloth, his solid body, and his room. At that point, one may become sensitive to the Spiritual Master, the Presence of the Condition of things, one who is already awake, the paradoxical man. He is, in person, that dimension which is Truth. He calls you constantly and roughens your feet. He intensifies the sunlight in your room. He does not awaken you to another place or dream, as if your mother shakes you awake to play in rooms protected or threatened by your father. Rather, he serves an awakening in which there is no realm, no implication, and no adventure. He does not awaken you to another place. He awakens you in place, so that even while the dream of living survives, the destiny or even noticing of all effects escapes you.

The Psychosis of Doubt

A talk by Da Free John

D A FREE JOHN: Many people claim to be religious and to be profoundly committed to traditions that belong to a higher view of human culture, but very few people have a sense of the powers behind the world, or an experiential understanding of the psyche, or a moral grasp of what it truly means to be religious, or a heartfelt commitment to how one must live in order to realize a truly religious life and destiny. True religion is to enter ecstatically into the Domain of Radiant Existence that is beyond the limited personal self, or ego, or body-mind. It is to engage in higher intuitive, mystical, moral, and emotional processes that lead into and then beyond the realms of the psyche and even all the realms beyond material visibility. It is a way of making positively creative changes even in one's "material" or physical life, as well as passing consciously beyond this gross physical life into another destiny, even while alive, and also at death. However, very few people have any understanding of this process, or even any hope that such a process may actually exist.

It is only later in time, in the recent centuries of objectively glamorous "civilization," that people have lost or begun to deny their psychic connection to the universe. And it is only in such exclusively materialistic or world-conquering civilizations that religion has become nothing more than a collection of behavioral precepts for downtown life, for how to manage your business, how to be completely fulfilled as a "person," and so forth. But true religion is not based on the emotionally dissociated superficialities of conventional worldliness. True religion is based on the <u>psychic connection</u> to Reality. There can be no true religion without profound psychic activity. True religion expresses the inherent disposition and motive of the psyche, or the intuitive, feeling core of Man. The contemporary religion of civilized popular societies has little or no psyche remaining from its psychic, feeling origins. The psyche is taboo to science and industry. Only the verbal mind is permitted to priest our destiny with all the automatic nonsense of meaningless, heartless rituals and objective beliefs. Such civilized religion is not based on a sense of the invisible forces with which we each need to enter into right association in order to live well and to be happy, in order not to be undone, bound up, smothered, and destroyed by the elemental movements in Nature. All true religion and spirituality are founded in the Way of the psyche, which contains a secret Pathway that leads beyond the Realm of Nature.

In order to live such a true religious Way of Life, individuals must enter psychically into the play of their experience in the material or objective universe. We must move beyond the self-bound stupidity of the verbal mind, which has no sympathy, no heart, no feeling, no psyche. We must move beyond the unhappy and degenerative stupidities of the mere bodily exploitation we inevitably engage when we are frozen in this mind without a psyche. The usual man in our time is limited only to verbal thinking and exploitation of his physical experience. Everything else is taboo, or else confounded by complications. The usual man cannot go beyond the hard-edged appearance of the physical body and the apparent objectivity of physical experience, because he is not permitted his own deep psyche. The psyche is the deep disposition of <u>union</u> with That which is Radiant and Alive. Only the unitary and self-transcending disposition of the psyche, rather than the separative and self-defining disposition of the conventional mind, can provide the foundation for true religion and a true humanity.

What is precisely and devastatingly wrong with the universal scientism of modern society and all the forms of mass politics that are derived from that scientism is that the modern scientific and political world-view does not permit the human being his psyche and the Way of the psyche. Scientism (or the disposition of scientific materialism) constantly obliges the individual to stand face to face with mere elemental experience and to deny all reality and hierarchical supremacy to higher and subtler dimensions, which in ancient times were commonly recognized to be the <u>fundamental</u> resource of human individuals and societies. Scientism denies our true connection to the energies and creative sources of the world. We are denied true religion by the mind of scientism and all of the social and political agencies of popular scientific or material culture.

Scientism is simply an analytical activity of the verbal mind. It is oriented toward the investigation of elemental phenomena without the "limiting interference" of psychic participation. Even when scientists consider phenomena that are not merely elemental, but that belong to the ambiguous realm of energies and the human psyche, they do not study these things through the psyche. They study them objectively, as if these invisibles were butterflies under a pin. But in order to investigate the higher phenomena of light-energy (or the hierarchy of processes in which "matter" is arising) one must ultimately enter into consideration of them through the medium of the psyche itself, through feeling, through intuition, through surrender to energy, through all the aspects of the mind and heart that precede and transcend the verbal consciousness.

The currently popular presumptions about the world do not permit us to recognize and acknowledge the invisible and psychically perceptible dimensions of existence. We are encouraged to watch TV and go to work and wait for science to save everyone. But science can never save anyone. Science is not a method of salvation. Salvation depends upon the awakening of the psyche of the human individual. There is no salvation (no fulfillment of Man) apart from psychic awakening. Science, however, is not a psychic activity or adventure. Therefore, it does not serve or awaken the psyche or the psychic Path of the individual. Science is nothing more than a useful method for the investigation and mechanical exploitation of aspects of the externalized or apparently objective and material universe. Such an enterprise can, if rightly used, produce useful technologies and benign changes in the environment, but it cannot improve our lot in any fundamental sense, because human beings are fulfilled and liberated only through psychic awakening, and psychic participation in the pattern and ultimate Condition of the universe. We must be awakened psychically, personally, emotionally, and deeply in order to be truly happy and free.

That the materialistic point of view of civilized scientism dominates human beings is a profoundly negative state of affairs, because such an application of science strictly anathematizes the awakening and the activation of the psyche of human beings. The propaganda of popular science is most profoundly about the anathematization and material limitation of the psyche. Whatever benign changes it may bring technologically, scientific materialism represents a trend in philosophy that is opposed to the psychic awakening of human beings. That is what is wrong with it. And as soon as anybody shows an inclination toward psychic life, toward the things of the psychic view of the world, toward mysticism, or toward religion (in the psychic sense, rather than just the downtown illusions of morality and self-fulfillment), he is considered crazy, bizarre, eccentric, an anachronism. And the popular cult of scientists is regularly represented in the press, animating benighted claims that the movement toward psychic experience is nonsense, falsehood, superstition, a sign of reaction to urban pressures, a passing phase in our material leap toward utopia and final collective knowledge.

The historical origin of modern scientism was in the rebellion of the verbal mind against the popular institutions that tyrannized it. Modern science was founded on a philosophical reaction to archaic exoteric religious institutions and other movements in human cultures that prevented the free and independent exercise of mental activity in the investigation of Nature. Scientism appeared as a righteous and, at the time, entirely appropriate, reaction to cultural oppression. Science arose as a revolutionary movement, which sought to permit the free exercise of the verbal mind. That revolutionary cultural reaction was fundamentally right and positive, and a major aspect of science and scientific influence is certainly positive. However, because of the philosophical exclusiveness of that original reaction of science, the popular culture of scientific and political materialism now supports a cultural psychology (or psychosis) that wants to exclude the psychic awakening and the psychic Path of our Destiny in and beyond the Realm of Nature. Therefore, such scientism represents a new kind of oppressive exoteric priesthood, a different kind of Church, against which others must now rebel. There must be the free exercise of the verbal mind and of intellectual inquiry, but there must also be the free psychic and Spiritual exercise of human individuality. Human beings must be permitted psychic association with the Great Universe. If such is denied them, they become crazy and dangerous. And that is exactly what has happened—these few hundred years in which the modern and materialistic scientific point of view has gradually become dominant have emptied human culture of its higher psychic associations and aspirations.

Now we are looking toward a future of technological domination, a heartless world, a human world without psyche. It is not only political totalitarianism that is represented in the image of the future of science fiction. It is a human world without human psyche or Transcendental Destiny. It is a universe without a psychic dimension, a merely physical universe rather than a psycho-physical universe. The current state of our so-called culture reflects the same lack. True culture depends on the awakened and heartfelt disposition of the human psyche.

The scientific community must understand and acknowledge that its positive aspect is its orientation toward free intellectual inquiry. The old exoteric religious institutions perpetuated an "understanding" of the physical universe that was characterized by uninterpretable poetic mythologies and all kinds of absolutist cultic nonsense. Fresh and direct inquiry into phenomena needed to be permitted. That aspect of the emergence of scientism was completely positive. The exoteric religious institutions that existed when scientism began to appear were not founded in universal Truth or a broadly communicated esoteric understanding of the "material" universe and the Way of Man. They were (and remain) downtown exoteric institutions, traditional cultic institutions, without great Adepts and without universal Wisdom. In throwing away this half-baked religion, however, we have also thrown away all <u>psychic</u> inquiry into the universe and its ultimate Condition or Destiny. Intellectual inquiry into the objective phenomena of experience certainly has its value, but psychic inquiry into the experiential universe is not only equally essential, it is primary, and it is more fundamental to the individual. Indeed, such psychic inquiry is absolutely essential for human happiness.

The attention of the psyche can move in any number of directions. There are Great Teachings and lesser teachings and false teachings. The dull conventions of downtown religion and the aggressive passion that one acquires in the streets and in the school of the common world are no Great Teaching at all. All of that is the lowest form of human communication, because it denies that the deep psyche is the fundamental nature of Man and that the individual must live by his psyche, not by the things of the world, not by the objects of

390

experience, not by the elemental, fleshy life, and not by thinking alone.

To "sin" is to "miss the mark," to be without a psyche, or to fail to accept the Way of the psyche, which is to be surrendered into the eternally all-pervading Life-Principle and to be identified with the Radiant Transcendental Being wherein all experience and the total Realm of Nature are arising. To "sin" is to fail to accept the Law of sacrifice, or self-transcending love. It is to be enamored of things themselves, to have lost the psychic and feeling connection to Reality, and to be turned in on yourself without free consciousness. To be awakened from sin is to "meet the mark," to be awakened in your psyche, in your heart. Man must live by his psyche, his unqualified feeling nature. He must enter psychically into relationship with the powers of the world, into relationship with the ultimate Power, the absolute God of the world. If he does not, he is deluded and seems to be destroyed.

The function of the Adept, or Spiritual Master, is to restore this understanding, this awareness, to reveal the true significance of all experience. The Adept Spiritual Master does not represent the glorification of any single convention of human experience. He is Awake in the midst of all experience, all the psycho-physical phenomena of human life. Therefore, such an Adept can establish (or reestablish) a culture based on the perfect Realization of Truth, in which all aspects of the structure of human experience are rightly understood. Man must realize a right sympathy with the etheric life of energy, feeling, and life-force; Man must also ascend through and beyond the etheric life in his astral, or mystical, higher mental, and intuitive structures of consciousness; and he must also evolve beyond the subtle inward dimension into the Transcendental Realization of Reality. We cannot even exclude bodily life in our Realization of the Absolute; we must become a sacrifice, even bodily, into the Absolute Being and Radiant Living Truth. Our action and adaptation while alive must represent a right relationship to that Absolute Reality, and, through that relationship, to all of the manifestations of the Universe and of Man that proceed from that Absolute. All things work together for the good of individuals who remain in right association with the Absolute Reality or Living God. They are awakened, they see through the limits of their experience, and they transcend the phenomena that bind and contain them.

The Adept Spiritual Master communicates the entire Way of the psyche, the Way of Life in Truth, and the right disposition toward all of the phenomena of experience. Therefore, he must criticize all of the forms of exclusive acculturation, all of the less than absolute religions and persuasions. You may hear me criticize all kinds of religious and psychic and mystical approaches to the Divine Reality, but I will not deny what is useful in them. I criticize the exclusiveness in every point of view and the limitation of experience and understanding that is evident in each kind of approach. Just so, I also constantly criticize the social and cultural conventions of ordinary worldly life, not because people enjoy themselves—true enjoyment is necessary and positive—but because there is no psyche in the dull and repetitive enjoyments of the usual man. There is no heart, no Truth, no Life in the popular design of our subhumanity.

The whole world is obsessed with the anathematization of the psyche, and to the degree that people become involved in the deep psychic life at all, they are involved in some little compartment of it, some creepy, petty, fascinated aspect of it that is not God-Realizing. I communicate the disposition of the heart in absolute terms, the Way of Life that involves the psychic or heartfelt relationship to everything. I communicate the Way of sacrifice, via the heart, or the psyche, to the Radiant Absolute Living Reality. In the process of this Way, through your awakening to the psyche, you will likely become fully aware of uncommon phenomena that are not discussed on television or admitted by the intellectual elite who presume to determine what we may know and not know. You are inherently and perfectly free to experience everything from ghosts and spirit forces to the most sublime visions and absorptions in the Great Light that shines above Nature and the body-mind. And you are also inherently obliged to transcend all experience through heartfelt understanding and the feeling sacrifice of the whole body-mind into the All-Pervading and Radiant Transcendental Consciousness that is the Seat of the world.

Just as scientific inquiry must be free, so also must psychic or religious inquiry be free of all kinds of nonsense and suppression. As it exists in the common world today, religion is largely comprised of accretions of nonsense, the archaic ideas and presumptions of very ordinary people. True religion can only be founded on the direct communication of Realized individuals, or Adepts, whose voices must be heard and honored in the world. People must begin to engage in truly religious forms of activity, a truly religious Way of Life. Likewise, science, or free intellectual inquiry, must also be permitted its freedom, its special function in the world. Nevertheless, the motive of science and its social influence in general must be purified of anti-psychic dogmatism. If the voice of science is not thus purified, it will more and more represent an evil influence in the world, an influence that seeks to dominate, suppress, and destroy the psychic potential and the psychic need of Man.

True Religion Is a Higher Cultural Motive Than Conventional Science

Conventional or traditional modern science is an expression of two primary presumptions. On the one hand, science is a method of enquiry, reflecting the analytical, "left-brained," extroverted tendency toward participation in elemental or sense-bound events. On the other hand—and as a consequence of the extroverted analytical disposition of its enquiry—modern science has become dogma or primary cultural doctrine. And that dogmatic and doctrinal presumption is utterly "materialistic."

"Science" propagates a great and negatively persuasive popular conception. It is the concept of "matter," which I have criticized in these essays. Scientific materialism is the dominant cultural or social, political, and technological motive of the present human epoch, and the trend of its propaganda represents the principal anti-religious or anti-spiritual motive of recent history.

Throughout this book, I have criticized that aspect of science which represents the materialistic trend in psychology and philosophy, whereas I have also made a generally positive assessment of the creative possibilities and discoveries of the rigorous intellectual method upon which science is founded. In the present essay, I am disposed to put true science (or the method that is science) into cultural perspective relative to the total structure of human consciousness.

Materialistic and propagandistic scientism represents, for the most part, a degenerative adolescent influence in contemporary society. That role of science is expressed via exploitative technologies and all the subhuman power politics of mass society. In comparison, false or exclusively exoteric traditional religion is associated with childish (or pre-adolescent) historical cultism. The dominant historical cults (or "great religions") serve to maintain a level of "order" in a subhuman mass society, but they demonstrate very little commitment to the universal esotericism of Transcendental Wisdom, and, indeed, their role is generally to suppress the open communication of such Wisdom (and its Adepts) in the world.

In the scheme of popular or subhuman society, adolescent scientism appears to be a motive superior to the relative childishness of myth-laden exoteric religious cultism—and so science has effectively dominated and nearly suppressed the religious consciousness of modern Man. However, in the scheme of a truly human social and cultural order, true science is not an adolescent motive or influence, and true religion is not a comparatively childish adventure.

False or childish religion is a species of magical mentality. It is associated with acts of willful hopefulness, in which desires for experiential consolation or change are formed into verbal and emotional "prayers" to the presumably real but invisible and mind-reading "God of Nature." Popular scientism is a cultural development that seeks to replace the magical processes of childish religion with technologies that actually fulfill the experiential desires of mankind. As such, science is a "method" for the answering of childish prayers. But such scientism is itself no closer to human maturity than the clever adolescent who offers secret pleasures to little children.

When science (or analytical enquiry) is extended as technology it duplicates (and, in terms of practical delivery, exceeds) the magical childishness of conventional religion. As such, science duplicates the natural human developmental pattern of growth from mere desire to willful fulfillment. Popular scientism or technology represents the triumph of the analytical intellect, expressed and implemented via the will (or the power of practical intention). If we view science in negative terms (as a propagandizer of materialistic philosophy and psychology), then we must view it as an essentially <u>adolescent</u> social and cultural motivation. However, if we can understand and make use of science as a truly human method and enterprise, then we can see that it simply represents the mentality or cultural adaptation of the third stage of human development.

The third stage of human life (which I have described within the context of seven fundamental stages) represents the development of the analytical mind and the will. True science is a cultural development of the third stage of human life, and, as such, it is superior and senior to the childish and subhuman magical mentality of false or conventional religious cultism.

However, true religion is not a development of the subhuman and magical egoic mentality. True religion is an expansion beyond the third stage of life, beyond the stage wherein we adapt to the analytical and broader understanding of the true intellect and to the self-integrating, self-expanding, and desire-implementing power of the will. True religion, or true and mature religious practice, actually begins in the fourth stage of human development.

In the fourth stage development of human life, the will is adapted to aspiration, or intuitive self-transcendence. True religion expresses the self-transcending motive, rather than the childish and adolescent motives toward unenlightened self-fulfillment. Therefore, true religion is a profound exercise of ecstatic surrender of the body-mind to the Living Principle or "Spirit" in which "matter" (or all psycho-physical events) is arising.

Seen as such, true religion is a superior or senior motive to true science, although such true religion is not antagonistic to true science and its benign technologies. In a truly human culture, the method and the extended enterprises of science (including technology and politics) are adapted to cooperative participation with the higher, universal, and profound esotericism of Transcendental Wisdom-Religion. Only true, universal, and esoteric religion is of ultimate and human cultural value, and only such true religion can provide the philosophical, psychological, and cultural basis for the advancement of Man or mankind beyond the level of our present impasse.

What Is to Be Realized?

396

There is only the Radiant Transcendental Being, Who is One. All beings and things and worlds are ultimately and Really only identical to That One, Who is God, the Divine Person.

Only God is Alive as everyone and everything. All beings and things and worlds are arising as spontaneous transformations or modifications of That One. God eternally Transcends the world and all beings, and yet the world and all beings are nothing but God. It is a Great and Passionate Mystery.

The individual being, manifest as the body-mind, is only a transformation or modification of the Radiant Transcendental Being or Divine Person. Wherever or whenever there is a psycho-physical being, the Radiant Transcendental Being is conscious as that limitation and feels Itself to be a particular being.

There is no internal self or soul within and independent of the body-mind. The individual body-mind is a modification or Play upon the Infinite, All-Pervading, Transcendental Being. The body-mind itself, in its contraction or recoil from the universal pattern of relations, suggests or implies the subjective internal self or independent soul idea. And once the body-mind or self pattern arises, it tends to persist, as a process of transformation, lifetime after lifetime, until there is Awakening to the Truth, or Translation into the Divine Domain—the Condition of Radiant Transcendental Bliss.

As the being adapts and evolves and achieves Ecstasy in the Divine, it Realizes its eternal inherence in That One and, ultimately, its Identity as That One. Such is Enlightenment, Liberation, or Salvation. Therefore, Enlightenment, Liberation, Salvation, or That which is to be Realized, is not a form of "status" or egoic achievement in this world, the after-death world, or the next lifetime, but it is the Condition of Love and Happiness, which transcends the body-mind, its experiences, its relations, and the world, even as the world continues.

The "being" that is Awakened to the Truth may abide simply as that Identity, excluding participation in the active pattern of the body-mind, its relations, and the world, and excluding as well the self-transcending gesture of Ecstasy in the Universal or Total Divine.

Such is the disposition in the sixth stage of life. Just so, the being that is only beginning to understand its circumstance in God may embrace the lesser disposition of abiding in a state of simple absorption of self in the Radiance of the Transcendental Being. Such conditional Ecstasy characterizes fulfillment in the fourth and fifth stages of life, and it arises when the self or body-mind becomes contemplatively absorbed in the Divine Power that is experientially perceived by or within the body-mind itself. But in the Fullness of the seventh stage of life there is perfect, total, and most profound recognition that the total body-mind, all beings, and the total world of possibilities inhere in an eternal Condition of perfect Identity with the Radiant Transcendental Being. Then there is no reaction either toward inwardness or release of self through internal or external experience. The total body-mind and its conditions and relations are recognized to abide in inherent Identification with That One. Therefore, there is simple persistence as Transfigured Bliss or Love, whatever arises. Every moment of experience is Realized to be equally and totally Profound. This continues, through all the acts and moments and transformations of the body-mind in Love, until the body-mind and its experience are dissolved, passed away, or Outshined by the Radiant Transcendental Being.

397

The Living God, the Beloved of all beings, has, from eternity, become a Great Sacrifice. The Radiant One has become the process of all possibilities. We are not merely the creatures or victims of God, created and set apart to suffer for some inexplicable reason. We are the very Sacrifice of God. God is Alive as us. Our lives are the creative ordeal to which God is eternally submitted. We need only Realize the Living One and thus become capable of this Divine Sacrifice, which is an eternal creative ordeal of Love that leads, step by step, toward a Most Wonderful Transformation. Once we transcend the illusion of our dark separate selves and enter into the Divine Process, we see clearly that the existence and destiny of the world and every being is the Fullness of Love-Bliss in a perfectly Transformed state that has become One with the Person and the Domain of the Transcendental Divine.

This is my Testimony and my Confession. And it is the same Testimony and Confession proclaimed by all the Adepts who have appeared to serve mankind on Earth.

The Presumption
of What Cannot Be Lost or Found

398

No action or condition actually separates us from God—but the experience of actions and conditions tends to awaken the presumption of separation from God.

No action or condition actually brings us closer to God—but, once we suffer from the presumption of separation from God, the strategic manipulation of actions and conditions may tend to awaken the presumption of closeness to God or even identification with God.

In any case, God is always already, presently and priorly, the very Condition or Truth of our manifest existence. And it is not the presumption of separation, closeness, or identification relative to God that actually Realizes the Divine Condition or Truth of existence. It is only the unqualified, direct, or radical presumption of God that actually or inherently Realizes God—and that presumption is effective only in every moment wherein the experiential actions and conditions of existence are actually or effectively transcended in the ecstatic presumption of God.

This is the fundamental Understanding, the secret of Freedom, Happiness, Pleasure, Wonder, Surrender, Love, and Life— because God is the very Essence or Substance of Freedom, Happiness, Pleasure, Wonder, Surrender, Love, and Life. It is only when God, or the Reality of the Radiant Transcendental Being, cannot be denied or even conventionally affirmed but only tacitly presumed (because It is Obvious, no matter what is arising as experience) that the body-mind abides already or priorly Free in God-Communion. And only such tacit God-Communion, Realized moment to moment, provides the Creative basis for truly human growth, higher transformation, and ultimate transcendence.

We cannot cease to be Free. Nor can we acquire or attain Freedom. We cannot cease to be Happy. Nor can we acquire or attain Happiness. We cannot cease in our Pleasure. Nor can we acquire or attain Pleasure. We cannot cease to Wonder. Nor can we acquire or attain Wonder or That which is Wonderful. We cannot fail to be Surrendered. Nor can we attain to Surrender by any effort. We cannot cease to Love. Nor can we acquire or attain Love Itself. We cannot finally die. Nor can we acquire Eternal Life by means of the manipulation or effort of the self (or body-mind), since only surrender of self permits inherence in the Life-Principle. But Freedom, Happiness, Pleasure, Wonder, Surrender, Love, and Life are our inherent Condition. And Truth is the tacit presumption of Freedom, Happiness, Pleasure, Wonder, Surrender, Love, and Life.

399

Will You Enter into Love?

A talk by Da Free John

DA FREE JOHN: True meditation is the transfiguration of the body-mind in the Radiance of Communion with God. That process is love, the release of all contraction and all the limitations to the native radiance of the being. When you are in love, you are truly meditating. The mind is attentive, the body is full, and you feel blissful. Therefore, to be in love is the paradigm, the archetype, the metaphor, of true meditation. However, love is the process that we are all seriously trying to avoid. To be in love is embarrassing and awkward. Our faces change, and we become foolish, not so ready-made, buttoned-down, cool, and strategic. We consent to be in love only on very rare occasions, usually when we have realized some romantic sexual association. Yet, to be in love, to be submitted into the Radiance of God, is the native state of Man. God is love. That is true enough.

Love is what you are all struggling with, you see. You would sit in meditation in a cave for twelve hours a day long before you would begin to get serious about the matter of love. You do all you can to see that you are pleasurably situated in your sexual relationship, in your work, in your household, or in your automobile. You work very hard to study and read about and think about and imagine and even perform meditative exercises. Yet love is the most profound, and the most difficult, activity to perform. Love is the one single act that you are most reluctant to perform—whether in public or in private.

The reason you are obsessed with desire to be released and consoled by experience is that you have fallen from love. You have become contracted and self-possessed. Therefore, you want to be satisfied, whereas if you could be released, if your heart could cease to be hardened, then the whole body would become full of light, full of bliss, as it is from time to time. Every now and then you catch a glimpse of real Life, and the Grace of the awakening to love is actually received and felt in those moments. But to become responsible for love at all times, under all conditions, in all relations, is the discipline that obliges you.

400

Your childish and adolescent self-possession and withdrawal from love have produced a false motivation toward spirituality and mysticism and all the worldly consolations of human life. Thus, you must "hear" the Teaching before you can begin this Way that I Teach, which is founded on a different realization from that of the usual man. Divine Realization is the Principle, not the goal, of this Way. To follow this Way is to be converted from your loveless self-possession and to struggle creatively with the conditions you have created in your life and with which you are confronted from hour to hour.

The test is this: Will you enter into Divine Communion? Will you enter into love, moment to moment, under the conditions given you? Or will you struggle with your mechanical tendency to be self-possessed, to be isolated in irony and fear and anger and guilt? It is not that you must become self-conscious about emotions that may arise. There is an exoteric religiosity in the world that falsely requires us to have no emotions—never to feel guilt, never to feel sorrow, never to be afraid. It is true, through Divine submission we must transcend chronic and reactive fear, anger, guilt, sorrow, irony, and the rest. But there are moments when any of these responses is completely appropriate, just as the physical body has reactions that contribute to its survival, such as pain. If you could not feel pain when touching something hot, you would not be able to protect yourself. Just so, we are emotionally equipped with survival mechanisms in the form of responsive emotions.

To be fiercely angry sometimes is good and necessary and right. It is part of our creative capacity to deal with things in this world that must be changed. On the other hand, chronic and petty anger, anger that is not rising on love and that manifests in a life that is not otherwise enlightened, must be transcended. But anger cannot be transcended through mere suppression—only through love, through understanding, through "hearing" of the Teaching of Truth, and through practical responsibility. When we become truly responsible at the heart and whole bodily, then all of our potential emotions attain their natural form and occasion, as do all of the functions of the body-mind.

You must enjoy the capacity to be much more exaggerated! The situation in the world suppresses our feeling. It makes us want to be relieved, to go to heaven, to be elsewhere, to drop out, to stop creatively influencing the circumstances of life. The more news you read, the more desperate you become. Therefore, you should continue to read the news, but you must also constantly consider the Teaching of Truth, and you must come to Life, you must Commune with Life and be enlivened by the Living God. You must begin to enjoy the capacity to be love, and, with others, you must create the human cultural environment in which you <u>can</u> be love.

In the "downtown" world of popular culture, we cannot look and feel and be happy; we cannot be lovers. We cannot be free and full of Life. We must be very serious, strategic, cool, ironic, and grown only to the level of the navel. You can observe, in all of your relations, the downtown, retarded, unexaggerated, self-possessed, Lifeless quality, your own fear of motion and emotion, gracefulness, and happiness. You are afraid to express happiness, and you are afraid to <u>be</u> happiness. In the conventional world, you must always be on guard, affecting immunity.

Observe your solemnity in your sexual intimacy, for instance. It is as if you were afraid that somebody is going to find you out. You are even afraid that the person with whom you are intimate is going to find you out! Being seen is one of the major problems of ordinary sexuality. Likewise, even though you propose to be involved in spiritual practice, you are afraid somebody is going to find out that you are not an ascetic. You constantly participate in cultural guilt. To presume to become involved in spiritual life is not taken lightly by the world. You must pay your dues for it. In worldly circles, to become serious about spiritual life is taboo, and once you have entered into the lesser cults of spiritual life, it becomes taboo to enjoy yourself, to be free and happy, to be sexually active, to have an enjoyable diet, to enjoy your relationships, to remain intimate with others.

You must begin to live beyond your childish guilt, fear, and self-possession. You must be confessed bodily, not only to the Living Divine Reality, but to your intimates. Devotional community is the theatre in which spiritual practice is engaged. Fundamentally, true spiritual practice cannot take place in solitude or in overwhelmingly worldly situations. It most naturally and inevitably is realized in the devotional community of those who are confessed in intimacy to one another, who oblige and permit one another to be love, to be bodily enlivened by the Grace of God, and to be happy even though mortal.

Once you enter into God-Communion, all your seriousness and problem-solving and thinking about birth, death, and experience—"Do I survive death or don't I?"—wondering about your ultimate destiny and all the time living as cool as a dead fish, waiting for Jesus—all of that comes to an end in true God-Communion. True God-Communion is Communion with the Living God, not just prayer to some abstract deity for help. The Living God is Present, absolutely Present, Radiant as your own feeling, Conscious as your own consciousness.

When you begin to awaken to this feeling-intuition and enter into God-Communion bodily, then all this puzzling about life and death, the meaning of the universe, the laws of nature, all the problematic wondering comes to an end. You may continue those investigations as an amusement, but you will be already happy and Full. The secret will have been realized. And in that Fullness of God-Communion, although we are without any knowledge about what existence is, there is nevertheless the certainty of immortality, the intuition that existence is not threatened. Forms of manifestation change and are threatened, yet whatever may occur after death is not the end of existence. Everything else may disappear, and at some point it will, but the fundamental matter of existence is never threatened. The future is not described or foreknown, but our existence is absolute, already identical to God. It is love.

Transfiguration

The following confessional prayer is given by Da Free John to all men and women who desire to realize their true and right relationship to the Being and Power Who lives and breathes all beings. Through heartfelt and prayerful offering of this Confession, we may be restored to the intuitive understanding and feeling of our own Divine Nature and established in our right relationship to and ultimate Identity with the Transcendental Being and Spirit. May all beings Awaken to Truth, so that they may make this Confession freely, openly, and with joy!

Transfiguration
(The Great Confession)

by Da Free John

L et the heart speak the Wisdom of the Unity of body, mind, world, and God:

There is neither one God nor many Gods.
There is only God.
All the one and many Gods are Idols of the One that is God.

God is the Radiant Transcendental Life-Consciousness, in Whom all places and beings and ideas appear and disappear.
There is no God but God, Who is the Transcendental Consciousness and Eternal Energy that Radiates in Man and in the world of Man.

That One Pervades and Transcends the world and Man.
That One is my God and my Eternal Self.

Every possibility, whether full of pleasure or full of pain, arises in God.

Every experience is a spontaneous and temporary modification of the Radiant Transcendental Life-Consciousness.

If I surrender to experience, I merely enjoy and suffer, according to the mood and complexity of my various thoughts, desires, and acts.

If I seek within my body-mind for God, I am confronted and deluded by states of body and mind.

If I seek outside my body-mind for God, I am confronted and confounded by the experience of all relations and events.

But if I surrender body and mind in the Radiant Transcendental Life-Consciousness, all experience Reveals the Living God.

God is not an Object of the mind or of bodily experience.
God is Transcendentally Present.

God is to be Realized as the Transcendental Subject or Eternal Self in Whom all knowledge and all experiences arise and dissolve.

Therefore, to Worship and to Realize God in Truth is to transcend the world and the body-mind of Man.

I am not separated from God.

Only my reflective and thinking mind seems to separate me from the Eternal Self or Transcendental Consciousness that is God.

I am not separated from God.

Only my reactive and loveless heart seems to separate me from the Divine Person, the Infinite Love-Radiance that is God.

I am not separated from God.

Only my bodily recoil from the universal demand of all relationships seems to separate me from the Eternal Domain, the All-Pervading Life-Power that is God.

I am not separated from God.

I must love, and trust, and surrender to the Infinite Consciousness that is beyond and prior to the world, the body, and the mind.

I must love, and trust, and surrender to the Eternal Life-Energy that is beyond and prior to the world, the body, and the mind.

God is the Living Truth.
God is the Way of Salvation.
God is the Eternal Master of Man.
By our acceptance of the Mastery of God, the Way of Salvation through God-Realization is Revealed.

Let the whole body pray in Truth:
I worship and bow down.
I surrender body and mind and all self-attention to the Living God,
Who is the Universal Life-Current and the Transcendental Self of all beings,
Who Radiates as Love in all directions,
Who is without center or circumference,
Who pervades and supports all the worlds,
Who consents to Awaken as Man by rising up in the lower roots of the body-mind, releasing all obstructions to the evolutionary Flow of Life,
Who Shines above the heads of those who are Awake, Transforming every part of them with Heart-Light,
Who is the Transcendental Heart, the Eternal Mystery, the Wonderful Truth, the Unyielding Paradox that finally Outshines the souls of all beings, every part of the body-mind of Man, and all the possible places in the worlds of experience.

Radiant God,
All-Pervading Current of Life,
Consciousness where I appear and disappear,
hear my breathing heart.

Awaken me,
to feel the Heart of Light and Love,
where this life and mind and body may dissolve.
I hold up my hands.

About the Author
and His Work

F rom his earliest years Da Free John has been graced with a most profound religious sensitivity, and this sensitivity or enlightenment has moved him to devote his entire life to serving the Divine awakening of others.

Early Life

Da Free John was born Franklin Albert Jones on November 3, 1939, in Jamaica, New York. Even during his childhood he consciously began to prepare himself for his future teaching work. He allowed himself to experience fully the suffering and delusion of ordinary human existence, and, as he grew, he explored every kind of experience and knowledge, both physical and psychic. In this manner he worked to discover and clarify a Way whereby other men and women might also awaken into ecstatic communion and unity with God.

He completed an academic education at two western universities (Columbia College and Stanford University), and he finished his academic career with religious studies at three Christian seminaries. He developed into a brilliant student, but all the while he was engaged in an intense experiential and inward investigation of all the phenomena of life and consciousness. He spent several years as a disciple of traditional spiritual teachers, both in the United States and in India. During this period he practiced esoteric yogic disciplines, and he realized and transcended the sublime processes of energy and consciousness described in the classic spiritual traditions.

Finally, in September, 1970, having fulfilled the traditional Eastern and Western approaches to life and Truth, and having understood both their strengths and limitations, Da Free John spontaneously resumed the enlightened condition he had known from birth. His body and mind were now completely realigned to infinite life, and he was fully capable of communicating that Divine life to others.

In 1972, having completed his own adventure of spiritual transformation and preparation for teaching others, Da Free John founded The Free Communion Church, now The Crazy Wisdom Fellowship. During the initial period of his teaching work, the relationship he enjoyed with devotees necessarily involved both spiritual intimacy and a great deal of personal contact. Da Free John thus communicated and demonstrated the Way of Divine Ignorance to those who approached him for spiritual help in the past. Even now he performs transcendental spiritual work in privacy for the sake of the world, but he lives in seclusion within the renunciate order of the Fellowship.

The Agencies of Spiritual Help

Da Free John has created the Teaching and all the levels of instruction and established the sacred environment of Vision Mound Sanctuary (a 600-acre retreat in northern California), and the community of those who practice his Teaching. Now and in the future, these are the principal agencies or transmitters of his spiritual help and influence. He leads no public life, nor does he have any outer obligations relative to the institution of the Fellowship or the practice of devotees. The Living Power, Presence, and Wisdom of Reality are openly accessible to all who approach the Fellowship, now and in the future, through the agents Da Free John has created.

Thus, he is regarded by devotees as the Teacher of the Fellowship, and he is honored as such through devotees' practice of the Way of life. Devotees do not engage in any cultic idolization of the Spiritual Master as an incarnation of God. They recognize him as a vehicle through which God has brought and continues to bring Grace

408

into their lives, but now that his own initial efforts have been completed, devotees are free to find and worship God directly and to be instructed and further Graced by the Teaching, Community, and Sanctuaries—the agents that he has created.

409

About
The Crazy Wisdom
Fellowship

Our Fellowship is aligned by inspiration to the Realization and summary Teaching proclaimed by the Western Adept Da Free John—and we are aligned by tradition to the highest Adepts of all traditions. Our Way of life is founded on the perfect Realization and highest Wisdom Teaching of the Adepts, rather than on the historical beliefs and suggestive metaphors of religious, mystical, and spiritual cultism.

We develop our practice on the basis of free and radical understanding of the psycho-physical limits of Man and prior transcendence of the conventional urge to solve the "Problem" of human existence through the search for knowledge and experience. We appeal directly to the Radiant Transcendental Being or Condition in which the world and all beings and states arise. And we find that the Way and the Truth Realized by the Adepts and proved in our practice provides a basis for understanding and positive unity with practitioners in all naturally human, religious, mystical, spiritual, or philosophical traditions.

Because of our unique philosophical and cultural orientation, we call ourselves The Crazy Wisdom Fellowship, signifying both our special alliance with the Wisdom of the highest Adepts of all traditions and our free orientation to the radical Way of Transcendental Realization communicated by Da Free John. The name "Crazy Wisdom" is taken from the tradition of free Adepts or "Avadhoots," who energetically proclaim the Way as a process of self-transcendence through God-Love, or direct Realization of the Transcendental Truth. The "Crazy Way" of surrender to Truth is founded in the "humorous seriousness" of Divine Inspiration—or that Love which the world calls foolishness. It liberates Man from bondage to the unenlightened conventions of the body-mind, and it Awakens both truly human and super-human evolutionary capabilities.

Therefore, the Way of life we value and embrace is the direct Way of Transcendental Realization, proposed in radical philosophical terms and expressed through a practice that transcends the conventional limitations of both oriental and occidental views of life, experience, knowledge, and the world.

We propose to create the culture of our Fellowship on a free basis, as a direct response to our philosophical consideration of life, prior to any resort to inherited or arbitrary conventions, ideals, or taboos. And we pledge to devote our Fellowship not only to the Realization and well-being of all its members but to love, service, cooperation, tolerance, and understanding in relation to all beings and all dimensions of human society.

An Invitation

The Laughing Man Institute is the public education division of The Crazy Wisdom Fellowship. It brings the practical and spiritual Teaching of Da Free John to the world. Presently many Students of the Institute actively live the Way of life described in the books of Da Free John, and many others study the Way and support on a regular basis the publication of the Teaching. If you are interested in further study of the Teaching, support of its communication in the world, or practice of the Way itself, we invite you to consider the other books of Da Free John and to write us at the address below for further information.

The Laughing Man Institute
P.O. Box 3680
Clearlake Highlands, CA 95422

Topical Index

A

Adepts, 4, 88, 300, 314, 315, 385-386, 391-392; and cultural influence, 56, 67, 195-197, 381-384; and comparative religions, 43-48; and evolution and evolutionary influence, 125, 349-352, 353-354, 355-369; Jesus as, 214-215, 321-329, 355; Krishna as, 315-317, 324-329

Adolescence, 37-43, 44; political reaction of, 91

Alexandria of Clement, letter by, 217-218

American spirit and narcissism, 67

Animals, evolution of, 370-371

Anxiety. *See* Stress

Aristotelian philosophy, 273

Asceticism, 162, 319, 325-327

Atman, realization of, 361

Atomic energy, 270-271

Authoritarian role of state, 74, 83-86, 90-91

Autonomic nervous system. *See* Nervous System

B

Baptism, 203-204, 207

Bhagavad Gita, 315-321, 324

Bhagavata Purana, 324-329

"Big Bang" theory, 269-272, 381

Birth, 246-247

Bliss. *See* Ecstasy

Body, 185-189, 342-343; and enlightened man, 229-230; and God-realization, 134-135; and light, 299

Body-mind, 292-295; and communion, 377-378; inspection of, 165-166; and stress, 239-253; and transfiguration of, 297-298

Brahman, realization of, 361

Brain hemispheres, 61-62, 116-117, 352, 357-363

Buddha, 5, 355-356, 281-287

Buddhism, 6-7, 282-287; and life-principle, 229-230

C

Chemistry of stress, 241-269

Childhood, 39-41

Christ. *See* Jesus

Christianity: criticism of, 193-198; cult of, 199-209; and life-principle, 229-230. *See also* Jesus

Church, 193-198; separation of state and, 78-82

Communism, 74, 91; cooperative communities and, 77

Community, 74-78, 92-102, 105-108

Comparative religion, 43-48

Cultism, 3-10, 48-51, 30-37; and Adepts, 381-382; allowable cults, 79; and the Great Religions, 193-198; and idols, 211-212, 227-228, 311; of Jesus, 198-208, 214-221

Culture, 13-17, 97-98, 139; of ecstasy, 108-110; evolution of, 355; higher culture of man, 352-353; and scientism, 57-59, 69-72, 393-395; verbal culture, 63-64

D

Death, 119, 187-190; and bodily enlightenment, 180; and star body, 264-265; and stress, 248-249; traditional method of, 312-314

Democracy, 97-99; and narcissism, 67-68; self-indulgence of, 75-76

Dreaming process, 361, 387

Drugs, 373; and State, 85

E

Eastern man. *See* Oriental man

Ego, 179, 331-335, 344-345; and consciousness, 295-297; dilemma of, 42-43; disunity of, 109; and God-realization, 134-135, 179, 181-185, 315-318, 395; and mysticism, 159-174; and space-time, 292-293; and star body, 263-266. *See also* "I"

Ego-death, 155, 159-174; and mind, 186; and mysticism, 173-174

Einstein, Albert, 271-275

E=mc², 271-280

Enlightenment, 143, 181-185, 228-230, 261-262, 297-298, 312-313, 367, 395; and drugs, 373-374; and energy, 253; and humor, 375; and spiritual master, 88-89, 363-368; and stress chemistry, 241-269

Energy, 268-280; and stress, 243

Eroticism and stress, 244-245

Evolution, 253, 263-269, 332-334, 357-363, 370-378; and love, 144-147; and mysticism, 354-356; of religion, 48-52

Existence of God, 22-27, 258-259, 398-399

Experience, 181-182, 236-238, 260-263; and ego-death, 159-173; and God-realization, 254-255; levels of, 181-182

Extrasensory abilities, 352

F

Faith, 72-73, 257-258

False religion, 30-33; and fear, 117; magical mentality of, 343; of science, 59-62

Families, 76; and community, 96-97

Fear, 119-121, 159-163; and laughter, 377; and madness, 167; and survival, 153-154

Feminine character, 125

Freedom, 67, 89; and community, 96-97; and indifference, 233-234; prior freedom, way of, 345-346; and separation from God, 398-399

Freud, Sigmund, 5

Fundamentalist religion, 80

Future religion, 346-347

G

Gautama. *See* Buddha

Genius, 3-10

Gnosticism, 218

God, 20-27, 142-143, 258-259, 398-399; and children, 39-40; exclusive God, 52-53; experiencing of, 289-291; and idols, 314-315; names of, 227-228; and nature, 15, 369-370

God-communion. *See* Communion

God-realization, 25-27, 172, 254-255, 315-318, 395; and ego-death, 161-162; and Jesus, 214; and laughter, 377; and sex, 134-135

Grace, 283-284

H

Hall, Robert K., 1

Hallucinogenic drugs. *See* drugs

Happiness. *See* Ecstasy

Heart, 189; mystery of, 357-358; and stress, 251-252

Heart chakra, 251

Hebrew tradition, 193-198, 214-215

Index of Titles

Essays and Talks of Da Free John in
*Scientific Proof of the Existence of God Will Soon Be
Announced by the White House!* (alphabetically
arranged)

The Books of Da Free John

All books are available at your bookstore or by mail from The Dawn Horse Book Depot. (See order form at the end of this book.)

THE INTRODUCTORY BOOKS—for those beginning the study of this Teaching

The Four Fundamental Questions
Talks and essays about human experience and the actual practice of an Enlightened Way of Life

"What are the questions that, if answered truly, would enlighten you and would lead you to practice the way of truth?" Thus we begin one of the most profound and liberating considerations of our lives. Using four challenging and deceptively simple questions, Da Free John skillfully exposes our conventional concepts of God and reveals the real Divine Condition of this and every moment of experience. He then discusses the true function of the Spiritual Teacher and summarizes a Way of life wherein we can realize true happiness. This brief book is the best introduction available to the enlightened Way taught by Da Free John.
100 pages, 2d edition, revised, $1.95 quality paperback.

Compulsory Dancing
Talks and essays on the spiritual and evolutionary necessity of emotional surrender to the Life-Principle

Here Da Free John talks intimately with his students about misconceptions in their understanding of God, relationship, and spiritual practice. He then reveals the process of emotional conversion in which God is tacitly obvious in every moment. His dynamic and often humorous conversations and his insightful essays free us of traditional concepts of the Divine and point the way to a new and heartfelt understanding of real religious experience.

"Da Free John talks sanely about real sanity. His subject is always the same: a way of living this human existence without fear and without obsession. He talks about surrender to God as only one who has done so can."
(Robert K. Hall, M.D., Co-founder of Lomi School and the Gestalt Institute of San Francisco)

180 pages, $2.95 quality paperback.

DA FREE JOHN'S MASTERPIECE OF PROPHETIC SOCIAL CRITICISM AND EVOLUTIONARY WISDOM—for those who have read the introductory books

Scientific Proof of the Existence of God Will Soon Be Announced by the White House!
Prophetic Wisdom about the Myths and Idols of mass culture and popular religious cultism, the new priesthood of scientific and political materialism, and the secrets of Enlightenment hidden in the body of Man

Both an urgently needed socio-political prophecy for our time and an evolutionary vision of timeless significance—this book is already capturing the acclaim of significant figures in the fields of psychology, politics, religion, and science. Destined to provide widespread controversy and debate, and sure to be adopted for courses in many fields by universities throughout the country.

"No one can really read [this book] without being changed in the process. It is like a rapid-fire succession of electric shocks, each carrying the message: Wake up! Wake up to your true spirituality and your true task on Earth! It is a great educational work . . . hard-hitting and unsparing in its critique of modern culture, its goals, its official religions, its official science. In modern society's time of troubles this is a much needed book."
(Willis Harman, President, Institute of Noetic Sciences)
430 pages, $12.95 quality paperback.

THREE PRACTICAL MANUALS

Conscious Exercise and the Transcendental Sun
The Principle of Love Applied to Exercise and the Method of Common Physical Action. A Science of Whole Body Wisdom, or True Emotion, Intended Most Especially for Those Engaged in Religious or Spiritual Life

427

Conscious Exercise is a proven system of simple formal exercises that strengthen, harmonize, and relax the body. In this beautifully illustrated, practical guide we learn how to stand, sit and walk with energy and feeling, how to perform two brief daily routines of exercise that bring strength and harmony to our lives, how to sit properly for meditation, and how to consciously breathe the energy of life. This unique book contains wisdom that is the very foundation of true spiritual practice.
272 pages, $5.95 quality paperback, $10.95 deluxe cloth edition.

Love of the Two-Armed Form
The Free and Regenerative Function of Sexuality in Ordinary Life, and the Transcendence of Sexuality in True Religious or Spiritual Practice

In Part One of *Love of the Two-Armed Form* Da Free John helps us to understand and transcend our emotional obstructions to love, relationship, and sexual pleasure. He then shows how the right use of sexuality can be an integral part of our spiritual and cultural evolution. In Part Two, he describes the process of *sexual communion*, the enlightened sexual practice that we learn and perfect as a life of spiritual responsibility deepens. Not a book for the casual reader, *Love of the Two-Armed Form* is a challenge to those who would truly understand emotion and sexuality and bring a positive, energetic disposition to all life.
475 pages, $10.95 quality paperback.

The Eating Gorilla Comes in Peace
The Transcendental Principle of Life applied to Diet and the Regenerative Discipline of True Health

In the midst of widespread confusion about health and happiness, *The Eating Gorilla Comes in Peace* is a humorous, dynamic, and radical investigation into the "wilderness of food," bringing real clarity and understanding to health and dietary practices. Topics covered include the right use of fasting and techniques for regenerating health; the proper transition to a vegetarian diet; the cure of physical and emotional imbalances with right dietary practices; and the optimum diet at various stages of spiritual development. Special sections are also included on the relationship between food and sexuality, children's diet, conscious conception and childbirth, and responsible relationship to the process of death.

"In my own experience as a practitioner, Da Free John's suggestions for life and health management have dramatically demonstrated their validity amongst my patients, which to my mind is the ultimate test of truth. For anyone interested in maintaining and raising their health, I recommend this book as the fundamental cornerstone."
(Bill Gray, M.D., N.D., coauthor of *The Science of Homeopathy—A Modern Textbook*)
600 pages, $10.95 quality paperback.

THE FUNDAMENTAL TEXT—for every student of spiritual life (We recommend that you read the two introductory books before reading this one.)

The Enlightenment of the Whole Body
A Rational and New Prophetic Revelation of the Truth of Religion, Esoteric Spirituality, and the Divine Destiny of Man

This epic work is a comprehensive and inspired presentation of the entire spectrum of true religious and spiritual practice. With brilliance and clarity, Da Free John discusses his own life and teaching work, the principles and revelations that are the foundation of the

Way of Divine Ignorance, the moral necessity of conversion to love, the esoteric understanding of the life and work of Jesus, and the actual process wherein the body-mind of Man is transfigured in God. This book is the principal source text of Da Free John's teaching and the fundamental text for all students of the Way that he teaches. 600 pages, $10.95 quality paperback.

THE SOURCE BOOKS

The Knee of Listening
The Early Life and Radical Spiritual Teachings of Da Free John

Da Free John's own account of the awakening, testing, and fulfillment of the whole Way that he Teaches. He describes the Condition of Enlightenment as he enjoyed it at birth, his years of struggling and miraculous transformation, and his ultimate resumption, in September 1970, of Perfect Illumination. The essays in Part Two interpret this Revelation with respect to all the spiritual and worldly traditions of the great search of Man. Written in the weeks and months immediately after his Re-Awakening, these essays demonstrate the eternal wisdom and perfect insight of the Enlightened Man. Foreword by Alan Watts, with a new, updated introduction.

"It is obvious from all sorts of subtle details that he knows what IT's all about . . . a rare being. . . .

"What he *says,* and says very well, is something that most people seem quite reluctant to understand. He has simply realized that he himself as he is . . . is a perfect and authentic manifestation of eternal energy of the universe, and thus is no longer disposed to be in conflict with himself."
(Alan Watts)

"A great teacher with a dynamic ability to awaken in his listeners something of the Divine Reality in which he is grounded, with which he is identified and which in fact he is. He is a man of both the East and the West; perhaps in him they merge and are organized as the One that he is."
(Israel Regardie)
271 pages, $5.95 quality paperback.

The Method of the Siddhas
Talks with Da Free John on the Spiritual Technique of the Saviors of Mankind

In his early teaching work Da Free John invited a group of ordinary people to discuss with him the principles of true spiritual life. *The Method of the Siddhas* chronicles the dialogues that took place. Often using humorous stories and parables, Da Free John answers questions, undermines traditional myths, and invites his listeners to share in "Satsang" or "Good Company," the sublime condition of relational love and understanding in the midst of an ordinary, pleasurable life. Although this book was originally published in 1973, it remains one of the most enjoyable and useful volumes of Da Free John's radical spiritual teaching.
364 pages, $5.95 quality paperback.

The Way That I Teach
Talks on the Intuition of Eternal Life

In this book of talks from 1977 Da Free John speaks about the struggle and joys of spiritual life. The dialogues with students elaborate on the principles communicated in his earlier works and compassionately provide wisdom that will aid anyone in spiritual practice. His ecstatic conversations reveal the esoteric mysteries of existence in a manner that truly awakens the basic religious sense of wonoe. or awe. *The Way That I Teach* invites all of us to create a culture of wisdom in which fear, sorrow, anger, and doubt are replaced by love, compassion, strength, and understanding.
261 pages, $5.95 quality paperback, $10.95 deluxe cloth edition.

The Paradox of Instruction
An Introduction to the Esoteric Spiritual Teaching of Da Free John

This book explains how we may awaken from the dream of suffering and self-possession and be restored to ordinary happiness and love. Comparing traditional approaches to religion and spirituality with the illumined realization of his own practice, Da Free John describes the stages of spiritual growth and his vision of the esoteric structure native to every human being and present in all forms of existence itself. His insights into the nature of ego, the condition of human suffering, and true awakening in God will delight and challenge many readers, particularly those with a philosophical bent. Available in clothbound edition only.

"*The Paradox of Instruction* itself is, in its scope, its eloquence, its simplicity, and its ecstatic fund of transcendent insight, probably unparalleled in the entire field of spiritual literature." (Ken Wilber)

327 pages, $10.95 deluxe cloth edition.

FOR CHiLDREN

What to Remember to Be Happy
A Spiritual Way of Life for Your First Fourteen Years or So

A delightful and easily understood message on how to feel and breathe the Mystery of Life and be always happy every day. When read aloud, both children and adults are delighted by its capacity to reawaken the sense of being alive and full of feeling in a wondrous World. Fully illustrated.

13 pages, $2.95 quality paperback.